THE *Christmas* WISH

Lindsey Kelk is a *Sunday Times* bestselling author, podcaster and internet oversharer. Born and brought up in Doncaster, South Yorkshire, she worked in London as a children's editor before writing her first book, *I Heart New York*, and moving to Brooklyn. Lindsey's novels include the I Heart series, *Love Me Do* and *On a Night Like This*. She now lives in Los Angeles with her husband.

You can follow Lindsey on Facebook, Twitter or Instagram @LindseyKelk, and sign up for her newsletter at www.LindseyKelk.com.

Also by Lindsey Kelk

I Heart series
I Heart New York
I Heart Hollywood
I Heart Paris
I Heart Vegas
I Heart London
I Heart Christmas
I Heart Forever
I Heart Hawaii

Girl series
About a Girl
What a Girl Wants
A Girl's Best Friend

Standalones
The Single Girl's To-Do List
Always the Bridesmaid
We Were on a Break
One in a Million
In Case You Missed It
On a Night Like This
Love Me Do

Cinders & Sparks children's book series
Magic at Midnight
Fairies in the Forest
Goblins and Gold

Novellas available on ebook
Jenny Lopez Has a Bad Week
Jenny Lopez Saves Christmas
Jenny Lopez is Getting Married

THE
Christmas
WISH

LINDSEY KELK

HarperCollins*Publishers*

HarperCollins*Publishers* Ltd
1 London Bridge Street,
London SE1 9GF
www.harpercollins.co.uk

HarperCollins*Publishers*
Macken House,
39/40 Mayor Street Upper,
Dublin 1
D01 C9W8

First published by HarperCollins*Publishers* 2022
This edition published 2023
1

A catalogue record for this book is available from the British Library

ISBN: 978-0-00-840786-5 (PB b-format)
ISBN: 978-0-00-8620134 (PB a-format)

This novel is entirely a work of fiction.
The names, characters and incidents portrayed in it are
the work of the author's imagination. Any resemblance to
actual persons, living or dead, events or localities is
entirely coincidental.

Typeset in Melior by Palimpsest Book Production Ltd, Falkirk, Stirlingshire

Printed and bound in the UK using 100% Renewable Electricity by CPI Group (UK) Ltd

This book is produced from independently certified FSC™ paper to ensure
responsible forest management.

For more information visit: www.harpercollins.co.uk/green

For my brother,
may we always ruin Christmas, one way or another

CHAPTER ONE

Bundled up against the cold, I stood outside my flat, waiting, until an ancient Volvo rolled around the corner, Mariah Carey's whistle tones filling the formerly quiet street. Shaking my head, I smiled as the car stuttered to a stop in front of me and the tinted driver's side window rolled down slowly to reveal the cheerful face of my cousin, resplendent in a pair of fluffy reindeer antlers. It was Christmas Eve.

'Ho, ho, ho, Gwen Baker! Have you been a good girl this year?' Manny asked in a deep and booming voice. He watched as I walked over to the car, struggling with my little suitcase and the several bags full of gifts hanging from my arms, making absolutely no move to help.

'Depends who you ask. What about you?'

'Depends on your definition of "good".' He reached over his seat to open the back passenger door. 'You'll have to chuck your stuff in here. I can't open the boot without the key and if I turn the engine off, it might never start again.'

I heaved everything into the car, filling the empty back seat with my precious cargo. 'I feel like I'm going to regret asking this, but where are your presents? Please don't tell me we've got to stop at the twenty-four-hour Tesco to do your Christmas shopping? Again?'

As usual, Manny was one step ahead of me. He patted the left-chest pocket of his jacket and grinned. 'Oh, ye of little faith. I've cracked it this year, everyone's getting Amazon gift cards.'

Slamming the back door, I climbed into the passenger seat and stared at him through a damp tangle of red-brown hair. 'Everyone? You're giving the kids gift cards?'

'Yes.' Manny's grin dissolved into a dismissive frown. 'Don't look at me like that, they're awful kids anyway. You ready to go?'

'Not in the slightest,' I replied as he gunned the engine.

'No sleep till Baslow!' He raised one fist in the air as we pulled out into traffic, only to be immediately stalled by a red light, both of us straining against our seatbelts when he slammed his foot on the brake.

'Sorry. Only legally required stops till Baslow!'

'I'll be impressed if we make it there at all,' I whispered as the light changed and we sped off into the night.

'I cannot wait to get home,' Manny declared once we were safely on the motorway and following what felt like half the country up north, headlights to tail lights all the way home. 'This year has been a bear and not the good, sexy kind. I thought Christmas was never going to come. On a scale of one to Elf, how giddy are you?'

He held his hand out for a sweet, more interested in a sugar fix than my answer. This was our deal, Manny

2

drove and I was in charge of the CD player and the tin of Quality Street, two very important jobs and both of them just about within my capabilities. I pulled out a Toffee Penny and put it right back. Manny was soft centres and nut-based truffles only. I got first dibs on the fudge, Dad got the hard toffees and Mum liked the big purple ones, a statement that caused no end of entertainment after a couple of Christmas brandies. My sister, Cerys, didn't like sweets. My sister, Cerys, was a monster.

'I'm trying,' I said as I passed him a Strawberry Delight. 'I just don't know if I'm in the mood for it.'

'Not in the mood for what?'

'Oh, you know. Christmas.'

He gasped so loudly, I almost rolled down the window to make sure there was enough oxygen left in the car for me. 'What's wrong with you? Are you sickening for something?'

I shook my head and popped a chocolate triangle into my mouth. 'No. I'm not really feeling the festive spirit, that's all. No big deal.'

'But you love Christmas. You're *obsessed* with Christmas.'

'Don't exaggerate, I'm not obsessed.'

'How many advent calendars did you have last year?'

I looked down at my nails, giving my shoddy home manicure a close examination.

'One.'

'Liar.'

'Two?'

'You're a liar who lives in a house of lies.'

'Fine, I had five,' I replied, ignoring his indignant caw. 'A Cadbury one and a Galaxy one.'

'Entirely reasonable. What else?'

'One from The Body Shop, a nail polish one,' I paused and sucked in my bottom lip. 'And one that turned out to be full of cat treats.'

'But you haven't got a cat?' Manny replied, confused.

'Yes, well,' I said, tucking my hair behind my ears. 'Didn't realize until I'd got it home from the supermarket, did I?'

The inside of the windscreen fogged up as he exhaled heavily. I reached forward to rub it down with my sleeve then cracked my window open. The heating was broken again meaning we had the luxurious choice of being freezing cold or red hot for the entire three-and-a-half-hour drive up home. Even though he spent more money fixing the Volvo than he would spend on buying a brand-new car, Manny refused to consider junking the old thing. It had belonged to his dad which meant the topic was not up for discussion.

'Right, let's make sure I've got this straight, last year it was five advent calendars, a fully decorated tree in every room of your house and a deeply annoying jumper that played "Jingle Bells" every time you breathed, and now I'm supposed to believe you've randomly gone full Grinch and decided to bah humbug the whole thing off?' he scoffed. 'I don't think so.'

'Not full Grinch. More like a partial Grinch, just the Grinch tip.' I unwrapped another chocolate and watched the cars blur into one another on the other side of the carriageway. 'I've had a lot on my mind, as you well know.'

A couple of months ago, I would tell anyone who asked (and plenty of people who didn't) that my life was perfect. I had an amazing job at Abbott & Howe,

4

one of the oldest and most prestigious law firms in England, and I was so close to being promoted to junior partner, I'd been having borderline erotic dreams about my new business cards. I lived in a lovely house in lovely west Hampstead with my lovely boyfriend and we were talking about potentially considering adopting a dog. Everything was moving in the right direction. At least it was until my lovely boyfriend declared he was leaving me for Justine, his receptionist, and I had to move out of my lovely house. Shortly after that, I had something of a meltdown at work and now, when I looked at myself in the rear-view mirror, it seemed likely that the RSPCA would put me up for adoption before they allowed me to take charge of a living, breathing animal.

'So now he's not only the chump who broke your heart, he's Michael Darden, the dentist who stole Christmas?' Manny asked with a scowl. 'I knew I should have punched him in the nuts when I went to pick up your stuff but no, you told me not to.'

My stomach performed a clumsy death drop into my pelvis. More than three months and I still couldn't hear his name without wanting to wash my hair in honey and headbutt a beehive.

'Like I said, you can't punch him in the nuts because it will make things weird if we get back together,' I said. 'And we *could* still get back together.'

Manny tightened his grip on the steering wheel but said nothing.

'I saw a TikTok that said men who are about to make a major commitment need to stretch like an elastic band, to test their boundaries before they come back to you.

Michael could be stretching.' I was babbling. I knew I shouldn't want him back, but I couldn't help myself. I missed brushing his blond hair out of his green eyes before we kissed. I missed the way he always put the coffee on before I woke up. I missed coming home to hear him shouting at the television then turning it off and pretending he was reading. I missed us. Everything fell apart when we did, and all I wanted was my life back the way it was.

'The only thing he's stretching is his receptionist's vagina. You are thirty-two, you are not allowed to get relationship advice from a fourteen-year-old on TikTok who has skim-read her nan's copy of *Men Are from Mars, Women Are from Venus* then made up a dance about it,' he replied. I bit my lip to stop myself from telling him it was actually a very well-choreographed routine. 'You've got to let him go. You've been in goblin mode for far too long – you don't go anywhere, you don't do anything and you haven't posted so much as a half-decent meme in weeks. I rely on you for all my astrology content, it's really not on. No one else cares about my moon sign, Gwen, no one.'

'Been trying to stay off Instagram,' I muttered, clicking my fingernails against each other. Michael hardly ever posted, but seeing his face hurt in just the right way. Nevertheless, Manny had a point. I felt all wrong. It was as though I'd been put through a hot wash and I'd come out the wrong shape. Fundamentally the same but irrevocably buggered. 'I'm officially changing the subject. Talk to me about work, are you excited to go back?'

'Yes?' I pulled the hood of my sweatshirt all the way

up and over my face. For someone who wanted me to cheer up, he was going the wrong way about it. 'Next question.'

'Are you going to tell your mum and dad what happened?'

'Absolutely not and neither are you,' I replied. 'I don't want to worry them.'

Or deal with how impossibly disappointed they would be if they knew what had happened.

'What if they want to be worried?' Manny countered. 'They are your parents, you know.'

'And they have enough on without me adding to their load,' I reminded him. My job was to smooth things over when Manny stayed out too late and didn't call, when Cerys got her nose pierced without permission, when Dad got drunk at Aunt Gloria's second wedding and told her it was about time she got a good seeing-to and Mum didn't talk to him for a week. Whenever we hit a bumpy road, I was there to smooth it out, with good grades, a smiling face and absolutely no drama.

'Anyway, it's not that big of a deal,' I added. 'I probably made things sound worse than they were when I told you what happened.'

He did not look convinced.

'I'm not sure how you could make it sound any better. I've had nightmares about it and I wasn't even there.'

And that was exactly why I couldn't tell my parents.

'I'm serious, there's nothing to tell them,' I insisted, fighting off flashbacks of flying staplers and high-pitched shrieks. 'Once I'm back at work, it'll be like nothing ever happened. All I want is for life to go back to the way it was, back to normal.'

'Whatever that means.' Manny took his hand off the gear stick to squeeze my knee. I smiled and covered his hand with my own. He truly was the best cousin a girl could ask for and I knew I was lucky to have him. Even if he did buy us Amazon gift cards for Christmas. 'I know it's been a rough couple of months but I think this is exactly what you need. Broken-hearted big-city lawyer comes home for a family Christmas in the country? All that's missing is for you to meet a member of the landed gentry who's fallen on hard times and needs free legal advice.'

'What if I get snowed in at the pub and meet a visiting prince from a very small Scandinavian country?' I suggested with a grin. 'It's a shame we don't have a family bakery that needs saving as well.'

'Or a failing shop that somehow has survived until now selling nothing but Christmas ornaments and is about to be put out of business by a mega corporation? Although you never know what Nan's been up to in our absence, I wouldn't put that one past her.' He held his hand out for another sweet and I rummaged around in the tin for his favourite. 'I'm serious though, let's make a pact. You are going to have a perfect Christmas. Twenty-four hours with your nearest and dearest, no worrying about ex-boyfriends or London law firms or how long it's been since you had your highlights done.' I reflexively reached a hand up to my sad hair. 'Nothing but pure, unadulterated, festive joy and more Ferrero Rocher than you can shake a stick at. Then, when we get back to town, we'll set fire to your sweatpants and all will be right with the world.'

'That does sound nice,' I admitted, warming to at least part of the idea. 'Everything except for the sweatpants.'

'Fine,' he said with a grunt. 'You can keep your elasticated waists but you have to give me a fifty per cent increase in goodwill to all men and promise to join in all my reindeer games.'

'Done and done,' I replied. A good lawyer always knew when to take the deal. 'We will have the perfect Christmas. Should be doable as long as we start on the Baileys before Cerys arrives.'

'Gwen Baker, the woman with the plan.' Manny held up his hand for a high five, only swerving into the next lane for a second. 'You always were the clever one.'

I turned up the volume on the CD player as the first bars of 'Last Christmas' echoed through the speakers, the festive spirit almost, *almost* upon me.

'If I'm the clever one, what does that make you?'

'The pretty one,' Manny replied, cranking the volume even higher, the swell of tinkling keyboards drowning out the sounds of the motorway. 'Obviously.'

'So obvious,' I agreed, clapping as the beat dropped. 'Thank you for the pep talk.'

'Any time,' he said with a flash of a smile. 'I just want my Gwen back.'

'All you want for Christmas is me.' I grinned and my cousin laughed.

'There's my girl,' he said as he pulled off the motorway. 'And here's our exit, almost there now.'

Out of nowhere, I felt a tiny flicker of excitement somewhere so deep inside it would have taken a crack surgical team to find its exact location, but still, it was there. Maybe this was what I needed. A couple of days away from London, my caring family waiting on me hand and foot and a never-ending supply of food, drinks and tiny wrapped chocolate we never ate any other time of the year even though they were perennially available and always delicious.

Maybe I would have myself a merry little Christmas after all.

CHAPTER TWO

'Anyone home?' I called through the open door of my parents' house. 'Twas the night before Christmas and all through the house the sound of the news at ten blared so loudly, I had to assume my dad had lost his hearing aids again.

'Here she is, here she is,' he bellowed, bursting out of the living room like an oversized toddler, cracked out on mince pies and late nights. 'Well? What's the news? Have they come to their senses and put you in charge of the whole bloody place yet?'

Since retiring earlier in the year, my father had transferred all his legal eagle ambition on to me. He'd always had grand plans, ever since I told him I was going to LCL to study law, just like he had, but lately things had got a bit out of hand. Casual monthly check-ins slowly became well-meaning weekly probes and, more recently, frighteningly frequent demands, more than once a day, wanting to know what was going on with my job. If I didn't answer his text, I got a phone call, if I didn't answer the phone call, we went to FaceTime. I was getting better at responding early for fear of him showing up outside my flat with a megaphone.

'Not yet, but there's still a couple of hours left in the day,' I quipped, my cheeks flaming as red as his festive pyjamas. 'Is Mum still up?'

'In there, still fannying around with the tree. You know your mum, she never stops.' Dad held out his hands for my suitcase. 'Go and say hello, I'll help Manny get the rest of the stuff out the car.'

'Thank goodness,' I said, rolling my eyes. 'He could use a hand with all those heavy gift cards.'

No matter how busy things were, I did my best to get home as often as I could, but it felt as though I'd hardly been up at all over the past year. Once for an ill-fated Easter weekend that ended in family-wide food poisoning and an up-and-down pop-in for Dad's big birthday and retirement party back in July, but when I entered the living room to a roaring fire in the hearth, Christmas cards on the mantlepiece and a real, towering tree taking up half the living room, my heart grew three sizes. This was exactly where I wanted to be.

'There's my little girl!'

Mum jumped up to her feet, hurling her entire five-foot-nothing frame at mine for a bear hug and then thrusting me into the armchair by the fire. My mother was like something straight out of an advert for vitamins marketed to the over fifty-fives. Petite and lean and always in motion, she simply never stopped. Up with the lark for a run around the village, healthy breakfast, packed lunch, off to school where she'd been head of science since I went there, yoga after work, cooked dinner on the table, smart silver and black bob, tidy cupboards, go go go. In my mind she was a blur.

'We were worried you wouldn't make it up,' Mum said, tidying away a box of chocolates she'd been hanging on the tree. They never went up until Christmas Eve because my dad quite rightly claimed being made to stare at chocolates you can't eat for an entire month is a human rights violation. 'They said the traffic was terrible on the news. Was the traffic terrible?'

'No worse than usual, it was fine, gave me more time to eat more sweets.'

'Do you want anything?' she asked. 'Something proper to eat? Something to drink? You look completely haggard. Oh, you're not well, I can tell. Are you ill? Is it flu? Or are you just not wearing any make-up?'

'Didn't sleep well last night,' I choked out as she yanked at my coat, wrapping the arms around my back and turning it into a straitjacket for one very brief, panic-stricken moment. 'I'll be right as rain in the morning.'

But I wasn't getting off that easily. She stood in front of me, her blue eyes boring into my brown ones, like a human lie-detector test. There was no upside to having a schoolteacher for a mother. She had seen it all.

'Are you really all right?'

I nodded. Somewhat true.

'Work's going well?'

I nodded. Entirely false.

'The new flat? How's that working out?'

Like living in a poorly ventilated bookshop stockroom that only had one window, barely functioning heating and a boiler that only warmed enough water for one tepid shower a day. Manny's friend Beck had described it as 'bohemian' when she showed me around but in truth it was a disaster.

'I love it.'

'And have you spoken to Michael?'

I attempted a casual shrug, but my shoulders got confused and forgot the second part of the motion, locking up around my ears instead, and instead of smiling, I just showed her my top teeth. I looked like a confused, constipated badger.

'I'm giving him space.'

An entire galaxy of it, against my will.

'You know you don't need to worry about me, Mum, everything is fantastic,' I lied, actively squeezing my shoulder muscles with my hands until they relaxed. 'Life couldn't be better, I promise.'

Aside from the aching, cavernous void in my soul that kept me awake at night and routinely sent me spiralling down a 3 a.m. YouTube rabbit hole, searching for bad acoustic cover versions of 'Someone Like You' performed by off-key teenagers in Idaho, while I shovelled chocolate Häagen-Dazs down my gullet in between gut-wrenching sobs.

But still, Christmas. Hurrah.

I beamed at the room around me. Manny was right, Christmas was going to be wonderful. Nothing to do other than eat myself into type two diabetes and occasionally change the channel on the telly. 'I should've known, you never give me any trouble. Thankfully I get enough from your sister and your cousin,' Mum said, her Welsh accent lilting as she clutched my coat to her heart. 'Now take your bloody shoes off, I've hoovered up in here.'

There really was no place like home.

* * *

14

'I didn't know if you were planning to stop at the services on the way up so I didn't make you a proper dinner.' She pulled me out of the chair she'd just pushed me into and led me, shoeless, into the kitchen before I could say a word. 'But I put a few bits out for you and Manny, you can help yourself.'

'There are enough sausage rolls here to feed the entire village,' I said as I came face to face with what looked like an entire stockroom of the big Tesco laid out on the kitchen table. Be still my grumbling tum. Mum and Dad weren't particularly adventurous eaters but if you made it in a mini size and whacked it in the snack section, they were all over it. The Bakers really did love their picky bits.

'Can't have Manny going hungry,' Mum replied, bustling over to the oven to remove a batch of mince pies. 'He's a growing boy.'

'We're both thirty-two and he's already six-foot-three,' I reminded her as I took my regular seat at the table, already halfway through a mini pork pie. Underneath the table, I subtly unfastened the top button of my jeans. Might as well start as I meant to go on. 'The only direction he's going to grow if he eats all this is outwards. I saw on the news it might snow tomorrow.'

'So your dad said, I'll believe it when I see it. Did he tell you your Aunt Gloria called right before you got here? Natalie's gone into the hospital, we might have a Christmas baby in the family if we're lucky.'

'Bloody unlucky for Natalie if we don't get a Christmas baby,' I replied as I swallowed the pork pie and grabbed a jam tart. 'I very much doubt she wants to be in labour for more than twenty-four hours.'

'You shot out of there like you couldn't wait another minute. Made a right mess of me you did, but it was worth it.' I choked on a bit of pastry. Since when was an episiotomy something to get nostalgic about? 'Your sister on the other hand, now she took her sweet time. Nearly two days I was in with her. Your dad had to go out and buy another box of cigars because he couldn't hold his water in the waiting room.'

'And he almost missed the birth altogether when he went out for a bacon sandwich,' I finished the story for her and we both smiled. It was not the first time I had heard it. 'Classic Cerys. Probably wanted to run through the numbers one more time before she made her appearance.'

'Bickering already and she's not even here yet,' Mum shot me a mild warning look. 'You're worse than the kids at school. I don't want any arguments tomorrow.'

'What was it you always used to say? I want never gets,' I replied with a smile. My older sister was my peacekeeper kryptonite, but then Cerys could get a rise out of a Buddhist monk.

Mum placed a brand-new jar of Branston's pickle on the table. 'My kingdom for a quiet Christmas. One day without you three fighting, that's all I ask for.'

'You never know.' I nabbed a cocktail sausage. 'Christmas is a good time to pray for miracles.'

'I'll give you a miracle,' she said, clipping me lightly around the back of the head. 'Go and get your cousin, I bet him and your dad are out there gossiping with the front door wide open.'

Pausing to slip on my trainers, I made it to the front doorstep in time to see Manny locking up the Volvo, my dad kicking at a slightly underinflated tyre with his slipper then clapping his nephew on the back. Manny put his arm around Dad's shoulders and the two of them laughed at a joke I couldn't quite hear. I smiled, lingering in the doorway so as not to interrupt.

I didn't remember much about my Uncle Jim, Manny's dad. He was a lorry driver so he worked away a lot and Manny and I were only nine when he died. An invisible patch of black ice, no one else involved, nothing anyone could have done. But I did remember how sad people were afterwards. Dad didn't cry in front of me or Cerys but his grief was always with us, hanging around the house like an uninvited guest: no one knew how long it might stay or when it might be polite to ask it to leave, so we quietly entertained it for as long as it cared to stay.

A week or so after the funeral, Manny moved in with us. Just for a little while, while Aunt Sue went to stay with her sister in Portugal to 'get herself together'. A few weeks turned into a few months and after a year or so, Aunt Sue decided she wasn't coming back and it became clear Manny was staying with us for good. It worked out perfectly for Dad, who had always wanted a son and missed his brother something fierce, and for ten-year-old Manny, who was completely alone and all at sea. The two of them needed each other and the universe seemed to know it, plus I'd been in the market for a brother ever since Cerys cut the hair off my Rollerblading Sindy so it worked out pretty nicely for me as well. Twenty years later, we were more twins than cousins, and I couldn't imagine our lives without him.

* * *

'Who wants a drink?' Dad asked as I placed the last of my presents underneath the tree.

'Me please,' I called, head lost in the branches. Mum's tree was a marvel, tall and full and swimming in ornaments, most of them even older than me. I lay on my back underneath it, sniffing up a great big lungful of its precious pine scent and felt every atom of my body relax.

'Use the nice ones,' Mum instructed when Dad reached for the everyday glasses. 'It's officially Christmas now these two are home.'

Shuffling out from underneath the tree, I sat cross-legged on the floor, watching him pour out sensible measures I knew would be doubled by this time tomorrow. Whisky for me, Mum and Manny, a Tia Maria and Coke for himself. Legend had it he switched to peach schnapps and lemonade for one heady summer in the early eighties but I refused to believe it.

'What's the plan of attack for tomorrow?' Manny asked, gratefully accepting his glass.

'Good question,' I said, shooting him the finger guns before receiving my own. 'Anything we should be aware of in advance?'

'You can always tell the lawyer in the room,' Dad clucked with puffed-out pigeon chest pride as I took a deep sip of the single malt. 'Nothing you need to worry about. Get up, do presents, your sister will be here by one, I should think.'

'Nan said she'd be here for half-eleven,' Mum said. 'Lunch at two, then it's open house at Dorothy's across the road as usual, there's someone there I want you to meet.'

'An old biddy who needs free legal advice,' Manny whispered in my ear.

'And I might have one or two surprises in store,' Dad added with a wink. 'A little bit of something to brighten up the day.'

I cheered, Manny groaned and Dad laughed, all while Mum chugged her whisky in one gulp. She took great pride in being the strongest drinker in the house, not that it was much of a competition. Dad was under the table after a sniff of the barmaid's apron, but Mum had the iron constitution of a particularly lairy ox, a trait I had sadly not inherited.

'Right then, I'm off to bed,' Mum declared with a double slap of the thighs. 'Someone has to be up at half past five to put the turkey in the oven and I'm guessing it won't be any of you. Are you coming, Steve?'

'Aye, I'll be up behind you as soon as I've finished this,' Dad replied, contentedly sipping his cocktail. 'Maybe I'll give you your present early.'

'You can stay out of my stockings, you randy old bugger.'

He winked as Mum put the Tia Maria back in the cabinet. 'She says that in front of you but it'll be a different story upstairs.'

It was always so good to know your parents were having more sex than you were.

'Don't you two be up all night,' Mum warned. 'You know Father Christmas won't come if you're not asleep by midnight.'

Manny looked over at me with feigned innocence. 'Did you hear that, Gwen? Auntie Bronwyn doesn't want you scaring off another man, all right?'

'Self-employed small businessman with working transportation who does things on the day he's actually supposed to do them *and* keeps his boots shiny?' I scoffed. 'Father Christmas is well out of my league.'

'I worry about you two sometimes,' Dad said, groaning as he stood before stooping to kiss me goodnight. 'Listen to your mother and don't be long for bed.'

'We won't,' we promised in chorus as they disappeared upstairs leaving us alone with the twinkling tree, carols playing in the background and most importantly, the open bottle of whisky.

'How are you feeling?' Manny asked as I sipped my drink.

'Surprisingly warm and fuzzy,' I replied.

'Perfection. Now all you have to do is stay that way.'

Closing my eyes, I listened to the carols playing in the background, the crackling flames of the fire.

'I have a plan,' I said. 'Don't worry about work, don't think about Michael and don't fight with my sister. Simple, right?'

'More simple than a meerkat trying to sell me car insurance,' Manny nodded. 'Fancy a top-up?'

'Go on then, since it's Christmas.' I peered up the chimney, just in case. No sign of red trousers, shiny boots or a sack full of toys. 'Besides, it isn't as though anything legitimately catastrophic can happen, is it? Christmas is only one day. How bad could it possibly be?'

CHAPTER THREE

The next morning, I woke up warm and cosy in my childhood bedroom, the central heating absurdly high as always and the smell of Mum's cooking wafting up the stairs, and I smiled.

It was Christmas Day and it was going to be wonderful.

I felt around under the bed, searching for my phone, the wall socket too far away and my charging cable too short to reach the bedside table. All my friends with kids had been up for hours, posting picture after picture of their kids tearing into piles of presents. New Barbies, first bikes, so much excitement. I tapped away at the screen, loving each one as it came up, my heart swelling at the joy of it all. If that wasn't the definition of Christmas, I didn't know what was. Making new memories and reliving old ones, all wrapped around each other like layers of wrapping paper. The year I got my roller boots and promptly decked it on the driveway, skinning both my knees in my nightie. Getting properly drunk for the first time on Christmas Eve with Manny and Dev, our friend from next door. Slipping my job offer from Abbott & Howe into Dad's stocking. The first time I brought Michael home to meet the family . . .

Nope, I reminded myself sharply, I was not going to think about Michael today. It was part of the plan.

It was nice to wake up in familiar surroundings for once. Getting dumped by the man you thought you were going to marry was in and of itself incredibly shit, and waking up every day in a strange flat, surrounded by strange things didn't make it any easier. I wasn't the one who'd chosen to end things, why did I have to leave? Aside from the fact it was technically his house and as soon as he made his announcement, he told me he'd already packed my bag and called me an Uber? Fairness had always been one of my biggest concerns in life and losing my dream man *and* my heated bathroom floor in one fell swoop still felt like injustice of the highest order. It definitely should have been one or the other, not both on the same day.

A text popped up in front of a photo of a toothless toddler on a skateboard and broke my train of thought. *Rhiannon Liberty Conners, born at 4.47 a.m. this morning. Mummy and baby doing well, best present we could have wished for!*

I tapped on the photo sent by my Aunt Gloria to see my cousin, Natalie, tired and emotional, damp blonde hair pushed back from her face, gazing down at the squishy pink lump in her arms. My baby cousin had a baby of her own. A tiny sob escaped my throat as I enlarged the photo of the newest member of the family.

'Happy birthday, Rhiannon,' I whispered a solemn oath. 'I promise I will always buy you separate Christmas and birthday presents.'

'Gwen? Are you up?'

Dad rapped on the door before poking his head into my room, beaming from ear to ear. 'What are you doing still in bed, chicken? *He's been*! Don't you want your presents?'

'Well, that's a silly question, isn't it?' I replied, bouncing out of bed and slipping my feet into a pair of red slippers. 'Give me a minute, I'm coming.'

'Bacon butties will be ready in five,' he called as he trotted off down the hall to bang on Manny's bedroom door. 'Up and out of bed or I'll eat them all myself.'

Now there was a threat that could get me moving.

'Simply having a wonderful Christmas time,' I sang to the Gwen in the mirror before giving her a wink and rushing off downstairs.

The tree lights twinkled in the semi-darkness of the living room, front curtains still closed, because you did not open the front curtains when you were all still in your pyjamas, according to my mother. Dad's promised bacon butties waited patiently on the coffee table and four mugs of tea sat in their four traditional spots, two on the side table, one on the corner of the hearth and one tucked away around the corner of the settee where I was less likely to kick it over, which I had only done once in thirty-two years but this family had the memory of an elephant. Christmas morning 1996 – when I spilt tea on her Sweater Shop sweatshirt before she had a chance to wear it – was only one among many things Cerys had never forgiven me for.

'How about a walk after this?' Dad said, looking at me and Manny as he lowered himself into his chair. 'Get some fresh air into the lungs?'

'Someone go with him,' Mum ordered. 'He won't admit it but he's got a bad hip.'

'I'll pass,' Manny replied. 'Bit worried my choked-up city lungs wouldn't cope with it.'

Sliding under the tree, I began sorting all the presents into piles.

Manny looked like a festive Adonis in nothing but a pair of black Calvin Klein boxers and a pair of reindeer antlers, entirely unfair for someone who only went to the gym to use the nice shampoo and take selfies. Not that I blamed him, I was sweltering in my red tartan pyjamas and dressing gown. 'What about you, Gwen?'

'Sorry, can't.'

'Why not?'

'Don't want to.'

I smiled sweetly as I handed him the first present.

'You'd think a bit of exercise would kill you,' he grumbled, holding the gift up to his ear and giving it a shake.

'Can you say for certain that it won't?' I asked. Dad sighed, giving up. 'Exactly,' I said, passing a shiny silver parcel to Manny. 'I rest my case.'

'Now, don't get too excited,' Mum said as I scuttled behind my gifts once distribution was complete. 'I told you we weren't going mad this year, it's mostly sensible stuff, socks and smellies and a few silly bits.'

Dad tossed a handful of red serviettes at Manny who already had tomato sauce running down his chin and scoffed. 'Don't listen to her, if anything she's got worse. There hasn't been a day gone by in the last three months when she hasn't come through the door with something to be hidden away in a cupboard.'

'Says the man who's already eaten and replaced an entire tin of Quality Street,' she replied. 'I obviously didn't hide them that well, did I, Steven?'

'Tis the season,' Dad said, proudly sipping his tea.

'OK, Mum goes first,' I ordered, my heartbeat quickening at the sight of all the shiny paper and sparkly bows. As far as I was concerned, presents were the best part of Christmas. Not in a greedy Scrooge way, it didn't really matter to me what was inside the presents, what mattered was the fact someone had taken the time, effort, and their hard-earned cash to go out and pick something with you in mind, wrap it up and give it to you as a token of their affection. A present was confirmation that you mattered, that you were loved, whether it was a bottle of bubble bath or a diamond ring. Not that anyone had ever given me a diamond ring, but obviously that was still something of a sore subject. Gift-giving was one of my love languages (along with physical affection, acts of service and a never-ending exchange of cat gifs) and Christmas gifts were the best kinds of gifts, because everyone gave and received at the same time. It was impossible to be unhappy when you were handing out and unwrapping presents, that was an indisputable scientific fact. Probably.

'You're up, Gwen.' Mum pointed to the large, rectangular box in front of me. The very last gift left. 'That one's from your dad. He even wrapped it himself.'

'Only the best for the best,' Dad said, flushing with pride. 'I know it's been a stressful year for you, this will help you relax.'

'If it's the codeine left over from your root canal, she has to share,' Manny said, pulling a brand-new black hoodie over his antlers.

'If you're very nice to her, perhaps she'll let you have a go with it,' Dad replied with a wink. 'I read an article in *The Lawyer* magazine that said Austin, Rhodes & Rollins gave them to all their partners last Christmas. It only seemed right that you should have one too.'

Ignoring the unpleasant sinking sensation in my stomach that came along with any mention of my job, I pasted a smile on my face and focused on tearing away the wrapping paper. What could it be? Bubble bath? A silk dressing gown? A weighted blanket so heavy it would pin me to the settee and trap me in their house forever?

No.

Oh no.

It was not any of those things.

Holding the box at arm's length, I looked up at my dad, horrified.

'Oh, you lucky girl,' Manny gushed, snatching the box out of my hands. 'Father Christmas brought you a vibrator!'

'What are you on about? It's the Gen 2 Cordless Personal Wonder Wand!' Dad replied, grabbing it away from him as I sat frozen in shock. 'It's a massager not a vibrator!'

'No, Uncle Steve,' Manny said, shaking his head. 'I'm both sorry and delighted to say you've bought your daughter a vibrator. And a good one as well, from the looks of it, very nice.'

'It's a *massager*,' Dad repeated as he read the back of the box, the look on his face less certain now. 'See here? Three speed settings, four massage patterns. *Massage*, Emmanuel!'

But my cousin was unmoved in his ruling.

'Yes, in that it massages vaginas,' he replied. 'No judgement here, she'll get a lot more use out of this than that salad spinner she got from Aunt Gloria.'

Dad tore open the box, removing the 'massage wand' from the packaging and wielded it over his head like a sex-toy-sceptre. 'They had them on *This Morning*!' he bellowed. 'They don't have vibrators on *This Morning*! Come here, Gwen, let me show you—'

'Steve!' Mum barked as I threw myself behind her, Manny rolling onto his back and hooting with laughter. 'Stop trying to vibrate our daughter!'

'It's a back massager,' Dad said one last time, staring forlornly at the massage wand and putting two and two together until he had no choice but to come up with 'sex toy'. 'You've all got dirty minds, that's the problem here.'

'Thank you, Dad, I'm sure it's brilliant,' I told him, gingerly taking the offending article out of his hands and holding it with the very tips of my fingers. 'And you know, my shoulders have been playing up, I absolutely need this.'

'Too right you do,' Manny commented, wiping tears out of his eyes.

'Shut up,' I replied sweetly. 'Thank you, Dad.'

'Right, that's presents done for another year,' Mum said with a smile so tight I was worried her face might snap. 'Let's get all of this tidied up before Cerys and her lot get here. Gwen, maybe you should put your presents in your room?'

She pulled a bin bag out of thin air like a sad magician, scooping up all the shiny, glittery wrapping paper and stuffing it deep inside the black hole of the plastic bag.

'It *is* a bloody back massager,' Dad grumbled as he disappeared into the kitchen to put the kettle on again, the official gesture of a broken man.

Everyone knew Christmas proper didn't start until Nan arrived. Just before twelve, Myfanwy James floated into the kitchen on a cloud of Chanel No. 5 and offered a flawlessly powdered cheek to Mum, then Manny, then me and finally, my dad. I hid a smile as she looked him up and down. Dad immediately and without a word of dissent tucked his loose shirt tails into his trousers.

Oh to wield such power.

'The turkey smells lovely, Bronwyn,' Nan said, Manny helping her out of her coat as she scanned the kitchen for invisible transgressions. 'What time did you put it in?'

'Half past seven.' Mum dabbed her brow with a gravy-covered tea towel. 'I'm basting every forty minutes, I'll have it out to rest in half an hour.'

'What kind of potatoes have you done?'

'Mashed and roast.'

'And did you get the vegetables from Reg? I told him to keep some to one side for you. I know you usually get yours from the *supermarket.*'

Somewhere out there, I was certain Mr Sainsbury's sphincter had just clenched and he didn't know why.

'I did. They were perfect, thank you.'

Nan nodded her approval and the little vein that was pulsing above Mum's right eye disappeared.

'All right then. Now, since it's Christmas, I'll have a drop of sherry if you've a bottle open,' she declared, taking herself off to the living room and leaving the rest of us to breathe a sigh of relief.

'Gwen, come and sit with me and Manny,' Nan ordered, holding her hand out for the extremely generous drink we watched my dad pour with a shaky hand. Even at eighty-three my nan was one of the most intimidating women to have ever set foot on this earth. Five foot two, pure white hair and sharper than those knives they sell on TV at three in the morning, she was my absolute hero. Maybe she wasn't quite as energetic as she used to be but she still drove her own car, always had at least three different books on the go and most importantly, took zero guff from anyone. When I was little, I used to tell people I wanted to be exactly like her when I grew up. All these years later and that was still the dream.

'Stand up, let me see that dress,' she ordered as Dad scuttled back into the kitchen and out of the way.

'Do you like it?' I asked. I gave her a dutiful twirl before smoothing down the soft, deep red velvet of my brand-new frock, one of the few late-night misery purchases I'd actually loved and kept. The high neck and long skirt felt formal enough for a family Christmas but the deep V in the back, cut just above my bra line, stopped it from feeling too matronly. Most importantly, the empire-line cut meant it was roomy enough to strap seventeen boxes of Jaffa Cakes around my midriff should the need arise and I very much hoped it would. Aside from the fact I'd stabbed myself with a little gold safety pin when I took the price tag off earlier, it really was the perfect dress.

Nan screwed up her face with distaste.

'It's awful.'

Or maybe it wasn't.

'What?'

'It's awful,' Nan repeated, as though it were an inarguable fact. 'It's hanging off you. Why would you buy something three sizes too big?'

'It's empire line, it's supposed to be loose.' I pulled lightly at the fabric I'd been completely in love with ten seconds earlier. 'You don't like it?'

'It looks like a tent,' she declared. 'I could get an entire circus under that thing, elephants and all. If you throw a dozen tables and chairs under it, we could rent it out for weddings.'

I fell back onto the settee. 'This style is very popular, Nan, it's sold out everywhere, it's meant to be loose. I wanted something that would be comfortable to eat in.'

'How much are you planning to eat?' she asked, incredulous as she unfastened the bottom button of her smart skirt suit jacket, a small snowflake brooch sparkling tastefully. 'Do you want to end up with gout like your grandad? Popular doesn't always equate to good, love. Smoking when you were pregnant was popular when I was your age. *Mr Blobby* was popular.'

She despised Mr Blobby. No one could tell you why, but God help him *and* Noel Edmonds if they ever bumped into my nan down a dark alley of an evening.

'Cerys is here!' Mum sang out from the kitchen and everyone in the living room froze. 'Someone get the door, I've got my hand up the turkey.'

Manny and Nan sat stock still, not moving a muscle.

'I'll go, shall I?' I said, standing up slowly.

'Get it and lock it,' Manny replied. 'What if I close the curtains and we're all very quiet?'

Nan knocked back the rest of her glass in one gulp. 'I know children are a blessing and I hate to say it, but I can't stand those kids.'

I paused by the tree, one eyebrow raised. 'You mean your beloved great-grandchildren?'

'Go and let your sister in and I'll have less of your cheek,' she tutted loudly. 'You've too much of me in you, Gwen Baker, that's your problem.'

'Biggest compliment ever,' I replied as I closed the living-room door behind me.

When my parents told six-year-old Cerys she was getting a sibling, she asked if she could get a pony instead. When Dad said no, the baby was already on its way, she tried to negotiate down to a dog, and I'd been nothing but a disappointing substitute ever since. It was impossible for us to be in the same room for more than twenty minutes without coming to blows and it had been that way for so long, ever since teenaged Cerys decided she was far too cool to have anything to do with her little sister and her nerdy cousin. But I'd promised Mum I would try, and if a virgin could give birth to a baby deity, perhaps Cerys and I could find a way to get along for a couple of hours. Admittedly it would be a bigger miracle than the baby in the manger, but a promise was a promise.

With a deep breath, I turned the lock, put on a huge smile and—

'Christ, it's roasting in here.' Cerys threw open the door and crushed me against the wall before I even had the chance to speak. 'Is the thermostat broken?'

Easing out from behind the door, I rubbed my probably-not-broken wrist, wondering whether or not I had enough strength left in it for one good punch. People who said violence was never the answer didn't have older siblings.

'Merry Christmas, Cerys. Good drive?'

'No such thing,' she replied, her eyes darting all over the hallway as she fished around for something in her enormous handbag. 'Have they painted in here? I told them to get a decorator to do it. I hope Mum hasn't had Dad up that bloody stepladder again, he's too old to be faffing about.'

'He's only sixty-five, Care,' I replied. 'Bit early to be putting him out to pasture.'

Through the open door, I shuddered when I saw Artemis and Arthur, my niece and nephew, leaping from their car seats and sprinting up the garden path towards me. The pair of them were terrifying, with red hair and wild eyes, and were unnaturally strong for children. Last Easter, I'd watched in horror as they tore a sealed cardboard box to shreds with their bare hands because Manny told them there was a bag of Percy Pigs inside. Not that I wouldn't have reacted in the same way but it was still very unnerving to see tiny children destroy something in less time than it took me to eat a Hobnob.

My sister paused and took a step back to properly look me up and down. While I had Dad's wavy, reddish-brown, hair and the solid Baker family build, Cerys took after our mum. Her hair was long and thick and black, and her petite body, once all sharp planes and angles, had been softened by the two terrors who ran straight past the pair of us into the living room where the presents lived. Even with two kids and a full-time job, she had an effortless grace about her. I had to work hard to look professional and put together, whereas Care was always elegant and chic.

'You look like shit.'

She was also extremely rude.

'Seriously, Gwen.' She dumped her bag on the chest of drawers at the bottom of the stairs and combed her hands through her shampoo-ad hair. 'You look ill. You look like you haven't had a good night's sleep in a month.'

'Well, it's probably closer to three so I'll take that as a compliment,' I said, letting the smile I'd been working hard to keep on my face disintegrate as she pushed past me and marched into the kitchen.

'If it isn't my favourite sister-in-law!'

Just when I thought things couldn't get more annoying, Cerys's husband swaggered into the house. Oliver was the opposite of my sister. Too big, too loud, too brash, he was a sledgehammer of a man with a thatch of strawberry-blond hair and ruddy cheeks that screamed 'Ask me the rugby scores, I definitely know them'. For years he'd been torturing us with his rudeness, his know-it-all attitude and impossibly blunt statements, and for the life of me, I could not work out what my sister saw in him.

Suffice to say, we didn't get on.

'Merry Christmas, Oliver,' I said, presenting him with my cheek against every better instinct. If my life was a horror movie, I would absolutely be one of those people who invited a serial killer into the house out of politeness and got murdered while they put the kettle on.

'Merry Christmas, Gwen,' he replied. 'I heard you got dumped.'

And who's to say my life wasn't a horror movie?

'And I heard you'd developed some tact,' I said sweetly. 'But then I suppose not everything we hear is true.'

'Shall we do your presents?' Mum asked as we all swarmed into the living room, Artemis and Arthur already under the tree scavenging for brightly coloured packages with their names on them. But before they could attack, Cerys shook her head, pressing her beautifully manicured fingers into her temples.

'I know it's early but can we do presents after lunch? I'm ravenous and my blood sugar is *extremely* low. I don't want to get a migraine when I've got to drive back tonight.'

'I knew you weren't eating enough the moment you walked through the door,' Mum said, leaping to her feet. 'I can have the starter on the table in two minutes, get yourselves sat down.'

'But it's only just gone one, we don't eat until two!' Manny protested. 'And we never do presents after lunch, we think people who do presents after lunch are weird! I'm not even hungry yet.' He held up a handful of orange and silver foil to be presented as evidence. 'I only just finished Gwen's chocolate orange.'

'Manny, please shut up,' I whispered, slapping the chocolate wrapper out of his hand. 'The sooner we eat, the sooner they can leave, meaning the sooner we can finish the bottle of Bailey's in peace. And don't think you're not replacing that chocolate orange.'

'Better earlier than later,' Nan agreed as she nodded towards the front windows where the skies looked heavy and full. 'They've forecast snow this afternoon.'

'Worst comes to the worst, everyone can stay over,' Mum said happily as Cerys physically removed Arthur from his presents and carried him into the dining room, literally kicking and screaming. 'That would be nice, wouldn't it?'

I looked at Manny, Manny looked at me and Nan shook her head.

'My advice is to say nothing,' she advised, ushering us into the other room. 'How else do you think I've lived this long?'

CHAPTER FOUR

'The table looks beautiful, Bronwyn, that's a very . . . interesting centrepiece.' Nan said as she sat down. Great-Grandma James's tablecloth was almost entirely covered by poinsettia-printed place mats, Mum's 'special occasion' coasters and every single condiment known to man, all positioned around what looked like a moderately sized holly bush that had been plucked straight out of the garden, woven through with battery-operated fairy lights and sprayed with glitter. On top of the holly sat an entire nativity scene, cast with Sylvanian Families, and I was almost certain those Sylvanian Families used to be mine. I stared at the one-eyed grey rabbit playing Mary as I took the middle seat next to Nan, Manny subtly crossing himself as he sat down on my other side.

'I made it myself,' Mum said with a blush as Oliver the man-child reached out to touch the leaves and promptly pricked himself. 'I've been taking floristry classes in the village, turns out I've something of a natural talent for it.'

'You know they say florists have the same psychological profile as serial killers,' Cerys said, as her husband sucked his finger beside her.

'I'll keep that in mind if I find the time for another hobby,' Mum replied with pursed lips as she dumped a plate of pâté on toast down in front of her eldest.

Lunch was the part of the day I'd worried about the most. All of us, sat around a table with nothing to do but talk to each other? Terrifying. Thankfully I'd memorized the last five local council newsletters and was completely up to date on sports, politics *and* Kardashian gossip – in other words, I was perfectly equipped to keep the entire family talking about anything other than me.

'Crackers?' I waggled a red and gold cardboard tube underneath Manny's nose.

'You certainly are,' he replied, slapping it away. 'Uncle Steve, shall I open the wine?'

'Way ahead of you.' Dad stretched his arm through the tinsel-trimmed serving hatch and grabbed a bottle of Pinot Noir off the kitchen counter. 'Who wants some?'

Everyone at the table, including the two kids, put up their hands.

'Come on then, Gwen,' Dad said, pouring wine while Mum set out the rest of the starters. 'I want to hear all about everything that's happening at Abbott & Howe. What cases are you working on at the moment?'

'Oh, come on, Dad.' I picked up my fork and poked at my pâté. 'No one wants to talk about work at Christmas.'

'We've been *very* busy this year,' Oliver declared before my dad could reply. 'Doubled our business, haven't we, Cerys?'

Somewhere behind the holly, my sister nodded.

'That's grand, Ol,' Dad said, grinning across the table before turning back to me. 'You know I love to talk shop, chicken, tell me everything. Any big mergers? Cut-throat acquisitions?'

'It's really not that exciting,' I replied with a weak smile. 'Mostly pushing paper around and sending emails. Besides, there's very little I can say, what with all the NDAs and what have you. But enough about me, what about that World Cup final, eh? What a match—'

'If things are too sensitive to talk about, you can just say.' I blanched as he patted my hand, looking more pleased than ever. 'Can't blame your old dad for trying to live vicariously through his daughter.'

'We brought on three new people this year,' Cerys said loudly. 'That's ten staff we've got at Adlington & Adlington now, not including me and Ol.'

'There's always money to be made in personal injury claims,' Dad gave her an approving but undeniably disinterested nod as he started on his meal. 'You've set yourselves up nicely there.'

'Set yourself up as ambulance chasers,' Manny muttered, earning a kick under the table from my mother as Oliver raised his glass, oblivious to the slight.

'Not that I didn't love my little practice,' Dad went on, thoughtfully spearing a tiny pickled onion and holding it up in the air. 'But I've always wondered what would have happened if I'd gone down to London after university instead of coming back home. I think I would have done really well at a place like yours. My favourite lecturer at UCL always said I'd have thrived at a Magic Circle firm. Very different that is, from a local solicitor's.'

'You wouldn't have met me for a start,' Mum replied

sternly. 'So you wouldn't have these kids and you wouldn't be sat here now, wondering what would have happened if you'd moved to London when you should be eating your starter.'

'Point taken.' He popped the pickled onion into his mouth and blew her a kiss.

With her pâté barely touched, Nan pushed her plate away and fixed her gaze on me. 'You'll be pleased to know I don't want to hear about your work.' She wrinkled her nose at the very thought and I relaxed, stuffing a giant forkful of my starter into my mouth. 'What I want to know is, what the bloody hell happened with you and Michael?'

All eyes turned to me as I choked on my pâté.

'Sorry,' I replied, reaching for my water glass. 'What was that?'

'Everything was all right last Christmas,' Nan pressed on. 'And weren't you here at Easter? He seemed fine at Easter.'

I felt a supportive hand on my knee and glanced gratefully at Manny.

'He didn't come with me at Easter, he was busy. Say, Nan, did I read in the council newsletter that they're closing the post office on Mondays? You must be furious . . .'

'Busy shagging his receptionist,' Oliver whispered loudly enough for everyone to hear and I shrank down in my seat, my cheeks flushed.

Nan sniffed with distaste. 'His receptionist? Surely not, Gwen, that's very common behaviour.'

'I know, I'm sorry, I wish he'd been more original but no, he went with a classic.' I laughed awkwardly, wondering whether or not this was a good time to hurl myself through the dining-room window. 'Anyway, about the post office—'

'He never was good enough for you,' Mum said, choosing to ignore the fact she'd been sending me links to engagement rings and wedding venues every other day for at least the last two years. 'You're best off without him.'

'The man is an imbecile,' agreed Dad. 'Doesn't know a good thing when he sees it.'

'I don't know,' Oliver countered. 'I've seen a photo of the new girl and she looks like a good thing to me. Fit as.'

'These things happen.' I cleared my throat loudly but even the fuzzy beaver shepherds on mum's nativity scene looked as though they had more dignity than I did in that moment. 'And you never know what could happen in the future. Sometimes couples need to take a break *just like the post office.*'

'I don't know about best off without him,' Oliver grunted, ignoring the fact that if looks could kill, I'd have had him sliced, diced and six feet under. 'But who wants to shag a dentist? Going around putting their fingers in other people's mouths all day. Disgusting, that's what it is.'

'And suing Marks & Spencer because some idiot fell on their arse in the changing room then taking seventy-five per cent of the settlement isn't?' I replied in a voice so shrill, the holly and the ivy trembled all the way down to their roots. 'Seriously, isn't anyone bothered about the post office? What if I needed traveller's cheques on a Monday? What if I needed stamps?!'

'Crackers!' Manny said loudly, waving his Christmas cracker in the air. 'For the love of God, let's pull the crackers.'

'And we haven't even had our mains yet,' Nan said, her eyes glinting as we all picked up our crackers and did as we were told for the very last time that day.

It wasn't even half past three by the time the turkey was cleared away from the table but Oliver was already glassy-eyed as Dad opened a third bottle of wine.

'Did you know I was a silver service waiter when I was at Magdalen?' he slurred, snapping at a napkin with his fork and spoon, clutched between his thumb and forefingers like salad servers. 'I'm amazing at this. Kids, watch Daddy.'

'For God's sake, Oli,' Cerys muttered as he dropped his cutlery, both children sniggering behind their hands. 'You're almost as bad as the kids.'

'That's not fair,' Manny said. 'He's much worse than the kids.'

She glared at him over the pointy grey ears of the Virgin Mary but he continued to drink his wine calmly, giving her nothing but a wink.

'Here comes the pud!'

By the time Mum came sailing into the dining room, carrying the most beautiful Christmas pudding I'd ever seen, things were almost back to normal. Against all odds, we'd made it to my favourite part of lunch – not the dessert itself, no one *really* liked Christmas pudding – but a very special tradition. The Baker family Christmas wish.

'None for the kids if it's got brandy in it,' Cerys said as Mum set the pudding platter in the middle of the table with a flourish.

I leaned in to give it a sniff then reared back, my eyes

watering. 'None for the kids then,' I told her, choking on the fumes.

'Oliver can't have any because of his nut allergy and don't cut me a massive piece because I won't eat it.'

'No one eats it, you mush it up and push it around your plate until we all agree we've suffered enough,' Manny said, checking the time on his phone then pulling a face. 'Let her get on with it so we can leave the table while we're still young.'

I nudged him with my knee. 'Expecting a call?'

He made a variety of mumbling, clucking noises under his breath before shaking his head and slipping his phone underneath his thigh, out of sight.

Hmm, I thought, curious. It wasn't like Manny to be anything other than spectacularly and brutally honest.

'You all know the drill,' Dad said, waving at the pudding platter. 'Whoever finds the sixpence gets their wish granted but you can't tell anyone what it is or the wish won't come true!'

'What about last year when Manny almost choked on it?' Cerys asked. 'He hardly kept that to himself.'

'And my wish clearly didn't come true, did it?' he replied, staring directly at her very drunk husband.

'It's a new sixpence this year,' Mum said brightly, a huge serving spoon in her hand. Ignoring our bickering was her superpower. 'I wasn't sure how hygienic it was to use the old one after . . . the unpleasantness.'

'She means when you threw it up,' Cerys stage whispered to Manny.

'Steve, have you got the matches for the pudding?' Mum's eyes glowed maniacally as she gestured to the glossy dessert.

'Matches, matches, matches.' Dad patted himself down, a gentle frown on his face. 'Must be in the kitchen, excuse me a mo.'

'If anyone's going to throw up this year, it'll be your husband,' Manny hissed, peering around the centre-piece at my brother-in-law. 'He's gone the full Bruce Bogtrotter over there. Don't poke him whatever you do, he'll explode.'

'Did I tell you Bernard and Lesley across the road put a pool in?' Mum asked in a high-pitched voice. Truly, her ability to block us out was astounding. 'They've done a nice job, it's in a greenhouse-type thing so you can use it all year round. She's going to let us do water aerobics on Wednesdays.'

Oliver clumsily rested one elbow on the table and pointed in Manny's general direction.

'Why are you so obsessed with me?' he asked, his tipsy tongue struggling to make sense of his 's' sounds. 'You've been staring at me ever since we got here.'

'That's because I've never seen a human put away that many potatoes in one sitting,' Manny shrugged. 'It's very impressive.'

'I think you fancy me,' Oliver replied with a sloppy chuckle. 'I think you're in love with me.'

Every muscle in my body clenched as my cousin set down his glass, dabbed the corners of his mouth with his napkin and cleared his throat.

'You, Oliver, are one of the most insufferable people I've ever met. And I've had drinks with Donald Trump's hairdresser.'

'Oh, I've touched a nerve!' Oliver chortled. 'He fucking loves me. Gagging for a bit of old Oli, he is.'

'Oliver, language!' Nan cautioned, tipping her head towards the kids who were far too busy with their phones to pay any attention to the adults.

'I can swear in front of my kids if I want to,' he grunted.

'No, you can't,' Cerys replied, snatching his wine glass out of his hand as he went to take another drink.

'Steve? Where are those matches?' Mum leaned across the table and rapped hard on the door of the serving hatch. 'Are you chopping the bloody tree down yourself?'

'I don't know why I'm in trouble when he started it.' A chastened Oliver crossed his arms over his chest like a petulant child. 'All I said was he fancies me. Probably does, you know what his lot are like. Can't help themselves, the poofs.'

'STEVE!' Mum bellowed. 'WHERE ARE THE MATCHES?'

The mild expression on Manny's face never flickered but I could see his hand clenched in a fist underneath the table.

'Excuse me, everyone.' He balled up his napkin and tossed it on the table before pushing back his chair with an ear-splitting screech. 'I've lost my appetite.'

'And now it's Christmas,' Nan said, sipping her wine as he strode out the room. 'Well bloody done, Oliver.'

'I can't believe you just said that,' I said as the back door slammed shut. 'You need to apologize to him right now.'

But even when he was as wrong as it was possible to be, Oliver was nothing if not committed to being a wanker. 'I don't need to do a sodding thing,' he sniffed, stubborn as ever. 'I only said what everyone else is thinking.'

'No, dear,' Nan replied with narrowed, fox eyes. 'No one was thinking that. Do you think it's possible you could be a latent homosexual yourself? I've heard things like this can happen when you're trying very hard to repress it.'

'Cerys?' I looked to my sister for help, but instead of cracking her husband around the head, she took a sip from his wine glass.

'I'm not getting involved.'

'You're going to let him speak to Manny like that?'

'I don't let him do anything, he's a grown man and he can think for himself. Stop trying to run Manny's life because you haven't got one of your own.'

This time even the kids turned and gasped.

I folded my napkin and placed it on the table, reminding myself of my promise. I told Mum I wouldn't fight with Cerys but, as a lawyer, I could argue that 'fight' was a very ambiguous term. It could mean don't verbally spar with your sister at the table or it could mean don't grab hold of her perfect hair and shut her head in a very hot oven, and right at that moment I definitely felt more inclined towards one of those over the other.

'I think I might pop out for a minute,' I said, resisting the urge to give her a slap and standing up instead. 'Go for a walk.'

'You're going for a walk?' Mum said with surprise.

'Yep.'

'In the middle of Christmas dinner?'

'That's right.'

'But it's bitter outside.'

'Maybe I'll freeze to death,' I suggested with a touch too much optimism.

'Found the matches! They were on top of the fridge after all that,' Dad announced, walking into the dining room with matches in hand as I walked out with tears stinging my eyes. 'What's going on? Where's she going? Where's Manny?'

'Oh, shove the bloody matches up your bloody arse, Steve,' I heard Mum sigh as I slipped out of the kitchen door and into the crisp, cold afternoon.

It was brass monkeys outside.

'I really am going to freeze to death,' I muttered, regretting my dramatic exit but refusing to ruin it by going back in for a coat. What sort of northern girl would I be if I did? Instead, I wrapped my arms around myself, pulling the sleeves of my dress down over my hands and marching on with purpose until the sound of raised voices coming from the dining room faded away completely.

Our long, rambling garden was a hide-and-seek aficionado's dream, full of tall trees and endless wildflowers that grew beyond Dad's carefully manicured rectangle of a lawn, and as soon as I was past the rhododendrons and around the corner, I couldn't even see the house anymore. It was just me, all alone with the beautiful winter garden. In summer, everything was full and green and lush, and the poppies grew so tall they completely obscured the low wooden fence that marked the end of the garden, just before the stream that ran down to the river. Even though it was beautiful, I had always preferred the garden in the winter. I loved to see the first frost blanket the lawn with diamonds. I loved the glossy red berries of our holly bush that popped against the greys and greens while the rest of the garden rested peacefully, preparing for the spring. Today the poppies were asleep under the ground and the old wooden fence was visible, bowed with age but still standing sentry, protecting us from the odd fox who couldn't be bothered to jump it.

'Manny?' I called, treading carefully in my tartan slippers. There was no sign of him.

'Where are you?' I muttered, hands on hips. 'Manny, it's only me!'

But wherever he was, he didn't want to be found. That or he'd gone to the pub and I was wandering around the back garden in nothing but my frock and slippers like a total walnut.

'If he has, I'll kill him,' I said, sitting on the rope swing that hung from our old oak tree. 'Provided I don't die of hypothermia first.'

Somewhere between too chilly to stay outside and too embarrassed to go back in, I swung myself back and forth for a long while, waiting for the fire in my belly to burn out. Eventually, I got used to the cold, my body digging deep to recall all those nights out without a coat in my teens and wrapping me up in a red-wine blanket. I was so mad at Oliver, so mad at Cerys and worst of all, mad at myself because perhaps she was right? Not about Oliver, obviously, he was a bigoted arsehole who ought to be slapped from pillar to post, but what she'd said about me struck altogether too close to home. I stared at my feet for a minute as a pair of fat tears threatened my lower lashes. I'd spent so long grafting, trying to make everyone proud, determined to get ahead, had I forgotten to get an actual life?

No, I decided, she was wrong, I had a life. Even better, I had a plan. Put the hard work in now, get promoted early, then, when all that came together, I'd have more time for marriage and kids, for the fun holidays and adventures my friends were always posting on Instagram. Michael knew I was ambitious when we met, he always said it was something he loved about me. A fresh flush of grief rolled over me as I thought back over all the times he'd introduced me to people, proudly telling them about my job before I even had a chance, his eyes shining with admiration and love. Yes, I worked long hours and yes, I had to put work first for a while, but the job demanded it, you couldn't half-arse a career in law, and there was nothing fundamentally wrong with that. It was a choice and I had every right to make that choice.

Just like Michael had every right to choose to shag Justine the Receptionist at a dental conference in Aberdeen and leave me three months later.

Swinging back and forth, I looked out over the fields and wondered. What was he doing today? Where was he? Had I crossed his mind at all? Last Christmas, we were here together and I had hoped to find an engagement ring under the tree. This year, I was here on my own and all I found under the tree was a five-pack of pants from my mum and a vibrator from my dad.

'Hello, stranger.'

Blinking back the unwelcome tears, I looked up to a tall, dark-haired man in a beautiful grey wool coat smiling at me from the neighbour's garden.

'It's a Christmas miracle,' I said, finding a smile amid my surprise 'Hello, Dev.'

Dev Jones moved in next door when I was twelve and he had just turned thirteen. Manny and I were playing football in the front garden when a car pulled up outside the empty neighbouring house and a lanky, dark-eyed boy with golden-brown skin and a mess of black hair climbed out the back, a Walkman in one hand and an acoustic guitar in the other. His Whites Stripes t-shirt was at least three sizes too big and his jeans hung down so low, the crotch was practically swinging around his knees. Manny paused, pulled a face and dismissed him without a second glance.

But not me.

I fell in love.

The whole world stopped as I watched him slope up his new garden path in slow motion, the *Romeo + Juliet* soundtrack playing in my mind and my stomach full of butterflies. I was transfixed. Until Manny kicked the football as hard as he could, whacked me right in the face and broke my nose in two places, which was how Dev Jones saw me for the very first time: screaming blue murder and covered in blood.

So it wasn't too surprising that my first love went unrequited.

'This might be a silly question but aren't you cold?' Dev asked as he stepped carefully over the low fence that separated our families' gardens.

'I was all right until you mentioned it,' I lied, a long-forgotten flutter in my stomach despite the fact there were still tears in my eyes. No matter how sad I might be, there would always be a place in my heart for my first crush. 'I suppose it is a bit chilly.'

'Here, I don't want to get in trouble with your mum if you catch your death.' Dev shrugged off his coat and draped it over my shoulders. He was still tall, still gorgeous; he'd always had his Indian mother's thick black hair and wide dark eyes, and now he was definitely less lanky than he used to be. When we were kids he was so skinny, he couldn't walk past our house without my mum trying to shove a mini Mars Bar in his pocket. Now here he was, a proper grown-up adult man.

Don't sniff his coat, I ordered myself as he sat on the swing beside me. *It's too weird. Do not sniff his coat.*

His coat smelled amazing.

'Everything all right?' he asked as I brushed the tears from my eyes.

'Yes?' I confirmed, even though it sounded more like a question than an answer. 'It's the cold, it makes my eyes run.' We hadn't seen each other in forever, there was no need to bother him with brutal honesty. I wracked my brains trying to remember when the last time might have been. It was years, at least eight, maybe closer to ten. The Joneses almost always went on holiday at Christmas and according to my mother, who quoted his mother with wide, rolling eyes, Dev was a very important doctor down in London and hardly ever had time to come up to visit.

'Not that it isn't lovely to see you,' I said, giving him a sideways glance through my hair. 'But you're the last person I expected to find down here. Your mum and dad didn't go away this year?'

He settled on the swing beside me and shook his head. 'Dad had to have an op on his knee and yes, my mother is furious, thanks for asking.'

'Your poor dad,' I winced. 'An operation and your mother's wrath, Merry Christmas, Peter.'

'He's not exactly living his best life,' Dev agreed before

lifting his chin to give me a questioning look. 'So what brings Gwen Baker down to the swings at the bottom of the garden on Christmas Day?'

'I was looking for Manny,' I explained, waving an arm around at absolutely nothing. 'Cerys and her husband were being awful and he stormed out. I thought he might be hiding down here.'

'Cerys was being awful?' A dimple I'd spent my entire adolescence dreaming about appeared in Dev's left cheek when he smiled. 'Did we just travel back in time twenty years?'

'Some things never change.' I laughed and tossed my hair seductively over my shoulder only to snag it on a tree branch behind me and almost rip it out at the roots as soon as I started to swing.

'So, how are you?' I asked as I attempted to casually untangle my hair without crying. 'How's things?'

'All good,' he said. Brief and to the point, classic Dev. 'You?'

'Oh, you know,' I replied, desperately trying to come up with a version of my life that sounded exciting and glamorous and Not Shit. 'There's so much going on, I don't know where to start.'

We exchanged tense smiles and I was still searching for the right thing to say when Dev let out an awkward laugh.

'I'm going to say it, this is weird.'

'But nice weird,' I agreed, echoing his laugh. 'It's been a long time.'

After our less than auspicious first meeting, Dev quickly became mine and Manny's third musketeer and I tried to nurse my crush with quiet dignity. Except for the time I sobbed myself to sleep after Dev got off with another girl at the village Halloween disco. And the Christmas disco. And the Easter disco. All the discos basically; Dev was much more popular than I ever was. Even though he went to a different school to me and Manny (a private school which meant he endured years of merciless mocking from the pair of us), we always spent our holidays and weekends together until we went our separate ways for university, me and Manny heading down to London and Dev vanishing up to Edinburgh. For years, I'd worked on a plan to get him to fall for me, somehow convincing myself I'd go off to uni and return home after the first semester, sexy and sophisticated, and Dev would finally see the real me and fall hopelessly in love. But no. I came home alone with a dodgy head of DIY highlights and Dev stayed in Scotland with his new girlfriend. His emails petered off from every day to every week to once a month, and after longer than I would have liked, I finally got a boyfriend of my own and Dev went from being the sole reason for my existence to someone I used to know.

It was altogether too easy to lose touch with even the most important people when you had almost every choice you would ever make still in front of you.

'Mum told me you're at some big law firm now, in London?' He looked at me for confirmation and I nodded. 'That's exciting, tell me everything.'

'More or less exciting than being a Harley Street surgeon?' I replied, my eyes flashing with genuine awe as I dodged his request. 'Tell me, do doctors really shag in supply cupboards all the time or have I watched too much *Grey's Anatomy*?'

'All I can say is I've never shagged in a supply cupboard,' he said, laughing again. It was nice to hear after the morning I'd had. 'But never say never. And I'm not on Harley Street. I moved to the Royal Papworth, in Cambridge in August. Would you believe I'm a cardiologist?'

'No offence but, no, not really. I mean, you think of cardiologists as being older, don't you?'

'I've terrible news for you,' he leaned in towards me and lowered his voice. 'We are older.'

'Wash your mouth out,' I replied with a grin. 'Seriously though, that's amazing, it must be so rewarding.'

'It is,' he said with a self-effacing half-smile. 'I know it's unbearably cheesy but I feel like I'm making a difference.'

I nodded solemnly.

'And you get to hold people's beating hearts in your hand like in *Indiana Jones.*'

'Sometimes, but it is frowned upon to do the chant during surgery.'

'Bloody NHS,' I sighed. 'You can't have any fun anymore.'

'Total killjoys,' Dev agreed. 'No sense of humour.'

A sense of ease curled around me as I rocked back and forth, the quiet, calm afternoon smoothing out any bumps in our long-lost friendship.

'Your fella's a doctor as well, isn't he? Or a dentist?' He tucked his hands into his trouser pockets, clearing his throat when he saw he'd caught me off guard. 'Mum mentioned it,' he clarified. 'I haven't been stalking you or anything.'

And just like that, the ghost of my Christmas past rudely butted in to ruin my Christmas present. The mood between us soured and I knew I couldn't sit there for another second.

'It's been nice to catch up but I should get back inside,' I said, standing abruptly and handing him his coat. 'It was good to see you, have a nice Christmas.'

'Good to see you too,' Dev replied. 'Merry Christmas, Gwen.'

He looked more than a little confused as I dashed back up the garden, leaving him alone on the swings. My heart sank into my slippers with every step and the tears I'd been fighting off came back with a vengeance, sliding down my face. I'd always lived a life according to my own choices, I thought sadly as I passed the rhododendrons again and the house came back into view. So why couldn't I move on? Why couldn't I choose to leave Michael in the past?

CHAPTER FIVE

'Look what the cat dragged in.'

Cerys was leaning against the kitchen counter with a tight smile on her face when I snuck back in, frozen hands tucked into my armpits.

'It would take at least ten cats to drag me anywhere and that's on a good day,' I replied, closing the back door then opening the fridge. I shouldn't have to deal with her without at least a snack. 'Have you seen Manny?'

'Upstairs. You're such a pair of drama queens.'

Do not fight with your sister, I reminded myself as my hands began to ball up into little fists. Her kids are weird, her husband is a frightful shithead and she can't eat gluten. She already suffers.

'He didn't have to be so sensitive, you know.' Cerys was not nearly as committed to the no fighting rule as I was. 'That's what Oliver and his friends are like, they're always joking about that kind of stuff.'

'It's only a joke if it's funny,' I replied, my anger rising again. Would it be *so* uncalled-for to plant her face first into Mum's trifle? 'Calling Manny names isn't funny.'

'He didn't mean it. Families say things to each other they wouldn't say to anyone else,' she snipped. 'You're not Twitter, you can't cancel my husband for one insensitive remark.'

'Cerys, your husband is an insensitive remark personified. Everything he does is insensitive. Even his breathing is offensive. Really though, have you ever taken him to have his sinuses looked at? I can hear them from here and he's in another room.'

'Gwen, are *you* all right?' my sister asked, giving me the kind of look you might bestow on a brave little dog that only had three legs. 'You seem so tense. Almost as though you got dumped and you're determined to ruin everyone else's Christmas because you're so bloody miserable?'

There was no winning an argument with my sister, never had been, never would be. The best thing I could do was to leave the room before we ended up wrestling under the kitchen table with me slapping Cerys with her own hand and shouting 'Why are you hitting yourself?' over and over until Mum came to separate us. Like last year.

'I might be miserable but at least I'm not delusional,' I said, stomping out of the kitchen with a chocolate biscuit in each hand. 'Your husband is a wanker.'

'And yours is non-existent,' she shouted back. 'Better luck next time!'

'It's only me,' I said as I sailed into Manny's room without knocking. 'Cerys said you were up here. You'll never guess who I saw outside and MANNY!'

I should have knocked.

My cousin was sat on the bed with his pants around his ankles, holding his phone at an awkward angle and taking a photo of an intimate part of his body that wasn't known for its photogenic qualities.

'Oh my God, *Gwen!*' he yelled, ditching his amateur photography session and scrambling for a pillow to cover his privates. 'What are you doing?'

'What am I doing?' I closed my eyes and covered my face with my hands at the same time, just to be safe. 'What are *you* doing?'

'Writing a letter to Santa, what does it look like?'

'If you send that to Santa, you're going to find yourself on the naughty list for the foreseeable,' I replied as I bumped, shin-first, into every piece of furniture in the room. 'My eyes! My poor eyes!'

'Why are you still in here?' Manny screeched. 'Get out!'

'I'm sorry, I'm going. I didn't see anything and we never need speak about this ever again.' I stumbled out onto the landing and slammed the door behind me, for the first time in my life wishing I'd stayed downstairs to talk to Cerys.

With my back pressed up against the landing wall, I tried very hard to erase what had just happened from my memory, but I was too late. It was already burned in like the licence plate of my dad's old Ford Fiesta, the *Live and Kicking* phone number and that time I came home late and turned on the TV to see Keith Chegwin wearing nothing but a hard hat. Why was Manny taking dick pics on Christmas Day? And more importantly, who was Manny sending dick pics to on Christmas Day? He'd been single forever.

'Gwen!' I heard Dad bellow from downstairs. 'Are you up there? Your mother wants you!'

'Are you even home if a family member isn't shouting your name from a completely different room of the house though?' I muttered to myself as I slunk back down the stairs and into the warm bosom of my family.

'Can I get anybody anything?' I asked, poking my head around the door to the living room on my way into the kitchen. 'Cup of tea? Glass of wine? Cyanide pill?'

'You can get your coat on,' Mum replied, clipping Arthur around the back of the head as she attempted to ram his arms into the sleeves of a neon orange parka. Artemis sat on the settee, already in her leopard-print puffer jacket, staring sulkily at an iPad while Dad, Cerys, Oliver and Nan all fussed with their own buttons, zips and belts. 'We're going over to Dorothy's.'

'But I haven't had my Christmas pudding yet,' I protested. 'Can't we go later?'

She grimaced as my nephew wriggled away, flapping his arms like a T-Rex crossed with a traffic cone. 'I've cleared it all away now, you can have some when we get back. Can you shout Manny down?'

'Um, he's on the phone.' Both literally and figuratively. 'He can meet us over there. Let me get my jacket and I'll come with you.'

'And maybe put a bit of blusher on,' Mum suggested, earning a warning scowl for her troubles. 'Humour me, Gwen, it's one day of the year. Would it kill you to make an effort?'

'I'm wearing blusher,' I said, waving a demonstrative hand in front of my face. 'I'm wearing a face full of make-up.'

'You'd never know it,' Nan said as she sailed by in

her wool topcoat. 'Why don't you borrow that nice lipstick your sister's wearing?'

But Cerys shook her head. 'No way. She's not getting her germs on my Lisa Eldridge.'

'And I'd rather smear my face with the blood of a sacrificial reindeer,' I added politely. 'If you want me to go, I'm going like this.'

My mother and my grandmother stared at me, mirror images of each other, both of their mouths disappearing into tight little lines in the middle of their faces.

'Fine.' Mum gave in first as Nan tutted with disappointment. 'Go and get the wine from the kitchen then. It's on the side in a gift bag. And lock the back door, we're going out the front!'

I grabbed my jacket from the end of the stairs on my way into the kitchen where two bottles of red sat on the counter in a glossy red gift bag. 'I know what'll put some colour into my cheeks,' I muttered, opening the fridge to find the bottle of cream liqueur beckoning me like the star of Bethlehem. Quickly unscrewing the lid, I took a deep, delicious swig, the creamy goodness drowning the unsettled feeling in my stomach, the scenes from Manny's room already melting away.

'Gwen?' I heard Dad call from the front of the house. 'Are you coming or not?'

'Coming,' I confirmed, closing the fridge, grabbing the wine and setting off out into the cold afternoon air with a warm, whisky glow in my belly.

Dorothy-Across-The-Road's Christmas Open House was a thing of legend. Every year for as long as I could remember our neighbour had welcomed all and sundry into her home for mince pies, cocktail sausages and cheese and pineapple on sticks, starting somewhere around mid-afternoon and ending when the last man standing passed out on her living-room carpet. When I was little, running around a grown-up's house unsupervised was a total thrill, but it wasn't until I was seventeen that my dad let me in on the real reason everyone looked forward to Dorothy's party so much; her rum punch. One cup made you merry, two cups made you jolly and three would see you unconscious until New Year, an idea that was becoming increasingly appealing.

'Come in, Bakers!' Dorothy's door opened before I even had a chance to knock, the lady herself ushering us inside with both arms. Somewhere between fifty and a hundred (and it was impossible to estimate with any greater degree of accuracy) Dorothy's not-at-all-natural red hair was piled on top of her head and she wore a white and silver caftan accessorized with fluffy white wings and a tinsel halo on top of her head. One glance at Nan's face was enough to confirm she did not approve.

'Don't stand on ceremony, coats off, let's get a drink in you,' Dorothy ordered as we moved through the hallway as one. From the looks of it, more than half the village was here already. 'My, Cerys, it's hard to believe your littles have got so big. I remember when you and Gwen were that age, feels like yesterday.'

Artemis and Arthur squirmed away from her effusive kisses, twisting and turning exactly as we had. I smiled at my sister, who replied with a scowl before grabbing her children by the scruff of the neck and directing them into the dining room, following their father who had already run off in the presumed direction of the punch.

'And Gwen, where's that handsome man of yours?' Dorothy asked, batting what looked like several pairs of false eyelashes.

'Oh, he's not here,' I replied, smiling politely.

'They broke up,' Dad clarified, a cartoon bubble that said 'yikes' practically hovering over his head. 'But you're better off without him, aren't you, chicken?'

Dorothy's halo bobbed up and down as she nodded in agreement. 'Nothing wrong with the single life. You know I never married and it never stopped me having my fun.'

'Certainly seems to have stopped her from dusting her skirting boards,' Nan whispered in my ear.

'Drinks!' I declared brightly. 'Why don't I go and find us some drinks.' Without waiting to find out what anyone wanted, I slid away from the rest of the family in search of peace or punch, entirely happy with whichever came first.

Dorothy's house looked like an explosion in a tinsel factory, every single room festooned with shiny sparkles in every single colour the good people at Chatsworth Garden Centre had to offer. And we were talking about a lot of rooms. Her house was a labyrinth and not the fun kind full of David Bowie and a load of Muppets. Every room flowed into another but none of them ever seemed to lead back the way I thought I'd come. The living room led to the dining room which led to the kitchen which led to another sitting room which led to a conservatory which was where I found myself, sat at a wrought iron table next to a shiny silver tree covered in miniature Santas who were doing unmentionable things to Mrs Claus. I draped my coat over the back of my chair and set two very full cups of rum punch carefully on the table, one for me and the other also entirely for me, a well-deserved Christmas present to myself.

Outside, heavy clouds filled the darkening sky and with only one flake of warning, snow began to fall, soft and silent. I checked my watch and saw it was almost six and frowned. The day seemed to be moving very slowly. And even though the house was packed to the rafters, I felt completely and utterly alone. Just me and the snow and my two cups of punch. So much for Christmas turning into a real-life Hallmark holiday movie. Where was a down-on-his-luck duke when you needed one?

'Can you believe the weatherman got it right?' asked a voice behind me right as I was about to give up and go home. 'First time for everything, eh?'

I looked over my shoulder to see a man. A tall, beautiful specimen of a man, with good hair and a lopsided smile and perfectly straight white teeth. Immediately I glanced around to see who he was talking to and realized after one moment too many, he was talking to me.

'Will wonders never cease?' I replied, packing away my sad thoughts as he came closer. Dear God, he was good-looking. As in cover-of-the-romance-novels-Cerys-used-to-get-out-from-the-library-then-hide-under-her-bed good-looking. 'My first ever white Christmas.'

'I've seen a couple at home,' he said, a thick Scottish accent curling around his words. 'Didn't expect to see one so far down south.'

I laughed at the idea of my 'Up North' being his 'Down South' and silently thanked the Christmas gods for sending him to say hello. If it turned out he was even tangentially related to any member of any royal family,

I would scream. He must have been about my age, but he was a big meaty man, much taller than me with short, dark blond hair, crystal-blue eyes. If it weren't for his Scottish burr, I'd have said Chris Evans had an identical twin we didn't know about, but not even Chris Evans was a good enough actor to pull off that accent.

'There she is!'

My eyes narrowed with confusion as Mum appeared behind the Scottish superhero and wrapped her arms around his waist, barely suppressed excitement all over her face.

'We've been looking for you everywhere. Gwen, meet Drew, Drew, this is my daughter, Gwen.'

'Pleased to meet you at last,' he said, holding out a hand. 'I've heard a lot about you.'

I shook his very strong hand while my mother pouted her lips and eyed him like he was a side of beef.

'Drew moved here from Inverness a couple of months ago,' she said, physically forcing him into the chair opposite mine, her tiny hands pressing down on his massive shoulders. 'He took over the butchers in the village, you know the one at the crossroads? His dad grew up here before he met his mum and moved north of the border but Drew hasn't been back here since he was a baby. Very funny, so charming, loves books, just like you. Anyway, let me go and get you both some drinks. You two sit here and . . . chat.'

I picked up my first cup of punch and threw it back in one gulp. So it was a set-up. My mother was trying to pimp me out to a charismatic butcher who had only just moved to the village with many sharp knives, knew how to carve up a carcass and had no friends or relatives in the area. It was almost as though she'd never seen an episode of *Law & Order: SVU* which I knew was not the case because I'd bought her the DVD box sets for Mother's Day two years ago (daffodils and bubble bath weren't nearly as educational).

'So, that's my entire life story, what about yours?' Drew sat back in his little wrought iron chair, making it look like dollhouse furniture.

'I am so sorry,' I said, forgetting his serial killer potential for a moment and instead wondering whether or not he could crush a walnut with his giant thighs. 'I don't know what my mum's told you but whatever she's said, I'm sure at least half of it is an exaggeration.'

'Oh, she's a proud mum.' His biceps curled against the sleeves of his white shirt and I felt myself go weak. I wasn't usually one for big burly men but I also didn't spend a lot of time in their company. 'She loves to pop into the shop and tell me what you've been up to.'

'That must be scintillating for you.' I paused and took a sip of my second cup of punch, marvelling at the sheer scale of the man. 'Drew, you're massive.'

'Thanks,' he said, hacking out a laugh. 'I do try.'

'I don't know why I said that.' I shook my head at myself, blushing crimson. 'Sorry, I don't get out much, I've forgotten how to talk to . . .' Don't say Greek gods, don't say Greek gods, don't say Greek gods. 'People.'

Phew.

'That must make working as a lawyer somewhat tricky?' he replied. 'I heard you're running a big law firm in the city?'

He was truly enormous. Drew was so big, he made Gaston look drastically malnourished. How many eggs was this man eating every morning?

'Something like that,' I deflected eloquently. 'So, aside from your dad being from here, what made you want to move all the way to Baslow?'

He scratched the underneath of his chin as he considered my question, a five-o'clock shadow already showing through his fair skin.

'Like Bronwyn said, the shop was available and I'd been looking for a while. I've always worked for my dad and I was ready to strike out on my own, I suppose.' Raising a giant hand, he waved around the room. 'Moving this far from home wasn't really in my life plan but I saw the listing, and you'll have to forgive me for sounding like an inspirational quote, but it felt like fate. The perfect shop showing up in the village where my dad grew up? As soon as I came to visit, I knew I had to take a chance. We've got to take chances in life, haven't we?'

'I thought you were a butcher, not a cheesemonger?' I replied, eyeballing my punch cups. How was I halfway through my second already?

'Full-time butcher, part-time cheddar enthusiast and always appreciative of a good pun,' Drew said, a bemused smile playing on his beautifully shaped lips. 'Do you not believe in fate, Gwen?'

'Fate? Me?' I laughed, a Katherine Hepburn-style, femme fatale laugh that definitely didn't make me sound like a senior donkey who had recently taken up vaping. I took another swig of punch and emptied my second cup. 'I don't know about that. I'd rather believe we make our own luck in life.'

'If you say so,' he smiled. 'I know better than to argue with a lawyer, let alone a fancy one from that there London.'

'That's me, Gwen Baker, fancy London lawyer.'

As I spoke, I couldn't help but notice my words were slurring slightly, as though my tongue had become slightly too big for my mouth. I stretched it out as far as it would go to investigate, ignoring the look of concern on Drew's absurdly handsome face.

'Gwen?'

I blinked and saw my mother standing over us with two fresh cups of punch.

'Mother,' I replied primly, tucking my tongue away. 'Is there a problem?'

'There's almost always a problem,' she set the drinks carefully down on the table without spilling so much as a drop, clearly more invested in my meeting The Hot Butcher than she was in arguing, at least for now. 'Here you go, Drew, this'll warm you right up.'

'Where's Dad?' I asked, pushing my glass away as the two of them clinked theirs together in a cheers. 'Hiding from Dorothy?'

Mum shook her head and casually rested one hand on Drew's shoulder, completely oblivious to the uncomfortable look of surprise on his face. 'He took Nan home and went to fetch his surprise. And he said something about getting the camp bed out of the garage.'

'Why would we need the camp bed out the garage?'

She pointed out the conservatory window and I saw the lawn was already covered in a thick, white blanket, with snow still falling steadily from the sky. 'Cerys can't drive back in this, can she? They're going to stay the night. She and Oliver will take your bed, the kids can sleep on the blow-up mattress in the living room and you're on the camp bed in the dining room. It won't kill you for one night.'

'He's a nice man and he's not bad to look at either,' she added with a wink. 'What? I'm sixty-two, I'm not dead.'

'You will be if you carry on like this.'

'Time waits for no woman,' she warned. 'Don't waste yours fretting over things you can't change. We're all very sorry it didn't work out with Michael but you can't spend the rest of your life waiting for him to come to his senses.'

A knock on the window of the conservatory made us both jump, Mum spilling what was left of her punch all down the front of my dress. On the other side of the glass, my dad was waving his arms like he was trying to direct a jumbo jet into Dorothy's garden. Fantastic, I thought as I waved back. Now I smelled like a cross between a clementine and a sailor on leave. If anyone asked, I'd have to tell them it was a new perfume from Jo Malone, Christingle and Sea Dog.

'What's he up to?' I asked as Dad beckoned us outside.

'Oh, you know your dad,' she replied, pulling on her coat. 'Ever since he retired, he's had far too much time on his hands.'

The two cups of punch sloshed around in my belly as I stood up and struggled to find my way back into my own jacket. Had the sleeves always been this complicated?

'You don't need to tell me.' I attempted to do the zip five times before the little metal pull slipped out of my fingers and I very nearly punched myself in the nose. 'I think I've talked to him more in the last six months than I have in my entire life.'

'He's proud of you, Gwen,' Mum said, successfully fastening my coat with one sharp tug. 'It's a big deal, isn't it? A woman doing so well at your age at a place like that?

We're both proud of you. Please humour him, for my sake. Some of us still work full time and he's more trouble than he's worth now he hasn't got anywhere to go all day. If only you and Michael had got engaged instead of splitting up, we could have set him on planning the wedding. That would have kept him quiet for weeks.'

A weak attempt at a laugh slipped from my lips.

'Yeah, that is a shame.'

'Never mind.' She led me out to the back door with a brisk smile on her face. 'Let's enjoy his surprise and just be grateful he's only obsessed with your job and not trying to explain NFTs to you. It's been six months and I still haven't got a bloody clue what he's on about.'

Twenty minutes later, we were still waiting outside in the freezing cold darkness, along with what seemed like every living soul in Baslow crammed into Dorothy's back garden.

'What is going on?' Manny asked, arriving just in time for whatever it was we were waiting for.

'Dad's up to something,' I said as I slipped my arm through his, teeth chattering through a conciliatory smile. 'I'm sorry about earlier.'

'Don't, I'm the one who should be apologizing,' he said. 'Not the sort of Christmas surprise you were after, I'm sure. May it never ever happen again as long as we both shall live.'

'Amen to that,' I agreed, leaning into a brief hug. 'But out of interest, who was it for?'

'Um, no one?' he replied, eyes darting around the garden. 'Look at the size of Dorothy's rhododendrons! Do they normally grow that big?'

'Oh my God, have you got a secret boyfriend?' I gasped, simultaneously outraged and delighted as his eyes widened with panic and a strangled sound escaped his throat.

'Evening everyone!'

Before I could press him for more details, we were interrupted by my dad, clapping his hands together at the end of the garden and waving his arms at the assembled masses. Never afraid of being the centre of attention, was Steven Baker. It was my worst nightmare, but Dad was never happier than when he was commanding a crowd.

'Every year Dorothy hosts this lovely open house for us all to come together,' he started, pausing for a smattering of applause that Dorothy accepted with a bow, her halo almost falling off her head. 'But this year, I wanted to make it extra special, give us all something to remember, and so I present to you, a very merry Christmas firework display!'

The whole village cheered as Dad stepped out of the way and with great ceremony, held a black trigger high in the air, pressing down on a bright red button as we all cheered.

And nothing happened.

'This is supposed to set them all off,' Dad said, stabbing at the button again and again, and again. 'Bloody thing isn't working.'

'Maybe it's wet?' Someone called out from the crowd. 'They might not work in the snow, Steve.'

'They'd want to work under the Atlantic Ocean for what I paid,' Dad muttered. 'Let me have a look at this. As you were, people! Won't be a tick.'

'You're not supposed to go back to lit fireworks, are you?' Manny said as Dad padded back to inspect his epic display with a torch, shining a pale white beam across the assembled explosives.

'Bugger me,' I breathed. 'It looks like he's about to declare war on the village.'

I'd never seen so many fireworks in one place. He had rockets, Roman candles, Catherine wheels and at least ten other kinds of firework I'd never even seen before. Right at the very back was a line of six cylindrical devices all linked together by one long fuse, all of them bearing the name 'Widow Maker'. Not troubling at all.

'Aunt Bronwyn, where did Uncle Steve get these fireworks?' Manny asked with concern.

She shrugged, rubbing her hands together before poking around in her pockets for a pair of mismatched gloves. 'I don't know, he told me he got some fireworks, I assumed he bought them from the supermarket after Bonfire Night.'

'I didn't know Tesco was a demilitarized zone,' I replied, pulling on Manny's arm. 'Come on, we've got to help him before he blows himself up. It can't be safe to have so many explosives this close to Dorothy's punch. Everyone here has to be at least ninety per cent proof.'

'What did I miss?' Oliver asked as he elbowed his way to the front of the crowd, knocking over two toddlers and a planter full of pansies on the way.

'Dad's set up enough fireworks to expose the earth's core,' I replied as Cerys and the kids joined him. 'I was simply suggesting we stop him before he blows himself up and takes the entire village with him.'

'I'm sure he knows what he's doing,' Cerys argued before pushing Arthur and Artemis slightly behind her.

'He used to do firework displays in the garden every year when we were kids.'

I turned around to see Dad shine his torch on one enormous rocket labelled 'Apocalypse Now'.

'I don't want to fight with you, Care, but I'm thinking maybe we don't want Grandad to blow himself to smithereens in front of the kids. That feels like one of those memories that might stick.'

She gave me another of her trademark condescending smiles and it took every ounce of my remaining self-respect not to whack it right off her face. 'Calm down and leave Dad to it, will you? Contrary to popular belief, you don't know everything. Also, you stink of booze.'

I knew I shouldn't rise to it, I knew I'd promised my mum and I knew I was thirty-two years old. But I simply could not help myself.

'What is wrong with you?' I snapped. 'If I said the sky was blue, you'd argue that it wasn't.'

'Well, technically it isn't,' she replied. 'The colour of the sky is determined by the scattering of electromagnetic radiation which we perceive as blue light for the majority of the day but at different times of the day, the sunlight comes through at different angles which is why we see red and orange light at sunrise or sunset.'

'Is it not exhausting being such a self-righteous cow all the time?'

'It's not all the time, just whenever you're near,' she answered, her voice hot. 'Why do you always think you know better than everyone else?'

'Nobody panic!' Dad shouted from the bottom of the garden as Cerys and I faced off. 'There's a loose wire, that's all. I'll have it all sorted in a minute.'

'I do not,' I blustered, heat burning out of my cheeks as our neighbours turned their attention away from my dad and towards the two of us. 'You're the one who thinks you're better than the rest of us because you went to Oxford and married a complete tit.'

'I don't think I'm better than you because I went to Oxford!' Cerys retorted.

'And I'm not a tit,' Oliver added.

'Shut up, Oliver,' we both said at the same time.

'Confirmed tit.' Manny put a mittened hand on my shoulder and squeezed. 'Come on, Gwen, leave it. Let's go home and I'll make you a hot toddy.'

'Yes, Gwen, leave it,' Mum said, an awkward smile on her face as she rolled her eyes theatrically at Mrs Ahmed from two doors down.

But there was no stopping me now, I was on a roll. Everything I'd been holding down rushed up to the surface: losing Michael, the nonsense at work, living in a shit flat, the time Cerys drew a moustache on my favourite My Little Pony.

'No!' I knocked Manny's hand away, all at once consumed by the rightful vindication of every wronged sibling ever to walk the earth. 'It's about time we had it out; what's the problem, Cerys? Is this because I got a job at Abbott & Howe and you're wasting your degree suing roadside cafes for making their coffee too hot?'

'Almost there!' Dad yelled, his face buried in a pile of gaudily decorated TNT. 'Let's have a countdown. Five!'

My sister's dark eyes burned black.

'That's it, Gwen, I don't care anymore. I've had it up to here with you.'

'Have you now?' I replied as half the village counted

down with my dad and the other half hung on our every word. 'Well, that makes two of us.'

'Four!' roared the crowd.

Dad dashed back up the garden and threw his arm around Mum's shoulders, blissfully unaware of the catfight of the century.

'I wasn't going to say anything because I didn't want to embarrass you in front of Mum and Dad,' Cerys snapped. 'But I don't know how you dare insult my job.'

'Three!'

'Hang on, have I missed something?' Dad looked at me and Cerys, burning with rage, and Mum and Manny, burning with embarrassment. 'Are you two arguing again?'

'Two!'

'Because it's a shit job,' I replied, prodding her in the chest. 'You're ripping people off for a living and you know you are.'

'At least I have a job,' she shouted at the top of her voice, before turning to our parents and bellowing with a victorious smirk. 'Gwen got sacked for attacking a client!'

'One!'

'Merry bloody Christmas,' Manny groaned as all the rockets exploded, Mum and Dad's shocked faces awash in red, green and gold light. 'And a Happy New Year.'

CHAPTER SIX

The ground beneath us shook as rockets whizzed up into the air, filling the snowy sky with multicoloured sparkles before the Widow Makers detonated with an ungodly roar. Gazing at the firework display, I wondered if there was still time to chuck myself on top of the Apocalypse Now rather than deal with the fallout of Cerys's accusation.

'Gwen?' Dad looked at me with misty eyes, his face a picture of confusion. 'What's she talking about?'

'Oliver's friend works at Abbott & Howe and he told us everything,' Cerys answered before I could even try to explain. 'She attacked a client, beat him up with a staple gun, and they fired her. It happened weeks ago and she hasn't had the guts to tell you.'

'That's not – not true! That's not what happened!' I protested, Dorothy's punch bubbling in my stomach as the Catherine wheels whirred into life, sparks flying everywhere.

'You mean you didn't attack a client?' Dad asked, heartbreakingly hopeful.

'No,' I replied weakly. 'I meant it was a stapler, not a staple gun.'

Right on cue, Apocalypse Now shuddered into life, whistling its warning before lighting up the whole sky with blinding white flashes. The look on my dad's face was not one I ever wanted to see again. The corners of his mouth drooped and his eyes were flat and grey, all the colour gone from his cheeks.

'Oh, Gwen,' he said sadly, reaching one hand out towards me and letting it hover an inch above my shoulder before he pulled it away. 'Oh dear.'

'But I can explain,' I started, tears burning behind my eyes. 'Let me explain.'

'I don't think this is the right place for this conversation,' he said, looking around at our interested audience. Without another word, he pushed through the crowd and disappeared around the corner of the house. Mum looked at me, her own features weighed down by disappointment. She inhaled sharply then shook her head, following Dad up the path.

'What was it you were saying about this being exactly what I needed?' I asked, my words sticking in my throat as Manny pulled me into his chest for a hug. 'A nice family Christmas, wasn't it?'

As the rockets finally ran out of steam and all little plastic tubes landed in the snow with a series of soft thumps, the whispers around us turned into murmurs and the murmurs escalated into good old-fashioned gossip. I looked over to where Cerys and Oliver were having what seemed to be an equally heated conversation, the look on my sister's face full of fury. I'd have thought she'd be more pleased with herself but what did I know?

'Don't stress yourself,' Manny said, stroking my hair. 'But if you'd told them when it happened, all this could have been avoided.'

I pulled away from Manny's hug, stung.

'If you don't mind, I could do without an "I told you so",' I said, wiping away a tear. 'This is exactly why I didn't want to tell them in the first place.'

'All I meant was—'

'I know what you meant,' I replied, cutting off his apology. Even in the chill of the snowy evening, I could feel the burn of every pair of eyes on me and shrank down into my jacket, pulling the hood up over my head. 'I can't be here, I've got to go.'

'Go where?' he called as I walked briskly away, hot tears trickling down my cold face. 'Gwen, where are you going?'

When I was little and things got too much, there was only one place I could hide where no one would find me. Between the back of the garage and the garden shed was a narrow gap, too tight for my dad, too claustrophobic for Manny and altogether too dirty for my mum, but just right for me. Holding my breath, I shuffled in sideways, only breathing out when I was on the other side, in my very own secret spot, a tiny clearing behind the two buildings that was closed in by hedges on either side. A light canopy of branches kept the spot mostly dry and shielded from the wind, and a well-placed street light kept it bright enough for me to see the smears of mascara on the backs of my hands. When I first started sneaking away to my hiding place, there was nothing there but an upturned plant pot for me to sit on, but over time I'd upgraded to a pair of sturdy wooden boxes, one for me and one for the only other person who knew about my den. The same person I saw shuffling down the gap between the garage and the shed a little while later.

'I thought I might find you here,' Dev said, brushing cobwebs out of his thick black hair. 'That was a pretty impressive scene between you and Cerys?'

'Oh God, you were there,' I covered my face with my hands as he pulled up the second box. 'Please tell me you've come to put me out of my misery.'

'Sorry. Took that pesky do no harm oath, didn't I?'

'You couldn't have run away and joined the circus, could you?' I groaned. 'Thanks a lot, Dev.'

Once when I was fifteen and he was sixteen, Mum and Dad were reading Manny the riot act over another late night with no phone call home and, not wanting to interrupt the argument you could hear from three doors down, Dev took it upon himself to climb on top of our garage to retrieve an errant frisbee. All well and good until he fell off the garage and landed in the hedge behind me. I took his falling out of the sky and landing at my feet as a sign that we were meant to be. Dev took it as a sign to be petrified of heights from that day forward, which I thought was a far sillier a response than mine, but most importantly, he promised to keep my secret spot a secret and to the best of my knowledge he always had.

'Want to talk about it?' Dev fished a handful of Celebrations out of his pocket and held them out to me. I hesitated for a second before choosing the mini Bounty. No one liked the mini Bounty but it was the polite thing to do. He looked at what remained and handed me the only Malteser in the bunch. 'I'm assuming it's still your favourite?'

'It is,' I admitted as I tore into the shiny cellophane wrapper, bottom lip quivering at the epic gesture. Only a true gent would give up his only Maltesers Teaser. 'Thank you.'

'You never were any good at asking for what you wanted,' he said, chomping into a miniature Mars Bar, completely unaware of how right he was. 'You don't have to talk about it if you don't want to, but as a trained medical professional, I am an excellent listener.'

'You always were,' I said, managing part of a smile. 'First of all, I didn't get sacked, that's not what happened.'

'But you *did* smack someone with a staple gun?'

'It was a stapler, not a staple gun, there is a massive difference,' I dropped my head back into my hands and let my hair fall all the way in front of my face. 'I've never done anything like it before, I don't know what happened, I really don't.'

'Never?

'Never ever.'

'What about that time you kicked Jason Broadhurst in the nutbag when you caught him copying off you in the GCSE mocks?'

'Fine. I've only ever done something like it once before,' I replied through my fingers. 'I have this insufferable client at work, Andrew Jergens. If there's a tech company in existence and Google, Facebook or Amazon don't already own it, you can bet it belongs to his dad. He lets his little prince run around with a couple of billion quid a year, buying up companies and pretty much running them into the ground.'

'Sounds like a fun chap,' Dev commented as he deftly unwrapped a Galaxy Caramel.

'Then I've oversold him,' I replied bluntly. 'He was in to sign some paperwork, banging on about some mega exclusive party he's planning in Italy and the next thing you know, he's inviting me to go with him.'

'The monster.'

I pushed my hair out of my face and looked up to meet Dev's eyes.

'It wasn't just an invitation to a party.'

'It wasn't?'

I shook my head.

'I'd rather not go into the details but it was made very clear that certain favours would be expected of me in return.'

'Oh.'

'I've worked with arseholes in my time, it comes with the territory, I can take a lot,' I whispered. 'But no one stood up for me, no one told him to shut up and we were literally in a room full of people. The next thing I knew, he had his hand on my leg and I lost it.'

Dev's expression clouded over. 'Hitting him with a stapler wasn't enough.'

'It was a stapler, a coffee cup and a reinforced three ring binder,' I replied. 'It's been a rough couple of months.'

I unwrapped the Malteser and popped it in my mouth, chewing as I relived my rage.

'He's awful, Dev,' I said, holding a hand over my mouth as I spoke. 'And it's been years of it, the inappropriate comments, the way he looks at me, at all the women I work with. But that doesn't make decking him OK, does it? When they go low, we're supposed to go high, not attack them with the entire contents of the stationery cupboard.'

He stifled a laugh before composing his features into a study of compassion.

'What happens now?' he asked.

'I've got a disciplinary hearing on the fourth of January. Harry, that's my boss, he doesn't think I'll get sacked since Andrew hasn't terminated his contract with the firm, but I can say goodbye to the junior partner position for the time being. Maybe forever.'

'He hasn't terminated his contract?' Dev looked surprised. 'What is he, a masochist?'

'Yes,' I replied. 'I think so. The next day he sent me two dozen roses with a card that said 'roses are red, violets are blue, you're a spicy filly, fancy a shag?'. It's wasn't an apology, he was still trying it on. I'd admire his tenacity if I didn't hate his guts.'

'And that's why they say there's no such thing as a good billionaire.' He rifled through his pocket again and handed me the rest of the Celebrations. 'Here, you need these more than I do. When did all this happen?'

'Two weeks ago,' I replied, the nightmare of it all still so fresh in my mind. Standing in Harry's office, mortified, while he um-ed and ahh-ed, muttering about the reputation of the company and stiff upper lips in the face of adversity and something about Winston Churchill before he eventually told me to pack my things and go home. 'I thought it would be OK as long as I didn't lose my job. Dad wouldn't have to find out.' Sniffing loudly, I forced all the unpleasantness deep, deep down inside where it belonged. Out of sight, out of mind as was the Baker way.

'That's the annoying thing about secrets,' Dev said kindly. 'They have a tendency to come out at the worst possible time.'

'He's going to be so upset,' I said, tearing into a tiny Snickers. 'All he wants is for me to make partner, I've let him down.'

'Your dad is a good bloke, I'm sure he'll understand when you explain.'

As much as I wanted to agree with him, I wasn't so sure.

'Dad is a good person but he's also very old school. I already know what he's going to say, that I should have risen above it and made an official complaint through the proper channels, and he's right, isn't he? You can't go round whacking people at work even if they are grade A wankers.'

Dev bunched his shoulders together and leaned forwards, resting his forearms on his knees. 'Maybe you're underestimating your dad here, Gwen. Remember how amazing he was when Manny came out? He's not a neanderthal, I think he would have understood.'

'And I think I know my family better than you do,' I replied. My voice prickled with annoyance. 'Just because my dad loves and supports his nephew doesn't mean he isn't going to be disappointed in me for the way I acted.'

'Yes, well,' he inhaled deeply through his nose and looked around my hiding place. It suddenly felt very claustrophobic, altogether too small for two people. 'It's been a long time, I don't really know him at all. Or you for that matter.'

That was it. I felt the red rage swallow me up and a torrent of words came tumbling out of my mouth unbidden. 'That's hardly my fault, is it? You're the one that went off to uni and forgot me and Manny existed,' I said, sharpening my words for maximum damage.

'You're the one who stopped replying to me!' He sat up straight, his straight black eyebrows lifted in surprise. 'Why would I waste my time writing to you when you couldn't be bothered to write back? I emailed you every day for months.'

I tutted and crossed my arms over my chest. 'Honey badger videos and one-line messages about your amazing girlfriend? Hardly a correspondence for the ages, was it?'

Dev stood up, a stony look on his face. 'Seems like you'd rather be alone. I'll let you sulk in peace.'

'Thank you, that would be wonderful,' I huffed. 'Merry Christmas, Dev.'

'Merry Christmas, Gwen,' he said, softening slightly. 'Whatever's going on with you, I hope you work it out sooner rather than later.'

I watched him go, barely fitting between the garage and the shed and making even more of a mess of his lovely coat as he went, and my frustration dissolved into shame. I'd never been the kind of person to lose her temper. Except when it came to Cerys. And Andrew Jergens. And Jason Broadhurst. But other than where those three people were concerned, I never lost my shit. Not that I didn't want to fully Hulk out at least ten times a day; I was a woman and a lawyer *and* I was on Twitter, I felt like flipping tables daily, but whenever those hot flashes sparked into life, I always tried to remind myself of something my dad told me when I started my training at Abbott & Howe: no one likes an angry woman. It was sexist, offensive and at least in my office, one hundred per cent true. For years, I'd done my level best to be professional, hardworking, calm and likeable, but now my rage felt like a can of Pringles, I had been popped and I could not stop. But there was no excuse for taking my frustrations out on kind, helpful, stupidly good-looking Dev. What sort of idiot lashed out at a beautiful man who willingly gave her chocolate? He didn't deserve it.

'I should go and apologize,' I said out loud, standing up and realizing there was something I needed to do more urgently. 'As soon as I've had a wee,' I muttered, wishing I'd put more time into Kegel exercises and less time into downing Dorothy's punch.

All the downstairs lights were out when I got back to the house. It was a little after seven-thirty, but Bronwyn Baker was not one to suffer a big light on in an empty room. Upstairs, I saw a dim glow coming from my parents' bedroom and the diffused light of the bathroom, glowing through the frosted glass. Keeping my fingers crossed that Cerys and Oliver were still out, I reached for the handle of the back door and turned it to the right. It was locked.

'Bugger,' I declared, the word puffing out in front of my face in little frozen clouds. I tried the handle one more time, jiggling it just so, before giving up and heading for the front.

Also locked.

And of course I didn't have my keys.

Standing on the front doorstep, I pondered my options. If I knocked on the door, Dad would answer. Dad always answered the door at night and I didn't think I could stand to see that look on his face again today. My phone was charging in my room so I couldn't call Manny and ask him to sneak me in. I *could* pop round next door and explain the situation to Dev's mum but in all honesty, I would rather wet myself and if I didn't get to a toilet shortly, that would be a very real option. Why did my ability to hold a wee completely disappear the moment I caught sight of my front door? If only there were a registered medical professional in the vicinity I could ask . . .

'I am not going to piss myself in my parent's front garden at the age of thirty-two,' I whispered, leaning against Manny's Volvo. 'There's got to be some way to get into the house.'

And there was. The downstairs bedroom window. Despite my parents' security concerns, Nan always left it cracked open whenever she stayed over due to the fact my father kept the central heating 'hotter than the fires of hell' (according to the budget-conscious, put-another-jumper-on Myfanwy). I could climb in through the window. Arming myself with a helpful stick, I clambered onto the boot of the car and wedged the stick through the window, pushing it upwards until I could reach my hand inside to open it all the way. It would still be a squeeze, I realized, comparing the size of the window with the size of my arse, but better to get stuck half in and half out a window like some sort of velvet-clad Winnie the Pooh than to wet myself outside and freeze to death in a puddle of my own wee.

Probably.

'Hello?' I called as pushed my head through the window and came face to face with a pair of heavy lined velvet drapes.

No response.

Sliding one arm through the window, I twisted myself around, immediately regretting the fact I'd been slacking on my *Yoga with Adriene* practice, and somehow forced my other arm inside.

'There we go,' I panted, as an unexpected gust of wind blew my dress up around my waist. 'Gwen Baker, ace problem solver.'

But the problem was only half solved. I rocked backwards and forwards like a human seesaw, attempting to inch the rest of my body inside as the sharp edge of the window frame cut into my ribs and the searing heat of the radiator wafted up towards my face. Nan was right, it was ridiculously hot. Swatting at a crack in the curtains, I heard the bedroom door open right as I reached the point of no return and my body gave in to gravity. My feet went flying up into the air as I crashed through the window, swaddled in the curtains, a muffled rip of fabric tearing as I went.

'Have that!' a loud, brave voice bellowed as I attempted to right myself. 'Burgling a house on Christmas Day, what kind of a monster are you?'

'I'm not a burglar,' I protested, fighting with my dress and the drapes as something heavy clocked me around the head. 'It's me, it's me! It's Gwen!'

The bludgeoning took altogether too long to stop and when I finally emerged from my velvet cocoon, Nan was standing over me, panting, with a hardback book held over her head.

'Who knew Barbara Taylor Bradford could inflict such damage?' I winced, poking at a newly tender spot underneath my eye.

Nan placed the book on her nightstand and let out a long sigh of relief. 'Sorry, pet. You might want to ice that, you're going to have a shiner and a half.'

'I had no idea you were so strong.' I stared up at her from the floor, almost afraid to move. 'Consider yourself added to my zombie survival team.'

'How was I supposed to know it was you?' she asked as she unravelled the curtains from around my legs and helped me up to my feet. 'What were you doing climbing in through the bloody window in the dead of night?'

'Nan, it's not even seven. You didn't hear me shouting through the window?'

'I was in the living room with the kids,' she explained as I sat on the edge of her bed, examining my war wounds. Scraped knees, tender ribs, nothing a chunk of Christmas cake couldn't fix. 'They're sat in the dark, ruining their eyes and playing some bloody game that's louder than the war.'

'Where's Cerys?' I asked warily.

'Oliver and Cerys went to the pub and your mum went upstairs to watch the telly. Manny had those little white plug things in his ears last I saw him and your father was knocking back a very stiff drink.'

'A double Tia Maria and Coke?'

'There was very little Coke.'

I gasped.

'He's upset then?'

'He wasn't jumping up and down and singing 'Frosty the Snowman', if that's what you're asking,' Nan replied. 'You caught him unawares, Gwen, no one likes to feel like a fool.'

'There was no need for him to know,' I said, my shoulders sloping at what I could only assume was the first of many tellings-off. 'I can't believe Cerys—'

'Leave your sister out of it and clean up your own mess. It was hardly her finest moment but that's not for you to worry about. Cerys has got her own troubles.'

'Like what?' I asked, incredulous. 'Her rich husband, her private-school kids, the massive mansion they live in or her thriving business that pays for it all?'

'You never really know what's going on in other people's lives,' she answered. 'Even the people you think you know best. I'd have thought you'd have learned that lesson this year.'

Pouting at my grandmother and her common sense, I stood up to examine the mess by the window. By some miracle, it looked as though I'd only knocked the rod off its brackets and not yanked it out of the wall completely and the curtains seemed to be intact. It was the first bit of luck I'd had since I opened the Gen 2 Personal Wonder Wand.

'Speaking of people I don't know that well,' I said, wrestling the curtains and the rod up off the ground. 'I saw Dev Jones outside.'

'Dev Jones from next door?' Nan's left eyebrow flickered with interest. 'Haven't seen him in a dog's age. Your mother tells me he's a doctor,' she added as I climbed on a footstool to heave the curtains into place. 'And he's engaged to be married?'

For a reason I couldn't quite put my finger on, my stomach plummeted at the news.

Dev. Engaged.

Somewhere deep inside me, thirteen-year-old Gwen

collapsed in a fit of hysterics while playing 'Hero' by Enrique Iglesias on repeat.

'He didn't mention it,' I replied in a squeaky voice. 'Good for him.'

'Good for him,' Nan agreed before letting out a tiny gasp. 'Oh, Gwen, your frock.'

Reflected back at me in the mirror on the front of Nan's wardrobe was a long, clean rip, running from my waist-band, all the way down the back of my dress. Dev was a successful cardiologist, engaged to be married, and I was a dumped, disgraced lawyer on disciplinary leave, walking around with my arse hanging out.

'I told you it was too big,' she said. 'A nice pencil skirt wouldn't have got caught like that.'

All at once I was very close to tears. My lovely dress, ruined.

Nan offered me a sympathetic smile, holding the velvet drapes in one hand and my skirt in the other. 'Don't get upset, sweetheart,' she said. 'I'll make you a new one out of the curtains like *Gone with the Wind*.'

'Thanks, Nan.' I gulped down my tears. 'After all, tomorrow is another day.'

Even though it was early, as soon as I'd used the bath-room, I shut myself away in the dining room and turned out all the lights, just a string of battery-operated fairy lights at the base of Mum's bizarre centrepiece twinkling away in the darkness. My apology tour could wait until tomorrow, the best thing I could do tonight was stay out of everyone's way. Lowering myself onto the camp bed with extreme caution, I stared up at the ceiling and replayed the events of the day in my head while the

Sylvanian Family Wise Men watched over me from the dining table. To think, only a few hours earlier I'd thought the worst thing that could happen was getting a sex toy from my dad.

So much for my plan, I thought sadly, the camp bed creaking beneath me. I was more worried about work than ever, I was definitely fighting with Cerys and now I was alone and squeezed between the furnace of a radiator and the dining-room table, all I could think about was Michael and how none of this would be happening if we were still together.

The best-laid plans of mice and Gwen.

'This is why Christmas only comes but once a year,' I whispered as I crossed my hands over my chest to keep them clear of the rusty, snapping springs. All I needed now was to lose a finger. 'No one would survive it more often than that. Thank God this one is over.'

And with that, I closed my eyes and went to sleep.

CHAPTER SEVEN

The next morning, I woke up warm and cosy in my childhood bedroom, the smell of Mum's cooking wafting up the stairs.

'Gwen? Are you up?' Dad rapped on the door before poking his head into my room with a huge grin on his face. 'What are you doing still in bed, chicken? *He's been!* Don't you want all your presents?'

'He?' I replied, pressing the back of my hand against my forehead, confused. 'He who?'

How had I ended up back in here? I hadn't gone to sleep in my room last night, I conked out on Satan's camp bed, burning my backside on the dining-room radiator every time I turned over.

Dad rolled his eyes and rattled his hands on either side of the door. 'You're a better lawyer than a comedian. Bacon butties will be ready in five minutes, up and out of bed or I'll eat them all.'

I stared at him from under the covers. My father was one of the world's greatest grudge-holders. He still drove twenty minutes out of his way to get his shirts dry-cleaned because the man at the dry-cleaners in the village 'looked at him funny' when he took his trousers in after Cerys's wedding more than fifteen years ago and tried to explain how they came to be stained after 'an incident' with a chocolate fountain. And yet here he was, stood in my bedroom, twelve hours after our fight and grinning from ear to ear.

'Dad,' I started. 'About last night—'

He cut me off with a knowing chuckle. 'Stay up too late, did we? I did warn you, no one wants to start Christmas day with a hangover. I'll get Nurofen out.'

'No, I mean about the work stuff,' I replied, rubbing my eyes and blinking. It seemed impossible that I didn't have at least a black eye, but my face wasn't tender and surely Dad would have mentioned a shiner. 'I should have talked to you before, I should have told you when it happened and I'm sorry.'

He beamed down at me with the kind of benign, paternal expression that did not belong on the face of a man who had given his daughter a vibrator for Christmas only twenty-four hours earlier, let alone everything else that had happened.

'Work stuff? What work stuff, chicken?'

'The stuff about my job?' I said slowly. 'About what happened at work?'

Now it was my dad's turn to look clueless. 'Gwen, what are you talking about?'

'Look, no one wants to pretend last night didn't happen more than me, but you might be taking it a bit far here,' I replied, trying out a laugh. 'There's moving on and there's complete denial.'

He held his hands out in front of himself to cut me off. 'Not another word, you don't have to explain yourself to me.'

I pinched my leg under the covers to make sure I wasn't dreaming. 'Are you serious?'

'Your mother has forbidden me from haranguing you about work,' he went on merrily. 'We can talk about it tomorrow. No work chat on Christmas Day.'

With that, he tipped me a wink and took himself off down the hallway.

'Oh my God,' I whispered, shrinking back into the bed. He's lost his mind. Mum always said me and Cerys would drive him mad but I didn't think she meant literally.

Dad taking refuge in a fantasy world of denial was one thing but that didn't explain why I was back in my bed when I'd definitely fallen asleep in the dining room. My heart began to beat a little harder than usual as I looked around, searching for clues. Nothing looked out of place, slippers by the bed, suitcase next to the chest of drawers and my red velvet dress hanging on the front of the wardrobe door.

My pristine, unworn, tags-still-attached, red velvet dress.

I climbed out of bed to inspect the fabric. Flawless. Not a single sign of a tear. It wasn't possible. Not even Nan could have done this overnight, she was an eighty-three-year-old woman who knew her way around a sewing machine, not one of the mice in *Sleeping Beauty*. Besides, I distinctly remembered pricking myself with the little gold safety pin when I'd pulled off the tags, the same little gold safety pin attached to the dress's label as though it had never been removed.

This wasn't good. This wasn't right.

Reaching under the bed for my phone I flicked the screen into life and felt a cold trickle of icy dread run down my spine. There it was. A brand-new, unread text from Aunt Gloria. *Rhiannon Liberty Conners, born at 4.47 a.m. this morning. Mummy and baby doing well, best present we could have wished for!*

'What is happening?' I muttered, my heart beating faster and faster.

'Morning,' Manny appeared in my open doorway, black boxer shorts, reindeer antlers, the same as yesterday. 'Oof, cuz, you look like shit.'

'Manny?' I looked up from my phone, desperate for something to start making some kind of sense. 'What day is it today?'

'Today, sir?' he replied with a terrible cockney accent. 'Why, it's Christmas Day.'

The screen of my phone began to blur in front of me and I realized it was because my hands were shaking. 'It can't be,' I breathed as the room began to swim in front of my eyes. 'Is this some sort of hilarious joke you all cooked up last night? Because it isn't funny at all.'

'Yeah, no, it's Christmas Day,' he said, showing me the screen on his phone. 'All day long, whether you like it or not.'

Thankfully I was right beside the bed when my legs buckled underneath me.

'What's going on?' Manny tucked his phone in the waistband of his pants and pressed his hand against my forehead, the tried and tested Baker response to any kind of crisis. 'Are you ill? You don't feel feverish.'

'No, but I do feel sick,' I replied, leaning forwards with my head between my knees. 'Manny, you're not going to believe me and I don't know how to explain it but today has already happened.'

'Oh, I believe you, it feels like we were just here. Shortest year ever,' he sighed as he sat down beside me. 'Come on, let's go downstairs and I'll mix you a mimosa.'

Looking up at my dress hanging on the wardrobe, I shook my head.

'I mean it, I have lived this Christmas Day already. Yesterday was today and today should be Boxing Day but it isn't unless you really are lying to me and Manny, I am freaking out.'

Manny pulled back to get a better look at me, saw the panic on my face and frowned.

'It's too early and I'm too sober for nonsense. What is going on?'

How was I supposed to explain?

'Christmas Day was yesterday. I went to bed last night and when I woke up this morning, it's like I've travelled back in time,' I said, trying to get the tremor out of my voice. 'I swear on Adam Driver's life.'

'Gwen,' he said, horrified. 'Think about what you're saying.'

'I'm telling the truth!' I insisted. How could I make him believe me? I hadn't felt this confused and frustrated since the *Sex and the City* reboot. 'I don't know how else to explain it. I've already lived through this exact Christmas Day. We opened presents, ate turkey, argued with Oliver, I saw Dev Jones from next door, there were fireworks, then Cerys went mental and told Dad about all the work stuff and it snowed and I had to sleep on the camp bed and, Manny, I swear to you. It's not déjà vu, it's not a glitch in the matrix, it's not a bad dream.

I'm telling you, I have already lived this exact day and you know I would never, ever lie to you.'

Manny stared at me, every possible expression flitting over his open-book face.

'So what are you saying, we're in a *Groundhog Day* situation?' he said eventually. 'And you're Bill Murray?'

'Yes. I'm Bill Murray.'

'Am I Andi McDowell?'

'No, you're the groundhog,' I replied. 'That or I'm having a complete psychotic break.'

He cocked his head to one side and raised his eyebrows, eyes wide with possibility. 'Well . . .'

'It's not a psychotic break,' I insisted, reaching out to slap his bare legs. 'This is real and it's scary and you've got to help me, Manny, I need your help.'

'I think that's the first time I've ever heard you use those words,' he said softly, taking a seat beside me on the bed. 'You never ask for help.' My lower lip trembled as I looked at him, my frenzy softening into fearful hope. 'I want to believe you, I really do. Tell me one thing that happens today, something you couldn't possibly know unless you'd been through it already.'

'Like what?'

He screwed up his wide mouth and wrinkled his nose. 'What are we having for dinner?'

'The same thing we always have for dinner on Christmas Day,' I replied. 'That's a terrible question, ask me something else.'

'Everyone's a critic,' he pouted. 'Fine. What am I getting from your mum and dad?'

Most of the events of the day were all too easy to remember and not because they were cherished memories

I would treasure forever, but I hadn't really been paying attention to Manny's gifts, I was far too interested in my own. Creasing my forehead with the effort of recollection, I saw him sat by the tree, cup of tea in one hand a bacon butty in the other and . . . 'Bedding,' I answered finally. 'You're getting bedding. John Lewis, very nice.'

He stared at me for a moment, an uncertain look on his face before he burst out laughing.

'You total knob, you almost had me there,' he groaned as he bounced off the bed. 'Very funny, Gwen. Get your arse downstairs, I want a bacon sandwich.'

'And it's going to snow this afternoon,' I said confidently.

'Thank you, Carol Kirkwood. That's hardly proof, is it? They've been saying that all week.'

'Oh, I know,' I jolted upright and jabbed my finger in the direction of his phone. 'I caught you sending a dick pic! In your room, after dinner, wearing nothing but reindeer antlers and oh my *God* why did I have to remember that?'

'What did you just say?' Manny reared back as though I'd told him I'd snogged Boris Johnson for a laugh.

'At dinner,' I explained, finding myself strangely energized. 'You had an argument with Oliver and you stormed out and I came upstairs to see if you were all right and you were . . . you know.'

I attempted to mime the act that hadn't even happened yet but would be burned into my retinas until the end of time.

'Please never do that again,' he warned, his face pale and bleak.

'How long have you had that dolphin tattoo on your

hip?' I asked as I narrowed my eyes at my cousin. 'And why don't I know about it?'

'You were never meant to know about the dolphin,' he whispered, yanking his boxers up over his belly button. 'I have protected that secret for *years*. What is going on?'

'I don't know,' I said again, hurling myself backwards into my pillows. 'But I would like to know who you're sending festive fap photos to?'

'Perhaps you should try to work out how you're defying the space time continuum before you waste any time on that,' Manny suggested as Dad bellowed both our names from the bottom of the stairs. 'We'd better go down before they send a search party. Now, do you want to tell your mum and dad what's going on or would you prefer not to spend Christmas Day in a straitjacket?'

'So, you believe me?'

An unbearable weight hovered over my shoulders as I waited for his reply.

'I don't know how or why but yes, of course I believe you,' he said, opening his arms for a hug and the heaviness that hung over me disappeared just for a moment. 'Whatever it is, we'll work it out.'

'I hope we work it out soon,' I replied. 'I don't know if I can relive this entire day all the way through again.'

'That bad?' he asked doubtfully.

'Justin Bieber's Christmas album bad,' I confirmed gravely.

Manny's hands flew up to cover his mouth as he gasped.

'We'll get through this together,' he promised. 'We've faced great adversity before. Remember when they took the Nutty Truffle Log out of the tin of Roses?'

'I thought I'd never get over it but I did,' I said, my confidence somewhat bolstered. 'You're right. If we can make it all the way through that *Last Christmas* movie, we can make it through this.'

'That's the spirit,' Manny cheered as we set off downstairs. 'Christmas Day the sequel, let's have it!'

The rest of the day went on as only I knew it would. I moved through most of it in a daze, too shocked and confused to really process what was happening. Occasionally I snapped to my senses long enough to look for hidden cameras in the house or a big blue police phone box outside, but by lunchtime, after Nan's savage review of my dress and Cerys's request for an early lunch, I found myself reluctantly resigned to the facts; I was officially repeating the worst Christmas Day on record.

'You could have warned me about your dad buying you a vibrator,' Manny hissed in my ear as I forced down my last bite of turkey. 'I almost choked on my bacon butty.'

'Your reaction was almost worth living through it again,' I whispered back while Oliver regaled the table with a thrilling tale about the time he successfully sued a pet shop for selling gendered mice, just as drunk as he had been the day before.

'What are you two gossiping about?' Mum eyed us with suspicion from the other side of her contemporary art masterpiece of a nativity scene.

'We were debating whether or not *Die Hard* is a Christmas movie,' Manny answered. 'Gwen says it is but I'm not sure.'

He was an evil genius. The one debate guaranteed to fire up any dinner table.

'Of course it is. The entire film takes place on Christmas Eve, at a Christmas party,' Cerys said, racing to take the bait. 'Bruce Willis has come home for Christmas, it could not be more of a Christmas movie.'

'Sorry but you're wrong,' Oliver argued. '*Die Hard* was originally released in July which makes it a summer blockbuster by definition.'

Cerys glared at her husband. 'But the concept of Christmas is pivotal to the plot of the film. There's a tree, there are presents, ergo, it is a Christmas movie.'

'Ergo?' He replied through peals of laughter. 'Er-fucking-go?'

'Oliver!' Nan said sharply. 'Language!'

As Manny opened his mouth to interject, I grabbed mine and Dad's empty plates and elbowed my cousin out of his seat. 'We're going to clear the table,' I said loudly. 'Should I fill the dishwasher?'

'Do you know how?' Mum replied, her eyes huge with surprise.

'Haha, very funny,' I replied, stacking plates along my arm as Manny cautiously pinched the edges of the gravy boat, a foul look on his face. 'Back in a tick.'

'I know you're going through something but I don't know why that means I have to endure menial labour,' he sniffed, once we were safely in the kitchen, door and serving hatch firmly closed.

'We're filling the dishwasher, not digging a trench. Stop whining, I need your help.'

'Fine.' He pushed the gravy boat across the kitchen counter with the tip of his finger until it fell into the bowl of soapy water waiting in the sink, his contribution complete. 'So we know you're reliving the same day, but do you have any idea why?'

'Not a clue,' I replied. 'But whatever the reason it's a cruel and unusual punishment. Why couldn't I be reliving last Tuesday when Dominos accidentally sent me two pizzas instead of one and a tub of Ben & Jerry's?'

'*Accidentally*?'

'Don't test me today, Manny Baker,' I warned, brandishing a dirty serving spoon in his face.

'These things don't happen for no reason, something must have caused it,' he said, ducking the offending utensil. 'Have you walked under any ladders recently?'

'Nope.'

'Crossed any black cats?'

'Not to the best of my knowledge.'

'Passed through an interdimensional portal?'

'I did fall asleep for a couple of minutes in the car on the way up,' I replied, dry as an overcooked turkey breast. 'Did you accidentally drive us through a Stargate when I was looking at my phone?'

'I would have if it had got us around that traffic outside Northampton any faster and this would be a small price to pay,' he said with a huff. 'What about a curse?'

'Who would go to the bother of cursing me? *Besides* Cerys.' I cut him off before he could suggest it. 'I don't think so. If it were a curse, I'd know. People love to tell you when they're cursing you, don't they? A curse on both your houses! Thinner! All that jazz. Otherwise what's the point?'

He considered my logic for a moment then nodded in agreement while poking himself in the stomach. 'I wish I knew who to piss off to get a go on the "Thinner" curse.

I'm all for body positivity but I can't afford to keep replacing all my jeans every time Cadbury brings out a new chocolate bar. Ooh, what if it's a spell?'

'It's not a spell and you're not a wizard, Harry.'

He looked almost as disappointed as he did when Dad had to explain why he wasn't getting a letter from Hogwarts on his eleventh birthday. 'I must say, you're being very calm about this,' he said with a sniff. 'I'd be wailing like Kate Bush in the "Wuthering Heights" video by now.'

Spoken like a true Hufflepuff.

'Maybe I'm in shock?' I suggested cheerfully. 'The running up and down screaming bit will probably kick in later, but for now it's a problem and I need to solve it.'

'Ooh!' Manny's face lit up with inspiration. 'What if you're dead?'

My cheerfulness was short-lived.

'If this was heaven, Chris Hemsworth would have fallen down the chimney dressed as Santa Claus, my bed would be made of Dairy Milk and we'd all be in Hawaii,' I replied flatly. 'But thank you for the positive thinking.'

'Fine, you're not dead, I'm only trying to help.' He rolled his eyes, hands tucked in the pockets of his navy blue trousers. 'But if it's not a curse and no one has put a spell on you, what is it?'

Turning on the tap, I rinsed off the dirty plates one at a time then stacked each one in the dishwasher. I hadn't entered any scary-looking caves or tried to travel through time and even if you put a gun to my head, I couldn't hand on heart tell you what a groundhog was. A bit like a rat but bigger? They definitely didn't have them in Derbyshire. I was scraping leftover sprouts out of their bowl into the bin when the doors to the serving hatch sprung open, Dad's head popping through as though he'd been shot, stuffed and mounted on the kitchen wall.

'You two are taking your sweet time,' he said, angling his arm for another bottle of red wine. 'Can you bring the pudding in when you're done?'

'Will do.'

Manny picked up Mum's homemade steamed pud, sat proudly in the centre of Great-Grandma Baker's antique pudding platter, a sprig of holly on top and slathered in brandy butter. Thankfully zero Sylvanian Families had been harmed in the making of this dessert.

'Where are the bloody matches?' he said, searching all the usual spots and coming up blank.

'They were on top of the fridge yesterday,' I replied absently as I stuck my bowl in the dishwasher, my mind wandering.

'Thanks, Mystic Meg.' He grabbed the matches and gave the pudding a sour look. 'Why she insists on serving it every year when no one likes it I will never know.'

'Because it's tradition. Traditions are important.'

'Then it should at least have the decency to be delicious,' he sulked. 'Come on, let's get it over with.'

'Be there in a sec,' I pointed to the rest of the dishes. 'Don't start without me.'

'Why not? You've already suffered through this once already, do yourself a favour and don't bother.'

Manny opened the kitchen door with his hip and carried the pudding into the dining room. I heard a chorus of cheers go up around the table.

'I didn't even get any bloody pudding though, did I?' I muttered to myself, staring into the remains of the parsnips and wondering whether or not it was worth putting what was left in the fridge.

And then it hit me.

I didn't eat the pudding.

'What if it's not a curse?' I said aloud. 'What if it's a wish?'

My pale reflection stared back at me from the kitchen window. Whoever finds the sixpence in their pudding makes a wish. What if the person who found the sixpence made a wish and trapped me here?

'That's got to be it,' I whispered, a very certain feeling running through my bones. 'It's that bloody sixpence. Someone made a wish.'

And, I realized as another cheer went up in the next room, there was every chance they were about to do it again.

'Nobody touch that pud!' I yelled as I tore into the dining room wild-eyed and desperate.

'Gwen?' Dad replied, serving spoon in his right hand. 'Are you all right?'

The Christmas pudding sat on the table in front of him, already alight, blue flames licking at its sides and flickering worryingly close to the centrepiece. Mum really had gone to town on the brandy this year. But I could google whether or not Sylvanian Families were flammable later, right now, I had to get my mitts on that pudding, *en flambé* or otherwise.

'Don't panic!' I shouted, immediately inciting panic around the table. 'I've got it!'

Without another thought, I grabbed the platter, flaming pudding and all, and turned around, running out of the dining room, through the kitchen, and was out the back door before anyone could stop me.

'Gwen! Come back!'

I heard Mum calling my name as I sprinted it down the garden, the flaming pudding rolling around in circles on the platter as I went. My slippers were long gone but I didn't stop to look for them, the sooner I got rid of this thing, the sooner things could get back to normal and that was worth a potential splinter and a pair of singed eyebrows. Puffing and panting as I reached the swings, I looked over my shoulder to see the entire family, bar Nan, watching from the other end of the garden.

'Is it the pudding?' Manny called.

'It's the pudding!' I confirmed with a yell. 'I have to get rid of it!'

'Yeet it!' he screamed joyously at the top of his lungs. 'Yeet it into the sun, Gwen!'

And yeet it I did.

With all the momentum of my spirited run, I pulled my arms back and hurled the pudding as far and as hard as I could, using the platter as a launching pad to chuck the flaming ball of suet and dried fruit over the fence. It flew through the air like a Christmas comet, the blue flames burning out as it arced gracelessly over the fence into the neighbour's garden and crashed, face first, into Dev Jones.

'Dev!'

I leapt over the fence and raced to the spot where he lay flat on his back, spreadeagled in his lovely grey coat and well-fitting trousers, his eyes closed.

'I didn't see you,' I said as I fell to my knees at his side. 'I swear I didn't see you!'

'That's a relief, I suppose,' he murmured. His eyelids fluttered open and his big, unfocused eyes met mine. In spite of his current condition, my former friend smiled as he realized who I was and in spite of everything else, I smiled back. 'Hello, stranger.'

'You're engaged,' I said, the words falling out my mouth before I could stop them.

'Good work, Gwen, you've concussed the neighbour.' Mum pushed me out of the way, crouched down on the ground beside me and took Dev's hand in hers, patting it gently. 'Now, Dev, can you hear me? Did you bump your head? Can you taste pennies?'

'No but I can smell brandy?' he replied, licking his lips.

'I'm calling an ambulance,' Dad said, turning back to the house. 'Don't move, young man!'

'No need for an ambulance,' Dev mumbled as the colour started to come back to his face. 'I'm fine, just surprised. There's nothing wrong with me other than getting knocked on my arse by whatever-that-was.'

I held the pudding platter out in front of myself, a last line of antique defence.

'It was a Christmas pudding,' I explained, picking a chunk of said pudding out of his hair. 'I threw it.'

'You threw a Christmas pudding at me?' he replied with a quizzical look. 'Why?'

The whole family stared at me, waiting for an answer.

'B-because there was a rat,' I stuttered. 'In the pudding.'

Oh, good one, Gwen. I silently slow-clapped for myself, my shoulders sloping with shame.

'There was a rat?'

'Yes.'

'In your Christmas pudding?'

'That's right.'

Considering I was a good lawyer, I had a terrible poker face.

'When I walked into the dining room, I saw it poke it's head out,' I went on, immediately breaking the first rule of how to tell a successful lie. Never give more information than is absolutely necessary. 'Obviously I didn't want the kids to see it and be traumatized. They bloody love *Ratatouille*. So I brought it out here.'

'All I know is that was a bloody hard rat,' Dev said as he sat up and looked around at the assembled Baker clan, all of whom were still staring at me.

'But you're all right, son?' Dad held out a hand and hauled him up to his feet with a grunt. 'No broken bones?'

Dev nodded, rubbing his hip, his gorgeous black hair barely even ruffled. 'I am. Trust me, I'm a doctor.'

'You know you could sue her for assault,' Oliver said, digging around in his pockets for a business card. 'Oliver Adlington of Adlington & Adlington, we specialize in personal injury claims.'

Dev stared at his outstretched hand, recognition flickering across his face. 'Oliver Adlington? Did I see one of your adverts in the toilets of a Little Chef?'

'That's right!' Oli cheered. 'We're trialling branded loo roll. It's got our logo and then it says, "We'll wipe the floor with them." Turns out there's a big crossover demographic between service station users and personal injury claimants.'

'I don't think we should be encouraging the neighbour to sue my sister on Christmas Day.' Cerys snatched the card out of his hand. Her eyes skirted over to me as she tucked it away in the pocket of her dress. 'At least wait until tomorrow.'

Dev scrunched up his face in disbelief, although which part he was struggling with the most was impossible for me to say.

'I really am sorry,' I told him, still kneeling on the ground as he dusted off the back of his coat. Sorry for hitting him in the head with a flaming pudding, sorry for snapping at him on the Christmas Day that never was, sorry for not replying to his emails all those years ago . . .

'No big deal.' He rolled his shoulders and turned his head from side to side, wincing just a little. 'I was having a very boring day until you attacked me with a dessert, but I think I will pop back in and take an ibuprofen just in case.'

'Perfect, he's going to tell his mother Gwen lamped him with a pudding and I won't be able to show my face at aqua-aerobics,' Mum muttered under her breath.

'Nice to see you all,' Dev said. He raised his hand in a wave to everyone but kept his eyes on me. An unexpected shiver of delight ran up and down my spine and I had to bite down on my bottom lip to stop myself from smiling. 'Merry Christmas.'

'Merry Christmas,' we chorused back, slightly out of time with each other and with varying degrees of enthusiasm. Still on the ground, I waved until he retreated out of sight, Dev Jones, gone again. A sensible but stylish slip-on shoe nudged me where I sat and I looked up to see my parents staring down at me.

'You saw a rat,' Mum said.

'Could have been a mouse,' I replied. 'Furry grey thing, white whiskers, pink tail. You didn't see it?'

'No,' she said as I mimed the whiskers with my fingers. 'I didn't.'

'Show's over, let's get back inside.' Dad put his arm around her shoulders as they peered at me with the exact same uncertain expression on their very different faces. It must be nice, I thought, to share everything with someone, right down to facial expressions. Even if those expressions were deeply suspicious and aimed squarely at me.

I rose to my feet, about to follow them in, when I caught sight of a small, smouldering ball out of the corner of my eye. The pudding peeked out of the long grass that grew around the stream, looking as tasty as it had ever been (which was to say, not very). I climbed to my feet and walked calmly over to the fence before pulling back my leg and booting it into the water. With one sad splosh, it sank into the stream, never to be seen again.

'And that's the end of you,' I declared, dusting off my hands as I set off to get on with my day and, hopefully, the rest of my life.

CHAPTER EIGHT

'Gwen? Are you up? *He's been!*'

I held my breath against an attack of accumulated carpet fluff that tickled my nostrils. The underneath of this bed hadn't seen a vacuum cleaner in months, Nan would be furious.

'Gwen?' Dad said again, mildly befuddled as he popped his head around the door. 'Where are you hiding?'

I said nothing.

'Must be in the lav.' He closed the door and made his way down to Manny's room to inform him of the status of the bacon butties. As the door creaked shut, I breathed out, the slats of the bed base above me, the cream carpet below and nothing but existential dread as far as the eye could see. Raising the bottle of Baileys I'd already liberated from the kitchen to my lips, I looked at my phone again.

Rhiannon Liberty Conners, born at 4.47 a.m.

Punting the pudding hadn't worked.

It was still Christmas Day.

* * *

The presents had been opened, Mum was in the kitchen, Dad out for his walk and Manny upstairs in the shower when I sat down at the dining table to gather my thoughts and fight off a panic attack. I need to come at this like it's a case, I told myself, all I had to do was find the facts and let them lead me to the answers. But it was hard to look at facts when you were reliving the same day for the third time and you'd necked a quarter of a bottle of cream liqueur before breakfast. The sixpence was the culprit, I just knew it, but knowing wasn't enough. Throwing the pudding away hadn't worked because the wish was already made, nothing I did to it now would change a thing. It was time to try another tactic. The first thing I did when building a case? Gather as much information as possible. Know thine enemy.

'Mum?' I called through the serving hatch. A clattering of saucepans confirmed she had heard me. 'Where did you get the new sixpence for the Christmas pudding?'

'Where did I get the sixpence?'

'Yes, Mum.'

'The new one?'

'Yes, Mum.'

Her neon pink face appeared in the serving hatch, completely consumed by Christmas-cooking panic. 'Amazon, I think.'

I'd been expecting her to say she found it down a little back alley or bought it from a man wearing a cloak and carrying a staff, but actually this made more sense. Amazon really did have everything, even magic sixpences.

'Have you still got the packaging?' I asked sweetly.

With a tut and a sigh, she pulled open a drawer,

rummaged for a moment then chucked me a small, blue cardboard box through the hatch.

'Thank you,' I said, turning the box over to read the back. The Little Silver Sixpence Company, a division of Globotech Ltd, a subsidiary of Phetazon Inc. Sixpence is not safe for consumption. If Sixpence is consumed, seek medical attention. Sixpence is not dishwasher safe. Wishes not guaranteed.

'Well, that's useful,' I said, making a mental reminder to go online and leave them a terrible review. Very shiny but may cause time loops. Two out of five stars.

'Will that be all?' Mum asked. 'Because I've still got to pull a three-course meal for nine people out of my backside with no help.'

Dropping the box back on the table, I waved a hand in her general direction and nodded.

'Very good, madam,' she said with a brief curtsey. 'Just once I wish one of you would offer to help.'

'What did you say?' I replied, my ears pricking.

'I said it would be nice to have some help, but don't you trouble yourself, Gwen, I'll do it all, as usual.'

The wish that had me trapped could only have been made by one of four people. Me and Manny left the table before the pudding was served, Oliver had his nut allergy and the kids weren't old enough to choke down the brandy butter, so it had to be Mum, Dad, Nan or Cerys. Perhaps, if I found out what they had wished for and made that wish come true, I could get myself out of my never-ending noel.

'Mum?'

I heard something heavy meet something hard, followed by an exasperated sigh.

'Yes, Gwen.'

'Is that really what you'd wish for?' I asked. 'If you could wish for anything?'

She paused, still with her back to me, her shoulder blades pinched so tightly together she could have held a Christmas cracker without dropping it.

'That or a million pounds,' she replied. 'And Hugh Jackman to bring the cheque.'

Abandoning the sixpence box, I left the dining room and poked my head around the kitchen door where she was already elbow-deep in a sack of spuds.

'I want to help,' I said, crossing the threshold into the kitchen. 'What can I do?'

'Sod off and stop bothering me?'

'I'm serious!' I grabbed a spare apron from the hook next to the pantry and pulled it over my head, glancing down to see I now had the body of a Chippendale. 'I want to help.'

Mum and her Cath Kidston apron raised an eyebrow.

'I do! I would have offered earlier but, um, I thought you liked doing it all on your own.'

A disbelieving scoff squeaked through her pursed lips as she pulled potatoes from the sack one by one.

'Or at least, I never bothered to think about whether or not you did,' I said, amending my statement.

'That sounds more like it,' Mum replied. She tightened her grip on the potato peeler and rubbed the bridge of her nose with the back of her wrist. 'I'm a sixty-two-year-old full-time teacher with an elderly mother to take care of, grandkids we babysit every weekend and let's be honest, your dad doesn't know his arse from his elbow, so when it comes to Christmas, yes I love it, but if I'm being completely honest, I also resent it. Shopping for presents, wrapping the presents, decorating the house, writing the sodding cards and on top of all that, I have to spend the entire bloody day cooking the bloody dinner while you all sit with your feet up. Why should all of it fall to me, Gwen, why?'

Very, very slowly, I leaned over to remove the sharpened blade from her hand.

'It doesn't just happen,' she added, her Welsh accent getting stronger by the second. 'All of this, none of it appears out of nowhere. I've been shopping for months – months! And what did your dad do? A smash-and-grab around Meadowhall last Thursday night. Took me three evenings to write the cards, an entire afternoon to put the tree up and I've been buying presents since January. And the food shopping? *The food shopping?*' She paused to launch an unsuspecting Maris Piper across the kitchen. 'I got into a fight with a woman over leeks. *Leeks, Gwen.* I slapped them out of the hands of a woman named Sharon because they were the last five leeks in all of Chesterfield and we *had* to have them or your nan would have a meltdown.'

'What leeks?' I asked, looking around at assorted vegetables that covered the kitchen top. 'I can't see any leeks.'

'Because there aren't any leeks! She got the leeks and I was asked to leave,' she shrieked. 'I can never show my face at the Tesco Extra in Chesterfield again, we shall have to drive all the way to Sheffield or start going to the big Asda and you know your dad hates the big Asda, *hates it.* All for bloody leeks. I don't even like leeks!'

'Were you not supposed to get your veg from the greengrocers?' I asked innocently. Mum's nostrils flared and her eyes widened and I shuffled back towards the door. I'd confiscated the potato peeler but there were an awful lot of knives within reach. 'Never mind,' I muttered. 'Supermarket veg is brilliant.'

But she wasn't finished. 'I don't spend three months shopping, twelve hours cooking and God knows how many more cleaning up after you all for the good of my health, I do it because no one else will. You asked what my wish would be, there it is, I wish someone else would make this bloody meal for once.'

And with that, she chucked another potato across the room and burst into tears.

'Oh no, don't cry,' I said, awkwardly manhandling her into a hug. This usually happened the other way around and I wasn't quite sure where to start. 'Don't get upset, I'll help you, I will.'

I gently shoved her in the general direction of the living room and sat her on the settee, lifting her legs onto the pouffe as she sniffed herself back to her senses.

'I'm sorry, I'm sorry,' she said, pawing at her eyes. 'Only, I'm so tired and it never stops. I thought one of you would have taken over Christmas duties by now but somehow I have more to do than ever, I never have a moment to myself.'

'How long have you been babysitting Arthur and Artemis?' I asked. 'What's that all about?'

She flapped her hand up and down as though trying to pull a date out of the air. 'It's not every weekend, more like every other weekend. You know how Oliver is, with his golf and his rugby and all that, and he's as much use as a chocolate teapot at home. Cerys needs the extra time to get on top of the house, you can't do that with two little kids under your feet, I should know.'

'And you don't?'

Mum let out a laugh so loud I was surprised the tree didn't fall over.

'Not to be rude, pet, but this is the first time any of you have ever asked what I need.'

The truth of it stung.

'Don't listen to me,' she said, rising to her feet as soon as she saw the expression on my face. 'I didn't sleep a wink last night, then I had to be up at the crack of dawn to preheat the oven, and—'

'Mum, no.' I stood back, one hand held out in front of me as though I might burst into a chorus of 'Stop' by the Spice Girls at any moment. 'I am going to make dinner.'

She sat back down slowly.

'You're going to what?'

'I'm going to make dinner,' I said, speaking firmly and clearly in my very best 'I know what I'm doing, don't question me' voice, most commonly used when ordering doughnuts. 'You're going to sit there, I'm going to take care of the food. The turkey's already in, isn't it? You've done the hard bit, leave the rest of it to me.'

'Don't take this the wrong way, pet, but do you know how to cook a Christmas dinner?'

I was a renowned expert in corporate law, I routinely went into Superdrug and only came out with the thing I went in for and three years ago, I wore a jumpsuit to a festival, went to the toilet four times and didn't even wee on myself once. I was a woman who could do difficult things. Compared to the jumpsuit thing, cooking a few vegetables and pulling a turkey out of the oven would be a piece of cake.

Mmm. Cake.

I pulled my phone out of the pocket of my dress and waved it in Mum's concerned face. The sum total of humanity's quest for knowledge in my hand and all I needed to know was how to cook some carrots. If the internet was going to take down civilization, the least I was owed was a decent recipe for root vegetables.

'Just because you haven't seen me cook, doesn't mean I'm not any good at it,' I replied, as much to myself as my mother. She hadn't seen me cook because I didn't cook, but I watched a lot of cooking programmes. Surely some skills had been transferred over by osmosis? All I needed was half an hour in the kitchen, some self-belief and, if *MasterChef* was to be believed, a good set of knives. It was all in the knives, they all said so.

'I've got this,' I said, brimming with unearned confidence. 'You put your feet up and relax.'

'I think I've forgotten how,' Mum said, awkwardly patting the sofa cushions on either side of her, still for the first time in my entire life. 'What should I do?'

'Watch telly, read a book, get angry about the *Daily Mail* online but read it anyway, fill an online shopping cart with things you've no intention of buying, the usual stuff,' I suggested, turning on the radio and filling the room with soothing Christmas carols. 'Try to relax. If you need me, I'll be in the kitchen.'

'And if you need me, I'll be right here,' she called as I rolled up my sleeves, striding into the next room to make my mother's wish come true. 'And all I have to do is cook a meal,' I said with a smile. 'How hard can it be?'

'Is everything all right, chicken? Oh, bloody hell.'

Dad entered the kitchen slowly, holding an arm across

his face to protect his eyes from the smoke that poured out of the oven and filled the room.

'Everything is fine!' I screamed as I flapped a tea towel at the screaming smoke alarm. 'Absolutely fucking marvellous.'

'I came to see if you needed any help?' he said, opening the back door and wafting it back and forth, sending clouds of smoke out into the garden. It was everything I could do not to get in Manny's car, drive down to London to hunt and kill Nigella Lawson. Easy Christmas dinner, my arse.

'Thanks,' I said, looking around the kitchen as plumes of thick black smoke continued to pour out of the oven. 'I can't imagine what set it off.'

'Gwen, what is that?' Dad asked. I saw him eyeing a bowl of lumpy white slop on the table, half of which was clinging to the front of my dress.

'It's the Yorkshire puddings,' I explained, holding up a sieve. 'The flour didn't want to mix so I thought, you know . . .' I mimed mashing the mixture through the sieve and the optimistic smile on his face dissolved to make way for a look of pure pity. 'Everything's good though. Completely on schedule, nothing to worry about. I wanted the oven to smoke like that, it was in the recipe.'

I grabbed the half-empty bottle of white wine that was sweating on the counter and took a deep swig.

'Do you want a glass for that?' Dad asked.

I shook my head as I put it back on the table with a heavy hand. 'I've already broken two, best not to risk another.'

'Right you are.'

If I could have read minds, I'd have sworn he was wondering whether or not Dominos delivered on Christmas.

'Well, I'll let you get on,' he said, sticking his hands in his pockets and backing up to the door. 'As long as we've got pigs in blankets, I'm a happy camper. You know my mum always used to make them for me on Christmas Day, they're the best bit of the meal as far as I'm concerned.'

'The pigs in blankets are fine,' I replied, edging over to the sink where twelve charred chipolatas wrapped in cremated bacon were welded to the bottom of a baking tray. 'It's all fine.'

Even though we both knew that wasn't entirely true, he went anyway, tapping away at his phone on what was *definitely* the Dominos app. I surveyed the disaster area that used to be the kitchen and grimaced.

Bugger.

This was not going to be as easy as I thought.

It took Mrs Jones a surprisingly long time to come to the door, considering I was knocking so hard I worried my knuckles might shatter the solid wood into splinters.

'Hello?' she said as she opened the door by a fraction, leaving it secured by the chain. 'Gwen, is that you?'

'It is, hello, Mrs. Jones. Merry Christmas,' I smiled my most dazzling smile as I rubbed the feeling back into my fingers.

She did not smile back.

'So sorry to both you but I was wondering, would you happen to have any spare bacon?'

I was doing my level best to look calm when in reality I felt like the Energizer bunny after three cans of Red Bull and a trip to the toilets with Donald Trump Jr. After our breakfast butties and my failed attempt at pigs in blankets, there wasn't so much as a bacon-flavoured Frazzle left in my mother's house. I considered wrapping the rest of the sausages in wafer-thin ham but even I had thought better of that one. Plus, I'd eaten most of the ham during a panic over the state of my Yorkshires.

The Joneses were my only hope.

'Bacon, you say?' Sunita replied, eyeing my Chippendale apron with reasonable alarm. 'We should have some, let me look.'

And then she closed the door.

I jogged up and down on the doorstep, my breath misting up the air in front of me. My mum and Dev's mum had never really got on. Our dads were fine with each other in the way that dads usually are, a shared celebration over a sporting event, mutual admiration of each other's cars and zero emotional connection, but our mothers had rubbed each other the wrong way from the off. Dev's mum was gorgeous, always elegant and put together, very much a walking advert for The White Company, and full price White Company at that, no sale rail for Sunita Jones. I remembered watching Sunita come home from her office job from the safety of my bedroom window and fantasising about owning a beautiful camel trench coat, just like hers. When I got my first promotion at Hampton's, I spend almost an entire month's rent on a Burberry trench coat and promptly left it in the cloak-room of a dingy Camden club a week later, never to be seen again, a painful and valuable lesson about the maximum amount I should ever spend on anything for myself. Bronwyn Baker always told us how she gave up trying to wear white clothing of any kind the moment she got her teaching degree. As she liked to say, busy prints hid the evidence better, a fact my friends in criminal law confirmed was true. Peeking through the window, I saw the inside of Sunita's house was still as impeccable as its owner. Dev and his dad wouldn't dare breathe too heavily for fear of leaving some sort of carbon dioxide stain on the Farrow & Ball paintwork. Not that there was anything wrong with wanting a smart, clean, minimalist home, it was just very far removed from the cosy, comfortable chaos in which I'd been raised. There were still days when I dreamed of being the kind of person who had a white cashmere throw tossed over the end of my mid-century-modern sofa, but I knew in my heart I would be a tea-stained hoodie on the back of the settee girl for life.

When the door reopened, I expected to see Sunita's standard look of disapproval but instead, someone else was smiling down at me.

'Hello, stranger,' Dev said, taking the door off the chain and opening it wide. A waft of warm air brushed over my cold skin. 'Long time no see. What are you doing outside?'

It was so nice to see him smiling again and without any pudding-related injuries.

'She came to borrow bacon,' Sunita replied as she pushed past her son to hand me a brown paper package, tied up with string. Bacon was one of my favourite things.

'My pigs need blankets,' I explained, clutching the packet to my chest. 'Had a bit of an accident with the first batch.'

'You burned them?'

'I incinerated them.'

'Devendra, you're letting all the heat out,' Sunita said, sliding herself between Dev and the door. 'We should let

Gwen get back to her cooking, it sounds as though she has a lot to do.'

'Yes, I should get back to it,' I confirmed, shuddering at the thought of returning to the scene of my many crimes. 'Thank you so much for this, you've really saved my bacon.'

Sunita stared me down and if I could have made myself evaporate on the spot, I would have.

'Quite,' she said, Dev beside her trying not to laugh. 'Merry Christmas, Gwen.'

'Merry Christmas, Mrs Jo—'

The words were only half out my mouth when she closed the door with slightly more force than was necessary and rattled the chain back into place.

'Bah, humbug,' I muttered, turning on the heel of my slippers and marching victoriously back to my kitchen.

CHAPTER NINE

My victory was short-lived.

'How am I supposed to do the roast potatoes, the roast parsnips *and* the pigs in blankets all at the same time as the turkey when they all need to be at different temperatures?' I wailed with despair, pressing the heels of my hands into my eyes until everything went dark. 'It doesn't make any sense, *Nigella*.'

Before I could drop my phone in the air fryer, a triple knock on the back door, both familiar and forgotten, made me jump.

'Twice in one decade?' I said, throwing the door open to find Dev on my doorstep. 'I am honoured.'

'I come bearing bacon,' he replied, presenting me with a plastic package of the bargain supermarket variety. 'The stuff Mum gave you is from that new butcher in the village, great for sandwiches, terrible for pigs in blankets. You'll never get the sausages to cook without burning the bacon first.'

'Like that, you mean?'

I gestured over at my first attempt like a 1970s game-show hostess.

'Fuck me, Gwen, what did those sausages ever do to you?' Dev set his bacon on the counter, took off his grey coat, unbuttoned his cuffs and rolled up his sleeves. 'Not to overstep my bounds but do you need some help?'

I opened my mouth to say a well-rehearsed 'No', but something stopped me.

I did need help.

'It's Christmas, you're supposed to be with your family.' Family, fiancée, same difference. 'I know it looks bad but really, it's all under control,' I said through gritted teeth. What was wrong with me? Even when someone offered, even when I really needed it, I still couldn't quite manage to simply say, 'Yes, I do need your help, thank you very much, might you know how one is supposed cook a parsnip?'

He picked up a packet of gingernuts. 'What are these for?'

I bit my bottom lip, my shoulders rising slowly up to my ears.

'The gingerbread and walnut stuffing?'

'No.' Dev opened the biscuit cupboard, a part of our kitchen he used to be very familiar with, and put them away. 'We're not even going into why not, just no. Right, I'm going to go out on a limb and say you don't cook that often?'

'How dare you?' I gasped, planting my hands on my apron's photoshopped Chippendale abs. 'For all you know, I could be a Michelin star chef.'

He picked up the Yorkshire pudding batter and turned the bowl upside down. The batter did not budge.

'Fine, you got me, this is my first go at Christmas lunch,' I said, collapsing onto a stool and dropping my head onto the counter. 'I don't know what happened, I did everything I was told, I followed Nigella's cooking plan and—'

'Wait, you tried to Nigella your Christmas dinner first time out the gate?' Dev sucked the air in through his teeth as he did a lap around the kitchen, picking things up and putting them down. 'Schoolboy error, Gwen, schoolboy error. When you're starting out you want your Delias, your Nadiyas, maybe an early Jamie, but you set yourself up trying to go the full Lawson on your first time. I'm sorry but I'm going to have to take over.'

'You're staging a coup on my Christmas dinner?' I replied, secretly delighted.

'You've given me no other option,' he said with a grave nod. 'I'm a doctor, I took an oath to do no harm and leaving you alone in this kitchen seems like one of the most harmful things I could possibly do as a human, let alone a medical professional.'

As he busied himself around the kitchen, lifting lids of pots and giving various pans a shake, I gnawed on the nail of my right thumb. It was impossible to overstate the size of my teenage crush on Dev. If they could find a way to harness the power of a teenage girl's obsession, the global energy crisis would be over in a single heartbeat. I did it all, wrote down every possible combination of our names to see which looked best, worked out our astrological compatibility, nearly set fire to the house trying to cast a love spell using a Body Shop Dewberry essential oil burner, I thought about him constantly. And now here he was, all grown up and in my kitchen as though no time had passed at all. I felt my pulse quicken the same way it did when we were still sixteen and just home from school with Dev scouring our cupboards for a mini Mars Bar. Naturally, his mum didn't believe in keeping sweets in the house.

'Right. OG pigs in blankets aside, this is all salvageable,' Dev proclaimed on completing his initial investigation. 'Challenging, but salvageable. We should be able to sort it in an hour or so.'

The sheer relief of it all. I dabbed myself down with a tinsel-trimmed tea cosy and forced myself to stop thinking about the tiny shrine I'd made to him in the bottom of my wardrobe. Every piece of evidence of our shared existence carefully archived in a Dolcis shoebox: bus tickets, photobooth strips, cinema stubs and a pair of his pants that blew off his washing line and into our garden and no I didn't feel good about keeping them but common sense doesn't really register with a fifteen-year-old girl in love.

'Tell me what to do and I'll do it,' I told him, blushing at the memory of the stolen boxers. 'Clearly I don't know my arse from my elbow in the kitchen but I take direction extremely well.'

Dev chuckled as he pulled a parsnip out of a sticky bowl and gave it a very thorough inspection. 'You must've changed a lot since we were kids. Rinse those off, dry them with kitchen towel then lay them out on a single sheet on that baking tray.'

'I've changed a lot, it's wild what time will do to a person,' I replied, examining the parsnip. 'Not that I'm questioning your methods, but these *are* supposed to be honey-glazed.'

'Glazed not drowned. If you put them in like that, the sugar in the honey will burn before the parsnips are even warmed through.' He gave me a look that suggested we would not be entering into a debate on the subject and I felt a distinct tingle in parts of my body that had not tingled in some time. 'I thought you said you take direction well?'

'Might have overplayed that part,' I mumbled as I gathered up the parsnips and terminated the tingling. It was pointless, he was engaged. Plus, he probably still remembered the time he came over to play video games with Manny and I ran into the room screaming and crying because I was convinced I'd lost a tampon inside me. It really was impossible to believe he hadn't fallen head over heels in love with me right there and then.

'Thank you,' I said with a small grateful smile. 'For offering to help.'

'Don't mention it,' Dev replied as he sliced open the packet of supermarket bacon like a pro. 'And for what it's worth, doesn't seem like you've changed all that much as far as I can see.'

I looked up to see the two of us reflected in the kitchen window and felt time slipping away. I was still a good foot shorter than him, my hair was still out of control and I still couldn't keep my eyes off him. Maybe I hadn't changed all that much.

'Some days I feel exactly the same as I did when I was sixteen and other days I don't even recognize myself in the mirror,' I replied, surprised at the honesty of my confession. But Dev always had been easy to talk to. 'Like, who is that old lady with the eye bags and what is she doing in my bathroom?'

'Perhaps she knows the man with the dark circles who keeps showing up in mine,' he grinned. 'I think you're probably the same person deep down. Are you still morally opposed to chicken on a pizza?'

'I don't know why it's wrong, it just is. I'm not even saying it tastes bad, it's not right.'

'Do you still hate golf and tennis?'

'How can someone whack such a small ball such long distances and make it go where they want it to?' I grumbled. 'It defies the laws of physics.'

'Speaking of physics . . .'

'Maths disguised as science. Sneaky and I don't like it.'

He laughed as he sliced the fat off a rasher of bacon with surgical precision. 'But your mum's a science teacher!'

'Manny too,' I replied with thinly veiled disgust. 'Can you even believe it?'

'Can't believe Manny ended up being a teacher,' Dev said as he laid each rasher of bacon out on a freshly foiled baking tray. 'I thought he couldn't leave school soon enough.'

'As much as he tries to keep it quiet,' I said, raising my voice over the flowing tap as I washed the honey off my parsnips, 'Manny is secretly a very good person. He hated school because he didn't have a good experience, now he's got the chance to make that experience better for other kids. It's kind of incredible when you think about it.'

'Wow.' Dev placed a small sausage at the end of each rasher of bacon and rolled them up slowly and carefully. 'Amazing level of selflessness from a man who once closed the entire school down by bringing in a live sheep on career day.'

'That was selfless in its own way,' I reasoned. 'We all got the day off and he spent a week in detention.'

'Teaching is probably a better fit for him. He would have made a terrible shepherd, always whining about how cold it was on the walk to the bus stop,' he replied. 'And what about you? You went into law, like your dad?'

'Yep,' I nodded, not exactly desperate to go into details. 'And Cerys is a lawyer too, you know.'

Dev cocked his head to one side and smiled. 'If anything, I'd have thought you'd go into teaching and Manny would be the lawyer.'

I glanced over my shoulder to see him hunched over the baking tray, intense concentration on his face. 'Why's that?'

'You always loved reading and he always loved arguing.'

'A fair assessment,' I admitted with a laugh. 'I think that was part of why he went into teaching too. He's serving a lifelong sentence for being a difficult teenager.'

'But you like your job?'

I shrugged and bundled my vegetables in paper towel.

'Yes?' I replied, sounding more non-committal than I'd planned. I held up the freshly washed parsnips for inspection. 'What shall I do with these?'

'Lightly drizzle them with the honey glaze,' he ordered. 'And I mean *lightly*.'

'OK, doc,' I said, sticking out my tongue as I dumped the vegetables onto another clean baking sheet.

'Corporate law aside, you seem like the same old Gwen to me.' He paused to clear his throat and I sucked in my cheeks to stymie my smile. 'I bet you're still carrying five different books around with you as well.'

Picking up the bowl of honey glaze, I turned away so he wouldn't see my face.

'I can't remember the last time I finished a book,' I admitted as I drizzled lightly. 'Every time I pick something up, I fall asleep. My brain can't process anything that isn't work.'

'Good thing you like your job then,' Dev replied softly.

'Yeah,' I agreed, my voice unreliable. 'It is.'

'Pretty sure I'm still exactly the same.' He tapped a heavy-handled carving knife against the chopping board as I placed the parsnips in the oven. 'Or at least I am according to my mother.'

'You're the same old Dev, are you?' I asked, leaning against the kitchen top as he deftly chopped the carrots, the turned-up cuffs of his white shirt straining against his strong forearms, and I had to remind myself I was only impressed with his culinary skills and not the way the muscles in his arms moved under his skin as the knife moved up and down. 'Still listening to The White Stripes and reading Terry Pratchett?'

'Why would anyone give up the classics?' he replied, the corners of his mouth edging upwards. 'Still the same, a bit more focused maybe. I'm a more concentrated dose of Dev.'

I pinched a chunk of carrot from the cutting board as he opened the oven door then tossed the rest of them in with the parsnips. Chomping it thoughtfully, I watched him shake the baking tray and check on the turkey. Dev had found his focus whereas I felt so diluted. Life had watered me down. He closed the oven door and turned to face me, one side of his mouth quirked up into a half smile.

'I think about getting in touch with you all the time,' he said slowly. 'Can't tell you the number of times I've looked you up on Instagram.'

'Then why didn't you?' I asked, my heart fluttering in my chest at the thought of Dev Jones sat at home, typing out my name. 'Scared I'd leave you on read?'

'Yes, exactly that,' he replied. There was something else about him that hadn't changed, he was still honest to a fault. 'People say social media makes it easier to stay in touch, but I think it makes it easier to drift apart. No one forgot about phone calls or letters but it's too easy to miss a DM or forget a text, isn't it? Emails get lost in the inbox all the time. Before you know it, it's too late to reply.'

Such wisdom from a man who once almost lost an eye trying to see if he could straighten his lashes using my GHDs.

'I can't believe we lost touch the way we did,' he added. 'I really regret it, Gwen. We were such good mates.'

'Me too,' I said, leaning backwards against the sink and forcing myself to meet his gaze. 'I definitely could have done a better job of replying to your emails.'

'And I could have put more effort into sending more than one line a week.'

We exchanged awkward smiles, the air partially cleared.

'Right, where are we at?' Dev clapped his hands, sending out a jolt of energy and clearing out the Eeyore energy that had descended on the kitchen. 'Carrots, parsnips and pigs in blankets, tick, tick and tick. What now?'

'Roast potatoes, mashed potatoes, gravy, Yorkshire puds, sprouts or stuffing,' I replied, pushing away a mountain of unresolved feeling and turning to the huge pile of veg still on the kitchen table. 'Pick your poison.'

'Roast and mashed potatoes?' he replied with a whistle. 'The decadence of it, Baker.'

'It's Christmas,' I said, attempting to toss a potato from one hand to the other and promptly dropping it on the floor. 'If you can't double up on carbs on Christmas, when can you?'

'Argued like the brilliant lawyer I'm sure you are,' he said, scooping up my fallen spud and pressing it into my hand. 'Let's do this.'

An hour later, Dev unrolled his sleeves and fastened the buttons at his wrist, flexing his fingers as I looked around the clean kitchen. The oven was full, the fridge was empty and a golden-brown turkey sat under a silver foil tent beside the sink.

'I really should get going,' he said before pointing at the bird. 'Don't forget, she needs to rest for twenty minutes.'

'Me and her both,' I said, completely knackered. Who knew cooking was such hard work? I made a mental note to hug my microwave when I got home. 'Thank you so much, I genuinely couldn't have done this without you, it's incredible.'

He ducked his head with faux modesty, a dismissive noise coming from somewhere in the back of his throat. 'Don't mention it, I love to cook and Mum never lets me,' he replied. 'How come you ended up on lunch duty anyway? Isn't this your mum's forte? I always loved her cooking.'

'It is,' I confirmed. 'But she needed a Christmas off. Actually, I think she needs more than one day off. She does everything for the family and we just let her, no questions asked.'

'But isn't that what mums do?' he replied. 'Take care of the family?'

'If you're lucky enough to get a good one,' I agreed. 'But it certainly isn't all they do and they shouldn't be the only ones doing it.'

'Good point, well made.' He pulled on his coat, patting down his pockets for his phone and his keys. 'What are you doing tomorrow? Why don't we go to the pub, have a proper catch-up?'

The idea of tomorrow itself was enough to make me swoon.

'If I make it through today, I'd love that,' I said, wiping my hands on my ridiculous apron, dreaming of a cosy corner in a country pub, cuddled up with Dev Jones. He was right, I really hadn't changed all that much.

He paused at the door, one hand on the handle, and looked up with a grin.

'What is it?' I asked, following his gaze.

Oh.

Mistletoe.

He leaned in towards me, the smell of him, the size of him, all of it overwhelming considering the only physical contact I'd had with a man was when the Deliveroo guy accidentally brushed my fingertips with his while handing over my most recent Nando's order. Dev's mouth brushed against my cheek, a scratch of stubble, the quiet click of lips parting, his breath prickling my ear. When he pulled away, I was a puddle. Who knew a kiss on the cheek could be so deeply erotic? His fiancée was a very lucky woman and I hated her guts.

'Merry Christmas, Gwen,' he murmured.

'Merry Christmas, Dev,' I replied, leaning against the kitchen cupboards, knees weak, as he let himself out. It was a lot. A magical moment with my childhood sweetheart *and* a fully cooked Christmas dinner? There was a chance Manny was right, this could be heaven after all.

'I don't know how you did it, Gwen, but that was marvellous,' Mum called through the serving hatch as she polished off her third helping of turkey. 'How long have you been hiding the fact you can cook?'

'And where did you learn to make Yorkshire puddings like that?' Dad added. 'Because it certainly wasn't from your mother.'

'Oh, you know, I watched a bit of *MasterChef*, that's all,' I shouted back as she clipped him around the back of the head. Manny passed the rest of the dirty plates back through the hatch, each and every one scraped so clean, I was able to stick them straight in the dishwasher. Dev was a confirmed culinary genius. Not that my family needed to know it.

'Michael is missing out,' Oliver shouted. I paused for a moment, taken aback by the almost-compliment from my brother-in-law. And by the fact I hadn't thought about Michael in hours. 'Although I shouldn't think it matters if that new gal of his is any good in the kitchen, if you know what I mean, looks like she's got the skills elsewhere.'

'Is everyone ready for pudding?' I called back, confident in my assumption that everyone knew exactly what he meant. Wanker.

'Yes, please,' Mum replied as she leaned back in her chair. 'I don't think I've ever felt so relaxed on Christmas Day. You've really made my wish come true.'

'You're relaxed because you've been drinking since half-ten,' Manny pointed out. 'Let's not give her any more credit than she deserves.'

But I didn't care, she said it. I made her wish come true. That was good enough for me and hopefully the nice people at The Little Silver Sixpence Company.

'Can you bring the Mini Rolls in for the kids?' Mum asked as I grabbed the matches off the top of the fridge to light the pud. 'They're in the pantry, I ran out of room in the fridge. Be careful, the bulb's out in there!'

The pantry wasn't huge but it was a long, narrow space that ran under the stairs, and like most pantries, very cold and very dark. When we were little, I was too scared to go in on my own and even now as a (relatively) sensible adult, I got a chill at the idea of poking around in the back without someone else in the room to watch my back.

'Where are they?' I shouted back, squinting into the darkness, matches still in one hand. 'If I go any further back, I'll be in Narnia.'

But no one could hear me.

'I bet that bloody lightbulb has been out for weeks,' I grumbled as I struck a match against the box. There it was. A big purple package on the back shelf, spotted at the exact same moment I stumped my toe on something extremely solid.

'Bugger,' I huffed as I dropped my match and the Mini Rolls disappeared into the darkness. Which genius had left something on the floor of the pantry when the light isn't working?

As I struck a second match, I saw right away which genius had left something on the floor of the pantry when the light wasn't working. My dad.

I'd stumped my toe on The Widow Maker and even worse, I'd dropped a match on Apocalypse Now and lit the fuse.

'Oh no,' I whispered, blowing out the second match that was burning its way down to my fingers. A frenetic white spark travelled down the firework's fuse as I huffed and I puffed, trying to blow the spark out, but it was no use. Dad's fireworks were about to blow the house down. I turned to run and warn the others but it was too late. Covering my head with my hands, I heard a boom, I felt the blast and somewhere in between the two, a packet of Mini Rolls went flying through the air with everything else in the pantry, me included.

CHAPTER TEN

'You set fire to the house?'

Manny stared at me, slack-jawed, his face ashen.

'Technically, I blew it up,' I replied, casually munching on a bacon butty the following morning, Christmas Day 4.0, right back where I started. 'Word to the wise, Dad's got a massive stash of explosives hidden in the kitchen so unless you like the smell of napalm in the morning, don't go in the pantry with any open flames.'

He pushed his breakfast away across the coffee table untouched. The presents were open, the TV was on and Manny's mind was blown. For some reason he wasn't taking the news of my eternal Christmas so well today. I couldn't imagine why.

'Were we . . . were we OK?' he asked.

'The house literally exploded so I'd have to say probably not?' I wiped a smudge of tomato sauce from the edge of my mouth and shrugged. 'But never mind, eh? All's well that ends well, or not, as the case may be. If at first we don't succeed and all that jazz. No point crying over severed limbs.'

For the first time, I was relieved when I opened my eyes to find myself back in bed on Christmas morning. Mum was furious when I backed her car into the fence the day after passing my driving test, I couldn't imagine her being exactly thrilled about me blowing up the whole house and everyone in it. Although Dad was the one who left enough explosives to alarm NATO in a blacked-out pantry so it could be considered a group effort.

'You seem awfully relaxed about this,' Manny said, still adjusting to my new reality. 'How are you not panicking?'

'Because I've already panicked and it didn't help. Are you going to eat this?' I asked, reaching for his bacon sandwich. For the last two days, I'd had to choke down every mouthful of food. Today I'd woken up ravenous.

He pushed the plate towards me. 'Do you have a plan? One that doesn't result in I don't know, killing us all?'

'I'm going to try Dad,' I replied, still very certain the wish was the thing. It was time to zero in on Steven Baker like an off-brand Terminator. Age: sixty-five. Profession: retired lawyer and enthusiastic Wikipedia editor. Known weakness: Tia Maria, spy novels specifically set in and around World War Two and those sad films where a dog saves someone's life then dies at the end. But what would he wish for? I had no idea. 'He asked me to go for a walk with him the other day and I said no.'

'You think your dad's ultimate wish is to go for a walk with you?' Manny scoffed. 'Wow, someone rates herself.'

'I think that's a good way to find out what he might have wished for,' I replied, flicking his ear as I stood up. 'Can you help Mum get lunch ready while I'm out? She shouldn't have to do all of this on her own.'

'Sometimes I think feminism has gone too far,' he warned. 'But yes, I suppose I can help, if only to guard the pantry.'

'We thank you for your service,' I said before calling to my parents across the room. 'Oi, Dad, I fancy a bit of fresh air. Do you want to go for a walk?'

My mother and my father stared at me. Mum's Hobnob broke in half and disappeared into her tea as my dad leaned forward and squinted in my direction.

'Who are you and what have you done with my daughter?'

'Oh you card,' I laughed, only sounding slightly hysterical. 'I'll go and get dressed. Be ready in ten?'

'I don't care if you're a pod person, I'll take it,' he replied, slapping his hands on his thighs. 'Care to join us, Emmanuel?'

Manny looked up from his comfortable position on the settee and pulled a face.

'I'd rather carve out my spleen with a reindeer antler.'

'Noted,' Dad replied with a nod. 'It's just me and Gwen then.'

'Father and daughter, out for a nice walk with no ulterior motives,' I said brightly. 'What could be more fun?'

'Not blowing up the house?' Manny suggested, earning a slap across the back of his legs as I skipped out of the living room and ran upstairs to get changed.

For as long as I could remember, I couldn't wait to get away from Baslow.

Life in the village was stifling, you couldn't so much as sneeze without everyone hearing about it. And if growing up under a village microscope wasn't frustrating enough, nothing guaranteed radical unpopularity in secondary school like having a teacher for a mother. Who wants to go round to a teacher's house after school? Who invites the teacher's kid to a party? No one who's planning to have fun at said party, that's who. Add to that the trauma of being Cerys Baker's little sister and you had the perfect cocktail of reasons a teenager might to want to escape. Six years older and a thousand times better than me at every last little thing on the face of the earth, there was evidence of Cerys's accomplishments everywhere I turned. Her photo on the wall at school, her prizes lined up on the shelves at home. Not that Mum and Dad put pressure on me to outperform my sister (as if that was even possible), most of the time they were too busy with work or dealing with Manny to worry about what I was up to. He wasn't a bad kid in the grand scheme of things, but he was certainly a self-described 'handful'. And who could blame him? If I'd lost my dad and been abandoned by my mum, I imagine I'd indulge in a little under-the-slide-at-the-park cider-drinking myself, but existing somewhere in between Cerys and Manny meant dedicating my entire existence to keeping the peace. Getting out of the village seemed like the quickest route to finding something that was all mine and I couldn't wait to cover the countryside with concrete, fill in all these wide-open spaces and lose myself in tall buildings and fast walkers.

'What's the plan?' I asked, following my dad over the fence at the bottom of the garden. The low winter sun sparkled on the frozen fields before disappearing behind a bank of clouds, and for the first time I found myself appreciating the comforting colour-palette of Baslow, all soft greens and warm browns. The limestone cottages and old oak trees, all gussied up with a little festive charm – a string of fairy lights here, a tasteful holly wreath there. It was beautiful, where I was from.

'No plan,' he replied, tapping his leg with the walking stick I'd watched him unwrap for the fourth time that morning. 'I like to wander.'

'Yes, but where to?' I pressed. 'You have to be wandering somewhere.'

'Nowhere. Wherever I feel like. And when I've had enough, I turn around and come back home.'

This was confusing. My father was a man who had a back-up plan for his back-up plan. He did not waste a second of his time, billable or otherwise, yet here he was, meandering off into the fields with a big grin on his ruddy-cheeked face.

Unfortunately for him, I was very much my father's daughter.

'Seriously though, where are we going?' I asked again. 'Because if we're going to be out longer than half an hour, I need to go back for snacks.'

Dad feigned a look of shock. 'You mean you haven't brought any?'

'More snacks,' I clarified as I pulled a Wine Gum out of my pocket and popped it into my mouth.

Across the fields, a few shafts of sunlight sliced through the clouds to paint Chatsworth House a gentle yellow-gold and beckoned us onward.

'Let's head that way,' Dad said, flicking his stick at the stately home in the distance. I nodded in agreement, following as he took long, confident strides along the hard ground. 'Nice to get out, isn't it? Get some fresh air into your lungs.'

'Very nice. The only fresh thing you'll get in your lungs around mine is the scent of . . .' I paused when I saw the look of dismay on his face, '. . . fine city living.'

'That takes us to my next question. How are things going in the flat?'

Tucking my hair into the collar of Mum's jacket, I gave a tight smile, deeply regretting having turned down her offer of a hat and scarf. It was bloody freezing.

'All good,' I replied. 'It's cosy.'

A less generous soul might have described it as 'unfit for human habitation' but I didn't need the lap of luxury to lay on the floor, scream-singing along to 'Driver's License' while obsessing over Michael's Instagram feed, did I?

'A flat above a bookshop must be heaven for you,' Dad said with a gentle chortle. 'Does the owner give you a discount?'

I thought of the towering to-be-read piles teetering on my nightstand and down the side of the settee and my conversation with Dev the day before. Books had turned into something I collected instead of something I read and that was depressing. For a fleeting moment, I wondered what Dev was up to, my cheek tingling at the memory of our mistletoe moment.

'You haven't said a thing about work,' Dad added when I didn't answer right away. 'Does it not quiet down around Christmas? We were always dead as a dormouse from the end of November, not that I was ever in the same league as Abbott & Howe, mind you, you're probably working round the clock every day of the year—'

'Let's not talk about work,' I said, trying to sound as cheery as possible. 'Surely there are more festive things to chat about? You know, politics? The global economy? I heard the Doomsday clock moved closer to midnight?'

'But I love hearing about your job,' he countered. 'What's the point of Christmas if not to catch up on all the important things in our lives?'

I slipped my arm through his, Mum's Regatta rustling against his wax jacket, and gave him a tight smile.

'Is work that important though?' I asked.

Dad stopped short and almost sent me face first into an unidentified pile of something brown and unpleasant.

'Once again I am forced to ask you, who are you and what have you done with my daughter?'

'I'm the same Gwen I've always been,' I promised as he chuckled, but somewhere inside I started to wonder. Who was that exactly?

If I ever made it to New Year's, I already had my first resolution. It was time to start exercising beyond walking all the way to the fridge and back. After an hour of walking up hill and down dale, I could feel every single muscle from my little toe all the way up to my arse and each and every one of them ached. My sixty-five-year-old father, on the other hand, strode on happily, the village far behind us and Chatsworth up ahead.

'What do you think Christmas is like in there?' I asked, nodding towards the great house, fantasizing about banqueting tables, centrepieces and eight-course lunch-eons. It was the kind of place that positively cried out for a Turducken.

'I'm sure theirs isn't that different to ours. Presents,

telly, turkey. That's all Christmas is,' Dad replied, kicking a large stone out of his way.

'You don't mean that,' I said, tilting my hips as I walked. My lower back was killing me. Seriously, I couldn't wait for January to roll around so I could join the yoga studio around the corner from the flat, go every day for six weeks then never darken their doorstep again. 'You love Christmas.'

He tested his walking stick against the edge of an inviting-looking bench, the highly polished pole rattling against the dull old wood, but he didn't stop. Instead, I noticed that his smile wavered and softened into something more complicated as we carried on walking.

'Love is a strong word,' he said. 'Bit of a mixed bag for me.'

'Because of Uncle Jim?' I asked.

He nodded and quickened his pace until he was half a step ahead, leaving me to feel the full weight of my foolishness. Of course it was hard for him, how could it not be?

'Don't get me wrong, it's still a happy time, you know there's nothing I love more than having all you kids under one roof,' he said, adding some starch to his stiff upper lip. 'But this time of year has a nasty trick of reminding you of all the things you've lost. Christmas is a celebration you're meant to add to, not take away from. Once a piece of the puzzle is gone, it never feels quite complete again.'

For a brief moment, all the things I'd lost over the last year flitted across my mind, but it wasn't the same, not really.

'I've never thought about it like that,' I said. 'I'm sorry, Dad.'

'Don't be,' he replied, an order as much as a suggestion. 'The sad only outweighs the happy if you let it, so I don't let it. Do you think your uncle or your granny and grandad would want me sulking away all Christmas? Certainly not. A bad attitude never helped anyone.'

He slowed to a stop and dug his walking stick into the cold ground. I stood beside him, relieved to see he was smiling again, a little misty-eyed perhaps but content enough, and I felt my expression lift to match his.

'They would have been so proud of you,' he said, staring straight ahead. 'My Gwen at a Magic Circle firm, hop, skip and a jump away from being a partner. You've always been the one with her nose to the grindstone, nothing you can't do when you put your mind to it. I do hope I'm still here to see it when you're running the place, chicken.'

My smile faded away. It didn't matter that it hadn't happened. I could still see the disappointment on his face, fireworks going off behind him, everyone whispering and staring. I wouldn't let it happen again.

'Dad,' I said slowly. 'If you could wish for absolutely anything, what would it be?'

He shook his head, still looking off into the distance.

'Come off it, I'm too old for wishes.'

'Humour me,' I pressed. 'Please?'

'Fine, if I must.' He rapped his walking stick against the ground three times. 'I would wish to have them all back, even if it was only for one day. I try not to dwell on what I've lost but as I say, it's harder this time of year. Must be the cold air, it makes your skin a little thinner.'

He was right, we all bruised more easily at Christmas. Too many long-buried feelings floating close to the surface.

'And did you know more people file for divorce in January than any other time of the year?' he added, catching me by surprise with a firm clap on the back. I stumbled forward a few steps, grabbing hold of a low stone wall to steady myself. The man was determined to see me on my arse before the end of the day.

'Cheerful thought,' I replied, rubbing my back. 'Long dark nights, forced family time, it does make sense.'

'Not to mention the fact there's nothing on the bloody telly these days. If me and your mother'd had to find the money to pay for Sky Atlantic when we first got married, we wouldn't have been together long enough to have you or your sister,' Dad said. 'Come on, we should head back before your mother sends out a search party.'

'We should talk about Uncle Jim and Granny and Grandad more often,' I said as we turned our backs on the buttery golden walls of Chatsworth House. 'I bet you've got loads of stories I've never heard.'

'Oh, never mind all that, I'm getting soft in my dotage,' he said with a laugh. 'Pretend I never mentioned it.'

'I'll do my best,' I said, weaving my arm back through his as we set off for home, my mind whirring with ways to make his wish come true.

After successfully keeping the peace between Oliver, Cerys, Manny and myself for an entire meal, I focused my attention to Dad's wish. He wanted more time with his lost loved ones, a task slightly more complicated than the one I'd tackled the day before, if only because I very much doubted Dev was as good at resurrecting people as he was at making Yorkshire puddings. There was a limit to what even the best doctors could do. I climbed up into the loft, fighting the very real urge to bin the whole thing off and spend the afternoon in the pub with Dev instead. If this worked and Dad got his wish, I could call on him tomorrow, say hello, catch up. Pulling the ladder up behind me, I felt around on the wall for the light switch. Years ago, there had been talk of a loft conversion, but after one too many episodes of *Grand Designs* my mum got distracted by the idea of an extension (they ended up doing neither), meaning the loft was left with a plasterboard floor laid on top of bare beams with one naked bulb, swinging from the rafters. In other words, it was a death trap and since I was not looking to meet another untimely end, I trod very carefully.

The box of family photo albums was tucked away in the corner behind stacks of dusty old CDs and tapes (Mum and Dad's extensive vinyl collection having been promoted back into the house proper after Cerys bought them a ridiculously expensive record player last Christmas, despite the fact we'd agreed on a £100 price limit on family presents). Wiping off the top layer of schmutz with a duster I'd brought for exactly that purpose, I pulled out album after album, their spines cracking with the effort of sharing their stories.

Dad never talked about his lost loved ones – the odd mention in passing maybe, but nothing more than that. There was exactly one photograph of my Uncle Jim in the house and that was a school picture of the two of them, high up on a shelf in the dining room. It was the same with Granny and Grandad Baker, just their wedding photo tucked away in the spare bedroom, even though Mum had dozens of photos of Grandad Collins around the house. It was something else I'd inherited from my dad, not so much keep calm and carry on, but pretend it wasn't happening and never, ever cause a fuss.

When Michael ended things, I didn't call Manny or my mum. I didn't trash the house or bang up his car, even though I could have pointed to several country songs as evidence to support that course of action. Instead, I took myself to a hotel, cried it all out on my own, and the next morning, perfectly calm, I texted Manny to ask if I could stay with him for a couple of days. Since then I'd kept myself to myself, avoiding my friends, avoiding my family, avoiding anything that wasn't work or sleep or streaming services. But, as my colleagues would apparently tell anyone who asked, bottling things up hadn't really worked that well for me in the long run, and I was starting to wonder if opening up might help my dad as well.

Next to the photo albums was another, newer box, the Sellotape holding down the cardboard flaps still intact. Flicking at the edge of the tape with my fingernail, I peeled it back to reveal a stash of DVDs in clear cases, each marked with a short sentence; Cerys's First Birthday, Silver Wedding Anniversary, Gwen's 18th, Manny's *X Factor* Audition. All our old home videos, transferred to DVD. Underneath our recent history was a stash of much older stories. Grandma Baker's 50th birthday, Manny's Christening, Our Wedding. Everything turned misty as I thought of all the special moments I'd accidentally lost over the years, snapshots of a life I'd lived and loved, but not enough to treat with care. This was love, this box, and it had to be Dad who'd done it, Mum couldn't even send me a photo from her phone without getting her thumb in the shot. It must have taken him weeks to do it all so why was it hidden away out of sight? Going through them all, one by one, I pulled out the evidence that best supported my case, and slowly tiptoed back across the loft. The last thing I needed now was to fall through the ceiling and break my neck.

'Famous last words,' I grunted as I dropped the ladder back onto the landing and climbed down with care.

Everyone but Manny was assembled in the living room, and given the fact I knew exactly what he was doing upstairs in his room, I let him be.

'Auntie Gwen, you're in the way of the telly,' Arthur whined as I knelt down in front of him and very much in the way of the telly. 'I can't see *The Grinch*.'

'I'll let you in on a spoiler,' I said, checking the cable that connected the DVD player to the TV. 'The ending hasn't changed from when you watched it last year.'

'Last year? Try this morning. He's been playing it round the clock since Halloween,' Cerys replied as my nephew started to scream at the top of his lungs until Artemis invoked sibling privilege and clobbered him in the face with a cushion.

'I thought we might all watch something else for a while,' I said, changing the channel to a chorus of groans. 'Come on, you don't even know what it is yet.'

'I know it's not *The Grinch*,' Arthur said, sulking in a huddle by his snoring father.

'Thank the lord,' Cerys whispered.

'What's this, Gwen?' Nan asked, sitting forward as an oversaturated picture crackled into life. 'Is it a porno?'

'Why would I show you a porno?' I replied, aghast. 'Ew, Nan.'

'You're such a prude,' she said, crossing her legs demurely at the ankles. 'I hear they're much better than they used to be.'

'It's not a porno,' I repeated as the same room we were in now appeared on the screen. 'Pack it in and watch.'

'Is that you, Nana?' Artemis asked my mother, pointing to a slim, dark-haired woman on the screen. She wore a bright red dress with extremely exaggerated shoulders, silver eyeshadow and a pink lipstick so frosted, you'd have had to pay me to put it anywhere near my face. The era was unmistakable. We had entered the eighties.

Mum raised a hand to her mouth, her eyes wide, as a much younger version of herself danced around the screen, quite literally rocking around the Christmas tree.

'It is,' she confirmed. 'Gwen, where did you find this?'

'It was in the loft,' I explained, holding up a handful of DVDs as the camera panned around to show a tiny toddler in front of a shiny silver tree. 'There's loads of them.'

'Oh my God, that's me!' Cerys jumped off the settee and onto the floor and landed beside me on the carpet. 'I remember that tree! I remember that dress! How can I remember that dress, I'm practically a foetus?'

'You kept it for years,' Mum replied, her hand dropping from her mouth to her chest as she beamed at the television. 'After you grew out of it, your Granny Baker altered it to fit your doll.'

Cerys sat back on her heels, touching the screen with her fingertips. 'That's right,' she breathed. 'Look kids, that's the same star on top of the tree that's up there today.'

'Wow.' Artemis twisted a strand of hair around her index finger, shaking her head at this piece of ancient history. 'The olden days were mad.'

'Artemis, you're nine, you think Taylor Swift is old,' I said as the picture crackled out and cut to Christmas dinner.

'She is old,' my niece mumbled under her breath. 'She's like thirty.'

'Oh my goodness, Mum, look at you!'

Before I could reply to my niece, a forty-something-years-young Myfanwy James waltzed onto the screen in a teal two-piece and distracted us all.

'Look at your hair!' Cerys gasped.

It was enormous. Two cans of hairspray and four hours of backcombing enormous. But the hair was nothing compared to the make-up, twin stripes of neon pink blusher ran down her cheeks, clashing with the baby-blue eyeshadow and beige glittery lipstick. The eighties were such a cruel decade.

'I will not apologize for being stylish,' Nan sniffed. 'You could take the shoulder pads out of that suit and wear it today.'

'Yeah, if you wanted to scare children,' Cerys whispered in my ear.

'Will you look at your grandad, what a handsome man.' Nan beamed as Grandad James appeared on the screen and I had to admit, she was right. With his thick black hair and deeply tanned skin in the dead of winter, even his extremely shiny double-breasted suit couldn't distract from his solid good looks.

After Grandad James came Uncle Jim, rugby shirt tucked into his high-waisted jeans, his curly mullet cascading over the neatly pressed white collar, and behind him, Granny and Grandad Baker. The picture went fuzzy for a moment as someone placed the camera onto the dresser to show the entire dining table. Dad's grinning head suddenly filled the frame, complete with the massive sideburns I remember being mortified by throughout my youth. He gave the camera a cheesy thumbs-up before settling down at the head of the table, everyone applauding as Mum came in carrying the turkey.

'Did you do this?' Mum asked, her eyes still fixed on the screen.

'Nope,' I replied. 'I think Dad did.'

I looked over my shoulder expecting to see a smile the size of Nan's eighties bouffant on every single face. Instead I saw five happy faces, a comatose Oliver, and a shell of a man that used to be my dad, staring blankly at the screen.

'Dad?' I said, scooting around to face him. 'Are you OK?'

He sucked in his cheeks and nodded once, his lips pressed together in a tight grim line. Then he tapped a soft fist against the arm of the chair, stood up, hitched up his trousers and walked out of the room.

Oh shit.

'Cup of tea anyone?' he called as he went.

No one answered, they were too busy watching the DVD.

An unpleasant sinking sensation in the pit of my stomach made me think this wasn't quite the magical wish-granting moment I'd been hoping for.

'Dad?' I said, closing the living-room door as I followed him into the kitchen. 'You all right?'

'More than, chicken.'

He kept his back to me as he filled the kettle, but from the ghost of his reflection in the kitchen window I could see that wasn't true.

'I was looking for the family photo albums in the loft and I found the DVDs with them,' I explained as I clung to the door handle, hovering on my tiptoes. A sad dad was almost as bad as a disappointed dad and my heart couldn't stand it. 'Why didn't you show them to us?'

He placed the kettle back on its hub and flipped the switch, opened the cupboard and took out two mugs. Then he opened the tea caddy and placed two teabags in the pot. Once the caddy had been closed and restored to its proper place, and a teaspoon retrieved from the cutlery drawer, he turned to face me.

My dad was crying.

'Oh, Dad, don't.' I rushed towards him and wrapped him up in a hug. 'Please don't cry.'

First I reduced Mum to tears and now Dad? I really was on a roll.

'I had all the old videos transferred when I lost my mum,' he explained in between sniffles. 'But when they came, I couldn't bring myself to watch so I hid them. I miss them all so much, Gwen, I really do.'

'I'm sorry,' I said as he blew his nose on Mum's commemorative royal wedding tea towel that was very much for display purposes only. 'When you said earlier, about bringing them back, I thought this would be a good way to remember them properly. It's like you always used to say about a complicated case, sometimes you've got to look backwards before you can go forwards, isn't it?'

He honked on the tea towel once more before setting it down on the kitchen top.

'I know you said Granny and Grandad wouldn't want you to ruin Christmas for everyone else but I don't think they'd want you to ruin it for yourself either,' I said as the kettle beeped to let us know it was ready, my dad's bottom lip starting to tremble once more. 'Keeping everything inside doesn't make it hurt less, Dad, you're just sealing it up to fester.'

And I knew that was true because I'd done it to myself. Burying my sadness hadn't made me any happier. Pretending I was fine had resulted in chucking a stapler at the son of a billionaire and a two-week suspension from my job. Hardly a stellar recommendation for the keep calm and carry on approach.

'You might be right about the videos,' he said quietly as he placed the lid onto the teapot with a decisive clink, two fat tears running down his cheeks. 'There's no point hiding them away in the loft, is there? Arthur and Artemis didn't even recognize them, they don't even know who they are.'

'Then let's go and tell them,' I suggested as he sand-papered his eyes with a manly sheet of kitchen towel. 'I bet they'd love to hear your stories.'

'Do you think so?' he asked, full of hope.

'Probably not, no, they *really* want to watch *Elf*,' I admitted, smiling when he chuckled. 'But it's Christmas and Christmas is about family. Not everyone gets a good one, do they?'

With a nose so red it would make Rudolph jealous, he kissed me on the forehead.

'You are getting very wise, chicken. Must take after your mum,' he said before taking the milk out of the fridge and splashing it into each of the mugs. 'It's no wonder you're doing so well at work if you can even make your stubborn old dad see sense, lucky them, I say.'

'Right,' I agreed, heart sinking back down into the pit of my stomach as I accepted my cup of tea with a big fake smile. 'Lucky, lucky them.'

By the time Dad and I sat ourselves down on the settee, the 1980-something Baker Christmas dinner had turned into the 1980-something Baker Christmas party. On the static-y screen, I saw brightly coloured paper crowns on top of everyone's massive hair, both grandads had taken off their ties and anyone wearing long sleeves had long since rolled them up. Everyone except for Nan, of course, she still looked immaculate. Granny, Grandad and Uncle Jim took it in turns to dance with tiny Cerys, and as big Cerys watched the scene play out, there was a smile on my sister's face that I hadn't seen in years.

'Happy memories, Care?' I said, poking her with my big toe.

'Yes,' she replied as she squeezed my foot until I squealed. 'Before you were born.'

'Who's that?' Arthur asked, putting down his Nintendo Switch to point at the screen as I rubbed the feeling back into my foot. 'The man in the stripy t-shirt?'

'That's my brother, your Great-Uncle Jim,' Dad said, hoisting his grandson up into his lap. 'He's Uncle Manny's daddy.'

Arthur's smooth little brow creased with confusion. 'Why isn't he here?'

'Uncle Jim died before you were born,' Cerys answered as my dad wiped away another tear. I rose to make a dash for the royal wedding tea towel but there was no need. Nan reached over to hand him a clean handkerchief from her handbag and Dad accepted it with a grateful smile.

'Handsome devil, was Jim,' Nan said, ruffling Arthur's hair as Dad dabbed at his eyes. 'Now I come to think of it, I'd say there's a bit of him in you, around the eyes. Don't you think so, Steven?'

'I do,' Dad agreed, sniffing into the hankie then stuffing it up his sleeve. 'Two good-looking lads, the pair of you. He loved video games as well, couldn't get enough of Pacman, he had the highest score in the village.'

Arthur scrunched up his entire face and for one minute, he really did look like my Uncle Jim.

'What's a Pacman?' he asked.

'Christ, I think I just felt myself age.' Mum pressed a hand against her forehead. 'Don't worry about it, Arthur.' She moved her hand to Dad's shoulder and he quickly covered it with his own. 'We should watch these every year, make it a Christmas tradition.'

'Anything's better than the bloody *Grinch*,' Cerys said. 'I'm in.'

Dad leaned over to nudge me gently in the ribs. 'Thank you, chicken,' he whispered. 'This is even better than what I wished for.'

Smiling, I sipped my tea and made a wish of my own, hoping that this time it would come true.

CHAPTER ELEVEN

Hope was a four-letter word.

The next morning, I knelt on the floor in front of my grandmother, my hair wild around my face, still in my pyjamas and without having even touched my chocolate orange.

It was still Christmas and I was not OK.

'If you could wish for absolutely anything, what would it be?' I beseeched, gripping her knees through her flesh-toned tights as though someone was coming to take me away.

When I woke up back in my bed again, exhausted from Christmases past, there were only two potential wishes left for me to take care of, Nan and Cerys, and the idea of spending my day making Cerys's wishes come true was a bridge too far. It had to be Nan, it just *had* to be.

'Gwen, what is the matter with you?' she asked, removing my hand from her leg. 'Have you been on the cooking sherry?'

'If you could wish for absolutely anything, anything at all in the whole world, what would it be?' I repeated, absolutely frantic. I could not and would not go through this again. 'There's no time for messing around, Nan, I cannot eat another mouthful of turkey, I cannot spend another evening at Dorothy's, I cannot look at a Gen 2 Cordless Personal Wonder Wand, you've *got* to tell me.'

'I will only ask you this once but are you on drugs?' she replied. 'Because you look just like Phil Mitchell on *Eastenders* when he was doing the crack cocaine.'

'I'm not on crack,' I confirmed with a violent shake of the head that did nothing to help my case. 'Please answer the question.'

'Maybe you're having an episode then.'

My response really depended on her definition of an episode.

'No, I'm not having an episode.'

Nan sipped her sherry, looking dubious.

'My Aunt Carol, your great-great-aunt, she had an episode once. She told everyone she'd been talking to fairies at the bottom of the garden and they gave her the electric shock treatment. In fairness it was the best thing that ever happened to her, she ended up leaving her husband and going to work for the BBC. Sometimes it does work.'

'I'm not having an episode. Or at least not that kind,' I replied, keen to move on but quite keen to find out more about my Great-Great-Aunt Carol another time. She sounded great. 'It's a very serious question, Nan. If you could wish for anything, what would it be?'

She swallowed and pursed her lips, snowflake brooch on her jacket twinkling like the lights on the Christmas tree.

'I'd do away with the internet.'

I slumped backwards onto the floor. 'You'd what?'

'I'd get rid of the internet. There's too much of it.'

There was no hope. I was going to be trapped in this Christmas for all eternity.

'You think there's too much internet?' I repeated. 'What does that even mean?'

'Barking at you from the minute you wake up,' Nan replied, scowling at the very thought of it. 'People don't need to know everything that's happening all the time, it's not good for them. Is it handy to be able to see the weather for tomorrow? Yes. Is it convenient to do a shop and have it delivered? No denying it. Do I need to know what some complete stranger on the other side of the planet thinks about Britney Spears at three o'clock in the bloody morning? Certainly not. I know what I think about Britney Spears, that's quite enough.'

'What *do* you think about Britney Spears?' I asked, incredibly curious.

'I think she's been through it,' Nan said with a ferocious look. 'And I should like to have a word with her parents.'

Me and her both.

'I'd get rid of ripped jeans while I'm at it,' she added before I could reply, her dark eyes lighting up with enthusiasm. 'They're disrespectful. Plenty of people out there can't afford nice clothes and you've got folk running around tearing things up on purpose and selling them for a fortune? Rude. And don't get me started on the terrible haircuts you see these days. I'm all for self-expression but they're taking it too far. Did I ever tell you about the time I burned my bra in the sixties? It was a very big deal back then, I only had two to my name.

They were much harder to get going than you'd think, your Aunt Gloria had to get hers started with a firelighter. I bet they go up a treat these days with all the bloody padding and whatnot.'

I held my hands against my face, pressing the fingertips into my eyebrows then sliding them around to my temples. This was going nowhere fast.

'OK, can we start again? Let's say, for example, you got the sixpence in the Christmas pudding after lunch,' I said, as cool as a deep-fried cucumber. 'Would you really wish for everyone to have the hair they were born with and no internet?'

She thought about it for a moment then wrinkled her nose. 'Probably not, pet.'

I sighed with relief.

'I want you and Michael to get back together, I'd wish for you to sort your love life out.'

Well, someone had relaxed a bit too bloody quickly, hadn't they?

'All I want is for you to be happy,' Nan said. 'And don't try to put me on, Gwen Baker, I know you're going to say you are, but are you? Are you really?'

I opened my mouth to tell her she didn't need to worry about me but when I tried to speak nothing came out.

'Seeing you kids happy is what makes me happy,' she added when I didn't reply. 'I won't lie, I was disappointed when your mother told me about you and Michael. You always seemed like such a good match, and he doted on you. I can't understand why the two of you couldn't work out your differences and make a go of it.'

Sat on the living-room floor, I stared up at my grand-mother, utterly incredulous. Getting rid of every pair of ripped jeans on the planet and destroying the internet suddenly seemed like the easy option.

'Are you serious?' I asked. 'You could wish for anything in the world and what you want is for me to get back together with Michael?'

'When you get to my age you understand what's really worth wishing for,' Nan said, dismissing my nonsense with a royal wave. 'Everyone wants to click their fingers and have it done these days, they don't realize you've got to put the work in. And as soon as it starts to get hard, they open the phone and order a new boyfriend or girlfriend or whatever you want to call it. You want to thank your lucky stars those apps weren't around when I met your grandad or you'd never have been born. I never could make a decision and stick to it.'

'No need to pull on that thread,' I replied, pulling a face.

Nan smiled as she reached for the remote control and turned on the TV. 'You asked.'

'You know what? Fine,' I said, rising to my feet, half wishing I'd chosen Cerys instead. 'I don't get to decide what you wish for, do I? One wish, coming right up.'

'If you say so, pet,' she replied. 'But while you're sorting out the wish could you get me a sherry?'

'I will drive to London and I will get Michael back,' I muttered as I went to fetch the Harveys Bristol Cream. 'Can't be any worse than blowing myself up, can it?'

'This is so much worse than blowing yourself up,' Manny said, sticking his head through the driver's side window as I attempted to coax his car into life. 'Admittedly you'd be dead, but least you'd have your dignity.'

'You wouldn't say that if you'd woken up on the same morning for the best part of a week,' I replied, checking my hastily applied eye make-up in the rear-view mirror. It was, as I expected, terrible. 'Besides, maybe Nan's right. I didn't try, I just left. Maybe I should have fought harder for me and Michael.'

'I did not live through all those hours of listening to you play the same Taylor Swift album on repeat for you to get back together with that bell-end,' he snapped. 'Sometimes there's nothing left to fight for.'

'Firstly, it was not the same album on repeat, it was the original version of *Red*, and *Red* (Taylor's Version), and I would thank you to note the difference,' I said, revving the engine as I stomped up and down on the clutch. 'And secondly, what if this is it? What if this is the reason I'm stuck here? You were the one who said I could use a little Hallmark holiday movie magic in my life, what's more romcom than getting stuck in a time loop until I make things right with my ex-boyfriend?'

'I don't know, getting drunk and shagging the neighbour?'

'The neighbour is engaged,' I replied, the memory of Dev's perfect forearms lingering in my mind for a moment too long. 'Unless you're talking about Dorothy?'

'As much as it pains me to admit it, I'm not always right!' Manny cried as I pulled the gear stick into reverse. 'I also said Chris Pratt seemed like a cool guy and that TikTok would never take off! Please don't do this, I'm begging you. Michael is a wanker. He looks like a squirrel, he never gets a round in and he treated you very shabbily. You deserve better than this, Gwen.'

'Squirrel or no squirrel, I have to do this,' I said, firing up my Spotify playlist and setting my emotional dial to 'determined' as the opening strains of 'All Too Well' (the ten-minute version) filled the car. I could not bear the thought of one more Christmas carol. 'I haven't spoken to him face to face since we broke up. I have to go and see him. After that, we'll see what happens.'

'Fine,' he groaned. It always took Manny longer than it should to know when he was beaten. 'If you're going to go, go. Have you got the address?' I nodded and gave him a thumbs-up. 'Text me when you get there and don't forget to tell him I hate him.'

'Will do and will do,' I promised. 'I think this might be it, Manny, I can feel it in my waters.'

'No,' he replied. 'That's my suspension. It's been shot ever since I shagged that guy from Beck's birthday party in the back seat.'

'And on that note,' I said, rolling up the window as he waved goodbye. With Taylor's voice blaring out of the speakers, I tore off down the road, on my way to Michael and hopefully, my destiny.

For me, Christmas wasn't Christmas unless I was at home, chock full of Mum's mince pies, Dad's terrible jokes, a stocking stuffed with satsumas and all the other clichéd traditional things that confirmed it 'twas the season. For Michael, Christmas was a cheeky week off work at the end of the year that would have been better spent anywhere else and he'd never really forgiven me for making him spend it with my family. Every year, around September, he floated the idea of going away, either on a proper holiday or a swanky staycation at some country hotel and every year I nixed it. My refusal to spend thousands of pounds on a Christmas jolly might not have been the straw that broke our relationship's back but, as I headed towards to The Elms, the very fancy hotel in deepest, darkest Hertfordshire Manny said he'd tagged on Instagram, I knew it was at least a factor. The Elms was the sort of hotel where reality TV stars got married and footballers pretended to play golf before getting hammered in the clubhouse. Two years ago, Michael sent me the link to their 'festive bliss' package and I replied with a gif of a budgie shaking its head. Two and a half grand for three nights when my mum was offering full bed, board and unlimited biscuits for free? It didn't make any sense. Best-case biscuit scenario at The Elms was if they had a mini packet of Walkers shortbread cookies tucked away with the coffee maker and what kind of Christmas was that? No, thank you.

The roads were practically empty on the drive down, but two and a half hours alone with Taylor Swift's back catalogue and my own thoughts still felt like an awfully long time. Four years Michael and I had been together. Four years of the most textbook relationship you could possibly think of. We met on an app, like everyone else. He took me to cool cocktail bars where smoking Old Fashioneds were served under a cloche, and restaurants that described themselves as 'gastronomic experiences'. He whisked me away on weekend minibreaks in Europe and took me to music festivals in the summer, his friends turning into my friends and my friends becoming increasingly annoyed by how bloody perfect he was. After a year, he suggested I move out of my shared flat and into his lovely west Hampstead home, a house that I could never afford, even as someone who had paid off her student loans and was bringing in a London lawyer's salary. But with Mummy and Daddy's help, Michael had bought it outright years earlier and me and my two suitcases of stuff fitted right in, like we were part of the classic but comfortable mid-century-modern furniture. After that, it was only a matter of time until we got engaged, everyone said so. Every weekend from April to September was someone else's hen do, engagement party or wedding and every weekend, that someone would pull me to one side, slightly pie-eyed and say 'You next!', as though it was already confirmed, part of some bigger plan. And I loved plans.

Except, I sniffed, as I pulled off the motorway, swiping at my eyes with the back of my wrist, things didn't quite work out like that, did they? After an extremely steady drive up the crunchy gravel driveaway, I hid Manny's decrepit Volvo in the back of the car park, apologizing to all the Jaguars and Aston Martins for its general existence. Pulling his buttery beige teddy coat off the backseat, I slipped it over my shoulders and glanced down at my red tartan pyjamas. Should I have taken the time to change before I drove down? Maybe, but Christmas wishes and the M1 waited for no man.

From the outside, The Elms looked like every other stately home-slash-hotel in England. Solid, square Georgian architecture and slightly foreboding in a public school kind of a way with its straight lines and regimented gardens, but on the inside it couldn't have been more different. Everything was shiny and new, all sleek glass and black marble with low light and brittle staff. Lingering inside the front door, my senses were overwhelmed by the smell of a thousand Diptyque candles burning at once and for a second, I completely forgot why I was there.

'Good morning, madam, can I help you?'

A grey man in a grey suit stared at me from behind the reception desk. The only nod to the time of year was a sombre arrangement of black, foliage-free twigs wrapped in fairy lights in the middle of the lobby which I took to be the world's saddest Christmas tree. At least, I assumed it was a Christmas tree, possibly it was a permanent modern art installation designed to scare children.

'It's miss, actually, just having a bad day,' I said, rubbing my ring fingers under my eyes and wincing when they came away black. I looked as though I'd just got back from a shift down the mines with my Great-Uncle Emlyn. 'I'm meeting someone who's having lunch here, can you point me to the restaurant?'

'Certainly,' he replied without making eye contact. Civil but disinterested. They probably didn't pay him enough to argue with old crones who wandered in off the street on Christmas Day. 'Luncheon is being served in The Orangery, down the corridor to your right. Perhaps your friend would rather come out to meet you? The Orangery is a formal dining experience, we wouldn't want you to feel uncomfortable.'

It was a funny thing to say because he was doing a very good job of making me feel incredibly uncomfortable without seemingly making any effort at all.

'I'm grand, thanks,' I said, aggressively tossing my ponytail over my shoulder only for it to flick all the way around and slap me in the eye. 'Merry Christmas.'

'And season's greetings to you,' he replied under his breath as I tiptoed, blinking, through the silent lobby.

* * *

It had been almost three months since I'd seen Michael and two and a half hours since I left home to see him, but now I was here, I still had no idea what I was actually planning to say. Michael, I still love you. Michael, let's try again. Michael, I'm trapped in a Christmas time loop and the only way to break it is to grant a wish and my nan really wants us to get back together? Probably wouldn't start with that one.

All I knew for sure was I wanted things back the way they were. Things started to go wrong for me the moment Michael ended things. If we could work things out, I'd be able to concentrate at work, knuckle down and get my promotion back on track and move out of my miserable flat and back into our beautiful home. . . and then what?

Pretend everything was OK?

Pretend he hadn't started seeing someone else behind my back?

Pretend I wasn't terrified he'd do it again?

My stomach churned, all the thoughts and feelings I'd done so well to ignore since I left swelling up inside me. Three months of Manny checking in on me every single day, three months of sleepless nights spent wondering what I'd done wrong, three months of blaming myself for his actions. I felt sick. There I was, telling my dad to let his feelings out, telling my mum she needed to put herself first and now I was about to beg the man who'd broken my heart to take me back? What was wrong with me?

I'd always been able to spot Michael in any room – with his pale blond hair and my heart tied to his, all roads led back to my love, and I saw him straight away, alone at a table right in the middle of the restaurant. The best table. A weak echo of the rush of happiness I used to feel every time I saw him washed over me. But this was not that. I wasn't excited to see him, I was anxious.

This was not what I wanted.

He'd changed his hair, I realized. He'd cut it all off short except for a little flick in the front. At some point in the last three months, Michael Darden had gone out and got a new haircut without telling me, for the first time since we met, and I realized, as I stared at him from the doorway of the restaurant, he would never tell me before changing his hair ever again. He would buy new shoes and get new glasses, he might even grow a beard if the mood took him, and none of it would have anything to do with me.

It hit me like a bolt from the blue, a series of tiny realizations leading up to one giant revelation, exploding one by one like Dad's fireworks. I'd lost weeks of my life wallowing and sobbing and singing along to my carefully curated *Now That's What I Call Misery* mixtape wishing for something that simply didn't exist anymore. I'd told myself over and over that if I could turn the clock back, everything would be OK, but just one look at this new version of my old boyfriend was all I needed to know that was not the case. I didn't want this man with a haircut I didn't recognize. I wanted the comfort and stability of our previous life – but that life was gone, forever. It was like getting back into a hot bath gone cold. Even if you added more warm water, it would never really be the same.

Backing up before he could see me, I breathed in through my nose and out through my mouth as if I was at the end of a rough spin class or had just eaten a particularly large sandwich. It was too much to take in, I had to get out of there. But before I could make a respectable exit, I saw a tiny brunette emerge from the ladies at the end of the narrow hallway, shaking her hands dry as she strolled along the corridor towards me in a lovely dress and high heels, looking every bit as though she belonged.

Justine the Receptionist.

'Well, this isn't good,' I whispered, looking to my left and then my right and realizing I was trapped. There were three options. Turn left into The Orangery and hope there was another exit of some kind, turn right and walk past Justine the Receptionist with my head held high, or I could hurl myself at the plate glass windows in front of me and pray for a merciful death. I knew the right thing to do and despite how attractive it might seem, it wasn't option three. I wasn't the one who shagged my attached boss behind Justine's back, I had no reason to feel small in front of her, but as I ran out of time I also knew I couldn't bear to be any closer to her than I was right now. And so, with a deep breath, I pulled up the collar of Manny's teddy coat and made a swift left turn into the restaurant.

If Classic FM was a restaurant, it would be The Orangery. Everything was muted and lush, quietly assured of its own splendour, elegant tablecloths, heavy linen napkins and an intimidating amount of cutlery at every single place setting. The diners were equally fancy, sleek and patrician and elbows-off-the-table, and I had walked in wearing my pyjamas and a battered, oversized teddy coat a giant man kept in his car in case of emergencies. So it was understandable when a fair number of people turned to have a look at me as I shuffled around the edge of the room, searching for an exit, Michael included.

Shit. Shit shit shit. Somehow my terribly flawed and poorly executed plan had failed.

His eyes widened with recognition and a scarlet stain crept up his neck as Justine took her seat and I stared back at him, every moment exploding with another flash-back firework. Bang, I don't love you anymore. Bang, I'm seeing someone else. Bang, you have to move out. Everything felt wrong from the fancy hotel and soft music to me being here in the first place. Not to mention the fact Michael was wearing a lurid red-and-green striped reindeer sweater, something he flatly refused to even entertain when we were together. It wasn't me, this glossy five-star Christmas, I wanted Mum and Dad's cosy dining room, the shouting, the laughing, even my awful sister. All the things that made Christmas Christmas. Looking at Michael now, sitting across from Justine, I could see it all so plainly. It wasn't me but it was them. They made sense together, which meant he and I did not. Panicking, I slid into an empty chair at the nearest table, taking a moment to recover myself before beaming at its three elderly occupants.

'Hello!' I exclaimed with an effusive smile, watching Michael watching me. 'Merry Christmas, how is everyone?'

'Who are you?' The man to my left asked, quite reasonably. The woman sat across from him reached for her handbag and held it close to her chest.

'My name's Gwen,' I replied, still with one eye on my ex as he whispered something to his new girlfriend. 'What's yours?'

'That's Patricia's seat,' said another older gentleman sat opposite me. 'You can't sit there, she'll be back from the loo in a minute.'

'She'll be longer than a minute,' the woman said with a flash of annoyance. 'She'll tell you she's never out of the toilet since her hysterectomy, but I've noticed it's usually more of a problem around the time the bill comes.'

Three tables up and two across, I watched as Michael rose from his seat, grim determination on his face.

'So, it's actually a funny story which I haven't got time to tell but I was wondering if you wouldn't mind all laughing really loudly as though I've just said something hysterical,' I said to my new friends. 'I'll give the cue.'

The woman peered at me over a tasteful holly and ivy centrepiece which I realized with a pang was all the worse for its lack of one-eyed grey rabbits. 'Are you wearing pyjamas?' she asked.

'Pyjamas?' I shook my head and pulled Manny's coat closed across my chest. 'No, these are very trendy co-ords, everyone's wearing them. Seriously, if you could all laugh right now, that would be amazing.'

'But you haven't said anything funny?' the first man replied. 'Why would we laugh?'

As Michael walked up to the table, I threw my head back, roaring hysterically and clutching my sides. 'Oh, you,' I gasped as I reached for a glass of wine that was not mine. 'Really, you ought to be a comedian. Tell me, have you ever considered starting a podcast?'

'Gwen?' My ex-boyfriend stood over me, his face a charming shade of beetroot and his arms folded across his chest.

'Michael!' I exclaimed. 'What a coincidence, fancy seeing you here.' I gestured towards him and then waved around the table at the three blank faces. 'Pals, this is my friend, Michael. Michael, these are . . . my pals.'

'We've never seen her before in our lives,' the woman whispered, covering her mouth with her handbag. 'Please alert security.'

'She's so funny,' I said, taking another glug of borrowed wine. 'Isn't she so funny?'

'I thought I was the funny one?' The man sat to my right dropped a crepey hand onto my thigh, gave it a firm squeeze and winked. I blanched. So this was how it felt to be hoisted by your own petard; I'd always wondered.

'What's going on?' Michael asked as I delicately removed the hand from my leg. 'Why are you here? And why are you wearing pyjamas?'

'They're called co-ords,' the woman replied sagely. 'But they do look like pyjamas, don't they?'

'It's been lovely to catch up,' I said, slapping the dirty old man's hand away as he reached out for a second squeeze of my leg. 'But I've actually got to dash. Enjoy your turkey, everyone.'

'We don't eat turkey,' the man who *hadn't* tried to touch me up under the table said with a sneer. 'This is a capon.'

'Apologies, I'm very common.' I stood up, took one last swig of Patricia's wine and raised my hand in a farewell. 'Merry Christmas, everyone.'

'Can I help you at all?'

A crotchety-looking man who was not the man I'd spoken to on reception but could definitely play him in a movie appeared out of nowhere and hovered beside the table. The little gold nametag on his jacket declared his name was Dick and I had no problem believing it.

'This woman is in my wife's seat,' declared the handsy man. 'She sat down and demanded we all start laughing, please have her escorted from the premises.'

'A minute ago you were trying to touch me up,' I pointed out indignantly. 'Come on, it's not like I was trying to re-enact *Dog Day Afternoon*, is it? I just sat at the wrong table.'

'And which table was madam supposed to be sitting at?' Dick asked.

A quick glance around the room suggested no one here was about to claim me.

'Now I think about it, I could be in the wrong restaurant,' I replied politely. 'Apologies.'

Clinging to what was left of my dignity, I turned to walk out of the restaurant as fast as my little legs would carry me. Which wasn't that fast, considering I was wearing the least aerodynamic coat known to man and there were several tightly packed tables between me and the exit, but it was still quite fast. At least fast enough to knock Father Christmas off his feet when he unexpectedly turned the corner into the restaurant.

We fell in slow motion, his arms windmilling as he toppled backwards, me on top of him, holding my hands up in front of my face. The sounds of screaming children drowned out the jaunty rendition of 'Santa Claus is Coming to Town' that played through speakers in the ceiling, and we hit the ground with a loud grunt. The soft padding of his belly broke the worst of my fall and I rolled off his prone body, my knee squishing something soft as I righted myself onto all fours.

'My balls!' Santa yelled, pulling off his lush, fake beard. 'She's bust my bloody nuts!'

'I'm sorry,' I cried, shuffling backwards on my hands and knees, attempting to reverse out of the situation and stop myself from making a joke about Santa's sack. It was not easy.

Knives and forks clattered onto plates and capons went cold as the beardless Old Saint Nick rolled around with his hands tucked up between his thighs. I scuttled away, staggering to my feet to survey the chaos but as ever, I could only see Michael, a look of true horror on his gorgeous, annoying face.

'What is going on in here?'

A smartly dressed, elderly woman stood in the doorway, little red handbag hanging from the crook of her arm, a sprig of holly pinned to her blouse.

'Patricia?' I asked, straightening the collar of my pyjamas. She gave me a silent nod. 'Your husband is a dirty old man.'

'Roger did this?' she gasped as Dick approached, his face like thunder.

'I think I'd better go,' I replied, skipping around her. 'Merry Christmas, Patricia. Enjoy your capon.'

'Gwen, wait!'

I was almost back to the Volvo when I heard Michael call my name. I turned to see him, the man I'd woken up next to every day until I didn't. His drainpipe trousers didn't suit him any better than his new haircut and I watched his chest heave from the exertion of running after me, a slight sheen of sweat on the recently revealed extra inches of his forehead. Was this really my Michael?

'What *are* you wearing?' I asked, holding a hand over my eyes to shield them from the sun.

'What? It's – it's an ugly sweater,' he replied, pinching the synthetic fabric and pulling it away from his body so he too could gaze upon Rudolph's glory, the reindeer surrounded by fairy lights and candy canes. It was too weird.

'I can see that. I suppose I meant *why* are you wearing it?'

'It was a present.'

No need to say from whom. He wouldn't even wear a pair of festive boxer shorts I bought for him a month after we met because he thought Christmas-themed clothes were tacky. That was when realization number two hit home. He was wearing the jumper because it came from her. Justine wasn't a rebound, it was the real thing.

'Why are *you* wearing pyjamas?' Michael asked, more than a little defensive. 'And isn't that Manny's coat? Is he here too?'

'No, he's not.' I shook my head and wished that he was. 'He says to tell you he hates you, by the way.'

He made a derisive noise I recognized, his 'I-suppose-you-think-that's-funny' scoff, the one that sat on the shelf next to his 'yes-I-suppose-so' grunt and 'OK-but-I'd-rather-not' sigh. I wondered if Justine recognized those noises yet or if he was still treating her to full sentences.

'What do you want?' he asked, blunt and to the point. To think his straightforwardness was something I used to admire about him. 'Why are you here?'

'I'm trapped in a Christmas time loop and the only way to break it is to grant a wish and my nan really wants us to get back together?'

Apparently I was starting with that one.

He opened his mouth to say something then changed his mind and shook his head.

'That's not even funny.'

'You're telling me . . .' I looked down at my wrist and gasped. 'One o'clock already? Oh well, must be off—'

'No!' Michael exclaimed, taking a big step forward. 'You don't get to show up at my hotel, scare a table full of pensioners, castrate Father Christmas then leave without an explanation. What is going on?'

'Firstly, they scared me more than I scared them,' I replied, digging my hands into Manny's pockets. 'And secondly, why can't I leave without an explanation? You left me for someone else without an explanation.'

When he ended things, I didn't know how to feel and even if I'd read every book ever written on the subject, I wouldn't have been prepared. The pain was constant, sometimes big, sometimes small, but it was always there. All this time I'd convinced myself the best way to make it stop was to pretend it wasn't happening, building temporary dams out of work, Netflix binges and entire selection boxes eaten in one go, but as I stood there, watching him squirm in a hotel car park, I knew I was going about it the wrong way. The only way to get through the pain was to let it in and ride it out. Every ounce of agony I'd held at bay for the last three months seeped into my bones, all the way through to the marrow. I let it burn and sting and settle, and much to my surprise, I survived.

'You hurt me,' I said, rolling back my shoulders and standing up straight.

Michael looked back at me, shocked. He was used to peacekeeper Gwen, the non-confrontational woman who always acquiesced for the chance of a quiet life, but that Gwen was gone and from the look on his face, he didn't quite know where to put himself in front of the new one.

'I can't believe you ended things the way you did,' I said, pacing up and down in front of Manny's knackered car. 'Four years over and done in five minutes. I can't even believe I'm stood talking to you now, I was starting to think I'd imagined you.'

'Clean breaks are always best,' he said, pausing for a moment as though he didn't have anything to add, even though he always did. 'If you love something, set it free. Better to let you go and all that.'

'Thanks, Sting,' I replied, flinging my arms out wide. 'I'm a person not a battery chicken, you didn't send me to live out my days on a nice organic farm so I wouldn't peck myself to death, you dumped me!'

'Battery hens don't usually have beaks,' he muttered. 'They cut them off.'

He looked over his shoulder at the hotel, checking to make sure me raising my voice hadn't upset it somehow.

'I didn't come to argue about battery hens.' I wiped my hands over my face, trying to remember exactly why I was there. Oh. Right. The wish. Bugger. 'Things weren't perfect between us, whatever that means, but I loved you,' I started, feeling my way around a conversation we needed to have even if I doubted I'd ever be ready for it. 'If you weren't happy, you should have said something. You don't wait until you've got someone else on the side to bin off the person you've spent the last four years of your life with. What you did was cruel.'

Michael shuffled around on the spot with his eyes cast

towards the gravel, the lights on his jumper twinkling merrily as he moved, completely out of sync with his mood.

'OK, that was wrong,' he said eventually. 'But what about what you did? Wasn't that cruel?'

'Me?' I squinted at him, dumbfounded. 'What did I do?'

'Good question,' he replied, the angry red spots blooming in his cheeks. 'What did you do? Nothing. You're obsessed with your job, Gwen, the only thing you care about is getting that promotion, you completely took us for granted. You didn't care about me, about us. All the parties you missed, the birthdays, my brother's wedding? Where were you when I needed you? You were at work.'

'I didn't miss your brother's wedding,' I countered quickly, frowning at the hazy memory of a marquee, a light-up dance floor and Michael's dad doing a striptease to 'You Sexy Thing'. 'I was definitely there.'

'You managed to squeeze in the reception, but you should have been there for all of it!' he shouted, scaring a flock of birds out of a nearby tree. 'I shouldn't have had to beg you to take a Saturday off to be at my own brother's wedding!'

My stomach lurched. He was right.

I was prepping papers for a merger because my boss had gone on a last-minute holiday and I'd missed the ceremony. And if I was being entirely honest, I'd missed it because I *volunteered* to prep the papers so my boss could go on a last-minute holiday. A rush of nausea washed over me and I very much regretted eating an entire six-pack of Mini Cheddars on the drive down.

'I – I'm sorry?' I stuttered, holding on to Manny's car

for fear of falling over. 'But I explained at the time and you said it was OK. Why didn't you say anything then?'

Michael screwed his face into an ugly scowl and shrugged. 'Because I already knew it was over.'

I took a step back as though I'd been pushed. His brother got married last autumn, more than a year ago.

'I hated your job,' he said, striding up and down the car park.

'You hated it?' I whispered. 'But you were always so proud of me? You always bragged about me to our friends, you encouraged me.'

'What was I supposed to do?' he asked. 'I hated your job, and what's more, I hated that hating your job made me look like an arsehole, like I was some old-fashioned chauvinist or something because I wanted my girlfriend to put me first.'

I was reeling. How could any of this be true?

'That's not fair, I put you first all the time. I moved to the other side of the city so we could live together even though it meant I had a longer commute. You made all our joint decisions, where we went, who we saw, what we ate. Whose idea was it to go vegan for six months, Michael? Not me! But I did it. I even stopped drinking Diet Coke because you told me to.'

'Diet Coke is poison,' he snapped.

'Poisonous and *delicious*,' I countered. 'My point is, I made a lot of sacrifices for our relationship, I did a lot of stuff because it made you happy, even if it wasn't top of my agenda.'

'Justine does things to make me happy because she wants to, not because I force her,' he said. 'Being with you, God, Gwen, it was like trying to butter cold toast.'

'Cold toast?' I pushed my fingers into my hair and squeezed my skull. 'First I'm a beakless chicken and now I'm cold toast?'

He swiped at a nearby bush and yanked his hand away, scratched and bleeding.

'Cold butter on cold toast,' he barked. 'Impossible! It was at my brother's wedding that I knew, but you always made things so difficult, pretending you were OK with my decisions then acting like some kind of bloody martyr.'

Biting my lip, I tightened my grip on the boot of the car.

'Justine puts me first.' Michael stepped away from the bush and dabbed at the scratches on his palm. It looked like it stung and I was not sorry. 'She cares about me, she takes care of me. Do you know she cancelled her own birthday party to come with me to my nephew's christening so I wouldn't have to go on my own? Can you even imagine that? She and I want the same things.'

I gulped down a big lungful of air. The christening was the weekend we broke up. He had taken a new girlfriend to his nephew's christening five days after I moved out of our home.

'Sounds more like Justine wants whatever you tell her she wants,' I said, choking out the words. 'Good job you're her boss, isn't it?'

'Don't be jealous,' he shot back. 'It's beneath you.'

'I think you'll find it isn't,' I replied triumphantly.

What an absolute twat. If I could have made my own wish, it would've been to have had this argument eighteen months earlier. If I'd known about *this* Michael, I might not have spent so many nights crying and scrolling through photos of us and placing unnecessary ASOS orders to soothe my pain.

'I fell in love with someone else, that's all.'

He said it as though it was perfectly reasonable, as though I was the idiot for not understanding. We were collateral damage. *I* was collateral damage. The path of true love never did run smooth, but no one liked to talk about all the people it steamrolled over en route to happiness.

'There was no big plan to mess you around,' he added, a gust of wind blowing his terrible Tintin hair up off his head. 'I wasn't sat at work thinking of the best ways to hurt your feelings. To be honest, once things started with Justine, I really didn't think about you at all.'

The sting of his words caught me off guard and when I breathed in, I found I couldn't breathe out.

'I fell in love with someone who *wants* to give me the things I need. I wish there had been another way to do it but there wasn't, or perhaps there was and I just didn't care. I don't know, all I wanted was for us to be over.'

'And all I want is to go home,' I said, all the air leaving my lungs at once, officially done.

'Justine moved in,' Michael said, turning away from the wind and scratching the corner of his eye. 'And before you hear it from someone else, I'm going to ask her to marry me on New Year's Eve.'

I didn't move, I couldn't. He was going to propose. I'd waited four years for something he was ready to give her after three months.

'When you know, you know,' he said with a smile, adding insult to injury.

My fingers curled around my car keys. 'Congratulations,' I replied. 'I'm so happy for you.'

'Really?' he sounded surprised.

'No, not really but I'm not as cruel as you so I won't tell you how I actually feel.'

If I wasn't sure before, I was now. I would rather live the same Christmas Day a thousand times over than go back in time and beg him to choose me over her. Whoever this man might be, in his skinny jeans and his ugly Christmas jumper, he wasn't the man I'd loved. This wasn't the same person who used to save me the crossword in the Sunday paper and put a bookmark in my book when I fell asleep on the settee, the man who ran me a bubble bath on cold mornings to ease me into my day. How had my wonderful Michael turned into this unpleasant stranger with such terrible hair? He was like a reverse butterfly, swaddling himself in a cocoon made up of nothing but malice and spite. And even though the idea ate me up inside, I had to wonder whether my Michael had ever existed in the first place. Was this who he was all along? Did I only see what I wanted to see? Somewhere along the line, I'd stopped paying attention and confused my idea of us with reality. I'd mistaken his rewarding my good behaviour for love and I felt terribly, terribly foolish.

'I think we've said everything we have to say to each other,' Michael sniffed, attempting to stick his hands in the pockets but only managing to wiggle them in up to his knuckles, his jeans too tight and the pockets too shallow. Still, he stuck out his chin in defiance, thumbs flapping by his unused belt loops, and all I wanted to do was laugh.

'Almost,' I replied, an unfamiliar emotion flooding through me and shining a light on parts of myself that had been lost in the dark for so long.

It felt like hope.

'I'm truly sorry for making you feel as though I didn't care about you because I did,' I said as I unlocked the car door and climbed inside. If I put my foot down, I could make it most of the way home before the snow started. 'And I hope Justine really is what you need and not just a reflection of your own bloody ego, for her sake.'

I slammed the door and cranked the engine, leaving him stood beside the car, mouth hanging open. It turned over on the first attempt. Hallelujah. Spinning out of the car park, gravel flying under my wheels, I turned the ancient stereo on and cranked the volume as high as it would go, tears of relief in my eyes.

'If there was one moment I wouldn't mind living over again . . .' I said out loud, watching Michael grow smaller and smaller in the rear-view mirror until he disappeared forever.

CHAPTER TWELVE

'Ahh, makes you grateful to be alive, doesn't it? The fresh air, the green grass, the friendly sheep.' Dad raised his arms high over his head, waving his walking stick like a finish line flag. 'Is there anything nicer than a brisk stroll on Christmas morning?'

'Jumping in the bath with the hairdryer still plugged in?' I suggested, marching slowly behind him, all wrapped up in Mum's coat. 'Fingers crossed those sheep aren't too friendly.'

When I woke up the next day, same place, same time, same bloody Christmas, I knew there was only one person's wish left to grant.

Cerys Cordelia Megan Baker.

So naturally I volunteered to join my dad on a five-mile hike to delay the inevitable.

Seeing Michael had changed things. I was still sad, but sad with a full stop. For months, he'd been draining all my battery, like an app left open in the background, and now I could delete him for good which left more energy for other things, like walks with my dad, avoiding my sister and pretending my existence wasn't defying the laws of space and time. I turned my face up to the soft shafts of sunlight that peeked through the clouds and for one brief, shining moment, with Jack Frost nipping at my nose, I felt good.

Right up until my feet slid out from underneath me and I landed flat on my back in a pile of sheep dung.

'You all right down there, chicken?'

Dad stood over me, shaking his head as though I'd done it on purpose.

'Grand,' I replied without moving. 'Thanks for asking.'

'That'll teach you to make fun of the sheep,' he replied, poking at a pile of dung with his walking stick. 'There'd better not be any on your mum's coat or you'll be buying her a new one.'

'Thankfully I think most of it is in my hair,' I said with a weak thumbs-up.

The silhouette of a man moved hurriedly towards us, his features blotted out by the low winter sun while a tiny white powder puff of a dog ran ahead, yapping loudly and dancing around me in a circle.

'Mr Baker? Gwen? Are you OK?'

I held my hand over my eyes and squinted. Dev's features came into focus as the dog hopped up onto my chest and settled right down.

'Hello, stranger,' I said.

'Hello yourself,' he replied, smiling when he saw I wasn't injured.

Each time I saw him, I noticed something new. His beautiful grey coat, his exceptional forearms and today, the sprinkle of salt and pepper at his temples, only visible when the sun shone directly on his hair.

'Did you fall or are you lying on the ground for fun?' Dev asked as he and my dad offered up an arm each and hoisted me back up to my feet, the little white dog looping in circles around us.

'You must not have heard about my new job as a government grass inspector,' I replied. 'All looks to be in order.'

Dad straightened his flat cap and gave Dev a knowing, manly nod. 'Wasn't watching where she was going, if you can believe it.'

'Gwen? Never!'

'I'm not usually a clumsy person,' I protested, relieved to know the time loop meant that somewhere out there, The Elms's Santa Claus could not refute my claim. Today he would be walking around with his testicles intact. 'There isn't nearly as much sheep shit to slip on in London.'

'But it makes up for it with other delights,' he replied before pointing towards the nearby stately home. 'Are you going down to the house?'

'We are,' Dad and I confirmed at the same time.

'Mind if I join you?'

'If you really must,' I said with a friendly shrug.

On the outside, I looked politely pleased, but on the inside I was happier than three French hens, two turtle doves and a partridge in a pear tree. A lovely countryside wander with a man whose time, place and date of birth I still knew by heart could be just the tonic. Dev would never call me cold toast. But at the same time, that annoying voice that loved to ruin things couldn't stop wondering where he was hiding his fiancée. Not that I was in much of a mood to discuss other people's happy relationships and really, there were a million possible reasons why she wasn't around. Maybe she was with her own family? Maybe she didn't celebrate Christmas? A lot of people met their partners at work and Dev was a doctor, she could be a doctor as well. A lot of doctors worked over the holidays, people didn't stop getting poorly because you wanted to gorge yourself on turkey and give your daughter a vibrator as a present. That was probably it: he was engaged to a beautiful, kind, intelligent doctor with naturally curly eyelashes that didn't even need mascara, wore her hair pulled back in an elegant chignon that always had one perfect strand falling in front of her face just so, who was most likely in surgery, literally saving someone's life while I lay on the ground covered in sheep shit.

What a bitch.

'I'm sure you've got lots of catching up to do, why don't you go on without me? I can't keep up with you kids anyway,' Dad declared, even though it was quite clearly a lie, he was twice as fit as I was, but I suspected we both still remembered the time he came in my room without knocking and found me making a collage out of photos of me and Dev and one of Cerys's bridal magazines. We never spoke of the incident again.

'Are you sure you're all right walking back on your own?' I asked as he fussed over Dev's dog until she rolled onto her back and did a small wee.

'Do I need to remind everyone who fell on their arse? Because it wasn't me.' He wiped his hand on the back of his trousers, the dog tucking her tail between her legs in disgrace. Striding off across the fields, he raised his walking stick in a farewell. 'Be back before lunch or your mother will have you. Merry Christmas, Dev!'

The little white dog bounced up and down around my knees, barking until I picked her up and nursed her like a baby.

'Pari likes you,' Dev said, rolling up the leather lead in his hand and slipping it into his coat pocket. 'That's a good sign, she's very wary of strangers.'

'She only wants me for a human heater,' I replied, turning to mush as she burrowed into the front of my coat. 'Is she yours?'

'My mum's. I borrowed her as an excuse to make an escape.' He smiled and swept his arm out in front of us with a gentlemanly flourish. 'Shall we?'

'We shall,' I confirmed, pushing his wonderful, beautiful-but-doesn't-know-it surgeon of a fiancée out of mind and leading the way.

Chatsworth House was always beautiful but at Christmas, it was out of this world. Giant fir trees decorated with twinkling lights lined the driveway and even just walking along the path towards it made me feel as though we'd been transported to a winter wonderland. When I was younger, I used to dream of what it would be like to live in such a beautiful place, imagining myself staring out of the top-floor windows and off into the woods. I loved the gardens and the ponds and the little arched bridges that crossed the river where I would pause and stare moodily into the water, as though I was secretly filming my own music video while Manny got lost in the maze every single time. By springtime, every inch of the house and gardens would be absolutely packed with tourists, but just for today it felt as though it all belonged to me and Dev.

'It's not open today, is it?' he asked, looking around the empty grounds. No one here but us.

'Don't think so.' It was years since I'd been to visit but she hadn't changed a bit. 'Pretty sure they're closed to the public on Christmas day.'

'We're not really the public though, are we?' he said with a devilish smile.

With Pari still nestling inside my coat, I gave him a questioning look.

'We aren't?'

Dev shook his head. 'We are a couple of friendly neighbours, stopping by to say hello, celebrate the season.'

'In that case it would be rude not to get a bit closer,' I reasoned, pleased to feel a flicker of excitement deep inside. 'What do you reckon?'

'Can't bear rudeness,' he replied. 'Let's go and wish them a Merry Christmas.'

We made our way around the outside of the house, catching up on our lives, the awkward shyness that hovered between us slipping away as Dev told me all the things about his life I already knew and he listened to my stories for the first time, again. The grounds were completely deserted. It was very obvious we weren't supposed to be there but politely walking around with a tiny dog who hadn't set so much as a paw on the floor hardly felt like the crime of the century. No self-respecting burglar would bring Pari as a guard dog. She was about as threatening as a feather duster.

'It always makes me feel like I'm in an Austen adaptation,' I said, choosing to ignore the fact Elizabeth Bennet would never have slipped in a pile of sheep excrement in front of Mr Darcy. 'Of course they didn't have water-proof coats and trainers back then. Might have lived longer if they had.'

'You wouldn't have lived this long in Austen's time no matter the outerwear situation,' Dev replied. 'I'd give you six weeks at most.'

'And why's that?'

'No TV, no films, extremely limited access to books, you can't sing, you can't play an instrument to save your life and if you didn't drop dead from boredom, you'd probably choke on your tongue from biting it so often.' He acknowledged my expression of outrage with a comi-cally outsized shrug. 'Am I wrong though?'

'Imagine spending every waking hour trapped in a room with my sister, waiting for a distant cousin to show up unannounced and propose,' I said with a shudder. 'Forget romance, those books are horror stories. I wouldn't need to bite off my tongue, I'd have already drowned myself in the lake.'

'There you go,' Dev grinned. 'Although it wasn't always a cousin who proposed, was it? Sometimes it was a family friend, a dashing neighbour.'

He gave a theatrical wink and I replied with a hollow laugh. If he'd made a joke like that when we were sixteen, it would have killed me on the spot. I simply would have ceased to exist.

'You wouldn't have fared any better than me,' I said. 'No computer games, no comics, you cannot dance to save your life and don't forget I've heard you play guitar. Neither of us would have been first choice to entertain our parents' guests after an eighteen-course dinner of freshly shot grouse and fourteen different kinds of jelly.'

'That's the one thing I'd be into,' he said, licking his lips and rubbing his belly. 'They were always eating jelly, weren't they? We don't eat it enough these days.'

'Speak for yourself. I always have jelly in the cupboard. You've got to get the proper cubes though, the powder isn't the same.'

Dev pressed his hands against his stomach, a hangdog expression on his stupidly good-looking face. 'God, what I'd give for a massive bowl of jelly and ice cream. Orange, no, strawberry, with an entire tub of vanilla ice cream. None of the fancy stuff, proper milk, sugar and stomach-ache after.'

'Sounds amazing,' I admitted. 'I wonder if Mum's got any jelly in the pantry.'

Right behind the Mini Rolls and the explosives.

'I've as much chance of getting any jelly as I have of my mother making a life-sized replica of Buckingham Palace out of cheese,' he replied, perking up more than a little. 'Actually, that sounds amazing.'

'With little water crackers for the windows,' I suggested, my own stomach rumbling at the thought. 'What cheese would you use? I'm thinking a nice solid mature cheddar, maybe a bit of red Leicester. Nothing too soft or crumby, you wouldn't get far with a Wensleydale.'

'Stop it, I'm starving,' he laughed. 'I'd even settle for an igloo made out of Babybels right now. Mum and Dad are off sugar and dairy so I've no hope. If it's not a potato, we're probably not having it.'

Pari barked to be put down and I watched as she raced away in front of us, smiling as the sun caught the salt and pepper in Dev's hair. He looked over and caught my eye, and I switched my gaze to the house behind him, my cheeks turning pink.

'I bet it's gorgeous inside,' I said, walking half a step faster and nodding towards the lights that twinkled through the windows. 'Have you ever been when it's all decorated?'

'Not since I was a kid,' he replied. 'You?'

I shook my head. 'I've always wanted to. I was supposed to go a couple of years ago, but I couldn't get tickets. My boyfriend didn't really want to anyway, this isn't his sort of thing.'

'Ah, the boyfriend. My mum said he's a dentist?' Dev said with a smile. 'But she has been known to be wrong before. Once. Before I was born. So the legends say.'

I tried for a casual laugh but failed. 'Ex-boyfriend and I'd rather not talk about him. Not worth the waste of oxygen.'

I was still too angry to get into it, too disappointed in Michael and myself. Plus, there was something else woven through my feelings, keeping them all tightly bound together, but I couldn't quite pull on the right thread to work out what it was.

'Got it.'

He tapped his fingers against his temple in a brief salute. He never was one to push too hard and I was grateful. Instead, he stopped underneath one of the windows, a golden glow shining softly through the glass.

'Want to have a look inside?' he asked.

'More than anything but I'm too much of a short arse,' I replied, jumping up and down. 'Maybe we should give them a knock and see if they'll let us in, you know, since we're locals and everything.'

'Or . . .' Dev checked quickly over both of his shoulders. 'You could climb on my back and have a peek.' He crouched down underneath the window, hands braced against his knees and looking up at me like I was the weirdo. 'Come on,' he said, slapping his thighs. 'Jump up.'

A brief vision of me, clambering on his back, falling off and both of us breaking a hip flashed through my mind.

'Absolutely not,' I said, standing firm. 'You can't go around looking through other people's windows, there's a name for people who do that.'

'Peeping Toms?'

'I was thinking "twats".'

He laughed but he did not move.

'Come on, Baker,' he said, gripping his thighs in readiness. 'You know you want to.'

'Baby Jesus, give me strength,' I whispered, trying very hard not to think about how those thighs might feel. I didn't remember him being quite so solid when we were teenagers.

'What are you waiting for?' Dev asked, still squatting. 'It's a cheeky look through a window, the world won't end if you climb on my back and check it out, I promise you.'

I dithered back and forth for a moment. On one hand, it felt dodgy but on the other, Dev Jones was bent over in front of Chatsworth House and demanding I climb on his back. And he was probably right, I couldn't bring on the apocalypse by peeking through a window. Said the girl who was on her sixth Christmas Day in a row.

'Fine, but I'm going on record as saying this is a bad idea,' I told him as I clambered onto his back, feeling my way upright against the rough stone side of the house and pressing my nose up against the glass.

It was more beautiful than I could have imagined.

The house, not Dev's back.

But also Dev's back.

Somehow, someone had popped inside my head and scooped out the Christmas of my dreams. The warm wooden floors and gilded ceilings, a huge fireplace big enough for me and Santa to climb inside at the same time, and one of the biggest, most beautifully decorated Christmas trees I'd ever had the privilege to witness with my own eyes. It was massive, at least twelve feet tall, and stood slap bang in the centre of the room, proudly showing off its baubles. Two wooden nutcracker soldiers stood sentry on either side of the fireplace, their mouths agape at the wonder of it all and I could have stared at it forever.

'Not to rush you,' Dev grunted under my feet.

'Let me get a quick photo,' I said, pulling my phone out of my pocket and holding it up to the window. But a picture couldn't do it justice and besides, I didn't really want a photo, I wanted to be inside.

'Dev?' I said, touching my fingertips to the window.

'Gwen?'

'This window's open.'

I pushed against the pane and felt it give. No alarms sounded, no sirens raged. There was nothing but a waft of tempting Christmas-tree scent and a complete loss of my senses.

'I'm going in,' I told him as I tucked my phone away in my pocket and opened the window all the way. 'Wait here.'

'You are joking?' Dev gasped, still stuck in the same position. 'Please tell me you're joking.'

This was not the kind of thing I would usually do. I didn't even like returning things to the shops because I was scared of judgemental sales assistants, but we were a long way from 'usual' right now. What was it they said? *Carpe Diem*. Eat the cake, wear the nice perfume, knee Santa in the balls, break into the stately home, if not now, when? And if my day was doomed to repeat itself for all eternity, the very least I could do was seize the shit out of it.

'Gwen,' Dev huffed, his body beginning to buckle under my feet. 'You're not really thinking about this are you?'

'Not really thinking at all,' I replied as I poured myself inside the house, Mum's jacket scratching against the sill, and landed in an undignified heap on the floor. Undignified but somehow unscathed. At least I was using this extra gift of time to get better at something, even if it was breaking into houses.

'Bloody hell,' I heard Dev mutter as a fluffy white face appeared in the open window. 'OK,' he said as I grabbed hold of a very excited-looking Pari. 'I'm coming in.'

Carefully placing Pari down on the floor, I stuck my head back out the window to see Dev backing up the path before taking a running jump at the house. I marvelled as he grabbed hold of the window frame, feet scrabbling against the 500-year-old stone walls, and pulled himself up and in.

'Impressive,' I remarked as he leaned against the wall, bent over double and panting as though he'd just run a marathon.

'Not to brag but I *have* been working out,' he gasped, flexing a very, very slender bicep. 'Promise you'll remind me never to try that again.'

'I promise to try to remind you,' I countered, smiling as Pari made herself comfortable underneath the Christmas tree and closed her eyes. We both felt like we were home.

From outside, the room looked lovely. On the inside, it was positively magical. The tree wasn't just big, it towered over me and as I gazed up at it, I felt all the years slip away. It was like being a little girl again, as though everything was possible and all my dreams could still come true.

Behind me, I heard Dev exhale.

'You should see the look on your face.'

'You should see the look on yours. Do you need a sit-down?' I replied, hiding my blushes behind my hair. 'Can you believe this is five minutes from our house and we almost missed it?'

'People don't always see what's right in front of them,' he replied lightly. 'Especially when it's been around forever.'

The corners of my mouth turned up but the smile didn't quite make it to my eyes. If Michael was to be believed, I was very good at that. I stroked a lush length of garland resting across the mantlepiece and raised my hands to my face. It smelled so fresh and green, as though it had been freshly cut that morning.

'Do you want a photo?' Dev offered. 'Or does my expert legal counsel think creating evidence a bad idea?'

'Worst idea ever,' I said with enthusiasm as I handed him my phone. 'But take a lot of different ones, I like to have options.'

He laughed, holding the phone expertly in one hand as I arranged myself in front of the fireplace, one leg kicked up behind me and my chin resting on the back of my hands.

'Nice, very nice,' he crouched down to get a new angle. 'It's giving modern Mrs Claus, it's giving "Santa Baby" the remix, it's giving I-just-broke-into-a-stately-home-would-you-like-a-cup-of-tea, I like it, I like it.'

'You're a very tolerant photographer,' I replied, offering up pose after pose as he snapped away. 'My ex hated taking photos, he never did more than one.'

'Welcome to the twenty-first century. He's going to struggle to get a new girlfriend if he doesn't know how to take a decent picture for Instagram,' Dev scoffed. 'Do you want a Boomerang?'

If he weren't engaged already, I would have proposed on the spot.

'Conveniently, he already had one before we broke up,' I said as breezily as humanly possible. 'I think she's more of a TikTok person. In that she's about twelve.'

Dev grimaced and dropped my phone down to his side. 'I'm sorry. He's clearly a terrible shithead.'

'So you've met him?' I replied, laughing.

After months of refusing to talk about him at all, it felt quite nice to drag Michael in a safe space. Metaphorical safe space, we were having this chat in the middle of a crime scene.

'It wasn't all on him, I have to take some of the blame. Not for the cheating, there's never an excuse for that,' I hastened to add. 'But he said some stuff that hit home a bit harder than I'd have liked.'

'Such as?' Dev asked, looking genuinely curious and not even the slightest bit judgemental. Not like the women on the returns desk in the Oxford Circus branch of Marks & Spencer who had apparently never bought a pair of work trousers in a rush then had to bring them back when they didn't fit.

'I'm a lawyer and sometimes I work very long hours,' I replied, feeling my way around this conversation. I took a moment while I searched for the right words, Dev nodding patiently to show he was with me. 'A while back, my boss told me I was being considered for a promotion, a huge promotion for someone my age, but that I'd have to take on more projects, volunteer for more stuff. Basically work twice as hard and twice as long until the big bosses decided I was worthy. Michael and I discussed it and he knew it wouldn't be like that forever, but it did mean I worked quite a lot of weekends, missed a few events here and there. Quite a few to be honest. He always said he was OK with it but . . .'

'But when it came to it, he didn't like you putting in all the extra hours?' Dev guessed.

'Turns out he wasn't that keen, no,' I said with a weak smile. 'I don't know. Maybe I should have given him more of a chance to have a say, maybe I wasn't really listening. He's perfectly within his rights to want to be with someone who isn't so focused on their career, isn't he?'

'And you're perfectly within your rights to be with someone who supports you in yours. Sometimes the things we want don't line up and you have to call it.'

'And sometimes people start shagging their receptionist instead of telling you that,' I replied. 'Things were good, once. He used to be supportive. I only wish I'd known that support was conditional.'

I sat down under the tree, beside Pari and scritched her behind her fluffy white ears.

'Obviously I'm biased, but it seems to me like he did you a favour.'

Dev sat down next to me and handed me my phone. I scrolled through the photos he'd taken, all of them perfectly framed, well-lit and shot from flattering angles. I was laughing and smiling in every single one. It was a long time since I'd seen a photo of myself where I looked so happy. I zoomed in on one of the photos, Dev's reflection caught in the mirror behind me. I wasn't the only one who looked happy.

'A really shitty favour wrapped up in a big "I'm a wanker" bow, but still,' he added. 'I am completely certain that you're better off without him.'

'And he's better off without me,' I laughed, looking up from my phone to see Dev staring at me.

'I can't imagine a world where anyone could be better off without you,' he said softly.

My eyes trailed up his body, the brown leather boots, his long denim-clad legs, the grey wool coat that draped perfectly over his broad shoulders. And then there was that face. Even after all the nights I spent lying in bed as a teenager, wondering what he would look like when we were grown up, I could never have come up with something so perfect. The lopsided smile, the dimple in his left cheek, the lock of hair that insisted on falling forwards no matter how many times he pushed it back, and those beautiful, beautiful eyes. Deep and dark and black-treacle brown, glowing with golden sparks as they locked with mine, a slight crease in his brow as though he was searching for something he hadn't expected to find.

'We should probably go,' I whispered, suddenly aware

that we were sitting awfully close together. 'Before someone hears us.'

Twisting around to take one last look at the tree, I shook off whatever it was that had come over me. Dev was engaged. As much fun as it might be, reviving a teenage crush wasn't going to help me move on and I wasn't looking to set myself up for two broken hearts in one calendar year. Down by my feet, Pari turned her head sharply and let out a short, sharp bark.

'Hush, Pari,' I hissed as she began growling at the closed door at the end of the room. 'You'll get us into trouble.'

Dev scooped up the excitable little dog and jumped to his feet as she started to yap over and over again. 'Come on,' he said, the threat of footsteps echoing down the corridor. 'We'd better get out of here.'

Still crouched down, I rushed to the open window, hoping I was even better at breaking out of a house than I was at breaking in. Without looking down, I climbed out, one leg and then the other, before hurling myself to the ground, landing on my hands and knees and rolling onto my side in time to see Dev launch Pari out of the window.

'Catch!' he called as she sailed through the air, legs kicking before landing on my stomach with a happy yelp, merrily licking my face.

'Coast seems clear,' I called, scrambling to my feet and spinning around to check every direction. 'Jump!'

But Dev did not jump.

Instead, he slipped both legs out the window then hung from the windowsill, his knuckles turning white as his feet scraped against the wall of the house.

'Stop kicking your legs and drop!' I hissed. 'It's not far, you're fine.'

'It's too far!' he shouted, legs still flailing around in the air. 'Will you catch me?'

'No, because you're twice my size and it's only a three-foot drop,' I howled. 'Dev, let go of the bloody window before we get caught.'

With an otherworldly wail, he dropped the whole three feet and landed flat on his backside.

'Maybe a four-foot drop,' I corrected as I pulled him upright. 'Five at best.'

'I can't breathe,' he gasped, patting himself down. 'I think I've broken my arse.'

'Dev, you are a doctor, you cannot break your arse. You're winded, that's all, you just need to walk it off.'

With absolutely no time for patience, I dragged him away from the house and across the grass as his breath came back in short, sharp bursts.

'Better?'

He nodded, limping, as his staccato breathing evened out and a man's head popped out of the open window above us.

'Oi!' he shouted. 'You two, stop!'

'Running it off would be even better,' I suggested, bolting away from the house at top speed. Pari leapt out of my arms and galloped ahead of us, proudly yipping at the top of her little lungs as we chased her, running as fast as we could.

'Which way should we go?' I asked, neon sparks flashing at the edges of my vision, my breath coming hard and fast.

'Doesn't matter,' Dev replied, catching my hand in his. 'Just keep going.'

My legs screamed with every step and every shallow breath I took scorched my lungs. If I was going to take up a life of crime, I was going to have to improve my cardio, I could barely speed-walk to Starbucks without passing out. But when I looked over at Dev, I saw a huge smile on his face and hope surged through me, firing up my tired muscles. We raced across the fields, wild and free and only feeling a little bit like I might be sick, putting one foot in front of the other until I couldn't tell if we were still running away or just running.

'I can't believe we did that,' Dev gasped, looking over his shoulder. 'Is he following us?'

'I don't think so,' I replied, slowing down only enough to look behind me, the house nothing but a dot in the distance. 'I can't tell.'

Even if he was, it didn't matter.

With Dev beside me, I felt as though I could run forever.

CHAPTER THIRTEEN

In the hours after Dev and I made our daring escape, I kept my phone close, still checking it every two minutes as I shovelled a third helping of turkey down my throat, searching for news reports about exceptionally good-looking people breaking into any stately homes, having a jolly good time and politely leaving in a timely fashion. So far, so nothing. Bonnie and Clyde, Mickey and Mallory, and now Gwen and Dev, two outlaws who played by their own rules, did what they wanted, when they wanted, but also made sure they were home in time for dinner.

A text from Dev popped up on the screen and I opened it immediately.

Can't believe we did that. I'm here until Tuesday, let me know if you've got time to hold up a bank/ get coffee x

'What are you smiling at?' Manny asked as I slid my phone into my dress pocket.

'TikTok of baby capybaras in Santa hats,' I replied before turning to my sister. 'Cerys, how about you and me pop down to the pub for a drink after dinner?'

The entire table fell silent.

Cerys stared at me as though I'd suggested we nip out to tar and feather Mr Regal at number 43.

'What did you just say?'

'I asked if you'd like to go to the pub after dinner.'

As unappealing as the idea of sitting in a room, alone with my sister, might be, it still beat the thought of starting the day over from scratch again. Best-case scenario, she made the wish, I made it come true, we all woke up on Boxing Day ready to gorge ourselves on my dad's famously rank turkey enchiladas. Worst-case scenario, she continued to find fault with everything I'd ever done and I got back from the pub just in time to chuck myself on the fireworks again.

'I thought it might be fun to put in some sister time,' I added. 'Have a catch-up.'

Whatever I was selling, Cerys was not buying.

'We have never been to the pub together in our entire lives and you want to start today?'

'You should go!' Mum practically screamed, banging a hand against the table, her eyes feverish with excitement. This was it, the sisterly bonding moment she'd been waiting for her entire life. Daughters who went on holiday together and wore matching pyjamas and texted each other to say something other than 'Are you going to Mum and Dad's on Father's Day or should I?'

'You should go,' Mum said again, more forcefully. An order not a suggestion. 'We'll look after the kids. And Oliver.'

A quick check on my brother-in-law, who was currently loosening his belt buckle by three whole notches, suggested the latter would be more of a challenge than the former.

'Fine.' Cerys flicked away a speck of dry mascara and continued to stare me down. 'One drink.'

'You never know,' I replied, savouring my turkey in the hopes that I wouldn't be eating it again for another year. 'You might even enjoy yourself.'

'Stranger things have happened.'

A chunk of dry white meat stuck in my throat and I coughed it down, banging on my chest and trying not to laugh.

'Oh, Care,' I chuckled as I dabbed at my watering eyes. 'You don't know how right you are.'

The walk to the pub was frosty in more ways than one. Cerys was silent the entire way except for the seven minutes she spent complaining about the Derbyshire mizzle ruining her new suede handbag and the only time I managed to stay silent was when I stopped myself from asking why she'd brought a new suede handbag to walk to the pub in the first place.

'What'll you have?' I asked, holding the door open and following her inside. The Baslow Arms wasn't especially busy, we'd finished lunch early and the afternoon crowd hadn't filtered in yet, a few overly keen regulars were propping up the bar and, I assumed, people who ate their Christmas dinner in the evening. AKA total weirdos.

'Whatever's drinkable,' Cerys replied. 'Which probably doesn't leave me with many options.'

'I seem to remember the sauvignon blanc was OK but I haven't had it since I was about seventeen so don't hold me to it.'

We walked over to a small round table in the corner, squeezed between the roaring fire and the bay window. I shrugged off my borrowed scarf and coat, hanging them on a hook on the wall, while Cerys took the chair closest to the fire. Her coat remained on.

'Nothing says a sophisticated taste in wine like underage drinking. I'll have a gin and tonic. Hopefully they can't find a way to fuck that up.'

'Gin and tonic it is,' I repeated, bowing under the Sisyphean weight of the task at hand. 'Are you going to take off your coat?'

'No.'

'Why?'

'I don't want to.'

I inhaled deeply through my nose and refreshed my smile.

'You won't feel the benefit when we leave!'

Cerys lifted her chin, her features impassive and inscrutable.

'I'm not planning to be here that long.'

'Two gin and tonics, coming right up,' I said, clapping my hands together and heading over to the bar.

Very few things in life were one hundred per cent guaranteed to bring me joy no matter what the circumstances. A hot bath full of bubbles, that video of Tom Holland dancing to Rihanna, correcting people who don't realize Taylor Swift writes her own songs were reliable examples of solid serotonin boosters, but there were few things in life as wonderful as ordering a gin and tonic in a cosy country pub. The pub hadn't changed much from when we were teenagers, me and Manny and Dev sitting at the wooden tables outside, taking it in turns to attempt to get served. My memories were a patchwork of freshly faked student IDs, too many vodka lime and sodas, and asking Manny to put Katy Perry on the jukebox then running over to change it to something cooler whenever a boy from the Upper Sixth walked in. My liver turned as I rested my elbows on the polished brass rail, a Pavlovian response to the sight of a bottle of cinnamon Aftershock behind the bar.

'What'll it be?' asked the charmingly gruff bartender.

'Two gin and tonics, please,' I said, smiling politely.

'Any preference on the gin?'

'Hendrick's?' I replied, wondering if I should have asked Cerys what kind of gin she wanted.

I paid for the drinks, optimistically leaving my tab open, and carried them back to our table. It was starting to fill up a bit, happy people slotting into their usual spots, laughing, joking and generally looking full of festive spirit.

And then there was Cerys.

'OK, out with it, what do you want?' She took a sip of her drink and stuck out her tongue. 'What's in this, hairspray? It's rancid.'

I *knew* I should have asked Cerys what kind of gin she wanted.

'Hendrick's,' I replied. If this tasted like hairspray, I'd wasted an awful lot of money on gin over the years when I could have been chugging cans of Elnett for the last decade. 'I don't want anything. I thought it would be nice for us to get out of the house for a bit, that's all.'

She wound the end of her ponytail around her finger, her shoulders hunched in on themselves as she valiantly forced her drink down. Her hair, which she had pulled up in a casual-chic chignon for lunch, had been hastily restyled when Arthur decided he needed to remove all the carefully positioned hair grips while we were eating and Cerys decided not to fight him on it. Now her thick black hair was yanked up and back into a ponytail so tight, just looking at it gave me a headache, with several unruly wisps frizzing up around her temples from our cold weather walk.

We didn't look alike, not really, but there were whispers of each other in our faces if you knew where to look. I had Dad's round eyes and Cerys had Mum's almond shape, but both pairs were inclined to narrow with suspicion as a default setting. Her lips were full with a perfect cupid's bow and spent a lot of time pursed together, while my smile was broad and easy but, according to all the Instagram ads I ignored daily, could use a shot or two of filler. Only our noses were identical, inherited directly from Nan. Small and narrow and a nightmare come hay fever season. I'd always felt mine was too petite for my heart-shaped face but on Cerys, it was perfect, balancing out her natural femme fatale features. In another life, she would have been a movie star, wandering into a private detective's office, wearing a big hat and begging Humphrey Bogart to find out what happened to her missing eighty-year-old millionaire husband. I'd be the secretary with one line of dialogue, secretly in love with Bogey and sat outside his office for the entire picture typing up nonsense.

'Why are you staring at me? Cerys asked, raising a reflexive hand up to her face. 'Are you trying to make me feel weird?'

'Why would I be trying to make you feel weird?' I combed my own unruly hair behind my ears, checking my wrist for an elastic band before remembering I'd used it to give Pari a ponytail before sending her home with Dev. 'Is it really that impossible for you to believe I just want to spend some time with you?'

She slammed her glass down on the table.

'Oh my God, you're pregnant and you want me to tell Mum and Dad.'

'Cerys, it would be a literal miracle,' I scoffed. 'Do you really think they'd choose me to bring the second coming of Christ into the world? The closest I've come to a spiritual experience is the second series of *Fleabag*.'

'Are you dying?' she asked with an ugly squint. 'Are you very ill?'

'I'm not ill, I'm not dying and the only immaculate conception I know anything about is Madonna's greatest hits album,' I assured her. 'All I wanted was to get out of the house and catch up with my sister. I want to hear about you, what's new with Cerys?'

She wrapped her hands around the glass and took a long, considered gulp.

'You're lying.'

I should have known she wasn't going to make this easy.

'How's work?' I asked, tipping half of my G&T into her empty glass. Unlike me, Cerys had inherited Mum's ability to put away the booze and since she refused to be convinced of my semi-altruistic motives, I figured my best line of attack was to simply get her drunk and get her talking.

'Fine.'

'And how are the kids? Doing well in school?'

'Well enough.'

'And things with Oliver, are they good?'

She nodded.

'Fuck me, Cerys. I feel like your mum asking about your day at school.' I rolled my head all the way back, arms folded in frustration. 'You're not going to give me anything?'

Her full lips puckered into the smallest possible pout as a Christmas medley began to play through the pub speakers. I waited patiently, head bobbing along to 'Do They Know It's Christmas?', while she stared at the wall behind my head.

'If you're that desperate to know, I'll tell you,' she said after two verses and a bridge, pouring the rest of my gin into her glass. 'The business is struggling because we expanded too quickly but Oliver won't sack anybody because he thinks it's "bad optics". We're mortgaged up to the tits on the new house and can't afford the three cars he insists we need but again, try telling Oliver. On top of that, I'm paying ten grand a term to put two kids through a school they hate, where they're learning absolutely nothing other than how to come home, tell me how awful I am then turn around and demand the newest iPhone and a pony.'

She picked up her glass and knocked it back in one.

'I'll go and get another round, shall I?' I suggested as she dropped her head into her hands and sobbed.

'Yes please,' she snuffled into her coat sleeves. 'And make mine a double.'

* * *

The whole time I was waiting at the bar, I wracked my brains for the right thing to say. I had two degrees, spent at least two hours a day absorbing all the wisdom Instagram had to offer and as everyone who had ever met me already knew, once, at a Q&A about *Hamilton*, I asked a question and Lin Manuel Miranda said I raised a good point. But right now when I was most needed, I couldn't come up with a single helpful thing.

'I'm sorry,' I said, handing Cerys a very full glass on my return. 'Is there anything I can do to help?'

The deafening pitch of her laughter was so loud, she not only attracted the attention of every single person in the pub, I was also fairly certain I could hear a car alarm going off in Huddersfield.

'You want to help me?' she wheezed, wiping at the edges of her eyes. 'Oh, I forgot how funny you are sometimes. No, Gwen, I don't imagine there is. It doesn't matter, it'll all be fine.'

'Wow.'

'Wow what?'

I gave her a small smile. 'You sound just like Dad.'

She slid her glass around in slow circles, condensation from the base shining up the dull, dark wood. 'I suppose I do. That must be where I learned it.'

'To be self-sufficient?'

'To live in denial.'

She didn't know how right she was.

'Quite good at that myself as it turns out,' I replied. 'I wish he'd passed on his uncanny ability to know which queue to choose at the supermarket instead.'

Cerys inhaled deeply then let out a long, noisy sigh.

'Please pretend I didn't say anything,' she said. 'I'll work it out, I always do.'

We sat across from each other, Cerys staring into her glass as though the solutions to her problems were hiding in an ice cube and me staring at the window, hoping they might fall from the sky. This had to be the wish, the reason I was stuck here. My sister needed help but what advice could I give? I was a childless, car-less woman, so bad with money, I once spent two hundred pounds on a mint condition vintage Mr Frosty on eBay when I was drunk. It wasn't even mint condition when it arrived, there was a crack in his little blue hat. I'd never been so disappointed in my life. Still thinking about the epic crappiness of the Mr Frosty, a radical thought blew through my mind. What if, instead of trying to tell Cerys what to do, I just listened instead?

'Would it help to talk about it?' I asked.

She closed her eyes and pulled the elastic band out of her ponytail, letting her thick black hair fall around her shoulders, and when she opened them, it was as though someone had asked her to describe the colour of grass and she was shocked to discover it was still green.

'It would help if you could get Oliver to listen,' Cerys said, still a little reticent. 'Every month there's more money going out than coming in but he won't have it. Every time I try to bring it up, he tells me we have to speculate to accumulate but I'm not sure that's the sound business advice he thinks it is. The only thing we're accumulating now is debt and I'm speculating about doing him in with a shovel.'

'And he's determined to keep the kids in their fancy school?'

Cerys nodded. 'He went to Queens so the kids have to go to Queens, doesn't matter that I went to the local comprehensive, he is insistent. I wouldn't mind so much if they didn't both hate it. All Arthur wants to do is sit in his room and read and Artemis would do well anywhere, she's terrifyingly sharp. Last week she asked me whether she'd have more power if she was a billion-aire, prime minister or if she married the next in line to the throne and I swear to God, Gwen, she was not joking.'

'What did you tell her?'

'I said why not all three and I'm more than a bit worried I've set the world on a very dark path.'

Swirling my drink in its glass, I watched the ice cubes clink against one another and fought the urge to impart my non-existent wisdom. It was time to let Cerys talk.

'I suppose I should be grateful she's got ambition, life isn't going to be easy for her,' she said, absently twisting her wedding ring around her finger. I noticed she wasn't wearing her Adlington family heirloom engagement ring but again, said nothing.

'At least not until she becomes Her Royal Highness, Prime Minister Artemis Windsor,' I replied. 'Do you think we'll all get to move into Buckingham Palace or should I start looking at the other available royal residences?'

Cerys's eyes softened just a little and she started to smile. 'She's not that different to me, I suppose, very focused, knows what she wants to do. I was the same when I was her age.'

'You wanted to be a billionaire dictator when you were nine?'

'Yes,' she replied, looking at me with surprise. 'You didn't?'

'When I was nine I wanted to be an author or a professional wrestler. Can't believe neither career worked out.'

'There's still time,' she said. 'Never give up on a dream.'

'Can't see me leaping off the top rope at this point but you never know,' I replied sadly. 'Did you really know you wanted to be a lawyer when you were that little?'

A big, genuine smile stretched all the way across her face.

'Without a doubt. When Mum was pregnant with you she was really poorly, morning, noon and night sickness for the whole nine months, so I used to go to work with Dad over the summer holidays.' She rested one elbow on the table, propping up her head, a dreamy look on her face as though she was recounting a love story, not the tale of a child being made to hang out in a local solicitors five days a week for six whole weeks in the summer. 'He put an extra desk in his office and I'd sit there watching while he went through his cases and I thought he must be the most important man in the whole world. All these people coming to him for help and asking him to fix their problems. You're going to laugh but I thought he was a hero, like he was Batman or something.'

She was right, I did laugh.

'A five-foot-seven Batman from Ilkley? Can't believe they haven't made a movie about him yet.'

'Maybe that's your book,' she replied with a grin before picking up her gin. 'Anyway, that's when I knew I wanted to work in law too. He always found the solution to a problem and I wanted to feel that way about the world.

What about you? When did you know you wanted to be queen of the world at Abbott & Howe?'

'I don't think there was a specific "A-ha" moment,' I admitted, searching my subconscious for an epiphany of any kind as Cerys snuffled a laugh into her glass. 'I just sort of did it.'

'You just sort of did it? What's that supposed to mean?'

'Silver Bells' tinkled into life over the speakers and I shrugged, keeping my shoulders halfway up to my ears.

'I don't know. Dad was a solicitor and you were a solicitor and I was good at all the right subjects.' I tapped the stem of my glass, keeping time with Bing Crosby. 'I knew I didn't want to be a teacher like Mum, nothing else was really calling out to me and everyone kept saying I should do a law degree, so I did.'

'Typical,' Cerys laughed softly. 'I should have known.'

'What's that supposed to mean?' I asked, my defences prickling.

'Do you have any idea how hard I have to work to keep my head above water while you coast along?' she asked, pulling the elastic band off her wrist and retying her hair into a ponytail so high, it pulled her entire face up with it. 'I slogged my guts out at school but what did it matter? Who cared about my exam results? Nobody. I was expected to do well while Mum and Dad dealt with you and Manny. I worked my arse off to get into Oxford and you're telling me you got better grades than me, a better degree than me and a better job than I did by accident? I don't know what would be worse, if you were lying or telling the truth.'

'That's not what I meant at all,' I said, trying to dig myself out of whatever hole I seemed to have fallen into.

'I only meant there wasn't any grand plan for me. Half the reason I did a law degree was to impress you.'

Now that really did make her laugh.

'Come off it, Gwen. As soon as Manny moved in, none of you would have noticed if I'd run off to join the circus.'

'That's not true at all,' I said. 'It wasn't like that.'

'It was exactly like that,' she replied. 'And now all I hear from Dad is how amazing it is that you got a job at a Magic Circle firm, nothing I do can compete.'

I tried to keep my mouth shut, I really did, but I just couldn't help myself.

'As if my job could even come close to competing with you and your perfect kids,' I snapped back. 'They've written me off as a sad old spinster at thirty-two.'

'God, I'm so sick of hearing about you getting dumped!' she exclaimed. 'You're not the first person on earth to go through a break-up. You're so used to everyone pandering to you, that's the problem. Baby of the family, everyone's favourite, poor little Gwen.'

Cerys always knew exactly how to set me off. It was a good job we'd never come up against each other at work; wailing 'I know you are but what am I?' then crying in the toilets never went over well with a judge.

'I am not the favourite!' I argued, extremely close to tears. 'They always paid more attention to you and Manny than they did to me and I never complained. I'm trying to fix things and you won't even let me.'

'Can you even hear yourself?' She lowered her voice to a mocking hiss. '*Nobody likes me, everybody hates me, I'm just going to study law*?'

I pushed my hair back from my face, trying to work out how we'd got here.

'Why are you so angry with me? All I said was I didn't grow up dreaming about being a lawyer.'

Cerys pushed her chair away from the table and stood up.

'Maybe that's why you're so happy to throw it all away now.'

I stared at her and she stared at me, each of us as stubborn as the other. Finally, she turned away, tutting loudly as she grabbed her handbag.

'Don't go!' I pleaded, jumping up to my own feet. We were so close to getting somewhere, even if I wasn't quite sure where that somewhere might be. 'Please don't leave, Care, I really want to talk about this.'

'Can you calm down?' she whispered, slipping off her coat and draping it over the back of her chair. 'I'm going to the toilet.'

'Oh,' I said, sitting down slowly. 'OK.'

'Drama queen,' she said, rolling her eyes. 'Try not to spill your drink on my coat like you spilt your tea on my Sweater Shop top.'

'It was twenty-five years ago!' I called after her.

She would never, ever let that go as long as she lived.

Moving my glass away from the edge of the table, I took a gulp of gin and looked out the window at the heavy white clouds. I'd spent years trying to live up to Cerys's example, earn her approval, and all this time she thought I'd been trying to outdo her. She was half the reason I'd gone into law in the first place, Dad being the other half. But what did that leave for me? I thought of all the things I'd inherited or learned from my family, my wavy hair, my round eyes, a superhuman ability to bottle up my emotions and a digestive tract that did not care for too much dairy. If only you could pick and choose your own traits or at least tailor them to your own needs.

'Don't use the toilets if you can help it.' Cerys sat back down at the table and squirted herself with hand sanitizer, a grim look on her face. 'Plus, someone left the door open to the basement; if you do have to go, try not to fall down and break your neck. Although if you did fall, we could sue, they're a death trap. So, Mum said you're living in a flat over a shop? That's depressing.'

'You're just going to change the subject?' I replied, opening my palms to her as she held out the little squeezy bottle. 'Pretend the last ten minutes never happened?'

'Ideally, yes.'

It really would be easier that way. Finish our drinks and go back to a comfortable, simmering resentment, but what was the point? Changing our relationship would be hard but whoever said worthwhile changes were easy?

'I know I haven't been the world's best sister,' I said, forcing out the words the same way I'd forced myself to eat Brussels sprouts every year. I didn't like them, I didn't want them but I knew it was the right thing to do. 'But I'm going to do better. I want to spend more time together, I want to know what's going on in your life.'

'Are you sure you aren't dying?' Cerys asked with suspicion.

'Almost positive,' I nodded. 'What if I came to stay with you and the kids for a few days? Or we could go somewhere like Center Parcs all together, I bet Dad would bloody love that. Or I could look after the kids while you and Oliver go to Paris for a romantic weekend away, that might help you two?'

'Are you trying to make things better or worse?' she said, shaking her head. 'If I went to Paris with Oliver right now, only one of us would come back alive. You can stop trying so hard, Gwen, you've made your point.'

'My point is I should already know all this stuff that's going on with you,' I exclaimed, ignoring the judgemental looks from the ladies at the next table for raising my voice. God help me, it was two of the women from Mum's aqua-aerobics group. I was in for it when this got back to her, Bakers did not air their dirty laundry in public. 'I should know your stuff and you should know mine and neither of us should be ashamed or embarrassed or trying to score points off each other. I can't go back in time and fix how we felt when we were kids but I can change how we feel today.'

'No, you can only change how *you* feel,' Cerys replied, pulling the sleeves of her dress over her fingers the same way I did when I was uncomfortable. 'You can't control other people's emotions.'

'But I can try to understand them,' I reasoned. 'And I can want them to be different. That's half the battle, isn't it? Understanding why things are the way they are and working to make a change?'

Cerys dropped her head back and groaned. 'So what? Now you're not just younger than me, cleverer than me and prettier than me, you're more insightful as well? How very dare you.'

'I am not prettier than you,' I scoffed. 'And I wasn't trying to be more anything I—'

'Gwen, I'm joking,' Cerys interrupted me with an unexpected laugh. 'You're right. You know I hate to admit it but you're right.' She took my hand off my glass and covered it with her own. 'And don't worry, I know you're not prettier than me.'

'You're such a bitch,' I whispered, turning my hand over to give hers a squeeze.

'A jealous bitch,' she corrected with a rueful smile. 'I'm so jealous of you, I can hardly stand it. I sit at home at night and I think about you living this amazing life in London with your incredible job and your glamorous friends and your gorgeous boyfriend, who admittedly turned out to be a wanker but still. I'm up here juggling Oliver and the kids and the business *and* trying to make sure we don't run out of toilet paper and there's nothing left for me. I mean, where does it go? What do they do with all that loo roll? Are they eating it? There's never enough, no matter how much I buy. This isn't the life I dreamed of and I took it out on you.'

'Michael used to go through a four-pack a week,' I said, delighted. 'Just him, on his own. One week I kept my own roll in the drawer under the sink to see how much he was using and it was nuts. I was genuinely worried there was something wrong with his insides but now I realize he just shits a lot.'

Cerys laughed again, a true, heartfelt cackle and it was the best sound I'd heard in ages.

'Four rolls in a *week*?' she replied. 'I hope his new missus is the heir to the Andrex fortune.'

'I hope he shits them out of house and home,' I replied smiling when she laughed again. 'He's *literally* full of shit, Care.'

She wiped her eyes with her sleeve, leaving black smears on her grey sleeve.

'Oliver got one of those Japanese toilets installed in our bathroom but he set the jet too high and it went up his arse and scared him so much he only uses the downstairs loo now. I hear him in the middle of the night, running down the stairs to make it in time.'

'Can't you turn the jet down a bit?' I asked.

'I turned it off months ago but why tell him that?' I recognized the look on her face as that of someone who took great comfort in winning life's small battles. 'I know he's not perfect, but we've been together for eighteen years, we've got kids, we've got a business. I always thought things would get less complicated when I got older, but it really is the opposite.'

She sat across from me nursing her drink, and instead of my older sister, I saw a younger version of our mother. A woman so frustrated with life, she was throwing down with a woman over leeks in Tesco. I didn't want to watch Cerys end up in the same place.

'You're hardly one foot in the grave,' I said, treading lightly. 'You're not even forty yet, you've got everything in front of you.'

'There are no simple choices once you've got kids,' she replied, matter-of-factly. 'And I don't mean that in a smug "You couldn't possibly understand" way, it just is what it is. Every decision I make, I have to make it with three people in mind. Would I love to get up, call in sick and sod off to Paris for the day? Totally. But who would take the kids to school? Who would pick them up? Who would remember whether it's football practice or ballet lessons or coding class?'

'Arthur plays football?' I asked.

'No, they're all Artemis. She's keeping her options

open in case she decides to bring down civilization via sports, the arts or tech.'

I really did need to get to know my niece better before she became the global supreme ruler and banished me to live on an oil rig with the deposed royal family.

'Can I ask you something?' Cerys said as I quietly wondered if any of the Windsors were better cooks than me. Fingers crossed. Deliveroo probably didn't drop off in the north Atlantic.

'Anything,' I replied.

'Do you like working at Abbott & Howe? Do you like your job?'

'That's a weird question,' I said, huffing out an almost laugh. 'It's a brilliant job, isn't it? Lucky to have it, everyone says so.'

'Right,' she turned her lips inwards, the edges turning upwards but not quite making a smile. 'I'm sorry about earlier. I shouldn't have said what I said. You're not responsible for the way Mum and Dad made me feel or for the way I make myself feel. I want to try harder as well.'

'You want to go on a family holiday to Center Parcs?' I asked hopefully.

'I'd rather kill myself,' she said kindly. 'But maybe we can make this pub thing a regular event.'

We sat quietly, drinking our gin in companionable silence. It was only when the snow began to fall, I realized what time it was. My drink was almost empty when Cerys's phone dinged inside her not-even-slightly-stained suede handbag.

'It's Mum,' she said, tapping out a reply without showing me the text. 'Checking to see if we've killed each other.'

'Tell her yes but I put up a good fight,' I replied, watching the snow start to gather on the ruby red Royal Mail post box across the street. 'Care?'

'Gwen?'

'If you got the sixpence in the Christmas pudding, what would you wish for?'

'No idea. I never get the sixpence because I never actually eat the pudding.' She put her phone away and took a deep breath in. 'I take it so Mum doesn't whine about it. But if I had got it, I'd wish to know why they're here.'

She nodded across the bar and I turned around to see two uniformed policemen walk up to the bar, speaking to the landlord in hushed tones.

'Oh shit,' I whispered as they all looked over in our direction at the exact same moment.

'What's wrong?' Cerys leaned back in her chair, glass in hand, temporarily without a care in the world. 'Worried they've come to take you away?'

'You're going to think I'm joking but yes, I am,' I replied, scooping up my coat and bag. 'I'm going to nip to the loo, if they come over here, tell them I went home.'

'Gwen, what are you talking about? Where are you going?' Cerys asked, eyes wide with alarm. 'What have you done?'

'Nothing.' I slipped out of my seat and onto my hands and knees, crawling around the back of her chair. 'Don't worry about it.'

'You just asked me to lie to the police and now you're on your way to hide from them in a pub toilet that is quite frankly unsanitary to say the very least,' she hissed, snatching at the collar of my dress. 'Tell me what is going on.'

'Gwen Baker?'

I looked up to see the two police officers, one man and one woman, glaring down at me. The woman looked slightly more stern than the man, but he looked more annoyed to be working at all on Christmas Day, so it didn't really feel as though I had a friend in either of them.

'Yes?' I squeaked from the floor.

'We'd like to speak with you in regard to a break-in at Chatsworth House this morning, would you mind coming with us?'

'You broke into Chatsworth House?' Cerys bellowed. 'Gwen Baker, are you on drugs?'

'No, Cerys,' I replied before smiling broadly at the officers as I rose to my feet. 'I am not on drugs and what's more, oh no, what's that outside the window!'

I was the clever one. The one who always had a plan. Except when it came to choosing what to do with her life, recognizing problems in her relationships and running away from the police. Everything flashed bright red as I hurtled towards the toilets, skipping around pub tables with hastily delivered 'excuse me's and 'beg your pardon's.

'Stop!' called the policeman. 'Stop right where you are!'

But I couldn't stop, momentum had got the best of me. Just as I reached out my arm to open the door to the ladies, the door to the ladies opened out towards me, knocking me off balance and sending me flying across the room.

Fantastic, I thought as I toppled backwards. Not only am I going to be arrested, I'm going to be arrested in the pub on Christmas Day in front of the women from my mother's aqua-aerobics class and I'm going to fall flat on my arse before they carry me away in handcuffs.

Only, instead of hitting the floor, I carried on spiralling backwards as though the ground had opened to swallow me up. It was only when I caught a flash of the terrified face of the policewoman on my way down, I realized what had happened. I had fallen through the open door to the steps to the pub basement.

Just like Cerys had said, they were a death trap.

Before I even had time to cry out for help, everything went black and Christmas number six was over.

CHAPTER FOURTEEN

My hands were still shaking when I woke up in bed the next morning.

'What are you doing still in bed, chicken?' Dad asked, popping his head around the door. '*He's been.*'

'He can't bloody stay away!' I shouted, throwing off the covers and leaping across the room. 'No, sorry, absolutely not. I'm not doing this again.'

'Doing what?' Dad stood on the landing, utterly nonplussed, as I pulled a jumper over my pyjamas and grabbed my handbag off the chest of drawers.

'All of it!' I replied. 'Christmas is cancelled!'

Not stopping to explain further, I dashed downstairs, grabbed a bacon roll and my dad's car keys and flew out the back door.

With my foot flat on the floor and hunched over the steering wheel like a less stylish (but more puppy-friendly) Cruella de Vil, I hurtled around the Peak District in my dad's car, aimless and directionless, both metaphorically and literally, since I hadn't bothered to bring my phone. The roads were

227

practically deserted as I sped up hill and down dale, circling reservoirs, occasionally honking at terrified ramblers with bits of tinsel woven around their walking sticks, and blasting Steven Baker's in-car CD collection out of the open windows. Nothing said confused, angry and possibly trapped in an eternal time loop like two Coldplay albums, The Best of U2 and the soundtrack to *The Greatest Showman*. The perfect soundtrack to my mental state.

What was I going to do? What if I was stuck here forever? There was so much more I wanted to do with my life. I wanted to fall in love again, I wanted to see the world, I wanted to know if The Rock would ever be president. This couldn't be it for me, it just couldn't. After three hours of driving, singing, laughing maniacally and occasionally sobbing, the car began to slow down. I jammed my foot on the accelerator but nothing happened. The engine sputtered, the car lurched forward for a few feet more then rolled to a complete stop.

Note to self, cars need petrol, I thought, cringing at the sight of the little orange needle hovering accusingly over the bright red E on the fuel gauge. High tech, high speech, Hyundai, my arse.

There was only one thing I could do and that was throw a tantrum.

The car rocked from side to side on the quiet country road as I thrashed around, restrained only by my seat-belt, beating my fists against the steering wheel and screaming at the top of my lungs. It wasn't fair, none of it was fair. I was trying so hard to help Mum and Dad and Cerys. I didn't push Michael in front of a car or anything, why was I being punished like this? When I was finally done, I opened my eyes, panting, and saw three sheep stood in front of the car, each looking less impressed than the last.

'Do you have a better idea?' I asked.

One of the sheep leaned down to grab a mouthful of grass and chewed slowly while the other two continued to stare at me.

'Oh, sod off,' I yelled, leaning on the horn, pressing it over and over and over until the woolly chorus of judgement dispersed. 'Sod off, sod off, sod off, sod off—'

A loud rattle on the passenger side window was enough to scare me out of my skin. An older man in a flat cap glared at me as I jumped so high, I hit my head on the roof of the car. His walking stick and backpack said 'rambler' but the fact we were on our own in the middle of nowhere added a fun frisson of 'serial killer' and I quickly locked all the doors with my elbow.

'Excuse me!' the man shouted when I did not wind down the window. 'Are you in trouble?'

Exactly the sort of thing a serial killer would say.

'Oh, no, I'm fine, thanks for asking,' I said loudly, looking around the front of the car for a weapon. Maybe I could chuck a Coldplay CD at him. Maybe I could play one of the Coldplay CDs. It would be enough to scare me away.

'You do realize that according to the highway code, a car horn should only be used to indicate danger,' the man said, his white mutton chops only adding to his stern demeanour. 'It very clearly states the horn should not be used to express annoyance.'

'Is that right?' I replied as my fear boiled away into irritation.

'Yes. Rule number 112, you can look it up in the copy I'm sure you have in your glovebox.'

He was not a serial killer but a do-gooder which was somehow even worse.

'So what you're saying is, I shouldn't press it now?' I said, hand hovering over the horn. 'When I am in fact very annoyed?'

'One should only use the horn to indicate danger,' he repeated, chest puffed out like one of the racing pigeons I was very certain he kept at home. 'I can't see anything that puts you directly in harm's way.'

'No but I can see something that puts you directly in harm's way,' I warned, the heel of my hand slamming into the horn over and over and over.

'This is a nice village, we won't stand for the likes of you!' he threatened as he backed away, taking long, speedy strides. 'I shall call the police!'

'Call them!' I shouted as he clambered over a stile and began to run-walk away, the most embarrassing of all walks. 'Go on, see if I care!' Collapsing against my dad's beaded seat cushion, I closed my eyes and stamped my slippered feet in the footwell. 'Please call them,' I muttered when he had disappeared from sight. 'It's the only bloody way I'll get home.'

Predictably, the angry rambler turned out to be nothing more than another man full of empty promises. After a whole hour of waiting for the authorities, I gave up, and abandoned the car at the side of the road. Without my phone, and entirely incapable of reading a map, I had no idea where I was, but my old pal, the highway code fanboy, had mentioned a village nearby and while it might be a nice village that wouldn't stand for the likes of me, I suspected it would still have a payphone that was less picky about its patrons. Armed with my car keys and eighty pence in change I'd found on the floor under the passenger seat, I set off to find help.

The skies were clearer on this side of the hills, fewer clouds in the sky and more patches of bright blue with long, hazy rays of winter sun shining down on the bare trees. It was beautiful really, cool and crisp and peaceful, the kind of day that gave life meaning. If you were the sort of person who actually had a life and weren't caught in an endless cycle of bickering siblings, vibrators from their dad and pigs in blankets. In spite of my promise not to think romantic thoughts about a taken man, I couldn't stop myself from wishing Dev was with me. If I ever got myself out of this situation, it might be nice to have an old friend back in my life. Cambridge wasn't that far from London, we enjoyed vaguely criminal activities, why shouldn't we be friends? It was entirely possible for two grown adults to enjoy a platonic relationship even if one of the two once used a rudimentary computer program to see what their future children would look like and had developed a mild but more recent obsession with his forearms. I might even like his fiancée, I thought as I followed the path of the rambler, hopping over the stile in my slippers. She was probably a wonderful person, the kind of woman who always had something insightful to say and sent her friends flowers just because. She was probably called Anastasia and taught Pilates on the weekends when she wasn't helping out at a donkey sanctuary, and didn't have social media.

'Maybe I'll just be friends with Dev,' I muttered, marching on in my PJs.

* * *

Fifteen fretful minutes later, a small limestone cottage with a neatly tended front garden came into view, but there was no one home. Five minutes later, I found another equally deserted house and ten minutes after that, I found myself in the heart of a tiny village, practically a hamlet if not for the beautiful, ancient-looking church in the middle of it all. I'd never really been a religious person, we weren't brought up with it as kids, but I did love a good church. There was something about the idea of a group of people getting together to say, hey, we haven't got trucks or diggers or cranes, and concrete is a good couple of hundred years away from being invented, but shall we build a massive building with massive glass windows and a big pointy bit on top to celebrate this thing we all believe in? As someone who couldn't put together an Ikea coffee table on her own, I had to respect it.

There was a small village green bordered by a post office, a pub and a bakery-slash-coffee shop, all closed, but outside the pub was just the anachronism I was looking for. Honestly, in this day and age, it would have been less jarring to see an actual TARDIS in the middle of the road than an old BT phone box.

'At least this one won't be smashed to shit and covered in graffiti,' I said as I pulled open the door to find a dangling cord with the handset missing and at least three dozen roughly sketched penises. I closed the door, defeated. Yes, I'd broken into a stately home, fallen down some very dangerous stairs, maimed Father Christmas and blown myself, my home and my family to bits, but I was not in the mood to freeze to death in my pyjamas, in a phone box covered in badly drawn knobs.

'Not today, Satan,' I muttered as I stalked across the village green. No, I wasn't a particularly religious person, but needs must when the devil shits in your teapot, it was time to seek help from his arch nemesis, the birthday boy himself.

Not having ever been to church on Christmas, I had no idea what to expect. The nave was empty, not a single soul to be seen on the wooden pews. My footsteps echoed off the stone floors and right away, I felt better. Even though I wasn't religious, a church still represented faith in something bigger than yourself and trusting that there was a plan. I couldn't think of anything I needed more than a little faith, apart from maybe a sandwich. I hadn't eaten all day and I was starving.

Wandering along the rows of empty pews, I paused and picked up a prayer cushion, turning it over in my hands. It was quite nice, navy blue with scarlet and gold embroidery. Michael's Catholic mum would have loved it and I might have tried to buy her one if her son wasn't a cheating shitbag and she hadn't sent me a Facebook message to say how nice it had been to know me and what a shame it was that we would never speak or see each other again less than twenty-four hours after Michael and I broke up.

'No cushion for you, Moira,' I whispered, placing it carefully back where I had found it.

On the other side of the aisle was a confessional. I'd always quite fancied a go in one but when I mentioned it on a day trip to Salisbury cathedral, Michael's Catholic mum crossed herself and went to light a candle.

But there was no Moira to stop me now.

'If you are up there, you probably think this is hilarious,' I muttered, letting myself into the dark wooden box. 'Before I start, you're not obliged to listen or anything, it's not like I'm a regular, and I know it's your son's birthday. You're probably very busy, so don't worry about sending me a sign or anything like that.'

I sat down on the wooden bench, my eyes acclimatizing to the semi-dark as I peeped through the little holes into the unoccupied other side. It was quite pleasant, all things considered. Made me wonder why we didn't have them across the board, who couldn't use a good confessional at the end of a stressful week?

'I'm not sure if there needs to be someone on the other side of the box for this to work,' I added. 'Like two tin cans on the end of a piece of string?'

Again, silence.

'I'll just start, shall I?' I rubbed my palms against my thighs, the fabric of my pyjama bottoms pilling underneath. 'My name's Gwen and I'm having a bit of a problem.'

Before I could explain what the problem was, the door on the other side of the confessional opened and someone sat down on the bench. I pressed my back against the wooden wall, startled.

'Hello?' A man's voice said through the partition. 'I thought I heard someone enter?'

I held my breath and closed my eyes. There was no point running away, I had nowhere to go and really, what was the worst that could happen? I was in a confessional, in a church and yes, I'd seen all the films with the scary nuns but I wasn't getting those vibes. They were almost always set in the seventies anyway, you didn't get possessed murderous nuns in Derbyshire in the twenty-first century. Very often.

'Hello?' the priest said again. 'Are you all right?'

'Hello,' I squeaked, my voice breaking like a twelve-year-old boy. 'Busy day?'

'You could say that,' he replied, clearing his throat. 'Any chance you're new at this?'

For someone who actually made her living by Being Clever, I felt extremely stupid. I knew less than nothing about this sort of thing, religion was always Michael's forte at the pub quiz. How was I supposed to know the law, learn about Catholicism *and* memorize the birth order of all the Kardashian-Jenner children and grandchildren? Simply couldn't be done.

'Reasonable chance.' I nodded, even though he couldn't see me. 'In that I have never done it before and I'm not entirely sure why I'm here.'

'Let's start at the beginning then. This is where people come when they have something to confess. They tell me what's troubling them and we talk it over. Does that sound like something you'd like to do?'

His voice was so friendly and warm and kind, I one hundred per cent believed he could reassure me about anything and everything, even the ending of *Game of Thrones*.

'I'm not sure it's so much a confession as a confusion,' I replied, trying to come up with the best way to describe my predicament without having to actually describe my predicament. 'It's a bit complicated.'

'Whatever you're about to tell me, I can almost guarantee, I've heard it before,' he assured me.

'Christ, I hope not,' I murmured. 'Sorry, inappropriate language, won't do that again.'

He took a long, calming breath in before he replied.

'Let's give it a try. Even if I can't help, I can listen, sometimes that's enough. My name's Father Declan, how can I help?'

'I've had a rough few months,' I said, trying not to stare through the holes. It felt so weird to be talking to someone I couldn't see, although that didn't stop me getting into a month-long feud about the musical episode of *Buffy the Vampire Slayer* with a TheChosenOne84 on Twitter, so I wasn't going to let it get in the way now. 'I'm not sure where I fit at the moment and I'm feeling a bit lost, a bit stuck.'

Also, I've been reliving the same day for a week and I'm two Christmas carols away from firing myself into the sun, I did not add.

'Is that important?' he asked. 'Fitting in?'

'Not in the schoolyard sense, no, but I'd like to know where I belong in the world. Me and my boyfriend broke up and I've been off work for a bit.' I paused and gnawed on my thumbnail for a moment. 'I'm not sure I know who I am without my job,' I admitted.

'Perhaps you're just you,' Father Declan suggested.

What a terrifying thought.

'Have you talked to your friends or family about all this?' he asked.

I pulled the sleeves of my jumper all the way over my hands until they completely covered the dodgy DIY manicure that should have been gone a week ago.

'No, not really.'

'Any reason why not?'

'I don't want to worry them,' I explained. 'They've all got their own problems and I've been trying to help them but nothing I do seems to make any difference.'

The confessional creaked as Father Declan shifted in his seat. 'It's commendable that you want to help the people you love but have you considered you might be putting a lot on yourself here? You're happy to shoulder the burden of others, but you have to allow them to help you carry yours. You can only take so much before you break.'

It was good advice, I just didn't know how it could help me out of my current situation.

'Tell me more about feeling stuck,' he said. 'What does that mean?'

The bright flickering possibility of telling him the truth dangled in front of me. There was a chance he'd believe me. He did work for the guy who sold the world on immaculate conception after all, although no matter how hard Yvonne Aylsford in Year Eleven tried to convince people that was what happened to her, no one believed her ever. Compared to some of the stuff that happened in the bible, my story wasn't that much of a reach. And if he didn't believe me, so what? We weren't likely to bump into each other in Tesco any time soon.

'It means, I've been stuck reliving the same day over and over,' I said, relief pouring off me as I said the words out loud. 'It doesn't matter what I do, who I help, who I hurt, no matter how hard I try, I keep waking up on the very same morning as though nothing at all has happened.'

On the upside, he didn't laugh.

Both sides of the confessional fell silent and I crossed my fingers, hoping he wasn't texting someone to come and take me away. After what felt like far too long for someone who did this for a living, he cleared his throat and I clung to the edge of my seat, waiting on his wisdom.

'Life can feel like that sometimes, can't it?' he said, his voice packed with wisdom. 'Like we're on a hamster wheel, reliving the same day, repeating the same mistakes. And Christmas can be the worst of it, going through the motions, acting out the same rituals and traditions as though nothing has changed even if everything is different to the way it was last year. Sometimes all we want is someone to hear us and acknowledge our pain. I hear you, child, I hear you.'

'Oh, for fuck's sake,' I muttered under my breath. 'I mean, thank you, that's lovely. Good to know.'

It wasn't as though I'd expected him to have the answer but a flat-out rejection of the concept was a little rich for someone who believed a man once turned water into wine yet didn't want to hear a peep about a Christmas-related time loop. As hard-to-believe miracles went, mine was nothing compared to feeding 5,000 people with five loaves and two fish. I couldn't even make a meal for Manny out of that.

'My advice is make the most of each moment, be present. I hope that's given you something to think about.'

'Surely has!' I said, slapping my hands against my thighs, officially confirming we were done. 'Right, I'd better let you get on. I'm sure the Christmas rush is about to start.'

'There are only twenty-four homes in the village,' he replied with a good-natured laugh. 'I've got all the time you need.'

'Time is the one thing I already have too much of,' I said, opening the door and preparing to head back out into the never-ending afternoon. 'Merry Christmas, I hope you have a good one.'

'Everything you learn today will help you tomorrow,' he called after me. 'Remember that.'

I paused outside the confessional, blinking up at the stained-glass windows.

'But what if there is no tomorrow?' I asked.

'Tomorrow is nothing more than yesterday's today. Think on it.'

I heard a gentle chuckle on the other side of the partition as I made my way up the aisle and out the front door.

'Just what I needed,' I muttered, bracing myself for the cold. 'A bloody riddle.'

An hour later, I arrived back at the car, a small can of petrol kindly donated by a nervous-looking teenage boy in the very tiny petrol station on the edge of the village in one hand, and the second of two Snickers bars, also kindly gifted, in the other. I had hoovered the first one in three bites the moment it was in my hand and there was a good chance I'd eaten some of the wrapper as well but it was fine, probably good roughage.

Removing the petrol cap, I replayed my spiritual coun-selling in my head and wondered if perhaps Father Declan wasn't the only one who had missed the point a bit. Admittedly, he didn't jump on board with my time loop problem but I wasn't really listening to his advice either. He was right, asking other people for help was something I found hard.

'But I did ask for petrol and a Snickers,' I said out loud, over the reassuring glug glug glug of the petrol going into the tank. 'So I must be getting better.'

As much as I needed to work on checking in with myself, I definitely needed to work on checking in on other people as well. Just because they said they were OK, didn't mean they were. I always said I was fine when I wasn't, whether I was suffering with period pains or had spent three hours crying in a corner about the fall of western civilization, so I could hardly expect other people to be telling me the truth when they said everything was fine and dandy.

As for the rest of his advice, that was a bit trickier. Be present, live in the moment, that was all well and good for yoga instructors on Instagram but what about the likes of me? At the side of the road, the same three sheep I'd come across earlier kept a reproachful watch.

'You probably know all about this living in the moment guff,' I said, swinging the empty petrol can in my hand. 'How does it work exactly? I thought we were supposed to make plans? I thought that was a good thing?'

They didn't reply, but to be fair, I'd been extremely rude to them when we first met. Plus, they were probably too busy being present to acknowledge me. From what I could tell, 'being present' usually happened on the top of a mountain, not on the number 95 bus when you were weighed down by four pints of milk, a frozen chicken tikka masala and two massive boxes of Persil that were on special offer. Who wanted to be present for that?

Every part of my life looked like the wrong end of a bad deal. I *was* stuck, and not just in a calendar day, I was stuck in my life. Most people dug themselves into a groove at some point, but this wasn't a groove, it wasn't a rut or even a hole. I was more like a dog tied to a pole in the back garden and running around in circles. The faster I ran, the shorter the rope became, and now I was all snarled up with absolutely nowhere to go. As I chucked the empty petrol can in the back of the car and turned the key in the ignition, a grim realization dawned. I'd tethered myself to a life I wasn't even sure I wanted and at no point had I stopped to ask myself why.

Until now.

I fastened my seatbelt with purpose, turned on *The Greatest Showman* soundtrack and pulled into the road. Getting stuck in an eternal Christmas until I could solve my family's problems was one thing, but forcing me to reflect on my own life choices was quite another.

Enough was enough, it was time to figure this thing out.

CHAPTER FIFTEEN

'I've got it,' Manny announced after I explained my predicament for the eighth time the following morning. 'You have to shag someone.'

I glanced up from my bacon butty with complete and utter disgust. '*That's* your solution?'

'It almost always is,' he replied happily. 'But think about it. You *want* to live in the moment and you *need* to grant someone's wish. It's got to be Nan, hasn't it? She didn't wish for you to get back together with Michael, she wished for you to sort out your love life. You're killing two birds with one bang. Gwen, you have to.'

He had presented the evidence and I, as a sworn upholder of the law, had no choice but to examine it further.

'Is sorting out my love life the same thing as hopping on a stranger though? Sorting out my love life probably means spending time alone to work out what I really want and need from a partner.'

'Said the girl who hasn't had a decent shag in years,' Manny replied. 'And don't look at me like that, I can tell by the number of jumpsuits you own Michael wasn't getting the job done. It's a little-known fact but there is a direct correlation.'

'I do like a good onesie,' I muttered without offering any further explanation.

'Under any other circumstances, I would support a period of self-reflection, but Gwen, we are not talking about normal circumstances. We're playing by fairy tale rules. It's true love's kiss or nothing.'

I took a questioning bite of my butty. 'I thought you said I had to shag someone?'

'True love isn't nearly as PG as she used to be,' he sniffed. 'Do you want to be stuck eating turkey and stuffing for all eternity?'

'No.'

The mere thought of another ball of Paxo made me gag.

'And do you want to be in a relationship?'

'Yes,' I admitted with the utmost reluctance. It still felt like I was letting the sisterhood down by saying it out loud, but I really did. I'd been single for years before I met Michael and while I knew it was better to be happily single than unhappily coupled up, I was sure that I wanted a partner in my life.

'Then where's the harm in testing my theory?' He pushed my hair back from my face and gave my cheek a strong pat that was just a hair's breadth away from a slap. 'Besides, a good shag never hurt anyone.'

'What about the time you put your back out with that guy from the Royal Ballet?'

'Should have known my limits,' he admitted. 'But I suspect the likelihood of finding a professional ballet dancer in Baslow on Christmas Day is slim to none.'

'You're not wrong there,' I said, already despairing of my potential options. 'The likelihood of finding someone under sixty-five with all their own hair and teeth is also slim to none. Might need to relax my stringent criteria a bit, any age, own teeth *or* hair.'

'Ooh!' Manny bounced up and down in his seat and pointed out the living-room window 'What about Dev? You said he's home?'

'He is home, but he's engaged,' I replied, flustered. One stray thought of his forearms and I immediately came over all unnecessary.

Manny shrugged. 'So?'

'He's *engaged* to be *married*,' I repeated, sadly locking the memory of rolled-up shirt sleeves and running across fields safely away. 'But . . . there was that man Mum tried to set me up with at Dorothy's party.'

'Is he fit?'

'He looks like Chris Hemsworth and The Rock had a baby and that baby grew up thinking both his parents were a bit puny and he ought to bulk up a bit.'

Manny's jaw dropped open. 'Then why are we sat here talking instead of lubing you up and throwing you out the door? I can think of no better way to live in the moment than for you to bang this man.'

'Then maybe you should shag him,' I suggested.

'Given half the chance,' he tutted in reply.

'He's too hot for me,' I said, shaking my head. 'I'm doing myself down but he's objectively very fit and I'm not good at chatting up very fit people. I've always seen myself as more of a long game gal. I've never been able to turn it on like that, I don't know how.'

'It's really very simple, men are biologically programmed

to say yes when offered sex,' Manny promised. 'It is genuinely harder to say no to a shag than it is to say yes.'

'And they let you teach science to children . . .'

'Whatever, it's true,' he grabbed hold of my hands and shook them hard. 'Come on, shag him for me. Shag him for your nan.'

As if I didn't feel sick already.

Could I really seduce Drew the Burly Scottish Butcher? His exes were probably all fiery redheads with legs up to their armpits who could hunt a wild boar for supper and still find time to give him seven thundering orgasms before bed. With my sexual history, I could just about commit to giving him an unenthusiastic hard-on and Müller Delight three days past its sell-by date.

'Who were you sending photos to?' I asked, tactfully neglecting to refer to the subject of said photos. 'When I walked in on you, I mean?'

'You mean the photos I won't take until half past three this afternoon?' he replied. 'He's no one, some random I got talking to on the apps last night, don't want to talk about it. Look, I know I haven't got the best track record when it comes to romance but that doesn't mean I'm not right.'

Manny had been single forever and not in a hyperbolic, I-haven't-had-a-decent-date-in-months forever, he genuinely meant forever. He was thirty-two and had never been in a relationship that lasted more than a couple of weeks. Not that he didn't get his fair share of action, but nothing seemed to stick.

'What happened to that man you took to that Halloween party? I thought he had potential.'

'He wanted to do a couple's costume after two dates.'

'Which couple?'

'Megan Fox and Machine Gun Kelly.'

'Probably not the one then,' I admitted. 'I'm sorry.'

'What's for you won't go by you,' he said, waving off my concern. 'But I've got a good feeling about you and this mega-yolked random. He's already got the parental seal of approval, I could practically see you ovulating when you mentioned him and most importantly, he's not Michael. I think this could be it.'

'I hope you're right because I don't know how much more of this I can take,' I put half my butty down on my plate and pushed it away. 'I'm even going off bacon sandwiches. That's not right, is it?'

'When a man is tired of bacon, he is tired of life,' Manny declared. 'Come on, let's get you upstairs and tart you up.'

I wiped my hands on my pyjamas and baulked. 'But the party doesn't start for another six hours?'

'Only six hours?' He picked up a chunk of my hair and let it fall back down to my shoulders. 'Well, let's do the best we can in the time we've got.'

Seduction had never been one of my strong points. Me and Michael went on three dates, got drunk, had sex and a relationship was born. The sex was fine, fantastic in the beginning, the way something new so often is, but we were never terribly adventurous or experimental. Once I accidentally left a magazine open on an article about pegging while I went to the loo and when I came back, Michael hadn't just thrown it away, he was shredding it along with his credit card statements and a recipe for vegan lasagne. Our whole affair was very bread and butter, I do this, you do that, you're done, I'm done, time for bed. More and more often we skipped the part where I was done but as time went by, I was far more concerned with getting to the 'time for bed' bit than I was with enjoying myself. My pleasure was never something I'd really thought too much about, sex was very much about keeping Michael happy. What I wanted, what I needed, I really hadn't thought about, inside the bedroom or out.

But now the whole world was open to me, I could do anything, do anyone. I could experiment and try things and find out whether or not I had any sexual predilections outside missionary, doggy style and me-on-top for the last two minutes. Did I like spanking? No idea, never tried it. What about role play? Something else I'd never tried, unless you counted that summer Michael took to wearing an awful leather flying jacket and aviators that he said made him look a bit like Tom Cruise in *Top Gun* if you squinted very hard.

I stared at myself in the bathroom mirror, willing myself to fall in love with the girl who stared back. I could be a daring, sensual, seductress. I could be an uninhibited, orgiastic temptress if I put my mind to it.

'Have you got any knickers that aren't big enough to carry shopping?' Manny called from the bedroom. 'Or shall I have a look in your mum's drawer for a thong?'

If I *really* put my mind to it.

Dorothy's party was as hectic as ever, the house packed from top to bottom. Breaking away from the Baker clan as soon as we walked through the door, I kept the trench coat I'd borrowed from my dad's old wardrobe tightly wrapped around me as I stalked through the maze of rooms seeking my prey. After several hours of prep, breaking only to shovel down lunch, Manny had finally deemed me ready to go forth and pull. My hair had been washed, conditioned, blow-dried and curled, my whole body scrubbed, shaved and oiled and after what Manny claimed were months of his life lost to begging the girls in Year Ten to get back to their biology textbooks instead of practising their eyeliner, through some sort of osmosis, the teacher had become the pupil. He was bloody handy with a make-up brush. My face was artfully blushed, contoured and shaded as if by a professional. He was wasted in that school, I thought as I glimpsed myself in a commemorative Rover's Return plaque. Why waste your days teaching kids how photosynthesis works when you could be at my house with an eyeliner pen, waiting to turn me into a verifiable goddess? I looked so good, I barely recognized myself. Even Cerys had managed a grudging 'well done for making an effort' before we left the house. Pouring myself a generous but not fatal measure of punch, I took myself off to Dorothy's conservatory and waited.

'Here it comes again,' I breathed as the snow began to fall on the other side of the triple-glazed windows. One of the only things I was still pleased to see every day. 'No such thing as too much snow.'

'Tell that to the man who just ran home to cover up his pigeons.'

It was Drew, my Prince Charming. Here to make a wish come true and built like an absolute brick shithouse.

'There she is.' Mum appeared over his shoulder, like clockwork. 'I've been looking for you everywhere. Gwen, meet Drew, Drew, this is my daughter, Gwen.'

'Pleased to meet you at last,' he said, holding out a hand. 'I've heard a lot about you.'

'Drew just moved here from Inverness,' Mum said, physically forcing him into the chair opposite mine, her tiny hands pressing down on his massive shoulders. 'He's taken over the butchers in the village, you know the one at the crossroads—'

'That's amazing,' I interrupted as Drew shook my puny hand in his meaty paw. I held his gaze as long as I could without turning to stone, such a brazen hussy. 'Mum, could you get me some punch? I'm running low.'

She pointed at the full cup on the table. 'What's that then?'

I picked it up, drained it in one gulp and put it back down.

'I'll go and get you some punch,' Mum said, something like grudging respect on her face. 'You two have a lovely chat.'

'Nice to finally meet you,' Drew said, clutching a thimble-ful of punch in his giant man-hand. 'Your mum talks about you all the time.'

'Please tell me she hasn't been trying to get you into her aqua-aerobics classes?' I replied, batting my absurd eyelashes.

'Aye, but that's not just your mum,' he laughed. His eyes crinkled, his accent warm and smoky, and I wondered how his arrival had impacted cholesterol levels in the village. 'They're a friendly bunch here.'

'Very friendly,' I purred. 'Do you like making friends, Drew?'

He spluttered into his punch and cleared his throat.

'Your mum said you're a lawyer?' he said, yanking

slightly on the collar of his Fair Isle jumper. 'That must be interesting.'

'Not as interesting as being a butcher,' I replied. Seduction tip number one according to the eighteen trillion YouTube videos Manny and I had watched while doing my hair, ask them questions about themselves. 'How did you get into that?'

'My dad was a butcher, and his dad and his dad.' He relaxed into his chair and I silently thanked Gen Z for the assist. 'Bit like you and your dad, isn't it? He's a lawyer as well, your mum said.'

'Mmm.' I licked my lips and tried not to gag on the mouthful of cinnamon-flavoured plumping gloss that came back stuck to my tongue. 'And what brought you to Baslow?'

'My dad's side of the family are from here. Moving this far wasn't part of my original plan but I saw the listing and you'll have to forgive me for sounding like an Instagram post, it felt like fate. The perfect shop showing up in the village where my dad grew up? As soon as I came to visit I knew I had to take a chance. We've got to take chances in life, haven't we?'

'We have,' I agreed, reaching across the table and clasping his hand in mine. 'Taking chances is so important.'

'Aye, OK.' He wriggled his hand free and picked up his punch. Discomfort written all over his gorgeous face.

'Do you enjoy it?' I asked, casually unfastening the buttons of my coat. 'Butchering?'

As soon as the words were out of my mouth, I regretted them. There had to be another term for it, surely?

'I do, there's an art to it,' he said, recovering his blinding smile. 'It can get in the way of my love life though.'

My fingers fumbled with the last button and I looked up sharply to make sure I wasn't imagining things. He'd mentioned his love life! This was it, I was in! With an incredibly sexy mountain of a man who could keep me in free sausages for life!

'I can't imagine a man like you has any problems in that department,' I demurred, running the belt of my trench through my fingers. Seduction tip number two, flattery will get you everywhere.

'Ahh, you'd be surprised.'

He looked off out into the garden for a moment before pulling his phone out of his pocket and swiping it into life. I was losing him, shit, I was losing him. What was tip number three? Let him know you're interested? Physical contact? Give him a blowjob in the back seat of his parents' car while they're driving it? No, I'd been watching too much *Euphoria*. I just needed to get him talking again. But it was so much more difficult to keep the conversation going with Drew. He wasn't nearly as easy to talk to as Dev.

Right on cue, over Drew's slab of a shoulder, I saw Dev walk through the conservatory door with his parents, all three Joneses still wearing their coats and presumably not because they were nearly naked underneath. Like me.

I caught Dev's eye and smiled, my whole heart filling with joy at the very sight of him. Recognition flickered in his eyes and he lifted the corners of his mouth politely before he turned away to speak to his mother. My heart deflated on the next beat. If only he could remember.

'Do you think you'd be a butcher if you hadn't got the idea from your dad?' I blurted out as Drew tapped away at his phone.

The Christmas Wish

'Good question.' He put his phone on the table and pulled a thinking face as I watched Dev disappear from the room, fighting off the feeling of sadness that came as he went. 'I became a butcher because of my dad but that's not why I *am* a butcher today. If I hadn't enjoyed it, I wouldn't have carried on with it. Must be the same for you, with the law? Would you have gone into it if it weren't for your dad?'

I wound the belt of my trench coat around my hand until it was so tight, I couldn't feel my fingers. 'I don't know,' I admitted. 'If I could make the choice again, I don't know what I'd do.'

'We make that choice every single day,' Drew said with a kind smile. 'Each morning when you get up and go to work, you're choosing it, aren't you?'

The thought had never occurred to me. He was right. I might have got into law for other people but I stayed because I loved it, didn't I? The long days, the late nights, the working weekends and cancelled holidays. The competition, the judgement, the constant panic that came with not feeling quite good enough and the overwhelming pressure that manifested in me chucking a stapler at my client's head. Who wouldn't love that?

I felt my fingernails pressing down into the palms of my hands and gulped.

'That's an awfully serious look you've got on your face there,' Drew said. 'I'm sorry, didn't mean to get so deep.'

'Don't apologize,' I replied, brushing away the niggle that was fast becoming a nag. I couldn't think about this now, I had something else to do, namely Drew. It was time to bring out the big guns. I shrugged my coat off my shoulders, revealing an obscenely tiny black dress

Manny had found in the bottom of my wardrobe. It was truly minuscule, skin-tight, the spaghetti straps straining against a chest that was apparently much bigger than it was when I was eighteen and thought wearing a sock with straps made for acceptable clubwear.

'If he doesn't go for this, he's gay,' Manny had declared when I finally pulled it down over my arse. I'd questioned the reductive nature of his statement out of a sense of social responsibility, but he made a solid case. Drew was single, new in town and so lonely, he had chosen to attend Dorothy's Christmas party alone and of his own volition. It didn't matter that I wasn't a master seductress, it didn't matter that I'd forgotten to toss my hair and laugh at his jokes, this dress would make my intentions perfectly clear. It screamed 'take me to bed or lose me forever' almost as loudly as it bellowed 'do not go near a naked flame' and from the look on Drew's face, it was a language he spoke fluently.

'That's quite an outfit,' he stammered before throwing back the rest of his drink. 'Are you, um, going on somewhere after this?'

'I don't know,' I cooed, leaning across the table to give him a better view. 'Can you think of anywhere . . . fun?'

'Oh no.' Drew stood up, his chair clattering to the floor behind him. 'I think, actually, I need to leave, right now.'

'Don't go!' I leapt to my feet and my right boob made a break for it out the front of my dress. I caught it just in time. 'Please, stay.'

'It's not you, you're great, you've got the wrong end of the stick, is all,' he said, looking away as I yanked my frock up, red-faced and dying inside. I was still trying to tether my breasts down when his phone pinged into life on the table and a photo appeared on the screen. 'Believe me, if things were different—'

'Oh!' I clapped a hand over my mouth as I realized it was a photo of a body part I did not possess.

'Shit,' Drew grabbed the phone and stuffed it into the back pocket of his jeans. 'I'm sorry, I'm so sorry, it's only that I'm . . .'

'Gay?' I suggested.

'Gay,' he confirmed, exhaling with relief. 'I'm so sorry.'

'Do not apologize,' I said, shaking my head and wondering how many more dick pics I would have to see before this infernal Christmas was out. 'You've done nothing wrong, there's nothing to apologize for and you don't have to leave. It's me, it's all on me. Mum wanted me to meet you, I didn't know, she *definitely* didn't know. You're great. You're brilliant. You're—'

'Gay?' he said again, this time with a booming laugh of relief. 'Really, I am sorry. You look pure gorgeous. If I could stomach the thought of it, I'd definitely have a go.'

I held a hand to my heart, extremely flattered. 'Really?'

'On my great-grandma's life,' he replied, waving his now blank phone screen in the air. 'I might call it an early night, go home and reply to my friend here.'

'Go, go,' I said, accepting a kiss on the cheek. 'May you receive nothing but the best dick pics of all time.'

Right at that moment, Mum returned with two cups of punch, full to the brim. Drew gave her a friendly nod as he bolted out of the conservatory and I sank back into my chair, wondering if I could borrow a caftan from Dorothy.

'What did you say to him?' Mum asked, her scandalized eyebrows attempting to break free from her forehead. 'And what are you wearing?'

'I didn't have to say anything. Drew is gay, Mum,' I replied, gratefully accepting one of the cups and letting myself sink into its cheap, reliable embrace. 'He is a gay man.'

She crumpled into his empty chair, her dreams shattered. And I didn't mean the dreams of setting him up with her daughter. 'Are you sure? He could be bisexual. Or pansexual! Kelvin, the head of maths, says he's omnisexual now but he's never been the same since he got hit in the head with a shotput on sports day.'

'Maybe it knocked something into place.' I pulled my trench coat over my apology of a dress as Bernard from down the road walked past our table, his eyes bulging out of his head. 'And sorry but no, he's good old-fashioned gay. You tried to set him up with the wrong child, I'm afraid.'

'No point trying to sort him out with Manny,' she sighed before helping herself to the drink she'd brought for my doomed date. 'No one's good enough for that boy, not even Drew. You're *sure* he's gay? He wasn't trying to reject you politely?'

I glared at her, clutching my coat closer to my chest.

'I was sure until you suggested otherwise.'

She pinched her shoulders together in a shrug as she sipped her drink. Just as I was thinking of making my excuses to go back to the house and get this day over with, Manny arrived, looking far too good for this party in close-fitting jeans and his new black hoodie, a hoodie I would be stealing to wear as a dress if he wasn't careful.

'What did I miss?' he said, looking around the room. 'Where's your man?'

'I'll get myself back on booze duty,' Mum offered, giving him her seat. 'You'll want a drink for this one.'

Manny looked back at me, confused as I pulled my beautifully blown-out hair back into the cack-handed ponytail of defeat.

'Turns out I'm not Drew's type,' I said diplomatically. 'By a long stretch.'

'Ah, Gwen, I'm sorry. So what, you go to bed and go through all this again tomorrow?'

'Looks like it,' I replied, turning to see Dev and his family chatting to Dorothy outside in the garden. Perhaps tomorrow we could go for another walk or he could help me with the cooking. The thought of spending more time with him was the only thing I had to look forward to.

'I know what will make you feel better,' Manny said. 'Let's go home and get rat-arsed and scream at *Love Actually*.'

'It's not only how badly Alan Rickman treats Emma Thompson, it's the whole gross Keira Knightley Andrew Lincoln bit. You can't tell your best friend's wife you love her just because it's Christmas, not ever,' I explained as we stood to leave. 'And Christmas is most certainly not the time to tell the truth. It is the complete opposite. Lie through your back teeth until you're safely into January, people.'

'Save your rage for the film,' Manny said soothingly. 'You know we're going to be doing this when we're eighty, don't you?'

I laughed. 'Unlikely. You'll be off on a yacht somewhere with your twenty-one-year-old lover while I scream at Andrew Lincoln all alone in my rocking chair.'

'We both know I'm destined to be alone forever,' he replied, fastening the belt of my coat for me and cinching it a bit too tightly for someone who had a passing interest in breathing. 'I imagine your kids will like having fun Uncle Manny around so much when they're little but by the time they reach their teens, I assure you they will find me both creepy and tragic.'

A freezing cold gust blasted my privates as someone opened the conservatory door and I very much wanted to be at home in my pyjamas.

'You couldn't be tragic even if you were head-to-toe in neon pink spandex and doing the "Tragedy" dance at a Steps tribute show. You're amazing,' I said. 'You're clever and funny and unreasonably handsome. Plus you never run out of milk, what a bloody catch.'

'Doesn't change the facts. If you'd thrown in how much I love Britney Spears, we'd have to dance out to the sounds of the Village People while people threw rainbow confetti at us. I'm a good old-fashioned tragic gay, Gwen, no two ways about it.'

'If loving Britney makes you tragic then we've all got a problem.'

'Didn't like to say, but . . .' He set his face with the same determination as when I tried to convince him to do Dry January. 'Don't make a big deal out of it, this is who I am and I'm fine with it. Sad Manny. His dad died, his mum left, he can't get a man to go out with him for more than a month to save his life. I'm more tragic than a *Real Housewives* reunion.'

I couldn't believe it. He'd always insisted he was single by choice, that he loved living alone and meeting new people, and that it wasn't strange for a gay man in London to have not been in a serious relationship at his age. I wasn't a gay man in London, who was I to question him? It never, ever occurred to me that he was lying to me.

The last time I called him out on his never-ending stream of Instagram thirst traps, he told me they were for no one's benefit but his own, nothing more than a record of his youth and beauty so he could look back on them when he was an old crone, held together by Botox, filler and the firm grip of a much younger lover. Who would argue with a defence like that? Not this legal professional. But looking at him now, hands tucked away in the pouch of his sweatshirt like a sad kangaroo of a man, my heart ached. No one should ever have to feel that way about themselves, let alone someone as wonderful as Manny.

'No one person is as bad as that. You couldn't hold a candle to the tragedy of Erika Jayne and you know it,' I replied. There was no way I was going to let him spend another second of his life believing these things about himself. Cerys needed someone to listen but Manny needed someone to speak up. 'The things that happened to you are really shit, incredibly, monstrously shit, but that doesn't mean you are intrinsically tragic as a human being. It means life can be a real kick to the knackers, that's all. You didn't cause any of those things, none of it was or is your fault.'

'I appreciate the vote of confidence, I really do, but with every year that passes another little bit of hope gets sucked away.' He wound his hands around each other inside his pouch and it looked as though an alien was about to burst forth out of his belly at any moment. 'I know it's not my fault my dad died, but it's harder to convince myself I had nothing to do with the fact my own mother abandoned me with you lot right after the funeral. She didn't even text me today, did you know that?' I shook my head gently. I didn't know.

Manny never talked about his mum so I never asked. 'I haven't been in a relationship because who would want me? What could I possibly be worth to anyone when my own mother can't be arsed to pick up the phone to her only son?'

His eyes brimmed with tears and I immediately hurled my body at his, trying to smother his sadness with my love.

'I can't explain why your mother does the things she does, no one can,' I told him as he wiped his eyes on my arm. 'But I do know you didn't do anything wrong back then and you're not doing anything wrong now. She's the one at fault and she's the one who is missing out on one of the greatest human beings who ever graced this planet with their existence.'

'I wish I believed you,' he snuffled into my shoulder. 'Maybe if I did, I wouldn't be exchanging dick pics with Scottish butchers on Christmas bloody Day.'

'Well, let's not ruin the day completely. It's like Cerys told me, we can't control other people, you have to start believing it yourself,' I replied before pulling sharply back from the hug. 'Wait, what did you just say?'

He looked up at me with red-rimmed, watery eyes.

'That I wished I believed you?'

'No, the other part,' I said, climbing out of his lap. 'This bloke, he's a Scottish butcher?'

'Well, that's what he says,' Manny replied, tapping his fingers underneath his eyes and trying to destroy any evidence of tears before my mother returned. 'He's probably slicing Billy Bear ham on the deli counter at Morrison's. You know it's not even ham? Probably never even seen a pig.'

'This butcher, is he local?' I asked, vibrating with excitement. A dick pic wasn't quite the same as a glass slipper but maybe Drew was *someone's* Prince Charming after all.

Manny shrugged. 'Somewhere in a twenty-mile radius I suppose, I didn't change my location settings.'

'Right, you're coming with me.' I yanked on his arm, pulling him across the conservatory.

'Where are we going?' he asked as I led him through Dorothy's living room, kitchen, sitting room and right out the front door. 'We should be cheering for sexual harassment in Ten Downing Street by now. That's another problem with that film now, it really isn't on for the prime minister to shag the tea lady, even if she is Martine McCutcheon.'

'We're going on a mission,' I replied. 'Hugh Grant can wait.'

He stopped halfway up the garden path and refused to move. I yanked on his arm but it was like trying to drag a shed. 'Gwen, we should be inside looking for the love of your life. Don't waste time on me.'

'No time spent on you could ever be a waste,' I said, stopping to squeeze both his hands in mine. 'You deserve your happily ever after just as much as everyone else.'

And I was going to make sure he got it.

'What is this?'

Even under the sodium-vapour glow of the street lights, Manny's face was ashen.

'It's a butcher's shop,' I said, pointing at the sign out front. McIntyre's Meat. Not subtle. How had my mother not known?

'And why are we here?'

'Billy Bear ham?' I waited for him to put two and two together, watching as he frowned, his forehead turning into a concertina of confusion. 'Oh, for God's sake, the man you've been sending photos to is Drew the Scottish butcher, the one Mum tried to set me up with!'

'Absolutely fucking not.'

It wasn't quite the rush of gratitude I'd expected but nevertheless, I persisted.

'You're going in there,' I said, pointing at the door to the upstairs flat. 'Ring the doorbell.'

'No.'

'Why not?'

'Because I don't want to.'

Where had I heard that before?

'Manny, I say this with nothing but love and the frustration born of having seen photos of your penis *twice* now,' I paused to take a breath. 'Ring the bloody doorbell.'

He made a disgruntled sound in the back of his throat and once again refused to move.

'Worst-case scenario, you see each other, you're not keen and Mum has to start going to a different butchers,' I reasoned, sliding my arm through the nook of his elbow to whisper in his ear. 'But best-case scenario, he could be the one. Drew could be the love of your life.'

I rested my chin on his shoulder and looked up at my cousin with wide, Disney-heroine eyes. 'You've already seen his knob, it would be rude not to say hello.'

'You know nothing about my people,' Manny grunted. 'But fine.'

With a joyous shriek, I jabbed at Drew's doorbell before he could change his mind, dancing around on the spot, then pausing to rearrange my boobs as they attempted to break free of their Lycra restraints once again.

It was just like a movie. Drew opened the door, a golden glowing halo all around him from the upstairs light, his beautiful Fair Isle jumper pushed up around his elbows, his hair artfully mussed as though we'd disturbed him from thinking some very deep thoughts or, even better, watching an episode of *Emily in Paris*. His eyes rested on me for a moment then he turned his gaze to Manny. It felt as though the air around us was on fire, charged with a trillion volts of oh-my-God-just-kiss-already.

'Drew!' I exclaimed when neither of them so much as spoke, moved or breathed. 'I'd like you to meet my cousin, Manny. Manny, this is Drew, a butcher who just moved here from Inverness.'

Manny looked at Drew, Drew looked at Manny and in that moment, something wonderful happened.

'Mr_Meat_88?' Manny said, his eyes wide.

'If_You_Seek_Manny_69?' Drew gasped.

'Ew,' I whispered.

But it didn't matter. Obscene screen names could come and go but whatever it was running between my cousin and his hot butcher was very real. My heart soared at the expressions on their handsome faces, their smiles growing with every passing second. I hadn't looked at anyone or anything like that since I found out the freezer shop down the road from my new flat sold past-their-expiry-date Cadbury's Creme Eggs all year round. Love is love is love is love and no man, woman or threat of food poisoning could stand in its way. The two of them inched closer together, one magnet drawn to another.

Hot, sexy magnets that I did not need to see any more of because one of them was my cousin.

'Well, this has been fun,' I said as I slowly backed away down the street. 'But I have some really important stuff to do that involves being anywhere else but here. Manny, I'll see you later.'

'Probably not,' he called without turning away from Drew. 'But thank you.'

'Any time,' I replied, doffing an invisible cap and strutting all the way home.

CHAPTER SIXTEEN

It was almost 4 p.m. on Christmas Day number nine and I was exhausted. So far I'd helped make lunch, got all the videos down from the loft, taken Cerys to the pub and introduced Manny to the love of his life. Again. Now I was back at Dorothy's open house, hiding in Dorothy's bathroom, trying to have five minutes' peace before Dad set off his apocalyptic fireworks. I was officially out of ideas when it came to the wish. If Manny was right and I was supposed to be sorting out my love life then I was going to be stuck here forever, but at least I would be stuck with people I loved. And also Oliver.

The last week had opened my eyes to so much, the struggles that go on behind closed doors, the problems we keep buried, the sheer dedication it took to make perfect Yorkshire puddings every time. Even if I was here for all eternity, I wondered if I would ever truly be able to learn everything about my family and I'd already known them for my whole life. At least I might manage to make a dent in my Netflix queue.

* * *

Much like Dorothy herself, the bathroom where I'd taken refuge was a work of art: Barbie's Dream Bath made life-size. Pink bath, pink sink, pink toilet, pink blinds, pink towels, pink shower curtain, pink soap, pink loo roll, pink-hued conch shell on the top of the water tank. Everything was pink because Dorothy wanted it pink and she simply hadn't allowed anyone to tell her otherwise. Dorothy was an icon. We could all learn something from Dorothy, I thought, as I rested my head against the flocked wallpaper and closed my eyes, just for a minute.

I got exactly seventeen seconds before someone started banging on the door.

'There's someone in here!' I yelled as the handle rattled, the ancient bolt loosening against the door.

'Are you nearly done?' the interloper called back. 'I'm going to piss myself out here.'

Washing my hands and chuntering under my breath, I gave the bathroom a sad parting glance, and let myself out, Bernard from the end of the cul-de-sac pushing past me with his flies already undone.

'Thanking you,' he said, shoving me out of the way and slamming the door shut behind him, an unmistakable sigh of relief echoing through to the landing.

'Charming,' I muttered as I checked to make sure my red velvet dress wasn't tucked in my knickers. It was nice in the bathroom. Peaceful. You could learn so much about someone from their bathroom, what products they had, what state their towels were in, did they have a big bottle of budget bubble bath, sexy oils or a big glass jar of bougie bath bombs?

'And now I really want a bath,' I said with a sigh, reluctant to re-join the party. There was no point seeking out relaxation at home, between Oliver's guffawing and the kids screaming, it was about as calming as a communal changing room. All I wanted was to dip my head under warm water and drift away until it was time to go to bed and start my day all over again. It would be nice to pretend I was somewhere else, to escape reality for an hour or so.

The bathroom door opened and Bernard walked out, zipping up his fly and giving me a nod.

'I'd leave it a minute,' he said, nodding back at the bathroom. 'Merry Christmas.'

'Noted,' I replied, wondering what Lesley saw in him. He must have had something pretty special up his sleeve (or down his trousers) to keep a good woman like her around.

And that's when I remembered.

'Wednesday morning aqua-aerobics,' I whispered, running down the stairs and out the front door, leaving my coat and my cares behind.

My mother had vastly undersold Bernard and Lesley's pool.

After popping home to 'borrow' the key that was hidden in the kitchen drawer where Mum kept All The Things (including but not limited to half-used birthday candles and a slimline Lett's diary from 1989), I let myself inside the giant glass structure behind Bernard and Lesley's house, a cloud of humidity swallowing me whole as I stepped out of the real world and into paradise. Whatever I was expecting, this was not it. The greenhouse itself was the size of a small aircraft hangar with an enormous heated pool in the middle, a sunken hot tub at one end and a cold plunge at the other. Sun loungers and palm trees had been placed at precise intervals along either side while grapevines trailed up the glass walls and along the peaked roof, blocking out the house, the village and the rest of the world. The only light came from the large round lamps under the water and everything shimmered and moved as though it wasn't quite real. I was in heaven.

Everyone would be busy at Dorothy's for at least another couple of hours, especially with the fireworks, which gave me plenty of time to play anywhere but here. I didn't have a swimsuit and I didn't care. Father Declan would be so proud; I was living in the moment and swimming in my knickers. With excited, fumbling fingers, I peeled off my dress, tossed it across one of the sun loungers and dove straight into the deep end in my mismatched underwear.

Everything felt better underwater.

The pressure pushed on my ears, muffling every single sound and tempering my thoughts. My eyes stung when I opened them, but only for a moment and I blinked as the whole world turned bright blue. All around me, my long unruly hair fanned out floating, weightless, and every single worry I had ever had was washed away. I swam around the bottom of the pool, skimming my fingers along the textured surface until my lungs began to burn, forcing me back up to the surface to take a big, life-affirming breath. I was alive. I was still here.

And I wasn't the only one.

'Hello, stranger.'

'Dev!' I exclaimed, losing my footing and plunging right back under the surface. How would I explain this? Was he going to call the police? Why hadn't I put on a nicer bra that morning? Why had I worn knickers that barely covered half my arse? I resurfaced with hair plastered all over my face, spitting out a mouthful of water.

'Nice dive,' I heard him say as I pushed my hair away and wiped my eyes dry.

'Thanks, I've watched *The Little Mermaid*, like, loads of times. What are you doing here?'

'I feel like I should be asking you that,' he replied, walking around the pool towards me.

I doggy-paddled to the side, my heart pounding from the shock of being discovered and the joy of being discovered by Dev. It was three days since our Chatsworth House adventure and absurd as it seemed, given all that was going on, I'd missed him.

'I was leaving for Dorothy's and I saw you skulking off down the street,' he said, and I was relieved to see he was smiling.

Clinging to the edge of the pool, I pressed my body against the wall so he couldn't see my makeshift bikini. 'So you followed me?'

'Not in a creepy way!' Dev replied, his fantastic eyebrows protesting his innocence. 'I thought you'd be on your way to Dorothy's as well, I was trying to catch up with you. Then you took a detour.' He squatted down in front of me, a fully-fledged grin on his face. 'Do Bernard and Lesley know you're here?'

The air prickled as I dropped my chin into the water and shook my head.

'Technically, I had a key, so it's not really breaking and entering.' Not like the time we climbed through a window and broke into Chatsworth House I most certainly did not say. 'But I did see them at Dorothy's,' I added, an invitation in my voice. 'They won't be back for ages?'

'I haven't got my bathers with me,' Dev replied, patting down his grey coat and his not-at-all baggy trousers.

Sod it. If ever there was a time to be present, it was now. Present, in a pool, in my pants, with Dev. For nine confusing days, he had been the bright spot in all of my misadventures, the one part I wouldn't mind reliving over and over. Pushing away from the wall, I sculled backwards across the water, desperate for him to stay.

'Neither have I.'

'Gwen Baker, village rebel,' Dev said, his decision made. He unlaced his boots and shucked off his coat, dumping it on the same sun lounger as my dress then paused as he took hold of the hem of his jumper. 'Excuse me, are you watching me get undressed?'

'No, of course not,' I replied, glad to be able to dip under water before he saw me blush. When I popped back up, he was stood at the deep end in a pair of tight blue boxers, quickly rearranging himself before he dove into the pool, slicing the water in two with long, clean strokes.

This is fine, I told myself as I checked the integrity of my bra straps. It was not designed for an underwater frolic, but M&S underwear had never knowingly let me down before. Just a casual swim in the neighbour's pool with a hot grown-up version of the boy you were in love with when you were thirteen and you're both in your pants. What could be more Christmassy?

If nothing else, it certainly felt like a gift.

'This is incredible,' Dev called, swimming back towards me, the light scattering of black hair on his chest glistening under the low lighting. 'New life goal, I definitely need my own pool.'

'Darling it's better, down where it's wetter,' I replied with a seductive laugh before cutting myself off with a grimace. Wait, was that actually quite rude? Thankfully, it looked as though Dev didn't know his Disney and rolled over onto his back, sailing by without comment.

'If this was in my back garden, I'd never leave.' He grabbed hold of a neon pink pool noodle that was floating in the corner and wrangled it into submission. 'I was having the worst Christmas possible until I saw you.'

'Really?' I replied. 'Did you wake up to find yourself trapped in a never-ending time loop that seems to be forcing you to confront what a complete and utter disaster your life is, how you barely know the people closest to you and how you might be stuck here forever?'

He wrapped the pool noodle around his back and under his armpits, one eyebrow raised.

'Very funny,' he replied and I let out a silent sob. 'OK, so not the worst Christmas possible but this was not the day to discover my parents have become a screen-free home.'

'That actually might be worse,' I admitted. 'No telly? At all?'

'No telly, no tablets, no e-readers, no laptops, no smart phones.'

'Have they never seen *The Shining*?' I asked, horrified at the thought of Christmas with the family without the reassuring glow of the television on in the corner of the room.

Dev laughed and let his eyes settle on me with the same smile on his face I'd seen at the bottom of the garden on that very first Christmas Day. The same smile he always had when we were together. Here was a man who was genuinely happy, simply because he happened to be in the same place at the same time on the same floating space rock. It felt impossibly good to see someone light up simply because I existed. It hadn't happened in a long time.

I swam over to the side to select a floating device of my own. Which was better, a far-too-enthusiastic-looking unicorn or a very judgemental flamingo? I went with the flamingo. My cotton knickers ballooned with water as I swam back over to Dev and I prayed the elastic would hold up. Walking around in a top half only was all well and good for the likes of Winnie the Pooh and Donald Duck but not for the rest of us.

'How about yours?' Dev asked. The water lapped against the side of the pool and his voice echoed off the steamy glass ceiling. 'Shall I take an educated guess and say it isn't going that well?'

'Today was lovely actually,' I said, thinking about how happy everyone had been when I left them at Dorothy's. 'Knackering but nice. And extremely complicated. I'm having a bit of a crisis.'

He scooped up a handful of water and doused his thick black hair, slicking it away from his face. 'Maybe I could help? I'm quite a good listener.'

The first thing I'd learned over the last nine days: ask for help when you need it and accept help when it is offered. I rested my forearms on my inflatable flamingo and opened my mouth to speak, not quite sure what was going to come out. There were still so many problems for me to tackle, but there was one thing that had been on my mind ever since my drinks with Cerys and it was about time I tried to figure it out.

'It's my job,' I said. 'I always thought I knew exactly what I was doing and now I'm not so sure.'

'You're a lawyer, aren't you?' Dev asked and I nodded. 'What is it you're not sure about?'

'All of it,' I laughed. 'Everything. If you'd asked me three months ago, I would have told you my job was everything to me. If you'd asked me two weeks ago, I would have had a nervous breakdown at the thought of losing it. But now . . . now I can't stop wondering why I'm even doing it.'

'As far as I can tell, there are only two good reasons to stay in any job.' He blinked as a drop of condensation fell from the ceiling onto the tip of his nose and I couldn't help but smile. 'Because you have to or because you want to. Do either of those reasons apply here?'

Resting against my flamingo, I kicked my feet gently, sending myself up to the far end of the pool where the grapevines covered the panes of glass, casting a dark grotto-like glow over the deep water.

'If I leave, the last ten years have been for nothing,' I said as Dev followed me into the deep end. 'I'm worried I might have wasted an awful lot of life.'

'There's still a fair bit of it in front of you,' he replied. 'You can't stay in a situation when it isn't right because you've put the time in, trust me.'

'Maybe.' I was treading water and dangerously close to being out of my depth. 'If I left, my dad would be so disappointed in me.'

I felt traitorous to say it out loud to another person but, at the same time, I was relieved.

'So?' Dev said simply. 'It's not your dad's life, it's yours.'

The idea took me by such surprise, my feet forgot to find the bottom of the pool and I disappeared under the water. So much of our lives were propped up by other people's expectations – parents, partners, teachers, bosses – but what were my expectations of myself? When I looked for them, all I found was a great big gaping hole. Between trying to live up to my sister's example and my dad's ambitions I'd forgotten to have dreams of my own. All this time I'd been following someone else's plan and the world had cleverly convinced me I'd made it for myself.

And to think, I was supposed to be the clever one.

For the first time since I walked through the office door, I allowed myself to imagine jumping instead of being pushed. It felt like freedom.

'If I left Abbott & Howe,' I said quietly, my voice was a pencil not quite ready to write it down in pen. 'Who would I be? What would I do?'

'You?' He shook his head as though he couldn't believe I didn't already know the answer. 'Gwen, you could do anything.'

It was like I'd been living my life inside a tunnel. A long dark tunnel with a speck of light at the end and nothing else but pitch-black darkness all around me. Without notice, I'd been thrust out into the light and I was surrounded by endless possibilities that had been there all along. How had I never noticed them before?

'I could do anything,' I repeated slowly, waiting for the words to sink in. 'But what exactly?'

'I don't know, you could be a writer?' Dev replied, his beautiful brown skin glowing golden in the half-light of the pool. 'Or an astronaut. Goat farmer. Marine biologist. Plasterer. Croupier. Chef.'

So he really *didn't* remember our other Christmases.

'Librarian. Podcast host. Engineer. Make-up artist. An alien on *Star Trek*. A motorbike courier. An international super spy. I would back you at anything you chose to do with one exception.'

'And what's that?' I asked.

'Singer,' he said, shaking his head. 'Sorry, but if you were planning to be the next Adele, someone had to tell you.'

'No, that's fair,' I replied. 'Why on earth did they let me play Rizzo in the school play?'

'It's been sixteen years and I still ask myself that question all the time,' he grinned. 'There are *not* worse things you could do.'

I flicked my hand at him, sending a tiny splash in his direction. 'I can't believe you remember that when I've spent so long trying to forget it.'

He laughed at my look of surprise, his huge dark eyes sparkled, just the way they did when we were kids. He floated towards me, his face inches away from mine.

'I could fill a library with my memories of you, Gwen Baker,' he said before pushing off the wall and sailing away down the pool.

'I'm going in the hot tub,' Dev yelled as he climbed up the pool steps, boxers clinging to his body in a way that made me wonder how committed to my morals I really was. Where was his fiancée and why was she allowing him to walk around the world unchaperoned when there were vulnerable, horny women out here? I let my flamingo carry me up the pool after him, watching as he fired up the jets and climbed into the hot tub, melting under the bubbles.

'You've got to get in here,' he called. 'This thing is incredible.'

'OK, knickers, don't let me down,' I whispered as I let all the water out of my submerged bloomers and climbed the steps, one hand on the railing and one on the elastic. The shock of the cooler air put a skip in my step and I clambered over the side as quickly as possible. Was my entrance elegant? No. Was the hot tub pure, unadulterated, red-hot bubbly bliss? Abso-bloody-lutely.

'This is going to sound really weird,' Dev said, closing his eyes and stretching out across the circular tub. I mentally traced the slope of his shoulders, the wiry definition of his upper arms, relieved his spectacular forearms were under water and out of sight, and pulled my knees into my chest, huddled in a ball to stop our toes from touching. No good could come of physical contact.

'What is?' I asked, carefully keeping my hands, feet and every other body part to myself.

'It's got to be ten years since we last had a proper conversation, hasn't it.' He slowly rolled his head from side to side, pressing his neck against the hot jets. 'So why does it feel like I just saw you yesterday?'

'Not yesterday,' I smiled. 'More like three days ago.'

'Ha-ha,' he replied as though I was joking. 'I'm serious, it's like picking up right where we left off. I can't believe we ever lost touch.'

This was something else I'd learned over the last few days, I realized. Know when to say you're sorry.

'That was entirely my fault,' I said, shuffling further away from him. 'I stopped replying to your emails because I was jealous.'

He opened his eyes and lifted his head.

'You were jealous? Of what?'

'Your girlfriend,' I replied. 'I was insanely jealous because you had a girlfriend.'

Something that was all the more difficult to admit given it was as true today as it was then. It was undeniable. My crush on Dev Jones was officially back and bigger than ever. He brushed the hair out of his eyes, moistened his lips then leaned forwards towards me.

'You do know I had a massive crush on you when we were kids, don't you?' he said.

'You did not!' I pulled back my arm and sent a giant splash in his direction only just missing our clothes on the sun lounger. 'That is mean, Devendra Jones, you shouldn't joke about things like that.'

'But I did!' he protested, laughing as he wiped his face with one hand and defended himself from a second attack with the other. 'From the first moment I saw you. I bet you don't remember, it was the day we moved in and you were playing football with Manny in the front garden and I saw you and it was instant, *pow*, look at *her*. Then he whacked you right in the face with the football and you screamed so loudly I thought the world was ending. I went inside to get help but when I came back out, you were gone. That was it, I was totally smitten.'

'You're so full of it,' I said, covering my face with my hands. 'You did not have a crush on me.'

'Did too, for years,' he argued, beaming from ear to ear. 'I remember when I was seventeen, I used to lie in bed at night listening to "Sex on Fire" by Kings of Leon, thinking about you.' His smile faltered for a second as my eyes bulged out of my head. 'I don't think I really understood what the song was about to be honest.'

'At least it wasn't "She Bangs" by Ricky Martin,' I replied, and he laughed.

'I used to put my hand on the wall and pretend you were doing the same thing on the other side,' Dev shook his head as I cackled happily. 'What an idiot.'

'Our houses aren't attached,' I pointed out, almost hysterical. 'How was that going to work?'

'I don't know, I was a very emo teenager.' He moved slightly, blocking the lamp behind him and the hot tub was plunged into darkness for a moment. 'It's not like you were lying awake on the other side of the wall thinking about me anyway.'

'Well that, Dev Jones, is where you are wrong,' I replied, my laughter bubbling away until all that was left was a smile I doubted would ever leave my face. 'And I still don't believe you because I had the biggest crush on you that anyone has ever had on anyone. Including Manny's crush on Justin Timberlake which was so intense, he bleached his hair during fresher's week and wore nothing but double denim for six months.'

We sat quietly for a moment and I could hear him breathing over the sound of the bubbles. Under the water, his toes brushed against mine and neither of us moved away.

'You really had a crush on me?' he asked, no trace of a smile left on his face.

'Yes,' I replied, breathless. 'I really did.'

'And I had a crush on you.'

'Allegedly.'

'Nothing alleged about it. Why do you think I was always hanging around with you and Manny?'

'Because you moved here when you were thirteen and you didn't know anyone in the village and didn't have any friends?'

'Yes, OK, that is true,' he admitted. 'But other than that it was because I spent every third minute of every single day wondering what it would be like to kiss the girl next door.'

I swallowed hard as he moved across the hot tub, the water up to his waist, and stopped right in front of me. He moved slowly, raising his hand to sweep a single strand of hair away from my forehead, just the very tips of his fingers touching my skin.

'And now,' he whispered, inching closer, 'here we are.'

'Here we are,' I whispered back, alive and electric. All I had to do was reach out. All I had to do was touch him. Never in my life had I wanted anything more than this moment, I'd imagined it so many times, fantasized about it, dreamed about it and now we were here, not even a heartbeat away from a kiss. But in all those dreams and fantasies, Dev was mine and mine alone. He didn't belong to someone else.

'I'm sorry, I can't,' I said, clasping my hand around his and sadly pushing it away. It wasn't supposed to be like this, even if I was the only one who would remember it. Dev pulled back, the muscle in his jaw ticking as he gritted his teeth and retreated to the other side of the hot tub. He stared at the palm tree in the corner until the clouds that covered his face began to clear.

'Because you have a boyfriend.'

'What? No!' I exclaimed. 'Because you have a fiancée!'

'I don't have a fiancée?' Dev replied, looking as confused as I felt.

'You don't?'

'Nope. I *was* engaged but we called it off months ago.'

'What?' I was completely incapable of processing this information. Dev was single? 'Why? How? When?'

'It's not much of a story, I'm afraid. It just wasn't right,' he said with a half shrug, as if it was the most casual thing in the world. 'She wanted to get engaged before her thirtieth birthday and we'd been together for ages, so on paper, it seemed to make sense. A week after her birthday, after I proposed, we both realized it didn't. So we called it off.'

'You called it off?' I was still struggling with the concept. 'Amicably? No one cheated, no one left, no one had sex with their receptionist?'

Dev frowned. 'That's a very specific question but no, not to the best of my knowledge. I don't think she has a receptionist and mine is a sixty-year-old lesbian who's been with her wife since they were eighteen so I don't fancy my chances there.'

'So,' I took a deep breath in and held it, the heat of the hot tub suddenly overwhelming. 'You're not engaged?'

'I am not,' he confirmed, that dangerous smile very slowly returning to his face. 'And you don't have a boyfriend?'

'No,' I replied. 'No boyfriend. No girlfriend. No partner of any kind.'

'That's interesting, isn't it?' He moved back towards me, gliding through the water until his hips pressed against my knees and I realized I was still holding my breath. Relaxing my legs, he slid between my thighs and I blew out a long, slow exhale.

'So interesting,' I whispered.

Wrapping my arms around his neck, I pulled him in closer, Dev's hands exploring my hips, my waist, my back, his touch igniting sparks across my skin. This. This was how it was supposed to be. The hot water swirled around us, tracing the path of his fingertips along my body, and I slid my hands up into his hair. I hardly dared to open my eyes, but I had waited for this for so long and I had to see it all, remember it all. How his teeth caught on his bottom lip, the way his eyes filled with wonderful disbelief. Excruciatingly slowly, Dev dropped his head towards mine and I could feel his breath on my face, our foreheads resting against one another, teasing out the moment until I couldn't stand it for a single second longer. I brushed my lips against his, just barely, as if to test the moment. Was this real? Dev's lips on my lips? Dev's heart beating hard against my own? Everything turned hazy as our lips met, colours, shapes and feelings, a sharp intake of air, the smell of the chlorine on his skin and water lapping against my body when I pulled away. He pulled me back to him, holding my body so tightly I gasped, and when he kissed me again, time stopped and nothing else mattered. I was completely lost and, for once, I had no desire to be found.

It could have been one minute or one hour, I really couldn't say, but I pulled away first and when I was brave enough to raise my eyes to Dev's, I saw all my longing reflected back at me.

'Well,' he said, still holding me close enough to feel every hard line of his body.

'Well,' I replied, not quite sure what to do with myself.

'We could go back to mine,' he said, a promising growl in his voice. 'But my mum says I have to keep the door open when I have a girl over.'

I laughed but it really wasn't very funny. I felt as though I might explode but it seemed rude to explode in someone else's private pool, especially when you weren't supposed to be there in the first place. With endless regret, I slid my hands down his neck and rested them on his chest, widening the gap between us. So this was what it felt like to be in the moment. I had never felt so present in my life. Certainly not in my four years with Michael.

'If you could wish for anything, what would it be?' I asked as he ran a line of kisses down my neck and along my collarbone, each one exploding on my skin and making me gasp with delight.

'Anything?' Dev murmured.

'Anything.'

'The same thing I've been wishing for since I was thirteen.'

'We really should go somewhere,' I murmured as my resolve weakened and his lips found their way back to mine, irresistibly drawn.

'We are somewhere,' Dev replied, whispering directly into my ear and unlocking every ounce of desire in my body. 'And there's nowhere on earth I'd rather be.'

We melted against one another, my legs locked around his waist as my back scraped against the tiles and I pressed my mouth to his as hard as I dared, forcing every single thought out of my head. Somewhere above us, fireworks exploded in the sky and just for a second, as Dev moved against me and my back arched against the wall of the hot tub, I found myself wishing this moment would never end.

CHAPTER SEVENTEEN

The bottom of the garden was quiet the next morning. The perfect place for me to sit with myself before the day began. There was so much to do, the walk, the lunch, the pub, the party. I clutched my cup of tea and settled on the swing, looking out over the fields and revelling in that weird sense of calm that blanketed the outside world on Christmas morning, like we'd all agreed to treat it like a Sunday even if it wasn't one. Although maybe it was? I couldn't really remember anymore, it was just like lockdown all over again, baked goods were plentiful and time meant nothing.

I'd tried everything I could think to try but the wish still hadn't been granted. I'd helped my mother, found a way for Dad to reconnect with his loved ones and if last night didn't count as sorting out my love life at Nan's request, I didn't want to know what would. I'd even gone above and beyond, helping Manny and Cerys for extra brownie points, but I was still here on Christmas morning number ten with more questions than I had answers. But perhaps, I thought as I blew on my hot tea before taking a sip, that was OK.

Three months ago, I was so sure of my place in the world. I was a proud, ambitious workaholic on the fast track to partnership at my prestigious job. I was Michael's girlfriend, hoping to be promoted to fiancée any day. I was the youngest of the Baker kids, the one who happily kept the peace and had an unrequited crush on the boy next door. Now I had to wonder how much of that had ever been true. Were any of us the people everyone thought we were? Good Time Guy Manny was lonely. Tough as Nails Cerys was afraid. Mum was overwhelmed and my dad had never truly found a way through his grief.

Then there was Dev.

What did I know about Dev? He was kind and funny, a good cook and a good listener. He cared about people so much he'd made it his career and when I closed my eyes, all I could see were flashes of the night before, his hands, his mouth, his body against mine. It was entirely worth the almost twenty-year wait. Every time we saw each other, he told me the truth when I asked for it. Dev had shown me who he was, I didn't need to guess, he was an open book.

Which left only me.

I wasn't sure of anything anymore. When someone waved a red flag you were supposed to stop, not wave back and keep on going because the map you'd been following for ages told you to. Roads changed, bridges crumbled. Old maps needed to be replaced with new ones. Sometimes you had to find a new way to get to your destination.

Sipping my tea, I felt the chilly wind on my face and breathed in.

All this time I thought I was in control, but like so much else in my life, that control was an illusion. Manny had been right to throw my Ronan Keating CD out the bedroom window when I was ten, and not only because it wasn't very good but because Ronan was peddling a dangerous message to impressionable youths. Life was not a rollercoaster and you did not just have to ride it. It was more like one of those rental scooters that had popped up around the city: mostly fun, sometimes unpredictable, but frequently impossible to control and occasionally trying to kill you.

A robin landed on the fence at the bottom of the garden, hopping back and forth and showing off his scarlet waistcoat before taking off into the Joneses' garden. I smiled, hoping he might land on Dev's windowsill. If he didn't have any telly to watch, the least the universe could do was send him a bird to keep him entertained. It hurt, knowing he wouldn't remember the night before when he woke up, but I couldn't change that. There was no point breaking my heart about something I had no control over. Like Manny always said, what's for you won't go by you. If we were meant to be, we'd find a way.

Finishing my tea, I stood up and stretched.

The funny thing about reliving the same day over and over was that the only person who had to live with the consequences of my actions was me. Nothing really mattered anymore.

And when nothing matters, it's much easier to see what really does.

* * *

'I've got an announcement to make.'

I tapped my knife against the side of my glass once we'd finished our mains, the whole family sat around the table, lolling in a tryptophan daze.

'You're going to burn that awful dress?' Nan guessed, raising her wine in my direction. 'I support your decision entirely.'

'No,' I replied, glancing over at Dad and reminding myself that whatever happened, the chances of it sticking tomorrow morning were slim to none. I could do this. 'I'm leaving Abbott & Howe.'

No one said anything at first. Manny reached for my hand under the table and gave it a squeeze, Oliver and Cerys shared a smirk and Mum looked straight at my dad, bypassing me completely. Nan refilled her glass and shrugged.

'I don't see how that helps you get that frock out of your life but all right. Cheers to your future.'

'You're leaving?' Dad said slowly, as though he was struggling to make two and two equal four.

'Yes, Dad.'

'You've been headhunted?' he guessed, a slim thread of hope in his voice. 'Denton Henry have offered you partnership?'

'No, Dad.'

'Then where are you going? Why would you leave?'

It was a good question but I had a good answer.

'Because I don't want to be there,' I told him, thinking back to my conversation with Dev. 'And I don't have to stay. I've got a little bit of money saved up, it's not like I'm spending a lot on rent right now, and I'll find another job. I've had a lot of time to think about it and I've made a decision. It isn't the right place for me.'

I waited for a rush of triumph, a clean and clear internal sign that I'd done the right thing. But all I felt was the unpleasant queasiness that came from eating too many potatoes.

Mum stood up, grabbing empty plates and stacking them loudly on top of each other.

'I'm going to clear the table,' she declared. 'Gwen, help me put them in the kitchen? We can talk about this later.'

'No, I'm afraid I don't understand,' Dad said, placing a hand on my forearm before I could make a move to help her. 'You can't just leave a job. Not when you haven't got another one to go to.'

'She can if she's been sacked,' Oliver muttered into his napkin.

'Hardly,' Dad snapped. 'She's on track to be the youngest partner in the company's history.'

'Youngest female partner,' Oliver corrected. 'My friend Felix Johnson made partner at thirty-three. And I very much doubt she's looking at promotion since . . . the incident.'

'Felix Johnson whose dad is a senior partner,' I replied calmly. 'And I wasn't sacked. Technically, I'm on leave.'

But Dad wasn't in the mood for technicalities. His normally placid face began to puff up with irritation. My father did not like to be the last person in the room to know what was going on and I could hardly blame him for that.

'Gwen, what's he talking about?' he asked. 'What incident? Why are you on leave?'

I folded my napkin into four neat squares and placed it on the table where my plate had been.

'I cobbed a stapler at a sexist pig and now I'm facing disciplinary action.'

'Oh my,' Nan said, taking a sip of her wine.

'But this isn't about that,' I insisted as my dad turned puce. 'I'm not leaving because I've been fired, I'm leaving because I want to. Every day I go to the office and work a stupid number of hours to make more money for an awful man and dozens more awful men just like him. There's nothing in it for me except a pat on the back from the boss, the promise of more work, more hours and eventually the chance to slack off a bit while some other poor girl works herself into the ground for the chance to repeat the cycle again and again and again.'

From the expressions on their faces, no one other than Manny seemed to understand why this would be a problem.

'There's a poster in the women's toilets that says "Pressure creates diamonds",' I said, picturing it in my mind. 'That's messed up. They haven't got the same poster in the gents and I know that for a fact because I went in once when I was bursting and the only thing in there is a picture of Denise Van Outen ripped out of an issue of *Nuts* magazine that is probably old enough to vote. But that's beside the point, which is, why are we celebrating treating women like bits of rock? I don't want to be pressured into being the hardest substance on earth, Dad, I want to be happy.'

'I can't believe I'm hearing this,' he said to no one in particular, picking up his fork, putting it down then picking it up again. 'She wants to be happy? Jesus wept.'

Manny reached over and plucked the fork out of his hand, passing it through the serving hatch to my mother. 'You'll be telling me they've got a live, laugh, love poster in the staff room next.'

'It's a law firm, Manny,' I replied. 'All three of those things are forbidden on company time.'

'I'm not talking about the bloody poster!' Dad roared. Everyone fell silent and in the kitchen, I heard a sharp smash as Mum dropped something breakable on the floor. Dad had never raised his voice to me my whole life. Manny? A million times and he'd definitely had stern words with Cerys a few times when she was a teenager, but me? Not once. I'd never given him a reason until now. 'You are not giving up that job. Do you know how difficult it is to even get your foot in the door at a firm like that?'

'Yes, I do,' I replied. 'Because I did it.'

'Then what on earth is wrong with you?' The atmosphere in the dining room darkened faster than the sky outside. 'I would have done anything for an opportunity like this and you're going to throw it away because you want to be happy?'

On a different day, it would have worked. The thought of upsetting my dad and leaving my job, abandoning a career I'd worked so hard for would have terrified me into taking it all back, but here at the table, trapped in my little time cocoon, it wasn't scary at all. Why would I escape one never-ending loop then willingly walk back into another one? I was just as trapped in that job as I was trapped in this never-ending Christmas.

'I do understand why you're upset, but Dad . . .' I paused, reminding myself this would all be over as soon as I fell asleep, blew myself up or fell down a steep flight of stairs. 'I'm not you.'

The colour of my father's face changed in splotches, turning from white to red like a Global Hypercolor t-shirt.

'You're going to waste ten years?' he asked, slapping his hand on the table. 'Throw away your career because you want to be happy? Do you think your Grandad Collins was happy down the pit? Do you think I was always happy in my job? Is Cerys happy? Is Manny happy? You're living in a dream world, Gwen. You're throwing everything away.'

'I am quite happy,' Manny replied. 'Not about everything, but—'

'No, you're not,' Dad interrupted and Manny's lips disappeared into a long thin line.

'Better to throw away ten years than waste a whole life,' I replied, searching for the strength to keep talking and finding it in a squeeze from Manny's hand underneath the table. 'I want to be glad to wake up in the morning, there isn't a time limit on that. If Mum wanted to jack in teaching and start a new career right now, she could. Nan too for that matter.'

'Good luck with that,' Nan replied with a cluck. 'You're not sending me out to work at my age. What would I do? Take tickets at the bingo? I'd rather you put me out of my misery.'

'What I mean is, it's never too late to make changes. Big ones, little ones, in-between ones. No one should stay in an unhappy situation if they don't want to.'

Dad didn't say anything but to everyone's surprise, Cerys did.

'Thing is, Dad,' she said, looking right at me. 'Gwen is right.'

You could have knocked me off my chair with a piece of tinsel.

'If she's going to change careers, she should do it now. It only gets more difficult for women as they get older and once you've got a family, it's practically impossible. But men do it all the time, don't they? At any age. I don't think she's throwing anything away, I think it's actually very brave.'

If I wasn't close to tears before, I was now. Cerys was actually standing up for me?

'That said, don't come crying to me when you're homeless in six months because we all know how shit you are with money,' she added. 'You're not coming to live with me.'

That was more like it.

'You've both lost your minds,' Dad snapped, flicking his napkin out of his lap and tossing it onto the table. 'Your mother is going to have to talk some sense into you, she's the one that reasons with children all day. I'm not sitting here and listening to this.'

Still muttering under his breath, he stood up and walked out of the room, leaving the door wide open in his wake. Not the first Baker to exit this Christmas dinner in a dramatic fashion, but certainly the most unexpected from the looks of everyone still sat around the table. Even Artemis and Arthur looked up from their iPads with vague concern.

'Are you going to go after him?' Manny asked as the back door slammed shut and the kids went back to staring blankly at their tablets.

'What's the point?' I sagged with an uneasy mixture of success and defeat. I really had thought this would feel better.

He tilted his head to one side in agreement, activating his only wrinkle, the little line on his forehead from where he was constantly raising one disbelieving eyebrow. 'Not that I'm not supportive, but on the way up you said you were excited to go back to work?'

'I was excited to go back to pretending nothing is wrong,' I replied, eyeing Cerys through the Sylvanian centrepiece. 'After some careful consideration, I've come to realize that won't work in the long term.'

'Careful consideration in the last twelve hours?' he asked.

'And then some,' I said. 'You're going to have to trust me.'

'I always do,' Manny said. 'I've got your back.'

Across the table, Cerys picked up her wine and glugged it down as she stared at her husband who was busy fashioning himself a sailor's hat out of his napkin.

'In case anyone was wondering, your grandad was quite happy down the pit,' Nan said. 'I'm not saying they were singing and dancing down there, but he got to work with his friends and buy a house for his family and he didn't do it so his grandchildren could spend their lives working themselves to the bone in jobs they hate. I think he'd be very proud of you right now, Gwen.'

The tears I'd been holding back bloomed and trickled down my cheeks, one by one.

'But he would hate that sodding dress.'

'Thanks, Nan,' I said, raising my glass in her direction. 'Good to know.'

CHAPTER EIGHTEEN

'Manny, Cerys, do you want to go to the pub?'

An hour had passed and Dad was still stewing over my announcement, pottering about in the garage and refusing to come back inside. Ever since I saw his head bobbing up and down over the top of the Hyundai, I'd been physically restraining myself from running out to tell him it was all a big joke and I wasn't really going to quit and I was so sorry. But it wasn't and I was and even though I was sorry, I knew I shouldn't be. It was my choice, my life, I had to make my own decisions whether he liked them or not and we both had to learn how to live with it.

'Fuck, yes,' Manny said, standing up immediately, his gold paper crown slightly askew. Nan had been dozing in the armchair since we finished dinner but I was almost certain she was faking it.

'The pub?' Cerys said, not nearly as enthusiastic as Manny. 'With you two? Now?'

'We can schedule something in for a later date if you

like,' I replied, popping Manny's reindeer antlers onto Artemis's head. 'But I could use some fresh air and a large drink right now.'

Her inscrutable expression flickered for a split second then she pushed herself out of her armchair, up to her feet. 'Ol, can you keep an eye on the kids for an hour?'

'Why can't we leave them with your mum,' he whined, pausing the poker game he'd been playing on his phone while the rest of us watched our old home movies. 'I want to come too.'

'I don't mind!' my mother piped up, her head popping around the living-room door as though summoned from the ether. 'You can leave them with me.'

'He can look after his own kids for an hour on Christmas Day, it won't kill him.' Cerys looked back at Oliver, who was already back to his poker game. 'In fact, why don't you come with us?'

Mum shook her head, tea towel in one hand, serving spoon in the other. 'Too much to do. And what about Dorothy's?'

'We can go to Dorothy's later,' I promised, taking the tea towel out of her hand as Manny grabbed for the serving spoon. 'It goes on for hours. And we'll finish the washing up when we get back, it's not going anywhere. Come to the pub.'

She looked at the three of us as though we'd suggested she run through the streets naked and slathered in brandy butter.

'I suppose one quick drink wouldn't hurt,' she said, testing the words before she committed. 'OK, let me get my coat.'

'Quick, before anyone changes their mind,' Manny said, rounding up the Baker women and herding us all into the hallway. 'First round's on me.'

'I'm not going to ask you about your job,' Mum said as she settled into a warm corner of The Baslow Arms. Manny and Cerys stood at the bar, poking and pushing each other while they waited to order and I tried to telepathically remind Manny to bring back some peanuts. Against all odds, I was hungry again.

I gave her a disbelieving look as I took off my coat and hung it on a hook on the wall.

'I'm not,' she added. 'Your dad's a proud man and, despite my best work, he's still very old-fashioned about a lot of things like work and money and lifting a single bloody finger to help me around the house, but I did a good job with you. If you're sure this is the right thing to do, you've got my backing.'

'Wow,' I replied. 'Thank you.'

Then she leaned forward in her seat, finger wagging in my direction. 'But what I will say is, that doesn't mean I won't worry. We didn't have a lot of money growing up, we weren't as comfortable as your dad's side of the family and that's always in the back of my mind. If you were still with Michael, I'd be less concerned. On your own without a job, that's a lot, isn't it?'

She wasn't going to ask me about my job but she was going to panic about me becoming a penniless spinster. Classic mothering.

'I'll find another job,' I promised, the tiny creases around her eyes deepening slightly as she formed a thin line with her lips. 'And I really, truly, honestly could not be better off without Michael in my life. He's happier without me and I will definitely be happier without him in the long run.'

I'd confirmed that last night in Bernard and Lesley's hot tub.

'All you want as a mother is for your kids to have an easier go of it than you did,' she replied, wringing her hands together as she hunched over the table. 'I know you all make fun of me for always thinking the worst but when you grow up without very much, it's hard to imagine the best.'

The expression on her face was a familiar one, I'd seen it when Cerys told her she wanted to go to Oxford and when Manny came out. Supportive but with concerns. She knew Oxford would be hard for Cerys after going to a local comprehensive. She believed Manny should love whoever he wanted to love but she also came from a generation that believed his life would be more difficult because of it. She didn't quite understand that they had to be true to themselves and do what felt right, even if it wasn't the easier option. It had to be hard, acting as a human bridge between two such different generations, especially when the younger one spent most of their time rolling their eyes at you.

'This is for the best,' I said as Cerys and Manny made their way back from the bar with a bottle and four glasses. 'Abbott & Howe isn't a good place for me. I never told you this but when I was a trainee, I used to eat my packed lunch in the toilets because I was so embarrassed that I couldn't afford Prêt every day like everyone else, and Mum, sometimes I still do it. I eat my lunch in the ladies because it's too stressful to eat at my desk and there's no time to leave the office. That can't be right, can it?'

'No,' Cerys and Manny chorused as one as she poured the wine and he distributed the glasses.

'I thought it would change when I qualified but it didn't change. Now I've been there ten years and every time I buy a new pair of shoes or some ugly, expensive suit I would never normally wear, I think, this is the outfit that will make me feel like someone who belongs here, but it never does.'

'If he was talking to you right now, your dad would tell you that's all in your head,' Mum said, picking up her wine and swirling the ruby-red liquid around the glass. 'My little girl belongs in any room she walks into.'

'And he might be right,' I admitted. 'But why keep fighting with myself when I could leave and do something else? Life doesn't have to be the thing you choose when you're twenty-one.'

'Or the person you choose when you're twenty-one.'

All eyes turned to Cerys and she quickly cleared her throat.

'Or however old you were when you met Michael, I don't know,' she corrected. 'That's what I was talking about.'

'I think it's brilliant,' Manny declared, raising his glass in a toast. 'You've been fucking miserable for years, fading away in front of us. I can't wait for you to get out of there.'

'You didn't think to mention it before now?' I asked, clinking my glass against his.

'Would you have listened to me?'

'No.'

'Shut up then.'

I looked at my mum, my sister and my cousin as they sipped their wine, every single one of us smiling. Until we tasted the wine.

'Manny, what is this?' I asked, gagging.

'It's cheap, Gwen, it's cheap,' he replied, glugging it down. 'Some of us live in London on a teacher's salary.'

'I've drunk worse,' added my mother, spoken like a lifelong educator.

'I haven't,' Cerys said, spitting it back into the glass. 'Gin and tonic anyone?'

Mum rubbed my back with a comforting hand and Manny filled her glass up to the brim while she wasn't looking. 'Your dad will come around,' she said. 'It might take a while but he won't be upset with you forever.'

'It'll all be forgotten by tomorrow,' I promised as I looked out the window just in time to see the snow begin to fall. 'I can almost guarantee it.'

One bottle turned into two and two turned into we might as well do another bottle since it's only a glass and a bit each, and by the time we set off home, we were going to be really quite late for Dorothy's party and the snow was thick on the ground. Manny and Cerys marched on ahead, singing the dirty version of 'Good King Wenceslas' while Mum and I strolled along behind them, arm in arm.

'It was nice to get out,' she said as we turned the corner to our house. 'I feel like I'm on a treadmill most days. I thought it would get better after your dad retired but he never bloody leaves me alone. What's for breakfast, what'll he do for lunch, what am I making for dinner, what do I want to watch on the telly, where are we going on the weekend. He's forgotten some of us still have a job. If it's twenty more years of this, I might upend everything as well and come to live with you.'

'You need to set boundaries,' I replied, as though I had any idea what I was talking about. 'They sound fun, I've heard about them on the internet.'

'And you need to duck!' she said, letting go of my arm and diving into an oversized azalea bush.

But it was too late. By the time I realized what she was talking about, Manny had already hurled his first snowball at my head.

'Oh, you ARSE,' I yelled, brushing snow out of my hair, my ear throbbing. 'I'm going to kill you!'

'I'm not part of this!' Mum sang as she ran across the road to Dorothy's house. 'Don't any of you bloody dare throw anything at me or I'll have your guts.'

'I've got to get a picture,' Cerys said, cackling beside the front gate and, digging around in her pockets for her phone. Until Manny sent a snowball flying in her direction.

'Manny, you wanker!' she exclaimed, forgetting all about her phone and bending over to launch her own attack. It wasn't her fault, all human beings were genetically coded to return fire in a snowball fight, no matter who, where or when.

'Have that!' she grunted, chucking her puny snowball at Manny and missing by a country mile.

'Ha!' he screeched. 'You're shit! You couldn't hit me if your snowball was the size of a basketball and I was ten foot wide.'

'He's right,' I said grimly as I sidled up beside my sister. 'You are shit. We both are.'

'So what do we do?' she asked as he began assembling an arsenal at the side of his car. 'You're even worse than I am.'

'She is! Because she's slow *and* she's short,' Manny shouted. 'You'll never beat me!'

I squinted at him with new-found determination.

'We can't beat him in a snowball fight but who says we have to?' I whispered. 'Let's just beat the shit out of him.'

Cerys's eyes lit up and she nodded in agreement, a silent deal was struck.

'Now?' she asked.

'Now!' I confirmed.

Without warning, we charged at Manny and knocked him off his feet. He sprawled out on the ground, all six feet of him writhing in the snow with Cerys straddled across his chest while I grabbed hold of his madly kicking legs.

'Why are you ganging up on me?' he screeched. 'This isn't fair.'

'Life isn't fair,' I yelled, wrapping my arms around his knees as they kicked madly.

Cerys grabbed a handful of snow and started stuffing it down the front of Manny's jumper as he screamed blue murder. He was still squealing when I heard someone loudly clear their throat and looked up to see Dev on the other side of the garden gate staring at the three of us, Pari straining at her leash.

'Oh good,' he said, looking relieved. 'Mum thought someone was being murdered.'

'Someone is!' Manny choked. 'For fuck's sake, Dev, help me!'

He laughed politely and took a step backwards. 'Sorry, mate, I'm Switzerland. I don't want any part of this.'

'Some neighbour you are,' he wailed hysterically as Cerys dumped more snow down his trousers.

Dev looked down at me, still squatting on my cousin's shins, his smile tempered by the years that had passed for him since we last spoke. But for me it was all so different. All the time we'd spent together over the last ten days came rushing back, all the conversations, the little things and the big things he'd helped me understand about myself, about my family, about everything – and he didn't even know it. Then there was the kiss. That first, perfect kiss. I thought about teenage Dev lying awake at night in his room, pressing his hand against the bedroom wall, listening to a song I assumed was about irritated vaginas, and teenage Gwen snogging her pillow, pretending it was him and there was no way I could stop myself.

'Good to see you all,' he said, tugging on Pari's leash. 'Merry Christmas.'

'Dev!' I yelled, scrambling to my feet. 'Wait!'

I threw my arms around his neck and planted my lips on his. I felt him freeze with surprise, hesitating for a moment before he melted against me. A soft sigh escaped my own lips as he dropped Pari's leash and pulled me even closer.

A perfect second first kiss.

'That was unexpected,' he murmured, dazed and delighted as we broke apart. 'Did Father Christmas only just get the letter I sent him when I was thirteen? I know the post is slow, but that would be ridiculous.'

'Sometimes it takes people a really long time to get the message,' I replied, my hands still resting on his shoulders. 'But better late than never.'

Snow fell from the sky and flew up from the ground, swirling around the two of us as though we were standing in our very own snow globe, freshly shaken.

'I should get back inside.' Dev's eyes lingered on mine as Pari ran joyous circles around Manny and Cerys who were still wrestling outside the front door. 'I only came out to see what all the screaming was about. We're about to eat, but I would love to see you before you leave. Maybe we could meet up tomorrow or something?'

'If there is a tomorrow,' I replied, only a little sadly. 'I'm all yours.'

He smiled so wide the dimple in his left cheek popped. 'Is that a promise?'

'One way or another, I will see you tomorrow,' I nodded, biting my lip to stop myself from tearing up. 'I hope you don't forget.'

'As if I could forget a kiss like that,' Dev replied, picking up Pari and walking back towards his parents' house.

Dad was upstairs when Cerys and Manny called a truce, exhausted and soaking wet through. He didn't meet us at Dorothy's party, he didn't put on his firework display and he didn't come downstairs for a cup of tea when we all arrived home either. By the time everyone decided it was time for bed (everyone except for Manny who was last seen snogging Drew the butcher's face off in Dorothy's conservatory), the only person who had spoken to him was Mum and it didn't look as though their conversation had been the highlight of her day.

Opening the dining-room door, I crept along the hallway to the kitchen, the dulcet tones of Buddy the Elf whispering through the walls even though Artemis and Arthur were definitely supposed to be asleep by now. Upstairs, floorboards creaked and taps ran, but all the lights were out, signalling that another Christmas Day was almost over.

'Might as well stuff myself stupid,' I whispered, making a beeline for the fridge. My appetite was back with a vengeance today.

'I've warned you about the gout,' said a voice in the dark. 'And I'll not sit up all night rubbing your legs like I did your grandad's.'

I flicked on the light above the oven to see Nan sat at the table, calmly drinking a mug of something hot and steaming while my heart pounded against my ribs.

'Christ on a bike, you scared me half to death,' I said between deep calming breaths. Death by grandmother would have been an interesting one to add to the list.

'Blasphemy on Christmas Day,' she tutted. 'Your great-grandma would've had your guts for garters. There's some Horlicks in the pan if you want some. There's half a bottle of Baileys in it, don't tell your mother.'

'Good job I didn't drink the whole bottle myself this time,' I said, grabbing a mug from the cupboard and helping myself. Nan sipped her boozy Horlicks and watched me, smiling like the cat who'd not only got the cream but had also bought the cow for good measure.

'What are you grinning at?' I asked as I pulled out the chair opposite her.

'I heard you've been up to no good with the boy next door,' she replied.

'Depends on your definition of good.'

I took a tiny sip and then a giant gulp. Horlicks with Baileys was obscenely good, why had no one tried this before?

Nan gave me a knowing wink, bathed in the golden glow of the light on the extractor fan. Mum always said she had been remarkably beautiful in her day, my nan, but I'd say she still was, if you bothered to look.

'Last I heard he was engaged,' she said, patting her hair into place for me. 'I hope he's filled out a bit, he always was a lanky little thing. Couldn't stop a pig in a ginnel, that one.'

'Definitely not skinny now,' I assured her. 'Filled out very nicely as it happens. And hasn't been engaged for months, just so you know.'

Her left eyebrow rose like a Welsh Bette Davis.

'Well, I'm glad. I know you're not supposed to say things like this these days, but I don't like to think of you down in London on your own. I'd be much happier knowing you've got someone taking care of you, making sure you're happy.'

'It was one kiss, might be a bit early to be giving him that kind of responsibility,' I replied. 'Actually, I don't think you should rely on any one person to make you happy.'

'Definitely not a man,' Nan agreed.

'I reckon it's more of a DIY project,' I smiled. 'But I'm all right, Nan, I'm OK.'

'Really?'

'Even if I'm not that happy right now, I will be,' I said, certain now that I meant it.

She nodded slowly and I blew on my hot drink. It really was good. Could spiked Horlicks be my million-dollar business idea? Was this the reason I'd been kept here for ten long Christmas Days? To share this wonder with the world?

'As long as you're not lonely, that's all I need to know,' Nan replied. 'It's the one thing I wouldn't wish on anyone.'

'I have been,' I admitted, only fully understanding the truth of it as I spoke. 'Being with someone who didn't want to be with me, working at a job where I never felt like I belonged. Those things made me lonely. I cut myself off from a lot of people for a long time because I was miserable. But maybe loneliness isn't always a bad thing, perhaps it's more of a reminder.'

'How's that, pet?'

I thought about the deep, dark emptiness inside me, the one I was still nursing when Manny and I drove home for Christmas. The one I'd tried to fill with endless ice cream and Taylor Swift songs and online shopping and lying awake until 3 a.m. reading the Wikipedia entries for every single episode of *The OC* on my phone. No wonder none of that had worked (although Taylor really had tried). You simply cannot cure loneliness on your own. Ten days ago, there was a void in me. Now, I was full to bursting with love and hope and dreams of what might happen next.

'Loneliness is how you know something is missing,' I said. 'Feeling lonely means you haven't given up hope.'

'And that's why you have always been the clever one.' Her smile softened and flickered at the edges. 'I've been lonely ever since I lost your grandad.'

She stated it so simply, as though it was simply a fact and not the most heartbreaking thing I'd ever heard. I was so little when Grandad died and I didn't really remember him. I couldn't imagine how it must feel to spend thirty years of your life missing someone. My face began to crumble, bottom lip trembling, but Nan remained stoic as ever.

'Pssh, don't look at me like that,' she said, flapping a slender hand in my direction. 'What I mean is, I don't want that for you. Whatever else it might be, I do know loneliness can be very cruel. You can't pick and choose when it visits and it often overstays its welcome, sometimes it stays so long you get used to it and forget to ask it to leave. I would hate for you to fall into that trap.'

I blinked back a tear before she saw and sniffed subtly into my mug. I definitely wasn't the cleverest one at this table.

'I promise, I won't,' I said. 'All that stuff I said at lunch, that applies to you too. You could still find someone else?'

'Of course I could, do you know how many men have tried?' Nan looked pleased as punch. 'And not just men. Can't say I wasn't curious when Miranda from the WI invited me on that ladies-only Greek cruise last summer.'

'Wow, OK,' I said, blinking. 'You do you.'

She stirred her drink with a little silver teaspoon, a misty look in her pale blue eyes. 'I'm happy with my lot. You read about all these people falling in love at a hundred years old, running off with a fancy man half their age, but who can be doing with all that faff? It's not for me.'

'Sometimes the faff is worth it though,' I said, keeping my voice light. 'Don't you think Grandad would've wanted you to have someone to keep you company?'

'No he bloody wouldn't!' she guffawed, breaking the quiet spell that had settled over the kitchen. 'He'd want me still in my widow's black, wailing at the edge of a cliff and cursing the gods for taking him away. He always said if he went first, I couldn't remarry unless they were richer, cleverer or better-looking than him and I always said that would never happen because that man didn't exist. I'm very happy to have been proven right. They broke the mould when they made your grandad.'

She patted my hand and let her gaze wander off, her eyes glazing over as they went, reliving fragments of a life well lived. I pinched a strand of damp hair that had escaped from my topknot and pushed it back behind my ear before she could do it for me. She looked so happy. I wanted that. To sit in the kitchen with my grandchildren on Christmas Day, remembering a life full of joy. Dangerously close to tearing up again, I turned to look out the window and watched the last few clouds melt away, leaving a perfect inky blue sky dotted with diamond stars and a near full moon. It was almost impossible to see the night sky from my flat in London and not only because of the smog and light pollution. The only window that didn't face the alley where the bins lived was directly opposite the flat of a man who liked to stay up all night screaming at video games and really quite frequently playing with himself. Manny came over once and tried to keep count but gave up by 10 p.m. I mostly kept the curtains drawn.

'Here.' I turned back to see Nan hiding something in her hand. 'I've got one last Christmas present for you.'

A shaft of moonlight fell through the window and sliced the table in two as she uncurled her fingers.

There it was.

The silver sixpence.

'Is that the sixpence from the pudding?' I asked, sitting on my hands, too afraid to touch it. How could such a tiny, inconspicuous thing cause me so much trouble?

'It is.' She placed the coin on the table, pushing it towards me with her index finger.

'So you made the wish?'

'No,' Nan replied. 'I didn't want to waste it. Couldn't think of a single thing I might ask for that would make my life better than it already is.'

'But if you didn't make a wish then why . . .' My voice faded away and the sixpence winked at me in the silvery moonlight until I made myself pick it up. 'You could wish for anything,' I said. 'You could wish for more time with Grandad.'

'Oh, Gwen, love.' Nan's sad smile reappeared as she stood up slowly. 'Wishes are for the future, not the past. What's done is done and we all have to live with it, that's how life goes. Besides, I cannot imagine going through Brexit with your grandad. He would have gone mad, we'd be having a second Bonfire Night in his honour. And think of the man with an iPhone? Jesus, Mary and the donkey, it would have been the end of our marriage. I'd never have been able to watch *Pointless* in peace and I do like that Richard Osman. He writes books now, you know?'

'You really didn't make a wish?' I asked again, cradling the sixpence in my palm very, very carefully. 'Nothing at all?'

'I did not make a wish,' she confirmed. 'It's all yours.'

I didn't know where to start, everyone needed something. Mum and Dad, Cerys and Manny and even though she claimed she didn't, my beautiful, lonely Nan.

'I just want everyone to be happy,' I whispered.

'That's a lot to ask of a sixpence.' She placed her mug and teaspoon in the sink, on her way to bed. 'Make a wish for yourself then make it come true, don't leave the important things up to anyone else, not even fate.'

It was sound advice.

'I'm off to bed,' Nan said with a tiny ladylike yawn. 'I only came to make that Horlicks to help me sleep. That bedroom's like a furnace, your father must be made of money the way he heats this house.'

Whenever a major decision had to be made in the Baker household, it was made at the kitchen table. So many decisions had been made here, big and small, difficult and easy, from which pizza toppings to get to which universities to apply to. The close proximity to the kettle made it a far more sensible choice than the dining-room table, plus the back door was right there in case anyone needed to make a speedy exit. I could still remember the happiness on my dad's face when we sat here together and filled out my application for the Abbott & Howe trainee scheme. We went through the best part of an entire box of teabags that day. Now I could simply wish for anything in the entire world and make it happen, no debate necessary.

When I closed my eyes, the first thing I saw was Dev. I could wish for him to fall in love with me and whisk me away to a life of endless bliss. Imagine it, the two of us together for ever. But how dependable and legally binding were these wishes? What happens after the happily ever after? As someone who did not consider direct-to-DVD Disney films canon, I realised you never really did find out what happened after the credits rolled. Were there any loopholes when it came to wishing on a star? As a lawyer, I would like to see the contract first.

Imagine if you only found out Prince Charming was actually a racist who never cleaned the toilet *after* you married him? Poor Cinders. You had to assume divorce law was complicated in those times. *The Little Mermaid* was the perfect example of someone who didn't read the fine print. Make a deal with a Sea Witch, almost end up as plankton. And I never had been convinced of their happily ever after, emotionally healthy young men don't marry a sixteen-year-old fish-child simply because they're very pretty, good at karaoke and their dog likes them. That marriage was doomed from the start.

I didn't want Dev to be with me because I'd wished for it. Life was about choices, me making mine, him making his. As someone who struggled to choose between a hoisin duck wrap and a pole-caught tuna baguette at lunch, I couldn't think of anything more romantic than someone choosing you and you choosing them right back, every single day for the rest of your lives. Wishing for it wouldn't feel right.

Placing the sixpence on the table, I pushed it around in circles with the tip of my finger, thinking of everything that had happened over the last ten days. Confronting Michael, fixing things with Cerys, telling my dad I'd decided to leave my job, and so much more. I'd done those things all by myself, I made them happen. I had so much more power than I knew. I hadn't been stuck for the last ten days, it had been much longer than that. Months. Years maybe. But no more.

'All I want is tomorrow,' I said, sliding the coin off the edge of the table and squeezing it so tightly, I was sure it would leave an imprint on the palm of my hand. 'That's my wish. I wish for tomorrow.'

It wasn't very romantic. It wasn't dramatic or spectacular, but it was more than anyone had the right to ask for. To wake up in the morning and find the world still turning.

Slipping the sixpence into my pocket, I walked over to the sink and washed out my mug, looking out at the snow-covered garden. Everything sparkled with stillness, not a single footprint in the snow, and I wondered if it would still be there when I woke up or if I'd be right back where I started. You could keep your endless riches and your prince charmings.

A tomorrow would be more than enough for me.

CHAPTER NINETEEN

I woke up to the sound of someone banging on my door and calling my name.

'Gwen? Are you up?'

So the sixpence hadn't worked.

It was crushing. I'd really believed it might be different this time. I stayed under the covers, refusing to cry, and tried to think happy thoughts. Chris Hemsworth's triceps, Cadbury's Caramilk chocolate, Bennifer getting back together. I had been gifted with an eternity to read all those daily deal books I'd downloaded to my Kindle and never, ever even opened. Or at least start a couple of them. I would find a way to deal with this. I would find a way to survive. Except I didn't have any Caramilk and all the shops were closed.

I would never eat Caramilk again.

'What are you doing still in bed?' asked the voice at the door.

'Contemplating existential dread,' I said, choking back a sob from underneath my blankets.

'Well can you do it somewhere other than the dining room? I want to hoover up before lunch.'

My dad wanted to hoover? I wasn't even sure Steven Baker knew what a vacuum cleaner was. I threw off a blanket that was not my duvet and rolled into the red-hot radiator, searing the flesh on my arse and waking me right up.

'What day is it?' I yelled, fighting with the camp bed as I scrambled upright. The disembodied voice at the door was not my father's, it belonged to my mum, and I wasn't in my bedroom, I was in the dining room, right where I'd gone to sleep the night before.

'It's Monday, Boxing Day,' she replied, standing over me in a pair of jeans and the deep green jumper Cerys gave her *yesterday*. 'How much did you have to drink last night?'

The sun shone brighter, the sound of children's laughter filled the air and the world even smelled sweeter – or had Mum finally uncorked the bottle of Estée Lauder Beautiful I'd watched her unwrap ten times? Didn't matter. Whatever it was, it was glorious. My life had meaning again. The promise of Caramilk was back on the table.

'I don't believe it,' I said, scrambling around on the floor for my phone. There it was. December 26th. Zero texts from Aunt Gloria and one WhatsApp from Manny that just said 'thank you' seventy-four times in a row with an aubergine emoji at the end.

'Gwen, are you feeling all right?' Mum asked as I leapt to my feet, the camp bed snapping shut like a Venus flytrap behind me.

'Better than all right,' I replied, sweeping her up in a

giant hug and squeezing until she squealed. 'I'm amazing, everything is amazing. It's Boxing Day, it's the day after Christmas. It's the best day ever!'

She fought me off with a Dyson stick and gave me a suspicious look. 'Who are you and what have you done with my daughter?'

I laughed once then clapped my hand over my mouth, afraid I wouldn't be able to stop if I started. It was tomorrow, yesterday's today, and I'd never been so grateful for anything in my life.

'Everything that happened yesterday, it really happened? You remember it?' I said, winding my hair up into a bun on top of my head. It needed washing! Because today was a new day!

'I don't know what's got into you this morning but yes.' Mum picked up my fallen blankets and began to fold them, one by one. 'Despite the amount of punch I put away at Dorothy's, I remember everything that happened yesterday. It was a fairly eventful day.'

It was. It was eventful. I tore the curtains open and saw the garden still covered in snow.

'Can you please attempt to help me by tidying up your mess in here?' Mum asked as reality slowly began to settle on my shoulders. 'I've got a hangover from hell, your father's buggered off on his walk and he's barely talking to me, Manny hasn't come home yet, your Nan's refusing to let the kids put the telly on so they're screaming blue murder, and I've got four extra mouths to feed at lunch since Cerys and her lot stayed over.'

'I will tidy up and I will help with lunch but there's one thing I have to do first,' I promised, kissing her on the cheek.

'Hopefully it's not in the bathroom,' she said with frown lines forming brackets around her mouth. 'Oliver blocked the toilet and I don't know where your dad's hidden the plunger. Where are you going?'

I smiled.

'To finish a conversation I started yesterday.'

'What's the rush? Today isn't going anywhere.'

'I really hope it is!' I called as I dashed out the room and bounded up the stairs.

Dad was easy to find.

The trail of footprints down the garden led me right to him, striding down the bridle path along the edge of the stream. I spotted him, wax jacket, flat cap, not five minutes away from the house, and broke into a sprint to catch up.

'Dad!' I cried. 'Dad, wait!'

He turned around, walking stick in hand.

'What's wrong?' he asked with a look of alarm. 'Is it your mum? Cerys?'

'Nothing's wrong,' I panted as I came to a stop, pressing my hand into my side.

'But you're running?'

'Sometimes I run,' I replied, wondering how normal it was for a thirty-two-year-old woman to start seeing stars after running for roughly two and a half minutes without stopping. 'I wanted to talk to you.'

'Because you've changed your mind?' Dad asked, his hopes briefly up.

I shook my head and his face fell. Without another word, he turned around and carried on walking.

'I haven't changed my mind and I need you to understand why,' I said, jogging in front of him and blocking the path. 'When I was little, you always told us we could do anything when we grew up. Well, that's what this is. This is me, doing anything.'

He stabbed at the ground with his walking stick. 'No,' he replied. 'This is you giving up. I raised you to believe in hard work and just rewards, not turning your back on a perfectly good career.'

'And I will work hard,' I countered quickly. 'But it'll be at a place that's right for me.'

He poked at something in a patch of bracken, refusing to look at me.

'I never had you pegged as a quitter.'

The hurt in his voice was sharpened to a point.

'Quitting isn't the same as failing,' I replied, trying to ignore the sting. 'I'm going to do something else with my life, Dad, maybe something amazing, and it'll be because you taught me not to settle for anything other than the best. Or would you rather I went back and spent the rest of my life unhappy?'

'I never said I wanted you to be unhappy,' he chuntered under his breath. 'But I don't want you to have regrets either. If you leave Abbott & Howe now, none of the other big firms will take you. Not after all this . . . nonsense. Word gets around, you know.'

'I do know and that's why I don't want to work in a place like that.' I thought of the dark corridors and the wood-panelled walls and the awful men in suits slogging their guts out to make money for other awful men in suits and then I thought a about never going having to go back there, and I smiled. 'You would hate it there, Dad. Everyone's miserable, no one's got any kind of life *and* they banned sugar from the office because the partners paid a nutritionist to do a peak performance diet plan that said we could only have low-glycaemic-index snacks and half a banana in the afternoon.'

That got his attention.

'You mean you can't have a Mars Bar with your afternoon cup of tea?' he asked, stunned.

'Most days I don't have time for an afternoon cup of tea,' I replied, shaking my head. 'I just throw coffee down my throat and hope it'll keep me going until home time, which is usually somewhere around eight o'clock if I'm lucky.'

'Eight o'clock and they won't even let you have a Mars Bar?' Dad whimpered. 'It's inhumane.'

Even though he looked surprised, none of this was new information. He knew I worked absurd hours for old men who dedicated their lives to keeping the world just the way they liked it, and he had encouraged me do it with a smile on his face. Because once upon a time, he wanted to be one of those men. Like Mum said, he was old-fashioned about a lot of things. But he also loved his kids. It was time for him to accept that things had to change.

'I don't know where I'm going to end up,' I said, choosing my words carefully now that I had him somewhere close to onside. 'But it'll be somewhere I feel like I belong. Where I don't have to work for shitheads who say and do disgusting things I haven't even told you about because well, it's embarrassing and ugly and not the sort of thing you want to tell your dad who is so proud of the fact you work for them. Wherever I go next will be better.'

'And it'll be somewhere you can eat a sodding Mars Bar whenever you want!' he replied, completely fired up even if he was choosing to focus on one of the lesser problems with my job. 'I'm sorry, chicken.' He pinched his shoulders together then let them slump down. I know the job isn't a walk in the park, but it's still hard for me to understand walking away after putting in all this time. Couldn't you change things by staying? Shake it up a bit from the inside? This is *Abbott & Howe* we're talking about, Magic Circle, top dog. It's what you've always wanted.'

'No, it isn't,' I corrected gently. 'It's what you always wanted. I just wanted to impress you and Cerys. Plus, I thought working in a law firm would be more like it was on *Ally McBeal* but no, no one sings, no one dances, there's zero Robert Downey Jr and I've not seen hide nor hair of a dancing baby.'

'Your mother bloody loved that show,' Dad muttered. 'Don't mention it when we get home, it's bound to be streaming somewhere and I cannot sit through all of that again.'

'You've got a deal.' I wound my arm through his, feeling something like peace all around.

'I won't pretend I'm not concerned,' he said, straightening the flap of his cap. 'And I do hope you give this a lot more thought before you hand in your notice, but whatever you decide to do, well, it's up to you, isn't it?'

'Yes, it is,' I agreed, turning my face towards the light that broke through a bank of low-hanging clouds. That was good enough for today. 'Shall we go on down to Chatsworth or do you want to go back?' I asked.

He looked down at my muddy trainers, borrowed coat and grey face. 'I'm not sure you'd make it,' he said, steering us back in the direction of the house. 'Let's get you home and put the kettle on.'

'Thank you,' I muttered. My legs were jelly. 'I'd have died before we got halfway across the field.'

'Whatever you do next, make sure it's something that mostly involves sitting down,' Dad advised. 'Long-distance runner is not going to be your thing.'

'I need a job where I can sit on my arse all day, drink a lot of tea and eat Mars Bars,' I replied. 'Any ideas?'

Dad scrunched up his face with concentration. 'Have you considered running for prime minister?'

'I *was* thinking about getting out of central London,' I replied with a thoughtful sniff. 'But now I think about it, I do quite fancy the country house and company car.'

'They'll let anybody run a country these days,' Dad said, cheerfully striking the ground with his walking stick. 'Worth keeping it in mind.'

'Always worth keeping in mind,' I agreed, marching along beside him.

The sun shone brightly when I stepped out the front door after lunch. Even though it was blinding outside, the air was still frosty and the snow was still on the ground, deep and crisp and even. It crunched under my feet as I practised my lines in my head.

Hi Dev, about the whole kissing thing yesterday, I've been trapped in a time loop so I know you used to have a crush on me plus we almost did it in Bernard and Lesley's pool the other night so . . .

I caught the eye of a tiny sparrow perched on a frosty white branch.

'No, you're right,' I said. 'Probably a bit much.'

The sparrow quite rightly flew away.

I didn't know what I was going to say. Dev was the

one who had pulled me through the last ten days. The one person I still wanted to see even when I could hardly bear to open my eyes. He helped me see how brave and bold and downright stupid I could be if I put my mind to it and he made me feel things, in my heart and in my M&S underwear, that I thought only existed in books and films and all those songs I'd learned by heart but never truly believed. I felt strong with him. He reminded me of a time in my life when every door was unlocked, just waiting to be opened. Somewhere along the line I'd confused a closed door with a locked one, but Dev had reminded me I was the one with the key. All I had to do was turn the handle and walk on through.

To me, Dev was everything.

To him, I was a woman he hadn't spoken to in a decade who randomly snogged him in the street twenty-four hours earlier.

It's going to be OK, I told myself as I opened the latch on our garden gate and turned onto the footpath between our two houses, pulling my jacket closer around me.

Don't overthink it.

Easier said than done now that all my decisions were set to stick.

Dev opened his door at the first knock. His dark hair, dark eyes and face lit up to see me and I smiled, my head full of ten days and twenty years of things I wanted to tell him.

'Hello, stranger,' I said.

'Hello yourself,' he replied. 'I see tomorrow did come after all.'

'At last,' I nodded. It was all I could do to meet his

eyes, feeling twelve years old again, knocking for the new neighbour.

'I've heard they're pretty regular, these tomorrows,' he said, grinning. 'They happen almost every day.'

'Almost,' I laughed, every part of me filled with pure joy. 'But not always.'

'I'm glad you're here.' Dev grabbed his coat from a shiny silver hook beside the door and joined me on the front step. 'I was starting to think I was imagining things yesterday. I ended up sat in my room, listening to my old CDs.'

'Bit of Kings of Leon?' I asked, almost fainting clean away when he laughed.

'How did you know?' He reached for my hand, his fingers winding through mine as our palms pressed against each other, warm and safe and full of promises. 'So where do you want to go?' Dev asked as we set off down the garden path.

'I don't know,' I replied, floating as much as walking. 'Why don't you surprise me?'

He paused in front of the gate, his grin fading to a soft, searching smile. Something that felt a lot like love shot through me, lighting up my darkest corners and leaving me on unsteady legs. But Dev wouldn't let me fall. He held my face in his hands and traced my cheekbone with his thumb before leaning down to kiss me, the warmth of his breath tingling against my cold skin, the heat of his lips running up and down my spine.

'Why don't we surprise each other,' he suggested. 'See where we end up?'

'That sounds like a very good plan,' I replied before pressing my lips against his again.

It was a very good plan indeed.

CHAPTER TWENTY

Next Christmas . . .

'MERRY CHRISTMAS!'

Arthur and Artemis answered the door wearing matching festive pyjamas, out of their tiny minds on too much sugar and the unbearable thrill of Christmas Eve.

'Auntie Gwen! Uncle Manny!' Arthur squealed as Artemis looped her arms around my waist and squeezed tightly enough to bust an internal organ. Not my liver, I prayed as I prised her off, anything but my liver. It was needed.

'Get out the way, I'm desperate for a piss,' Manny shouted as he peeled them off, waving at Cerys as he ran upstairs to the toilet.

'Good drive?' Cerys asked, holding her arms out for the bags and bags of presents I retrieved from the back seat of Manny's new car. RIP the Volvo. She served so well for so long but had finally gone to the great car park in the sky and Manny was taking it like a champ.

'Terrible drive,' I replied. 'Is there a bottle of anything open?'

She grinned. 'There's a bottle of everything open. Red wine in the living room, white wine's in the fridge. You know where it is, help yourself.'

'I don't,' Drew said, walking through the door carrying his bag, Manny's bag and my suitcase, all in one hand. 'I need a whisky, a very large whisky.'

'Manny was a handful on the way up,' I explained as he set our bags down and swapped them for my niece and nephew, tossing Artemis up onto his shoulders and throwing Arthur up into the air.

'Why change the habit of a lifetime?' Cerys replied. She cocked her head towards the living room and Drew moved quickly, the kids clinging to him like barnacles. 'Mum's got the whisky open, they're in there.'

'How are you settling in?' I asked, following her into the kitchen. Nan's kitchen. The last time I was there was to pack everything up into boxes. Now, full of Cerys's pots and pans and colourful Le Creuset pots it looked like a home again, the same but different. It was hard not to feel a little sad.

'Oh, you know, it is what it is,' Cerys fanned one hand in the air, opening various cupboards, pulling out tubs of peanuts and packets of crisps. 'Artemis is doing well in the new school but Arthur's been a bit of a terror. Someone has found his confidence. His teachers recommended I put him in drama classes. And sign him up for football. And Tae Kwon Do.'

I couldn't help but be impressed. Who knew he had it in him?

'And how are you doing?' I asked.

She poured a packet of sweet chili crisps into a big green bowl and laughed.

'I'm knackered, all the time. Constantly exhausted. But do you want to know the messed-up thing?'

I nodded, immediately stealing a handful of crisps.

'Even though I'm doing everything on my own, it actually takes less time than it did with Oliver around. It's quite freeing, knowing you're the only person who's going to clean the toilet rather than seething about the fact that there's another adult in the house who isn't going to lift a bloody finger.'

'I know exactly what you're talking about,' I assured her, shuddering at a flashback to the time I tried to explain to Michael how to use a bottle of Toilet Duck. 'Is he coming to see the kids tomorrow?'

Cerys smirked as she popped the top of a tub of hummus. 'He's gone on holiday with his new girlfriend. Totty.'

'No.'

'Yes. She's his brother's wife's cousin or something? They introduced them because she wanted to sue Marks & Spencer for discrimination. She claims the rise of Percy Pig has made her a social outcast.'

I bit my lip to stop myself from laughing.

'Dare I ask why?'

'She's a pig farmer,' Cerys replied gaily. 'She farms pigs.'

'It's a match made in heaven,' I said, almost choking with laughter. 'She can chuck him a bowl of slop every night with the rest of them.'

A little bit of schadenfreude is allowed at Christmas, especially when it's for your sister's ex-husband. She tried to fix things, as she told me over several bottles of wine when she came down to visit at Easter, but he didn't want to face reality and eventually she had to make some hard decisions for her own sake as well as for the kids. I was so proud of her.

'Here she is!' Dad cheered as I walked into the living room bearing a platter of cheese. 'That's it, Christmas has officially started now.'

It felt so strange, celebrating in a house that wasn't our childhood home. The tree wasn't as big and all of Cerys's ornaments were colour-coordinated instead of a higgledy-piggledy colourful record of Christmases past. But that didn't matter. What was important was standing in a room with the people I loved. And the massive glass of whisky Drew held out to me in his giant bear paw of a hand.

'Merry Christmas, pet,' Mum said, turning her cheek up for a kiss.

'Good drive?' asked Dad.

'Why does everybody always ask that when they already know the answer?' I replied. 'Yes, Mum, it was the most wonderful drive ever, the roads were not full of lunatics, everyone drove very safely and Manny wasn't a complete nightmare from the moment we set off to the moment we arrived.'

'Talking about me?' Right on cue, Manny strolled into the room all dashing smiles and hugs for everyone.

'Only to say how wonderful you are,' Mum gushed as Drew gave him a drink and a kiss on the cheek before turning back to the kids, accepting his role as a human climbing frame. Artemis and Arthur were almost as obsessed with him as Manny. Who knew true love could blossom from Christmas dick pics? It really did work in mysterious ways.

'You two should be in bed,' Cerys said, plucking her son off Drew's shoulders and grabbing her daughter's ankle as she climbed up his back. 'If you're not asleep when Father Christmas comes, you won't get any presents.'

Artemis gave a comically exaggerated frown, hands on her skinny ten-year-old hips. 'But you stay up later than we do, and you still get presents.'

'That's because we know Father Christmas,' Manny replied smoothly. 'We're all old mates.'

'Why can't we be friends with him?' Arthur asked. 'Doesn't he like children?'

'Doesn't want to get in trouble with the authorities,' he replied, shaking his head. 'Wouldn't look good, would it? An eccentric old man hanging round with loads of kids. You don't want to get Father Christmas cancelled, do you?'

'Manny,' Cerys warned under her breath.

'It doesn't matter,' Arthur mumbled into his chest. 'He doesn't exist anyway.'

Everyone gasped.

Cerys crouched down in front of her son and poked him gently in the shoulder. 'Are you sure about that? Because I believe someone asked him for a PlayStation and if he doesn't exist, how are you going to get one when they're all sold out?'

I felt a tug on the sleeve of my coat and looked down to see Artemis slip her hand into mine and pull me down to her level. Much to my delight, her hair had darkened over the last year and was almost the exact same shade of reddish-brown as mine, turning into my sweet little mini me.

'I already know there's no Father Christmas,' she whispered. 'I heard Mum and Dad arguing about who was supposed to buy my Barbie Dream Home like, five years ago but I didn't tell Arthur.'

'That's very nice of you,' I replied, not sure whether I was supposed to confirm or deny. She'd already grown up so much since Cerys and Oliver's break-up and I didn't want to push her down that road any faster than necessary.

'Here we all are,' Dad beamed as everyone settled into a comfortable spot. 'Everyone's home.'

'Almost everyone,' Mum corrected and no one spoke for a second.

'Do you need any help with anything, Care?' I asked before things could get too maudlin. Nan wouldn't want that. 'Happy to make a start on the veg for tomorrow.'

'Despite the fact I offered to host to save Mum the work, she turned up with half of Tesco in the back of the car,' Cerys replied, casting a look of disapproval at my mother. 'We've just got to throw it in the oven in the morning.'

'And I've got the bird in the back of the car,' Drew added. 'He's a beauty.'

'As long as it's not a capon,' I muttered into my glass.

Mum looked around the room, her bottom lip quivering and threatening to break at any second. 'This is the first Christmas we've had away from home since Cerys was born. Can you believe it?'

'We could do Christmas at ours next year,' Manny suggested, curling his hand around Drew's and beaming up at his love. I'd never been so happy and so heartbroken at the same time as I was when he told me he was moving back to Baslow in January and buying a house with Drew. I would miss him horribly but the two of them really were made for each other. Cerys wedged herself in between them and leaned forward to help herself to a handful of crisps.

'Before we commit, will you have a settee by then?' she asked innocently.

'The cheek of it,' he replied, swiping her snacks. 'Give us a chance to get settled. Not all of us conveniently acquired a house from our grandmother.'

'There was nothing convenient about it,' a voice boomed from the hallway.

Myfanwy James walked into the living room, a set of house keys in one hand, elegant black walking stick in the other, which she immediately used to crack Manny around the shins as he jumped up to hug her. 'Why are your jeans four sizes too big? Are you keeping ferrets down there? You want to get yourself a nice pair of trousers like Drew.'

Just as it always did, my heart doubled in size at the sight of her.

It had been an eventful year for Myfanwy. Right after Christmas, she had a fall and spent a regrettable two days in hospital after which the nurses called my mum, begging her to take Nan home. After she slipped again in March, it was decided (although not by Nan) that she shouldn't be living alone. She managed two months at my parent's house before declaring that the house was so hot, my dad was obviously trying to kill her, and finding herself a little bungalow in the Bluebells retirement community, fifteen minutes up the road. As soon as Cerys's divorce was finalized, Nan suggested she sell her massive house outside Manchester, pocket the cash and move into her old place down the street from Mum and Dad. Nan was like a new woman. She'd even started crocheting cases for the emergency buttons all the residents wore around their necks, finding a passion for design at eighty-three.

And that wasn't all she'd found.

'I parked in front of the house but I'm blocking the driveway,' Gerald said, striding into the living room, knocking the cold off his cap. 'I can move it if anybody needs to get out.'

'Nobody needs to go anywhere,' Nan said, easing herself into her favourite armchair with Manny's help. 'Especially me. Once I'm down, I can't get back up.'

'She's having you on.' Gerald gazed at her with such fondness, I had to cover my smile with my hand for fear of incurring Nan's wrath. 'She's up and down like a whore's drawers when it suits her.'

'Language,' she admonished, tittering in her seat. 'Now somebody get me a drink.'

Gerald moved to Bluebells for the company, he'd explained the first time we all went to visit and found him hoovering Nan's living room. His wife had passed away several years before, their kids all lived far away and all his friends 'kept popping their clogs' and even though he wasn't looking for love, he fell for Myfanwy the moment he saw her. She still insisted they were just good friends but as my dad pointed out, it was a bloody good friend who waited on you hand and foot, acted as your unpaid chauffeur and always seemed to be in your house whenever anyone called, morning, noon or the middle of the night. I didn't care, she wasn't lonely anymore and that was all that mattered.

Two drinks and several pounds of cheese later, the doorbell rang and Artemis thundered through the hallway to answer it at a speed only available to the under-twelves.

'Auntie Gwen!' she bellowed. 'He's here!'

Even though it was only seven days since I'd seen him last, the butterflies in my stomach fluttered when Dev walked in the room, grey coat on his back, easy smile on his face and, because he was perfect, Santa hat on his head.

'Merry Christmas, everyone,' he said before taking off the hat and handing it to a waiting Artemis. He bent down to press a quick family-friendly kiss to my cheek and my heartbeat quickened as our eyes met. Every time I saw him was like the first time, all over again.

'Hello, stranger,' I whispered.

'Hello, yourself,' he replied.

'Good drive, son?' Dad asked, asking the official first question of dads everywhere as he heaved himself off the settee to get my boyfriend a drink.

'Not too bad, I managed to get out earlier than I expected,' Dev answered with a polite nod, seating himself on the arm of my chair, his hand absently curling around the back of my neck. 'Thankfully, not that many poorly hearts to take care of this Christmas.'

'You're so good, you make me sick,' Manny said as Dad handed him a glass of red wine.

'I love you too, Manny,' Dev raised his glass in his direction before turning to me. 'Is that your giant suitcase in the hall?' he asked. 'What's going on, you planning to move in?'

I fingered my necklace, a very special silver sixpence on a chain that I never took off.

'I wanted to be prepared for all occasions,' I replied, nodding. 'Just in case I ended up stuck here for a while.'

'Seems unlikely we'd get two white Christmases in a row,' he said. 'Have they forecast it?'

I kissed him gently on the lips and smiled.

'Stranger things have happened, trust me.'

It really had been an eventful year. I didn't go back to Abbott & Howe. I sent in my resignation and was informed by HR that I had more than eight weeks of rolled-over holiday allowance accrued so I wouldn't need to work my notice. For the first few weeks, I didn't do very much at all other than read books, watch films and spend as much time with my friends and family as humanly possible. It was incredible. Then a friend of a friend asked if I was interested in taking on a maternity cover position at her law firm, still corporate but in the charity sector, and I said yes. Ten months later, I was still there and in two months, when the contract was up, I'd find something else. Something closer to Cambridge, I thought, looking up at Dev.

Kind, patient, brilliant Dev. We took things slow at first, so slow we were practically moving backwards. It was several weeks before I invited him to stay at my flat, weeks we spent really getting to know each other, as time ticked by for both of us. Thankfully, he was all the things he'd shown himself to be and so much more besides. Not only was Dev a good cook, he knew what a toilet brush was and wasn't afraid to use it. He loved to read almost as much as I did and I'd lost track of the number of weekends we'd spent lying at opposite ends of his settee, our legs entwined, lost in our books. And not that it was the *most* important thing but teenage Gwen would have been delighted to know the sex was ridiculous. It was so good it made me want to make new friends just so I had more people to talk to about it over brunch. Cerys was certainly sick of hearing me go on and Manny had barred the subject altogether. For someone who had been so dedicated to getting me a shag, he really hit his maximum quota of sex chat very early on in my new relationship. But regardless, it was immense. Who knew talking to each other inside and outside of the bedroom was the key to a happy and fulfilling relationship? Such a wild and unthinkable concept. But it wasn't all lazy Sundays and excellent sex, Dev worked long hours, his schedule was unpredictable and he brought new meaning to the term 'hangry'. Technically, it was more like 'hamotional'. I once found him sat in front of his fridge, practically in tears, because I'd eaten the last KitKat while he was at work and he didn't know how to cope. It turns out it's tricky to snack in the middle of open-heart surgery and when the boy got home from a long hard day of saving lives, he needed his KitKats. It was fair. So no, he wasn't perfect. He was a real human being with faults and flaws and an inability to close a cupboard door after he had opened it instead of a dreamy teenage crush who only lived in the pages of my diary. This Dev was real, and even better, this Dev was mine.

* * *

'Now that we're all here,' Dad stood up and raised one finger in the air. 'I've got a surprise.'

'Not fireworks?' I replied, sitting bolt upright and searching the room for flammable material.

'Even better.'

I watched as he lowered himself carefully to his knees and crawled underneath the Christmas tree. With his backside waving in the air, he backed out, dragging a large, solid-looking black box with him.

'Gen 3 Personal Wonder Wand?' Manny guessed.

'You're joking but I got some real use out of that,' I replied, pinching at my tight shoulders. 'Dad was right, it is a bloody good back massager.'

'Steven, sit down before you give yourself a heart attack,' Nan ordered as Dad dragged the box merrily across the room to the TV. 'I'm not spending Christmas visiting you in hospital, especially not the Northern General. That place was practically a gulag.'

'It's one of the best hospitals in the country,' Dev murmured in my ear.

'Don't say that any louder or you'll be spending Christmas in the garage,' I advised in a whisper.

'Come off it, Myfanwy, fit as a butcher's dog, I am,' Dad insisted as he opened the box with a 'ta-da'. Inside were what looked like hundreds of discs, all in little clear plastic cases, all of them labelled. He pulled one out and carefully placed it in the brand-new Blu-ray player that Cerys also got in the divorce (along with the flat-screen TV, his stereo, his record collection and anything else that might have brought Oliver joy). 'I had the rest of the family films transferred to DVD! And I thought we could watch one tonight, new Christmas Eve tradition.'

The TV blinked into life, Mum and Dad's living room filling the screen.

'Oh Christ, it's the nineties,' Cerys groaned as she appeared on the screen. 'If I see my Rachel cut, I'm leaving the room!'

'I bet you looked great,' Drew insisted as the camera panned around the rest of the family. Mum, Dad, Uncle Jim and Aunt Pauline, Granny and Grandad Baker, followed by Nan, and Grandad Collins.

'Such a handsome man,' Nan said as Gerald took her hand.

'A lucky man,' he replied and they shared a smile, Gerald looking at her as though all his Christmases had come at once.

'Not done yet,' Dad said, tapping the TV screen. 'Here comes the main event.'

'Oh no,' Manny gasped, all the colour draining from his face. 'It can't be.'

'What's wrong?' I asked as my mother and Cerys began to laugh. 'What is it?'

'You don't remember?' he said, holding his hands over Drew's eyes. 'Get Dev out of here, before it's too late.'

'No chance,' Dev replied as he scooted off the arm of the chair and onto the floor next to my dad. 'Whatever this is, I'm not missing it.'

'It isn't?' I whispered as a vague memory started to dawn. 'It can't be.'

'It is,' Manny pulled a cushion out of its cover and slid the red velvet slipcover over his head like a sack. 'It totally bloody is.'

Two tiny reindeers trotted onto the 55-inch screen, holding hands and bobbing up and down, staring directly into the camera. One looked extremely nervous while the other appeared extremely confident. Both of them looked ridiculous.

'Is that . . . is that you two?' Dev asked without taking his eyes off the TV.

'Please don't watch it,' I begged, collapsing onto the floor beside him and trying to cover his eyes with my hands.

'We're never having sex again,' Manny groaned from inside his cushion cover while Drew sat forward on the edge of the settee, his mouth hanging open with delight.

With my dad giggling behind the camera, Reindeer Manny and Reindeer Gwen took centre stage and burst into a spirited rendition of 'Rudolph the Red Nosed Reindeer', complete with choreographed dance routine.

'This is incredible,' Dev grinned as Artemis howled with laughter. 'Do you still have that outfit by any chance?'

'I bet they still know the moves,' Drew said. 'Come on, why don't you show us?'

'Yes, Auntie Gwen, yes!' Arthur said, grabbing my hand and pulling me up to my feet. 'Show me the dance!'

In an instant, the room was full of music. Artemis seamlessly connected her iPad to the stereo and everyone was on their feet, Drew leading cushion-headed Manny into the middle of the room, while our tiny counterparts continued to wiggle and hop on the television.

'I love this song,' Artemis yelled as she turned up the volume to 'Last Christmas', shouting along and bouncing around in a silly dance I suspected she'd be far too grown up to entertain this time next year. She grabbed hold of Dev's hands and pulled him into the middle of the living room, arms flailing wildly. Mum and Dad joined in with a gentle jive while Gerald twisted his hips in front of Nan's chair, giving her the world's most polite lap dance. We all danced around the room, Manny singing at the top of his voice and bouncing Artemis up onto his shoulders, Arthur hurling himself from left to right, stopping occasionally to swivel his hips like a baby Elvis, while Drew danced with Cerys, lifting her up off her feet as she cried with laughter. So much joy. So much love.

'I think this should be our song,' Dev said, pulling me into his arms as George Michael warbled through the chorus. 'Last Christmas, I gave you my heart.'

'It's not actually a very nice song when you listen to the lyrics,' I replied as he spun me around. 'You snogged her once and she doesn't remember you a year later? It was a Christmas party, George, she was clearly drunk, she doesn't owe you anything and you need to get over it. Don't be that man.'

'You pick one then,' he said, laughing. We laughed a lot. It was nice. 'There are plenty to choose from. "All I Want for Christmas is You", "Christmas Wrapping", "I Wish It Could be Christmas Every Day"—'

'Any of them except for that one,' I interrupted, reflexively reaching for my sixpence necklace. 'One Christmas is quite enough.'

Sliding my arms around his neck, I kissed him squarely on the lips.

'What was that for?' Dev pulled me in closer and the rest of the room seemed to slip away.

'Just for being here, for being you,' I answered. 'This is all I want for Christmas.'

'Wow, really?' He grinned, swooping me low to the ground and holding me there, suspended over the soft blue carpet. 'Maybe I should return all your presents then?'

'Well, no, that's silly, I wouldn't want to inconvenience you,' I replied quickly. 'Since you've already picked them and bought them and wrapped them and—'

He cut me off with a kiss and the whole world vanished. This was it. I had everything I could ever want, my family, my love and to top it all off, I had me. The happiest, truest version of myself, something I didn't even know was missing until a year ago.

I opened my eyes to see them all, laughing and smiling and dancing, and I marvelled at the wonder of it. I was so, so lucky. Whether we had a hundred years together or only today, it didn't matter. It was perfect.

And I wouldn't have wished for one day more.

ACKNOWLEDGEMENTS

More people than I can count helped this post-sinus-surgery fever dream transform into an actual book, but I will list as many as I can before we literally run out of pages.

Thank you to Rowan Lawton for being such a brilliant agent and even better person. I am so lucky to have you and everyone at The Soho Agency.

My undying gratitude to everyone at HarperCollins for pulling together to make this 'really simple idea' come to life – IOU Channing Tatum inside a cake. Lynne Drew and Lucy Stewart for bearing the brunt of it while remaining grace personified, and Martha Ashby for stepping into the breach and working her Sheffield magic when it was most needed, thank you. To Amy Winchester, Maddy Marshall, Holly MacDonald, Isabel Coburn, Alice Gomer, Kimberley Allsopp, Jean Marie Kelly and everyone else who makes these books a thing, I appreciate you so much and it's only thanks to you that I've been able to do this for so long.

Thank you to Cerys Sadler for lending me her name and winning the Young Lives Vs Cancer auction. The family wouldn't have been the same (or Welsh) without you.

The last couple of years have been a Whole Thing, haven't they? Well, they have, and I don't know how I would have managed to put pen to paper without the support/empathy/sage counsel/come-down-from-the-ledge pep talks of other authors including Mhairi McFarlane, Lia Louis, Marian Keyes, Kate Ruby, Lizzy Dent, Sophie Cousens, Andie J Christopher, Dorothy Koomson, Chip Pons, Anna Carey, Laura Kay, Kwana Jackson, Sarra Manning, Mike Gayle, Lauren Ho, Justin Meyers, Sally Thorne, Emily Henry, Jane Fallon, Sophie Irwin, Cressida McLaughlin, Lucy Vine, Claire Frost, Rosie Walsh, Gillian McAllister, Paige Toon, Giovanna Fletcher, Louise Pentland, Holly Bourne, Isabelle Broom, Andrea Bartz and heaps of other people I'm forgetting in this moment.

And to the people who smiled and nodded when I told them I was going to 'do a Christmas Groundhog Day book because it writes itself' and then watched me throw myself around for the next twelve months yelling 'It's so hard it doesn't make sense!', I owe you a Hawaiian vacation. Jeff, Bobby, Sarah Benton, Della Bolat, Julian Burrell, Kate Crowther, Kevin Dickson, Louise Doyle, Philippa Drewer, Olga Friedman, Emma Gunavardhna, Tal Harris & Kasia Kowalcyzk, Emma Ingram, Hal Lublin, James McKnight, Eleanor Moran, Danielle Radford and forever and ever, Terri White.

If you loved *The Christmas Wish*, why not try another of Lindsey's laugh-out-loud and totally swoonworthy romcoms . . .

Keep reading for a sneak peek at chapter one . . .

CHAPTER ONE

'If you ever want to know how someone really feels about you, ask them to pick you up from the airport at rush hour,' Suzanne said. 'No one in this town would willingly drive to LAX for anything less than true love.'

'Flattery will get you everywhere,' I replied as my sister pulled sharply away from the arrivals terminal of Los Angeles International Airport. She cut in front of ten other cars, all of them hitting their horns at the same time, sending us off with a chorus of discordant honking, as my suitcase slid back and forth across the boot of her SUV. I closed my eyes and clutched at my seatbelt, nerves already jangling with jet lag. It felt as though I'd left my brain somewhere over the Atlantic Ocean, several time zones behind me. Humans weren't meant to be up in the air for eleven straight hours, it simply wasn't right. My watch said it was 4 p.m. but my body said otherwise. Why was I awake? Why was it daylight? And why did I decide to watch the entire *Twilight* saga instead of sleeping? I had been a fool.

'You didn't have to come and get me,' I said, twisting against my seatbelt to get a proper look at Suzanne. 'I could have got a taxi.'

Life in California suited my sister. She looked happy and healthy, her blonde hair was freshly cut and coloured, her skin was glowing and there was something else I couldn't quite put my finger on, a kind of glossy sheen that she definitely didn't have when she worked in Slough.

'Phoebe Chapman, sister of mine, love of my life, you know I would go to the ends of the earth for you.'

I yawned and smiled at the same time, utterly exhausted but deliriously happy. It was almost two years since we'd been in the same place at the same time and they had not been the best two years of my life. The thought of this holiday was the only thing keeping me going for the last few weeks, sun, sea and sisterly bonding. It was just what I needed.

'Also, I was feeling guilty,' she added. 'I have to go to Seattle for a meeting. I'm leaving tonight.'

She slammed her foot on the brake, barking obscenities at a little red car as it pulled in front of us. The driver flipped up their middle finger and promptly sped away, drifting across another two lanes, the Fiat and the furious.

'What do you mean you're leaving?' I asked. 'They're making you fly all the way to Seattle for a meeting? Couldn't you Zoom in?'

'I'm so sorry, Pheebs, I need to be there. If I don't go and fix things today there'll be literally no internet by this time tomorrow.' She pursed her lips and two little lines, permanently etched between her eyebrows, dug their way deeper into her forehead. It was an expression I knew well. Standard Suzanne exasperation. She'd been working on it ever since I was born.

'But I was thinking, you could come with me if you want? You might like Seattle, it's an interesting place, there's plenty to do.' She paused to flick her fringe out of her eyes. 'Well, there's a few things to do. Not as much as there is in LA but there are shops and museums and things like that. There's the Space Needle. Oh, and there's this cool market where they chuck whole fish at you.'

'On purpose?' I asked, horrified.

A notification popped up on the screen of her iPhone and she actually growled. Whoever David Sales might be, I would not want to be him.

'The only thing is the weather isn't forecast to be that great this week,' she said, flicking the message off the screen without reading it. 'It rains a lot. And I mean, a lot.'

Seattle was sounding more and more appealing by the second.

'But if you want to come we could try to get you on my flight. Or the one after. Worst-case scenario, first thing tomorrow morning. I'll be in meetings most of the day but I could dinner in the evening, if you don't mind eating late.'

It was one thing to threaten me with a flying fish to the face but quite another to mess with my meal schedule. I looked out the window and watched my dream of a perfect holiday swim away upstream like so much Seattle salmon.

Suzanne glanced over at me, her hands gripping the steering wheel at ten and two. 'Or you could stick to the plan and stay at my house. If that's easier.'

'How long will you be gone?' I asked lightly.

'Two days. Three tops.'

She seemed to have forgotten I spoke her language fluently. 'Leaving soon' meant you'd be waiting an hour. 'On my way' almost always translated to 'I'm still at my desk' and two or three days meant she'd be gone for at least a week. Half my entire holiday.

'And you have to leave tonight?' I pulled at my suddenly too-tight seatbelt. 'You really have to go right away?'

Her tasteful diamond earrings caught the light as she nodded, dazzling me. 'Two trips to the airport in one day. Am I a masochist or what?'

'We've known that ever since you chose to do advanced maths at A level,' I said with a half-hearted smile. 'If you've got to go, you've got to go. Can't have the internet imploding just so you can babysit your little sister.'

'I'll make it up to you when I get back,' she replied, relieved. 'We'll go to a fancy spa or something, really push the boat out.'

Flapping a hand in the air between us, I waved away her non-apology. It wasn't her fault and it was only a few days. I could survive in LA on my own for a few days. And it was like Therese always said, there's no point getting frustrated about things you can't control.

'You can't help work,' I told her. 'I get it. I had to work last weekend, totally cocked up my plans.'

'Oh no, was there some kind of greetings card emergency?' Suzanne said, smothering a half-laugh with an apologetic grimace. 'Sorry, that was rude. I know your job is entirely as stressful as mine.'

'Rude but fair,' I laughed. 'The furthest I've ever travelled for a work emergency is to the big Tesco when we ran out of teabags.'

I smiled when she smiled, expertly pretending the jibe didn't bother me. I was used to it.

'Everything's going well though?' she asked as she fiddled with the air conditioning, setting it somewhere close to sub-zero. 'I *loved* that set of National Pet Day cards you sent me. Your best yet, I reckon.'

'Thanks,' I replied, shivering in my jeans and T-shirt and gazing longingly at the sunshine outside. 'They did really well.'

Head copywriter at the UK's third largest independent greetings card company was far from the worst job in the world but it didn't exactly inspire wonder and awe in people when they heard about it either. I couldn't quite remember her exact title, but Suzanne was head of something strategic for an app I refused to download for fear of never accomplishing anything meaningful ever again. Was she partially responsible for the downfall of civilization? Yes. Was she incredibly rich and seemingly happy? Also yes, so, did she care about the first bit? No, she did not.

'What else have you been up to?' Suzanne asked, steering the car and the subject in a different direction as she merged onto another motorway. 'Anything interesting?'

Nothing I wanted to tell her about, I thought.

Love Me Do, Lindsey's sun-filled, feel-good, hilarious romcom, is available to buy now!

Fern
Britton
Picks

Exclusively for
TESCO

EXCLUSIVE ADDITIONAL CONTENT

Includes exclusive content from the author
and details of how to get involved in *Fern's Picks*

Dear lovely readers,

Have you ever wished it could be Christmas every day? Then this hilarious, romantic and festive novel is your wish granted… Lindsey Kelk's latest feel-good read is the gift we all deserve this Christmas!

Gwen Baker is home for the holidays, single and in a career rut. What she needs is a Christmas miracle, but what she gets is family drama and undesirable gifts.

There is a bright light during these dark winter nights though, in the shape of her boy-next-door teenage crush, Dev. And she's destined to run into him day, after day, after day…

With laugh-out-loud moments and a heart-warming twist, this irresistible novel will fill you with hope and humour – it's the perfect antidote to any cold winter evening! I hope you love it.

with love
Fenny x

Fern Britton Picks

Exclusively for

TESCO

Look out for more books, coming soon!

For more information on the book club, exclusive Q&As with the authors and reading group questions, visit Fern's website **www.fern-britton.com/ferns-picks**

We'd love you to join in the conversation, so don't forget to share your thoughts using **#FernsPicks**

Lindsey's Guide to the
Perfect Christmas

Warning: contains spoilers

Since you are holding a copy of *The Christmas Wish*, I am going to assume it is now or will soon be the most wonderful time of the year. CHRISTMAS*.

If this book wasn't enough of a clue, I should probably mention now, I'm a big fan of the festive season. Huge. Massive. I can't even start to tell you how many holiday-themed items of clothing I own because it's both embarrassing and I've honestly lost count but basically, what I'm saying is, this is a safe space and you are in good hands. One of the greatest things about Christmas is the fact that it is both the same and different for everyone. There are commonalities that pop up everywhere – the same Christmas carols, the same food, the same drunk family member who passes out before teatime – and then there are all the things that make the season uniquely ours, whether that's your favourite cookie recipe, the film you watch *every* year, or the weird little ornament you made when you were seven that always finds its way onto the tree.

But even as a bona fide Christmas obsessive, I understand it can be a stressful time. The key to minimizing the urge to hide under the dining table with a bottle of Baileys before you've even hit Christmas Eve is preparation. Advance planning is your friend. The earlier we start, the less there will be to do when the

*if it's actually the middle of a blazing hot July, good for you, it's never too early

big day rolls around and the more time we can spend sat on the settee, watching Christmas movies and actually enjoying the bottle of Baileys we didn't feel compelled to drink while hiding under the dining table.

It is with great joy that I share with you some of my top Christmas tips – take what's useful, ignore what isn't, but walk away from the Christmas mocktail at your peril. The most important thing is you have a holly, jolly Christmas, whatever that looks like for you.

1. Get That Tree Up

I know it's controversial but truly, what are you waiting for? I used to put mine up on the first of December but one of the best parts of living in America is that they put it up the day after Thanksgiving. A whole extra week of tree! Nothing gives me the warm and fuzzies quite like a fully decorated, beautifully lit Christmas tree.

2. Bake Early, Bake Often

I love baking but it feels as though I never have the time. At Christmas, I make time because baking is the best and homemade treats hit different. Batch cooking is a winner here – make your dough, pastry, whatever and freeze half of it. Freshly baked cookies are only mere minutes away!

I always make mince pies, I always make gingerbread and for the last couple of years, I've added white chocolate & cranberry cookies to my Christmas cooking rotation. They are easy, delicious and make a nice homemade gift. Seriously, people *love* food, and packaged right, people love to receive gifts you took the time to bake yourself. Not kids, obviously, ungrateful monsters, but I've found they go down a treat with relatives who appreciate your effort. You can also layer the dry ingredients in a mason jar and give that with a bottle of wine. TOO CUTE.

3. Start Shopping ASAP

Gifts are my love language and I'm a big fan of buying something when I see it, budget allowing, and hiding it away until it's time. For example, I buy my husband clothes every year because if I didn't, he would walk around in bin bags and while that's super cool if you're into that kind of thing, I prefer him in people clothes. So, I keep an eye on the end of summer sales at the shops he likes and bag a few bargains. He's happy and I've saved some money to spend on more gifts. My Yorkshire nana would be proud.

Another tip is to scour Etsy for vintage homewares. A pair of vintage cocktail glasses and a bottle of something makes a thoughtful gift that works both for booze lovers and as a stylish standby in case you need something in a hurry. Go and have a look! It's a sexy sustainable gift option and more affordable than buying brand new stuff.

4. Wrapping Sucks and Takes Too Long

Wrapping presents is like painting a room: I get all giddy about choosing the colours and how it will look when it's done, but when it comes to covering furniture and taping the woodwork, it's tedious. Cutting paper and tying ribbons dozens of times is the same. These things aren't even for me! But the only way out is through – get everything ready, paper, scissors, tape, ribbon, more tape and paper because you will run out, and stick on your favourite Christmas movie. Or, and I must impress upon you that I don't approve of this myself, stick everything in gift bags and call it a day.

5. Never Underestimate the Power of Self-Gifting

Gifting is my love language. I love myself, therefore I must get myself a gift. Makes sense to me.

6. Christmas Eve Eve

I know I'm a monster but there is no such thing as too much celebrating. Christmas Eve tends to be a quieter affair around these parts, prepping for the big day and All The Cooking, so I like to celebrate Christmas Eve Eve with friends whenever we can. Whether it's a pop in and a hug or a full-on cocktail party, I'm happy as long as I'm seeing my favourite people (sometimes my favourite people are my cats, that's OK too).

7. Speaking of Cocktails…

I've included a recipe below, but please note that a mocktail easily turns into a cocktail with the addition of a measure of your favourite spirit, dealers choice. I like gin but it works just as well with vodka. Or tequila. Or whiskey. You get the idea.

8. Have a Christmas Day Plan

There is no way to stress this enough: do not go into Christmas Day half-cocked. Without a proper plan, you're bringing a chicken nugget to a roast turkey fight. If you're the one cooking, you need to know exactly what and exactly when, you need to know who's coming and what they will and won't eat (but they should eat what they're bloody well given, it's not a restaurant). Know what time people are arriving, have some film suggestions up your sleeve so you don't spend Christmas evening flicking through every streaming service known to man, and for the love of all that is festive, don't let my husband near your tin of Quality Street before the big day or there will be none left for anyone else. He learned the hard way to honour the sanctity of the Christmas cupboard. Most importantly, make sure you're not running around like a headless chicken (turkey?) all day – it's your Christmas too.

9. Have a Boxing Day Plan

Equally as important as a Christmas plan, even if that plan is to sit around in PJs all day and I strongly recommend it is.

10. Remember it's Just One Day

Unless you happen to get caught in a time loop and have to relive Christmas over several times in a row, remember it'll all be over soon. It's not an easy time of year for everyone and I know sometimes the run-up can leave us overwhelmed and disappointed come the actual day but really, it's just about celebrating what and who you love. If that means hanging out with your cat and eating Nutella on toast, I salute you. If it means getting together with fifteen of your most awful relatives and cooking for eighteen hours, go nuts. There are no rules, no wrong or right. Just have a lovely time.

The Little Donkey
(a Christmas Moscow Mule Mocktail)

150ml Ginger beer
75ml Cranberry juice
Squeeze of fresh lime
Cranberries to garnish

Questions for your Book Club

Warning: contains spoilers

- When we meet Gwen she is at a crossroads in her life. How did this inform your first impression of her? Did your understanding of her change as you learned more about her?

- The Baker family is both traditional and unconventional. How do you think their experience of loss has informed their family dynamics?

- It is clear from the first page that Manny and Gwen have a special bond – their sibling relationship is very different from that of Gwen and Cerys. How do you think this affects each of the characters, and the family as a whole?

- Did the book change the way you think about fate or destiny?

- Dev and Gwen split up with their respective partners in very different ways, for very different reasons. How do you think these experiences changed the way they approached love, and even each other?

- In this story, Dev and Gwen find each other again and again. How do you think their relationship evolved throughout?

- Christmas is itself a character in this book. What role do you think Christmas plays in the story? How do you think the story would be different if it was set over a different day?

The Good Servant

March 1932

Marion Crawford was not able to sleep on the train, or to eat the carefully packed sandwiches her mother had insisted on giving her. Anxiety, and a sudden bout of homesickness, prohibited both.

What on earth was she doing? Leaving Scotland, leaving everything she knew? And all on the whim of the Duchess of York, who had decided that her two girls needed a governess exactly like Miss Crawford.

Marion couldn't quite remember how or when she had agreed to the sudden change. Before she knew it, it was all arranged. The Duchess of York was hardly a woman you said no to.

Once her mother came round to the idea, she was in a state of high excitement and condemnation. 'Why would they want *you*?' she had asked, 'A girl from a good, working class family? What do you know about how these people live?' She had stared at Marion, almost in reverence. 'Working for the royal family . . . They must have seen something in you. My daughter.'

On arrival at King's Cross, Marion took the underground to Paddington. She found the right platform for the Windsor train and, as she had a little time to wait, ordered a cup of tea, a scone and a magazine from the station café.

She tried to imagine what her mother and stepfather were doing right now. They'd have eaten their tea and have the wireless on, tuned to news most likely. Her mother would have her mending basket by her side, telling her husband all about Marion's send off. She imagined her mother rambling on as the fire in the grate hissed and burned.

The train was rather full, but Marion found a seat and settled down to flick through her magazine. Her mind couldn't settle. Through the dusk she watched the alien landscape and houses spool out beside her. Dear God, what was she doing here, so far away from family and home? What was she walking into?

When the conductor walked through the carriage announcing that Windsor would be the next stop, she began to breathe deeply and calmly, as she had been taught to do before her exams. She took from her bag, for the umpteenth time, the letter from her new employers. The instructions were clear: she was to leave the station and look for a uniformed driver with a dark car.

She gazed out of the window as the train began to slow.

Available now!

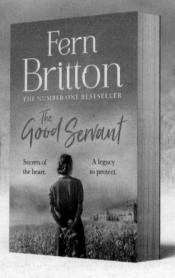

Our next book club title

With war raging on, there are still battles of
the heart to be won...

Wartime
Wishes
at
BLETCHLEY
PARK

MOLLY GREEN

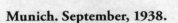

Munich. September, 1938.

When twenty-one-year-old Madeleine Hamilton is asked to smuggle
two young pupils to Berlin, she nervously agrees. But, when they run
into trouble on the train, it is Maddie's turn to be saved by a chance
encounter with a handsome man.

Bletchley Park. September, 1939.

A year later, Maddie is undertaking training in Morse code when a
familiar face shows up unexpectedly. The attraction between them is as
deep as it is instant, but Maddie knows one person holds the potential to
harm her country and her heart – and it is her duty to protect both...

**The third novel in Molly Green's moving wartime series set at
Bletchley Park, perfect for fans of Nancy Revell and Donna Douglas.**